Hiding in Plain Sight

AMY WALLACE

HARVEST HOUSE PUBLISHERS

EUGENE, OREGON

The author is represented by MacGregor Literary Inc. of Hillsboro, Oregon.

Cover design by Garborg Design Works, Savage, Minnesota

Author photo by J. Collin Atnip

HIDING IN PLAIN SIGHT
Copyright © 2012 by Amy Nicole Wallace
Published by Harvest House Publishers
Eugene, Oregon 97402
www.harvesthousepublishers.com

Library of Congress Cataloging-in-Publication Data
Wallace, Amy, 1970-
Hiding in plain sight / Amy Wallace.
    p. cm. — (Place of refuge series ; bk. 1)
ISBN 978-0-7369-4731-2 (pbk.)
ISBN 978-0-7369-4732-9 (eBook)
1. Mennonites—Fiction. I. Title.
PS3623.A35974I6 2012
813'.6—dc22

2011022642

Printed in the United States of America

12 13 14 15 16 17 18 19 20 / LB-CD / 10 9 8 7 6 5 4 3 2 1

To Jen Keithley and Sharon Hinck,
friends and critique partners extraordinaire.
You've made the journey a joy, the work a gift, and the
celebration better than chocolate. Along the way, you've
nourished my soul and brought life to my words.
I love you both for being the hands, mouth, and
red pen—I mean encouragement—of Jesus.

❧

ACKNOWLEDGMENTS

I'd forgotten how scary writing a novel can be. If it weren't for the persistent grace of God, my beloved family, and the amazing people listed here, this story would not exist.

My family continues to cook, clean, and lock me in my office until my work is complete. They also pray fervently for me and brainstorm passionately with me. Thank you for believing in me, cheering me onwards and upwards, and always showing me Jesus in everything you do.

Twenty-five people deserve a round of applause for storming heaven on your behalf and mine. This prayer group has prayed weekly for every aspect of this story and so much more. Thank you! You all prayed me through and kept me grounded on the truth—God is in control and I can rest there.

Thank you, Chip, for loving this story from the start and telling me I could do this writing thing when I was sure I couldn't. To Jen and Sharon, dear friends and loyal critique partners, you inspire and amaze me. Thank you both for everything!

I'm honored to be part of the Harvest House family. Special thanks to LaRae Weikert and Bob Hawkins for making this dream a reality. And to Rod Morris for your deft hand and wise counsel.

Special thanks to the many experts who shared of their knowledge and time to bring this story to life: Sergeant Amber Odom (Montezuma Police Department), Adele Goodman (Traveler's Rest B&B proprietor and inspiration for Emma), Amanda and Linda Yoder, Verna Wingard, Lisa Yoder, John and Amanda Washburn, Chip Cofer, Captain Chris Jackson (Louisville Fire Department), Tommy Woodsmall, Carrie Rey, and Jenny Collins.

Finally, to the One who controls it all despite my best efforts: Thank You for never letting go, for teaching me a new way when I preferred the well-worn path, for shaking my foundations and remaking them stronger, deeper, and centered on You. This story is Yours, Lord, may it make You smile. I love You, Daddy.

Be alert and of sober mind.
Your enemy the devil prowls around like a roaring lion
looking for someone to devour.

1 Peter 5:8

"I have told you these things, so that in me you may have peace.
In this world you will have trouble.
But take heart! I have overcome the world."

John 16:33

CHAPTER ONE

A shley Walters needed one thing tonight.

Rather than wait for what would never come, she climbed into her Silverado and headed toward the Mennonite farmlands. That peaceful area of town always calmed her.

Since she couldn't call Eric, she tossed her cell phone into the passenger's seat on top of her folded police uniform. Late shift was a rite of passage for newbies. She'd survived it on the Gwinnett County police force. She'd manage it here in Montezuma, Georgia, too.

With a glance at the phone, she fought the urge to pick it up and call her brother. The almost daily habit was a painful reminder that Eric wouldn't answer ever again. If he could have, he'd have given her his usual pep talk, probably with one of his priceless impersonations. Mickey Mouse and Boris Karloff were her favorites.

"You can do anything you set your heart to, Lee Lee. Everything God created you to do. And I'll be there cheering you on. Each and every step of the way."

If she could hear her big brother's words one more time…

She fixed her blurry eyes straight ahead and forced the painful shards of memory away. Work required an officer with complete concentration, not someone with one foot in the present and another one stuck in the past. She should have solved the ten-year-old cold case and achieved justice for Eric. But every lead hit a dead end years ago. Nothing but dead ends.

She passed the Montezuma Mennonite Church and turned left, heading back into town...and the present.

Even before her shift tonight, she had to live through the upcoming dinner party. The party she'd begged out of for an entire month, much to her sweet neighbor's dismay.

Emma had brought over dinner or chocolate croissants at least once a week, staying to hear about her day. She insisted that was what neighbors did in Montezuma. It was far more than that. Emma had extended friendship and a caring, maternal interest in her life.

So for Emma and the patience she'd shown, Ashley would enjoy tonight. This was an evening for firsts. Like the snow they'd had on Christmas a few weeks ago. First time in over a hundred years. That's about how long it had been since she'd enjoyed a party.

Deep breath in. And out. Tonight she'd have fun. Tonight she'd live in the present.

She pulled into the Traveler's Rest Bed and Breakfast parking lot and turned off the engine. Beside her, Emma's silver Escalade and a handful of other makes and models filled the small space. Cars lined the street, and in the frigid twilight, she catalogued every one. Twice.

Years ago, she would have turned to prayer to deal with a situation like this. Not today. It hurt too much. Maybe she should just head home and paint instead.

Before she could escape, Emma appeared at the porch rail, bright smile beaming. Ashley couldn't back out now. Not when the whole town had turned out for her belated "Welcome to Montezuma" party.

Ashley sighed as she exited her truck and adjusted her pancake holster under her black lambskin coat. Her red cardigan and matching tank top dampened, despite the January chill. She should have known better than to agree to this, but friends came few and far between for newcomers, especially a woman with a gun.

Brushing a few long black hairs from her shoulder, she stood rooted to the spot. She should have stayed home with a Jane Austen DVD and some caramel corn. Or better yet, gone into work early and rounded up a few criminals.

She calmed her breathing and stepped forward, the ever-confident cop persona in place.

Emma waved from the wrap-around Victorian porch. Compared to Emma's elegant Jackie O-inspired wool coat and shift dress, Ashley was way underdressed and frumpy.

"There you are, dear. Come in, come in. Let's get you out of the cold." The light breeze only mussed Emma's graying hair a tiny bit, and the evening light cast a rosy glow over everything.

Ashley took the porch steps one at a time, slow and steady. Tucked close to the house, three older gentlemen played a rousing game of checkers. Their space heaters added instant warmth to the cold night.

"I'm telling you, mister, I'm gonna school you nice and good if you aren't careful." One skinny man pointed a weathered finger at the other two.

"Oh, pishaw. You always say that and show nothin'." Another, more portly, gentleman grinned and jumped three red pieces with his black king. "How 'bout that?"

Ashley couldn't help but chuckle, and her shoulders unknotted a little. If nights like this were the norm, moving here was the best choice she'd made in a long time.

Emma slipped an arm through Ashley's and nudged her closer to the group. "George, Stan, Wally, have you met my new neighbor, Officer Ashley Walters?"

The men stood, and the sturdiest of the three hitched up his neatly pressed trousers and pointed to the checkerboard. "Join us? Old Stan could use an advisor. That's what George is doin' for me." Wally winked. "At least that's what he says he's doin'."

Emma shook her head. "Not yet, boys. Miss Ashley needs to meet a few others before you steal her away to play checkers." She tugged Ashley toward the front door.

"It was nice to meet y'all." Ashley dropped her voice. "I'll be back soon."

The men nodded and chuckled, returning to their game.

Inside, the bed and breakfast shone with spit-polished antiques, an elegant spread of hors d'oeuvres on the large dining table, and soft mood lighting. Magical. But that was Emma. Everything she touched turned out perfect.

"Thank you, Emma. This is so nice."

Emma's eyes twinkled as she hung their coats in the hall closet. "You're worth it, my dear."

Ashley's heart clenched. So this was what a doting mom was like. She had little experience in that department.

"Come, have some food." Emma led her toward the dining room table, introducing her as they went to a number of older Montezuma residents who all smiled their welcome.

Ashley waved as she followed on Emma's cute orange and pink heels. Her own boring black flats heightened her throbbing sense of awkwardness.

In the dining room, Emma thrust a small, blue and white plate into Ashley's hands, picked up silver tongs, and plopped a buttery, chocolate-filled croissant onto the plate.

The first bite melted in her mouth.

"You could stand to eat far more of these than you do."

She almost choked. Need to gain weight? Not in a million years. But rather than argue, she ate and allowed Emma to fawn on her other guests. The chocolate pastry tasted like sunshine and dreams. She closed her eyes and let everything else fade into the background.

"Excuse me?"

A smooth and decidedly male voice drew her back from chocolate heaven. She opened her eyes and fought not to widen them. His average build and thick, dark brown hair didn't startle her, but his thoughtful blue eyes hit the mark.

A quirk of a smile played across his clean shaven face. "I'm sorry to drag you away from your chocolate, but have you seen Emma? She asked me to meet her here." He glanced around at the older folks milling about. "I wasn't expecting a crowd."

Mr. Blue Eyes had no idea there was a party. Things started clicking.

Danger, Will Robinson.

Ashley wanted to bang her palm on her forehead. How could she have fallen for this setup?

"Emma was just here a minute ago." She leaned toward the newcomer. "But since you're the only one not my parents' age, maybe you could…"

He raised his eyebrows. "Keep you company?"

She couldn't help but join him in laughter.

Emma appeared out of nowhere. "Oh, delightful. Patrick, I'm so glad you've met our newest resident. She's a gem, is she not?"

"Actually, Emma, I've not been properly introduced." Patrick bent down toward the shorter woman. "In fact, I had no idea I was being finagled into attending a party."

"This was all Emma's idea." Ashley bit her lip to suppress any further outbursts.

Emma twinkled.

"Ah, so I see." He placed an arm around Emma's dainty frame. "Dear Mother Hen, are you playing matchmaker again?"

Again? The floor could have swallowed Ashley up and she'd have rejoiced.

"Oh, bother." Emma swatted Patrick's arm. "If you mean that granddaughter of Wally's, that was pure coincidence. One I quickly nipped in the bud, didn't I?"

"That you did. But not before she asked me to run away with her."

Emma huffed and turned away from them, fussing with the plates on the table. "She did no such thing."

Patrick winked behind her back.

With a nod, Emma turned and wagged her finger. "Dropped out of finishing school, that one did." She grabbed Ashley's hand. "But let's forget the past, shall we? Officer Ashley Walters, meet the dashing and very single Patrick James, marriage and family counselor."

He stuck out his hand. "It's truly a pleasure to meet you, Ashley."

"Oh. Yes." Ashley straightened and shook his hand like they were sealing a business deal. "It's good to meet you too."

"Well, I'll leave you two alone to get acquainted." With that, Emma disappeared yet again.

Ashley's stomach picked that silent moment to growl. Loudly.

Patrick nodded toward the table. "I'd be happy to fill a plate right behind you."

She turned back to the decked out table and aimlessly picked up food as she tried to dream up some intelligent bit of conversation. Nothing came.

And the gaggle of well-dressed, white-haired ladies standing in the hall and at the far end of the dining room didn't help with their waggling eyebrows.

Patrick filled his plate with more than she piled on hers. "How long have you been a police officer?"

"Five years. How about you? Counseling, right?"

Patrick nodded toward the back of the house. "There's a nice glassed-in patio out that way. Would you like to join me?"

"Sure."

All the ladies nodded their approval, as if it were any of their business. Ashley forced herself not to groan. So much for fitting into the close-knit community and finding her way around nice and slow.

She hustled to the nearest wicker couch, the only one situated against the house, and sat down. Patrick eased in next to her. The backyard stood still and empty, but there were no doubt listening ears hovering just out of sight.

"How long have you been a counselor?"

"Long enough to know when the business day is over and an enjoyable evening has begun." He took a few bites of salmon something. "This is wonderful. Emma is a fantastic cook. Just be careful what you say or it'll be tomorrow's special menu."

"Advice duly noted." She studied him over her second chocolate pastry. "You either haven't been a counselor long or you aren't happy in your job." Maybe she should have been a lawyer. Or a hunting dog. Or even slightly embarrassed at slipping into work mode.

It was safest there.

Patrick's eyes crinkled. "Neither, actually. I've been a marriage and family counselor for eight years, and I love my job. Most days. Today, not so much."

"Want to talk about it?"

"Not particularly. Since we've been set up on a blind date, how's about making the best of it? Tell me something about you."

"I'm from Atlanta, a native. Child of a busy interior decorator and a lawyer. Cop by night, artist by day."

Patrick nodded and focused on her eyes, as if what she said really mattered. A natural counselor.

Two could play that game though, and it was her turn. "Do you have family here?"

"Yes, my mother, sister, brother-in-law, and niece all live nearby."

"You grew up in Montezuma?" She nibbled on some crackers and pâté.

"It's really not an affliction. Let me guess, small-town life is a big adjustment?"

"How did you pick up on that?"

"Crossed legs, eyes scanning the surroundings. Short answers. And…" He leaned closer and lowered his voice. "Let's not forget the slight curl of your lip when you said the word *Montezuma*."

Busted. "Sorry. I moved here hoping for a slower pace and peaceful surroundings to paint. I found it." She shrugged. "I had no idea how draining constant quiet could be."

He nodded and waited in unnerving silence.

A glimpse at her watch provided a nice escape hatch. Long before she needed to head over to headquarters, she stood and dusted off her pants with one hand. "Thank you for making an awkward situation bearable."

He chuckled as he stood. "I hope it was more pleasant than that."

"Yes, it was. Pleasant I mean." A quick look toward the patio's interior door revealed Emma spying on them. "I'd better say my good-byes to Emma and all before I leave." She finished off the last bite of her pastry.

Patrick held out a hand. "Here, let me take care of your plate for you." He stacked the two plates and set them on the bench. "I was wondering…would you be free tomorrow? For dinner?" He ran a hand through his neatly trimmed hair.

"Not tomorrow, sorry. I work most Fridays and Saturdays."

He studied the wicker coffee table and slipped his hands into his jeans.

"But I'm off Sunday night."

His smile returned. "I know a great place in Americus. How 'bout I pick you up at seven for dinner?"

"You know where I live?"

"Emma's mentioned it a time or two."

Gotta love small towns. "Okay. I guess I'll see you then." She hurried over to where Emma and a few older ladies gathered, oohing over some potted plants. "I should be going. Thank you for the party, Emma. It was lovely."

Emma reached up with her hankie and wiped something from Ashley's mouth. "So glad you enjoyed the chocolate too, dear."

Oh, for the ground to swallow her. Right this second.

✐

Standing in front of her bedroom mirror, Ashley fastened her damp hair into a tight bun like the Mennonite ladies she'd seen at Yoder's restaurant. Then she strapped on her sidearm and took one last look in the mirror as she ran through a series of questions. Could she do it today? Could she stay safe and protect fellow officers and the public? Even if it meant using the gun she just strapped on?

Yes.

The day she answered no would be the day she turned in her badge and gun for good.

The drive to headquarters didn't take five minutes, but walking wasn't smart late at night, even in a small town. She parked her truck and grabbed her satchel of paperwork and manuals to study.

Inside the building, the heater blasted warm air in her face. It didn't reach all the way back to the squad room though. As soon as the shift supervisor concluded his debriefing, she'd beeline it to her cruiser and run the heater all night long.

Lieutenant Shafer stood at the front of the squad room, his dark features twisted in a frown as Ashley and Sergeant Culp settled in for their assignments. "We've just received a second call about a disturbance at Harvey's."

Culp stood, adjusting his duty belt over his paunch. "The rookie and I will have us a look around."

She hated being pegged a rookie by someone she'd have smoked in the academy. But she just smiled tight and said nothing. In Montezuma she was a rookie again. For now.

"Stay alert, you two." Shafer smoothed his plain blue tie. "With these recent burglaries and reports of drug runners up and down I-75, this disturbance call is nothing to sneeze at. We need to find out who's doing what and end it."

"Yes, sir." Ashley followed Culp out the station's glass doors and slipped into her squad car. Culp squealed out of the parking lot ahead of her.

They passed one sleepy or dilapidated building after another, Walnut Street's nightlife as active as a graveyard.

Thankfully, the radio remained silent on approach. Turning left into the deserted strip mall parking lot, she surveyed the entire area. Nothing out of place.

She parked in front of Harvey's grocery store and motioned to Culp. "I'm going 'round back. I'll radio if I find anything."

Culp walked toward the front of the store, smack dab in the middle of the Flint River Plaza.

She hustled to the left side of the strip mall, slipped around back, and watched the tree-filled area with a sharp eye. Nothing darted and no teens giggled in the dark.

But her neck hairs stood on end and her heart thudded.

She crept along the backside of the stores and stopped just before Harvey's loading dock, listening. Puffs of frosted air hung in front of her. For a long minute she eyed the silver walk-in freezer near the door.

A loud crash inside the building forced her Glock into her hand before she could blink. Not waiting on Culp, she proceeded to the back door and stayed low. The lock was busted and a beat-up hammer still lay on the concrete. Whoever their burglar was, he wasn't all that bright. Maybe high.

She keyed her mike. "Dispatch. 10-3, 10-33." She hoped Culp heard the code for radio silence and her emergency transmission. He'd better hurry.

Wedging her foot in between the open door and the frame, she nudged it wide enough to slip inside. Culp better hustle.

As soon as her eyes adjusted to the emergency lighting, the scene before her strained her brain. Nothing out of place. The office door to her right was still closed, no lights or movement beyond the glass. She tried the door. Locked tight. Not a burglary?

Banging on the other side of the metal doors leading into the grocery snagged her attention.

Culp slipped inside the back door, none too quiet.

She held her peace and waited to hear any change in the noise in front of her.

Nothing now.

Gun pointed down, she stepped forward and pushed open the metal doors.

The dimly lit grocery hummed. Every nerve ending stood at attention.

A flash of activity to her right shot her into action. "Police. Stop."

She snapped into Weaver stance and zeroed in on the now frozen form of a small, badly bruised kid with saucer-shaped brown eyes. His homemade clothes and a tattered coat hung limp around him.

He dropped an opened Little Debbie package, skinny white arms raised to the ceiling.

CHAPTER TWO

The boy's lower lip trembled. "I…I'm sorry. I meant no harm."

Ashley had been fooled by innocent-acting teens before, one that almost ended her life. She patted the kid down and found nothing on him. No wallet. No keys. Just a mess of food at his feet.

Culp holstered his handgun. "What's your name?"

The kid still held his hands up but stared at the Little Debbie on the floor at his feet.

"You can put your arms down." Culp chuckled. "You one of them Mennonite kids getting into trouble?"

The boy shook his head. His clothing said differently.

"What's your name?"

The outside door banged open. "What in tarnation is going on here, officers? I got called out of a deep sleep, and I'm too old to mess around this close to midnight." Ronald Harvey, grocery store owner and town councilmember, thundered inside and stopped short at the sight of the boy.

"Bradley? What are you doin' here, son?"

Ashley spun to face the gray-headed man wrapped in a down coat, still wearing his bedroom slippers. "You know him, Mr. Harvey?"

"I'm gonna go call the lieutenant and let him know the deal." Culp left without even trying to catch Ashley's eye. So much for watching each other's backs.

She focused back on Mr. Harvey. "You called the boy by name. Do you know him well?"

"Yes, I know Bradley. He's been shopping here with his family since he was little. Good kid." Mr. Harvey jutted his chin out and bent toward the boy. "This ain't like you, Bradley. What's gotten into your head?" He jerked up and opened his eyes wide. "Is this 'cause of your pa?"

Bradley blinked hard and fast and locked onto Mr. Harvey's eyes. "Is he worse?"

"Son, I…"

The boy blinked back tears. "Is he in the hospital?"

"No." Mr. Harvey sighed. "Let's get this mess cleaned up and we can talk." He touched Ashley's arm, nodding to the back. "Can I have a word in my office?"

The boy launched into cleaning up the mess of Little Debbie snacks, bread, milk, and meat. "I will clean this up, sir. I'm sorry. I will pay you back."

"That you will, son. We'll talk in a minute."

She keyed her mike. "Culp. Can you come inside?"

"No need, officer. No need." Mr. Harvey slipped into the back area of the store.

But not until Culp returned to supervise Bradley's cleanup efforts did she join Mr. Harvey in his office.

He sat behind a rickety desk piled high with stacks of papers. "Have a seat, officer." He motioned to the only empty space in the tiny office. "Can I call you Ashley?"

"Sure." Not standard procedure and not how she liked things, but by reputation Mr. Harvey was an honest man and an upstanding citizen. He'd call her by her first name anyway, whether she said yes or not.

"Ashley, I know this ain't how they do things up in your big city of Atlanta, but I will not press charges against that boy. He's been through enough."

"But, sir, he broke into your store and stole food. Whether you press charges or not, I need to call DFACS."

"Bradley's thirteen. A good boy." Harvey shook his head and studied the papers on his desk. "A good boy with a troubled past. Not that I give charity to everyone with a sob story, but Bradley's situation is different."

"How so?"

Mr. Harvey leaned forward, still not meeting her eyes. "I knew his real mom—"

Wood clattered on the floor right outside the door.

Harvey stood, face crumpled but kind. "Bradley?"

The boy appeared in the doorway, shoulders bent, face reddened. But when he looked up, his eyes were steel. "You know my mother? Tell me where she is." A wood-handled mop shook in his hands, and tears washed away the hardness in his eyes. "I came back to find her. No one else wants me."

"Bradley, let's get you home first." Mr. Harvey locked eyes with the boy. "We'll talk more later."

The boy hung his head and nodded, leaving the office more silently than he'd come.

"Regardless of what you've seen in Atlanta or here tonight, Bradley's a good kid. I don't understand why he's here or why he's a mess, but I'll get to the bottom of it." Mr. Harvey rubbed his eyes with the palms of his hands and flopped back into his chair. "No one even told him why they sent him away last August. He figured out part of it, but not all. They shoulda told him."

"Who?"

"His adoptive parents, Peter and Anna Yoder. They're part of the Mennonite community here, and I've known them for decades. They sent Bradley to stay with Peter's nephew in Indiana when Peter's heart condition worsened." Mr. Harvey shook his head again. "Peter just passed away a few days ago. I don't understand why no one's told the boy."

"But he stole from you." Ashley squirmed at the thought of sending this hurting young kid to juvie. "And he's been beaten. Did you see the bruises on his face?"

"They didn't come from his parents or anyone else in the church. I stake my life on that. They're a gentle people. And I intend to handle Bradley as they would. He'll work to pay off what he broke or took. No charges and no police needed. I'll take him on home to his mama now."

Ashley stood with Mr. Harvey. "I'll take him, sir. I need to find out how those bruises happened. It's my job." This child was not going to return to people who hurt him. Not if she had anything to do with it.

"As you wish, officer." He stepped around her and to the door. "I'll explain things to Bradley."

She followed him into the store and waited while everything was explained. Everything except the boy's adoptive father's death. Guess that was a family matter Mr. Harvey wouldn't enter.

The boy simply nodded and fought tears. "Thank you, sir. I'm sorry. Very sorry."

"I know, son. I'll see you in here on Monday morning."

All four of them left the store in silence. Mr. Harvey locked up with a temporary bicycle lock he must have found in his office. Culp returned to his car.

Ashley waited until Mr. Harvey drove away in his very old, gray Cadillac. "You'll follow me over?" That should have been a given.

Culp grunted.

She opened the back door of her cruiser and motioned for the boy to enter. A pang of guilt tugged at her insides. At home, she'd never thought twice about putting a surly teen in the back cage. But Bradley was different. Very different. Small. Scared. Innocent.

Or so she hoped.

Eyes wide, he did as instructed with no question.

She started her patrol car, heater blasting, and peered into the backseat. Bradley fixed his eyes on the moon following them through the otherwise dark night.

Turning onto Georgia 224, Ashley took a deep breath and cleared her throat. "Where do you live, Bradley?"

Wide lengths of unlit farmland stretched out on either side of them before the boy found his voice.

"Will Miller Road. Only white farmhouse there. Dairy farm on the left side."

She divided her time between the empty road and Bradley's dark silhouette. "You were hungry, that's why you broke into Harvey's?"

He hung his head. "Yes, ma'am."

"Will your parents be upset?" Her heart caught at the words. Bradley only had one parent waiting for him at home. She wasn't the right one to explain any different. Right now, she had to find out who caused the boy's injuries.

"Yes."

"Angry?"

His head jerked up, confusion crinkling his forehead. "My father will be disappointed. My mother sad. But they'll forgive. It's their way."

"Not yours?"

He lowered his eyes and turned to look out the window.

They were closing in on Bradley's home. "Where did those bruises on your face and arms come from, Bradley?"

He rubbed his right arm and winced. Those marks were new.

"Your family?"

Once again his head snapped up. "No. Absolutely not." Eyes down again. "It's what I deserve for my actions this week. It happened in Columbus, Georgia."

"What were you doing in Columbus?"

"Running away."

She pulled to the side of the deserted road and stopped. "Want to explain that?"

"I can't."

She turned in her seat and softened her tone. "Were you angry you'd been sent to Indiana?"

His eyes remained down. "I needed to get home to see about my father." At that the boy clammed up and stayed silent.

She returned to the road. Up ahead a short way, two older minivans dotted the large, flat front yard.

"That is my house. Please let me out here."

Nothing doing. They'd walk up the front porch together and she'd observe with her own eyes that it was safe to leave Bradley. She had to be sure.

From the well-lit porch, the curious faces of four women wrapped in dark winter coats tracked her progress up the long unpaved driveway.

She opened Bradley's door and gently took hold of his arm. "I have more questions. We'll talk again soon."

He nodded and shivered at the bitter cold.

Culp parked behind and nudged Ashley as they walked together up to the white farmhouse. "They'll handle it well. Let it go."

Bradley stayed by her side as they ascended the front steps and met the crowd of bonneted women at the door.

As soon as Bradley's foot hit the porch, an older woman in a dark homemade dress rushed forward and engulfed him in her muscular arms. *"Ach, dank Gott. Du bischt lewich."*

"I am sorry, Mamm. So sorry." His eyes overflowed as mother and son whispered words Ashley couldn't begin to understand. The three other women joined them.

From the looks of the reunion, Bradley was safe. And loved.

Bradley's mother turned to Ashley and startled. *"Denki...*Thank you for bringing my son home." She looked at their guns and badges. "Is there a problem? Has he done something wrong?"

"Your son can explain. We'll be leaving now." Culp motioned behind them with his chin.

It was well past midnight and there remained no official business here. Insisting on anything further right now was beyond the bounds of her badge and her decency.

They said their goodnights, and the women quickly shuffled into the house with Bradley and closed the door. She and Culp started back to their cruisers.

Culp opened his car door and paused. "Mrs. Yoder started speaking to you in Dutch."

"So?"

He chuckled. "They only use Dutch with kids and animals. Which one are you?"

"Ha-ha." She opened her car door and closed it quickly. Any more conversation with Culp would strain her civility.

Driving back to the station, Ashley replayed the entire scene at

Bradley's house. The simple dresses, the sad faces. The joy in their voices at Bradley's return. His apology and tears too. So why had he run away in the first place? Who bruised the kid? And what did Mr. Harvey mean by the boy having a troubled past?

She'd get answers to these questions and more whether the peaceful, sad ladies at Bradley's home wanted to chat or not.

She owed him that much.

CHAPTER THREE

Patrick James sprinted across North Dooly Street and headed toward the outskirts of town, following his usual route. Today he'd up his miles. He had time, and like every diehard runner he craved the adrenaline rush. The pounding of his ASICS on the pavement and the rhythm of his breathing helped calm his racing mind.

A flash of lights behind him forced him into the grassy shoulder.

Instead of moving past, a familiar truck slowed to match his pace. "You oughta come shooting with me today and give up this runnin' thing. It's for the birds. Huntin's time well spent."

"Let it rest, Chip."

His brother-in-law pulled his truck ahead and parked on the shoulder.

Patrick stopped and checked his watch. Thirty minutes down, thirty to go. He should get eight miles in, but not if Chip Jackson hogtied him into a chat.

Chip hopped out of his truck, his favorite camo getup backlit by interior lights. "It's the next to last hunting weekend. Come bag a buck with me. You need at least one this season."

Best friends since middle school, Patrick learned to hunt because

Chip loved it. In turn, Chip played pickup basketball with Patrick even though Chip hated shooting hoops.

Patrick sucked in a few big breaths. "Maybe next weekend. Unless I have plans."

Chip shook his head. "First you work too much and now you're ditching me for a girl?"

Patrick double-checked the deserted road and started jogging backwards. "I'll see you tomorrow at church. Lunch after?"

"Like always." Chip huffed and climbed back into his truck.

Patrick waved as Chip passed and then pushed his legs to make up for lost time. Soon, his mind cleared of all the patient files he needed to tend to and the frustrations of the past week. Patients who knew what to do to help themselves but wouldn't.

He altered his route today and headed toward Ashley's house. He'd run past it once in the month and a half she'd lived there. Emma had spoken of Ashley nonstop, but he hadn't been in a rush to meet her.

He didn't need a romantic entanglement à la Melanie again. Melanie had played him and left him with wedding bills for a wedding that never happened. She'd needed *space* and time with her guy friends.

Ashley was different. Just like Emma had said. She was beautiful and vibrant, strong and scared. Of what, he couldn't guess. But she wore that fear like armor.

Everyone had chinks in their protective mechanisms. He wouldn't pry, but she intrigued him, drew him in during their short conversation yesterday. Of the few women he'd spent time with socially, only Ashley asked if he'd like to talk about his tough week. Most just talked and raved about what a great listener he was.

Ashley's tenacity was a nice change.

He circled back through Ashley's neighborhood and headed home. Maybe he'd call her later. Might even ask her to church. Emma had said Ashley was a believer, she just needed a nudge to find the right church home.

Then again, maybe he'd wait. No need to rush.

A ringing phone greeted him as he entered his four-bedroom house. Kath. He'd call his sister back after a shower.

Ten minutes later, he cradled the phone between his right ear and shoulder as he whipped up an omelet.

"Kath, keep in mind I didn't ask for advice."

"Really, Paddy. You should call her. It's time."

Their mother had filled his baby sister in on everything last night, thanks to Emma's thorough party retelling.

"It wasn't your fault what happened with Melanie."

"I know, Kath. I still have no intention of rushing into a relationship like an acne-faced teen. Besides, I need to get back to the office and finish some paperwork."

"You can be so thickheaded. I just want to see you happy."

"I know."

"At least ask Ashley about the break-in at Harvey's last night. Make sure she's okay."

"What break-in?"

"Ask Ashley."

He'd have heard from Emma by now if Ashley had been hurt. Still, he should call. Kath didn't need to know about it though.

His tiny niece squalled in the background. "Sounds like Susie-Q needs Mommy."

"I'm not letting you change the subject, Patrick." Sounds of wailing grew stronger. "That's right. Tell Uncle Patrick he needs to talk to us and then call Ashley."

Peacemaking. That was what Dad had said Patrick did best. Even when he'd rather run, he still had a family role to fill and a sister to look out for. "Can we talk tonight? I'll call after work."

"Promise?" The squalling calmed down to a sad mewl.

"Have I ever lied to you?"

"No."

"Look, Kath, I need to get back to the office and—"

"Stop working on Saturdays. Go hunting with Chip and stay for dinner. We'd all love it."

Between Mom, Kathleen, and their redheaded Irish tempers, Patrick's peacemaking skills got a workout. "Next weekend, okay?"

"On the calendar. In pen."

"Yes, ma'am." He saluted like he did when they were younger. "Love you, Mother Dear."

"Talk to you tonight, Paddy. Call Ashley." She clicked off, leaving the silent house ringing with her demands. She meant well. She always had, and he loved her for it.

But he didn't need Kath's prodding. He just liked to give her something to cluck about. It saved Chip the mother hen routine and kept his brother-in-law from ruffled feathers.

Patrick made short work of his omelet and then wiped off the spotless countertops and sink. Without further deliberation, he punched in Ashley's number.

"Hello?" Her groggy voice made him second-guess the call.

"Sorry, Ashley. I was trying to catch you right after your shift." His clock said nine.

"Is this Patrick?"

"Yes." He paced the hardwood floor in his living room, his footsteps echoing as he walked.

"Sorry. Shouldn't have answered the phone half asleep. I got home an hour ago and hit the sack." She yawned and the sound of a muffled groan filtered through the phone line.

"I heard about the big break-in at Harvey's."

"How'd you hear?"

"My sister. Who probably heard it from Emma." There were actually a number of possibilities, all in the neighborhood between Ashley's Victorian and his smaller brick.

"And how did Emma hear about it? That was only a few hours ago."

Sitting down on the edge of his leather recliner, Patrick checked his watch. She still had so much to learn about small towns. "I was wondering if you needed to talk through anything from last night."

"You're really using that as a pickup line?"

"Would you be mad if I was?"

"Maybe not."

His cell vibrated on his belt. A new client. "I hate to phone and run, but I need to take this other call. I'll talk to you soon."

"I'm sure you will." He could hear the laugh in her voice. This day was looking better and better.

❧

Jonathan Yoder wished to be home. His hands itched for a rough piece of oak to carve out his frustrations. Instead, he frowned as he turned the heater in his truck up as high as it would go. It should have gotten warmer as he drove south, but this January was cold everywhere. And the farther he traveled from his carpentry shop, the more alert he grew to the different surroundings.

Things had been going so well with Bradley. He was sure the boy just needed a strong hand and constant love. "I gave that, Lord. What could I have done better?"

Truth and painful memories flooded his mind. He should have told Bradley the moment his Mamm shared the news of Peter's passing. But Bradley had been doing so much better, had been so much more content, happy even. No troubles for an entire week. He had planned a trip to Montezuma with Bradley for the funeral, to tell Bradley when they were on their way. But the boy was gone the day after Anna's phone call, and he had searched for him ever since. Had he heard the conversation? Did betrayal and more hot anger send the boy's feet running?

"Father, forgive me. I was not honest. I was wrong. Please allow me the chance to make things right with Bradley."

The gasoline gauge moved lower and demanded attention. He looked at the massive city of Atlanta all around his truck. His Uncle Peter had visited here before, and many of his relatives had ministered in the downtown streets. This was not a good place to get caught with an empty tank of gasoline.

He found a small gasoline station off the interstate and pulled up to a pump. Once he paid for the fuel, he returned to his truck and began to fill his tank. Not many vehicles around considering the traffic everyone at home had warned him about. It had been an easy twelve hours on the road, far easier than sitting in his lonely house after he had received news of Bradley's return home.

Two men stared at him and laughed.

Jonathan turned to prayer, the cold air and audience prompting him to hurry. Mary had very much disliked this part of traveling and going to the store.

If Mary had still been alive, Bradley would not have run. They would have told him the news together, and Mary would have held him close. Jonathan could not give that to him—a young mother to love him, comfort him. A mother to read to him and teach him about the farm she had grown up on in Goshen.

But what could he do now? God had taken Mary and their baby home. Jonathan trusted God would provide what he needed to help Bradley and Peter's widow, *God be with her*.

He ran a hand over his whiskered face. Two years had passed and still he had no desire to consider another wife. His family had been patient with him. Now with Bradley's trouble, this question of remaining single would come again.

He walked back to the gas station to purchase a soda and some potato chips, glancing around to see if the two men had left.

There was nothing but rows of chocolate snacks and beef jerky he was not interested in and a line of people waiting to purchase various items. Had Bradley stopped here when he fled Jonathan's carpentry store and too quiet home? It was good to know the boy had arrived safely in Montezuma, but it was hard to understand why he ran, how he made his way to Georgia. Anna did not know. Why had Bradley not spoken a word before he left?

He found a bag of Doritos and a Coke and took his place in line.

The two men from outside entered the store and stepped behind him in line, snickering.

"Whatcha think 'bout me becoming one of them A-mish?"

The two men laughed out loud.

Jonathan focused on his black shoes. Still, he could not miss a young woman ahead of him turning around.

The man behind him spoke again. "Remember that movie…what

was it? Where that mean old cop hid out on some A-mish farm? Wonder if this here guy is a cop or one of them religious nuts?"

"*Witness.* That was the movie." The second man spoke slower.

Jonathan had never heard of any such movie, but that would be no surprise to these men. The ways of his people were odd among the non-Mennonites he had met.

One of the men stepped on his heel as the line moved ahead. Jonathan ignored the accident.

"I think maybe he's one a them pacifiers or somethin'."

The young lady ahead of him glared at the man. "That's pacifist, you idiot. Don't you know anything?"

"Watch your trap, kid, or you could get hurt. And this big guy's not gonna protect you, ya know?"

Jonathan prayed in silence and kept facing forward. Once he had paid for his items, he walked through the glass doors, glad to put the incident behind him.

"Hey, weirdy, wait up." The man from the store yelled at Jonathan. This time there was more distance between them, but the footsteps were loud and fast.

Keys in hand, Jonathan climbed into his truck. And without making eye contact, he pulled out of the parking lot.

Even when he drove back onto the interstate, Jonathan's heart still pounded. He hoped the time spent in Montezuma would be far less interesting.

∽

Montezuma life continued its slow and boring pace as it had all the time he'd spent in this Podunk place.

He hated the smell of manure. How could people waste their lives scooping up cow droppings and cutting crops? He had bigger plans.

Yoder's restaurant was busy, but he slowed his steps to catch a glimpse of Prudence. All he caught was his reflection. Floppy brown hair covered his eyes. He ignored the strangers coming in and out of the restaurant and hurried across the asphalt.

The barking of puppies next to the gift shop caught his attention.

Two little blonde girls in long denim skirts and black coats ignored the cold afternoon and played with the puppies like they were the best things in the world.

The old white goat in his small metal pen hopped on the table, begging for food as usual. Dumb animal.

"Hi there. This is Chester. Want to hold him?" One of the little girls held out a limp, chestnut puppy.

"Sure." He crouched down and gathered the animal into his arms. "He's great."

One of the girls giggled. "He likes you. Maybe you should buy him. My mom says we can't."

He shook his head. "Sorry, I don't have a good enough place to keep him."

The older of the two sighed. "Oh well. Chester sure did like you. My big sister says dogs are a good judge of character."

He smiled. He hoped everyone forgot the stupid things in his past and started to see the new, mature person he'd become. He glanced around and saw more cars filing into Yoder's parking lot. He had to go. People would be looking for him soon.

With a wave to the girls, he walked away fast. Things should start going his way soon. He was ready to move ahead and do what had to be done. This time, he wouldn't care who got hurt in the process.

It wouldn't be him.

CHAPTER FOUR

Ashley meandered around her massive, silent house, her mind buzzing but alighting on nothing substantial. She'd dressed as if she were going to church, her long-sleeved maroon slip dress soft and warm and her black knee-high boots giving the older dress what she hoped was a stylish look. Margo would call sometime tonight and ask all about her date with Patrick. Her best friend would also inquire about her church prospects.

The answer would be the same. No. Not yet. The last time she'd gone…

The doorbell resounded through the halls. One last glance in her antique floor mirror and she made her way toward the door, dodging a few of the unpacked boxes. Mastering a glamorous glide remained her mother's skill, one Ashley had never acquired. She walked like a cop.

When she opened one of the white double doors, Patrick thrust a bouquet of multicolored tulips into her hands. At least she wasn't the only nervous one.

"Come on in." She stepped out of his way and closed the door after he passed, stiff in his dark blue suit. "Thank you for the flowers."

She sniffed the beautiful bouquet and quirked an eyebrow at Patrick as he followed her into the kitchen. "I don't have a Facebook page to list my favorite things, so how did you know about tulips?"

He grinned and a little tension slipped out of the room. "Need you ask?"

"Emma?"

"Montezuma needs no computers with our dear Emma around."

She pulled a crystal vase from one of the opened boxes still littering the breakfast nook. "This will look wonderful, don't you think?" After rinsing off the vase, she slid the thick stems into the tepid water and placed the arrangement on the cooking island.

Patrick stared at the jumble of boxes, eyes wide open and his mouth almost matching. She should have done more cleaning.

"Patrick?"

He twitched a little and met her eyes. "Oh. Sorry. Are you ready to go?"

"Sure. You okay?"

"Yeah, I'm fine. I'd forgotten how hard it was packing and unpacking a house alone. I'd be happy to help."

Ah, no way. "I'll get to it this week, thanks. I've stayed pretty busy with work."

He held out his arm. "I can imagine. New town, new work environment." His eyes flicked over to the kitchen clock. "I hate to rush out, but we need to get going to make our reservation."

She took his arm, charmed at his Southern manners. "I prefer being on time too. Casualty of the job, I guess."

Patrick helped her into her black wrap coat and closed the door behind them, the lock clicking loudly on the quiet street. He even opened the door of his Mustang for her. None of the high-brow dates arranged by her parents had acted this gentlemanly.

She studied his ultraclean car. No wonder her messy kitchen shocked him. She really needed to devote more time to unpacking. That or take him up on his offer to help.

The drive down North Dooly and out of Montezuma was quiet. Not nervous quiet, but a relaxed quiet, as if they were longtime friends.

Patrick stopped at a red light. "Guess with a cop in the car I should obey all traffic laws."

Rather than groan at the usual cop jabs, she paused on a memory that flitted through her brain. A fancy ballroom and Eric in a tux, chaperoning her senior prom. She'd laughed and joked with her friends back then, with Harrison. Maybe she could again. "Don't you always obey all the traffic laws?"

"Do you?"

"Touché." They laughed. "I used to, as a new beat cop. But…well, not always now. I should get back to that though. Need to set a good example here."

"You already are."

The Mustang's leather and a hint of Patrick's woodsy cologne created a heady scent. Or maybe it was just the compliment. Too few of those and she acted like a beggar at the first taste of bread.

"How exactly am I setting a good example?"

"I've heard tell of perfect incident reports, impeccable manners, and procedural excellence, just to name a few."

"From whom?"

Patrick shrugged. "Confidentiality being what it is, I'll never tell."

"The chief is in counseling? You don't say." She stifled a grin.

"I didn't say."

"Ah, but you insinuated. That goes a long way in a small town, from what I hear anyway."

"I'll give you one name."

She turned in her seat. "I might be okay with that."

"Culp is a regular at my brother-in-law's gun range. According to him, you just might get better than him someday."

So Culp was dishing about everything she'd already bested him on. She could live with that. Most of the time those behaviors got her approval from her parents but ribbing from other cops. Nice to know it hadn't this time.

In the quiet, she rested back into her seat and compiled a status report of the date. So far, so good, except for the initial assessment of her home. She'd learned to play the game so well it was habit. She just couldn't transfer the same procedural perfection to home life. She wasn't good enough to keep it all under control.

"Sorry I brought up work. I didn't mean for you to retreat into silence. Let's make a deal." Patrick kept his eyes on the road. "No cop talk and no counseling talk from here on out, okay?"

She turned a little in her seat to study Patrick's profile. "I'm that obvious?"

"A little jaw clenching." He glanced her way. "Mind if I play some James Taylor?"

"Sure, but aren't you a little young for his music?"

Soft strains of "Something in the Way She Moves" filled the car. She'd heard this one on an Atlanta oldies station a while back.

"Maybe not too young, but thanks. My dad liked a little JT in with his Alabama and other country."

"I prefer Rascal Flatts."

"A modern country girl."

He said it like a compliment. She'd take it. They settled into silence again as the trees and green flashed past the car.

Pretty soon, Patrick poked a thumb toward his window. "There's Andersonville. We should go sometime."

"Isn't it a POW museum?" She shuddered as they passed it. "Not my idea of a good date, you know?"

"But it's an important place to see, to ponder. I go there to pray sometimes."

She'd let that one go. It's not like she didn't pray for the men and women serving America. She did. Had. But graveyards and headstones were better left to others.

Patrick drove into downtown Americus past a huge castle-like hotel and parked on a side street. "I hope you don't mind walking a few blocks. This used to be one of my favorite places to come with my dad and just walk around downtown." He pointed to a candy store a ways down the road. "My sister and I begged to go there every time we came into Americus."

"Big sister or little?"

He grinned. "Little sister by three years, but she acts like my mom. I love her though."

Patrick held out his arm and they strolled toward the Victorian hotel. With no guests milling around the ornate lobby, she took an unhurried look at the rose chairs and delicate antique lamps and clocks while Patrick spoke with the uniformed man at the front desk.

"Ready to eat?"

Patrick escorted her to Amelia's restaurant. The pristine white tile floor, chocolate walls, mirrored fireplace mantel, and linen tablecloths were Victorian elegance at its finest. She stood still and stared, breathing in the beauty.

Wealth and beauty weren't new to her, but the history here called to her, welcomed her into another world where simplicity and elegance dominated.

Patrick smiled and held out a chair. "Glad you like it."

An aproned older woman glided toward them with two glasses of water, the ice tinkling with every step. "See here, Mr. Patrick, you enjoy this favor, you hear." The grandmotherly woman put down the glasses and turned to Ashley. "Ah, I see why all the fuss. You enjoy your time here too, Miss."

The woman hurried back out of the room. Ashley raised her eyebrows. "Why isn't anyone else here?"

"They're normally closed on Sundays."

"But not today?"

He placed a red napkin on his lap. "They heard you would be in town and decided to welcome you in style."

"You know the owner?"

"A good friend of my mother's and a romantic like Emma." He shrugged. "I couldn't pass up the chance to impress you a little."

"Well done." She scanned the table for a menu and found none. "Have you memorized the menu?"

He leaned close and whispered. "They're having a wedding tonight. The menu is filet mignon, garlic mashed potatoes, salad, rolls, crème brûlée, and true Southern iced tea, heavy on the sweet."

Even if the entire place hadn't opened just for them, all her favorite foods and a dashing companion hinted at a magnificent first date. She cocked her head. "Let me guess—you planned the menu because Emma knows my favorite foods too?"

He laughed. "I wish. But no, I asked about the meals tonight and guessed their selection would be acceptable."

"You guessed well."

Her cell phone buzzed in her purse. Margo. She debated not answering, but her best friend would continue calling until she did.

"From your look, I'd say that call is important." He nodded to the still noisy phone.

"I'll just be a second." She grabbed her purse and dashed to the ladies' room near the hotel entrance. No one was in the sitting room, so she returned Margo's call.

"Not answering because we're having too much fun?" Margo's thick Southern accent filled the phone line. Ashley missed that *Gone with the Wind* drawl her best friend had perfected in elementary school.

Ashley whispered like she was sharing a high school secret. "We're at this massive, unbelievably beautiful restaurant…all by ourselves."

Margo giggled. "And you're enjoying it?"

"Enjoying it, yes, but it's weird. He talked about his sister earlier. It hurt, you know? The past is still present. I can't pretend it isn't."

A long sigh. "Ashley, please. Eric wouldn't approve of his death defining you. It's been ten years."

Sometimes the veil between past and present whispered paper thin. "Stop lecturing. I only need one mother."

"No church?"

"Margo, enough. Okay? My timeline, remember?"

"I'm praying for a magical evening. This Patrick must be something for you to accept a date this quickly. I shall call him directly." Margo's affected twang hit a high note. "And offer my sincerest congratulations."

"Thank you, Scarlett. Call you later."

Ashley returned to salads and rolls that smelled like heaven in a comfy kitchen.

Patrick stood and pulled out her chair. "They taste just like you're imagining."

His ability to read her expressions so well should bother her, but it didn't. Being understood was its own cure for anxiety.

Every taste of dinner melted in her mouth.

Their waitress beamed as she approached the table. "Are you ready for dessert, child? It'll keep that smile on your pretty face for a week."

"Absolutely." They didn't do Southern manners like this in Atlanta. She loved it.

"Tell me about your painting." Patrick dabbed at his mouth with his napkin. "There was an easel in the living room and some paints in your kitchen."

Bless him for not scolding her like Mother for leaving things spread all over. "I've painted since I was about six. Art has always been my escape, my personal therapy."

"Cheaper than visits to my colleagues, I'm sure."

Not if she added in the private lessons her parents had agreed to in exchange for her attendance at social events. "Probably. I try to keep it simple at home. Landscapes mostly. Dreams, sometimes. Oils and a little watercolor."

"I'd love to see your work sometime."

"Maybe next weekend after I finish settling in."

He grinned like a kid in a candy store. Margo would cheer. Ashley didn't want to unpack the psychology behind the easy way she'd let Patrick past her defenses. She just wanted to enjoy tonight before yesterday and tomorrow stole today's sweetness.

∞

The evening progressed better than Patrick could have hoped. Ashley's willingness to not force conversation and yet talk freely placed her miles ahead of any of the other women he'd dated.

As they walked outside into the cold night, he offered her his arm and Ashley took it. They strolled down West Lamar Street. He loved this area. The green striped awnings, the brick storefronts. It always ushered in good memories of Dad and Saturdays spent fishing or sometimes just driving around these small towns of his heritage.

"So, do you and your dad still walk around here often?"

"No. Dad died when I was nine."

Ashley stopped, compassion filling her eyes. "I'm so sorry. I shouldn't have asked."

"It's okay, honest. I don't mind talking about him. Everything good

I learned, I learned at his knee. It's important to remember and give weight to the good, forgive the bad."

"It's not always that easy."

"What do you mean?"

She stared straight ahead. "I lost a family member too, and I can't just remember the good and forgive the bad. There's a lot more to dealing with grief."

He stopped walking and faced her. "Did you lose this family member recently?"

"No. My brother died ten years ago."

"I'm sorry. Were you and your brother close?"

"He was a year older than me, but more like my twin. Our parents were busy being young urban professionals, so Eric and our nanny were the only family I had most of the time. But Eric made it wonderful. He taught me how to play basketball and shoot his BB gun. He listened to my silly make-believe stories and acted like they were the most well told adventures in the world. He even shared his desserts when I lost mine for talking back."

"I can't imagine you would talk back." He prayed the teasing eased her sad memories a bit.

She half smiled. "Yeah, well. I might have been a little rebellious as a kid. Eric kept me in line, made life fun."

"He sounds like a great guy."

"He was. Thanks for asking about him. I know it's not great first date conversation."

He met her sad green eyes and held her gaze. "I'd rather you be yourself than smile your way through a date."

She'd allowed him inside a vulnerable part of her life, and it deepened his appreciation for her. He prayed for comfort to heal the haunted sadness still encircling her.

Ashley stopped in front of an empty storefront. When Patrick was younger, there hadn't been any unoccupied buildings here. Now they dotted the downtown. Store after store closed.

"How long ago did this store open?"

"I used to come here as a kid, so a pretty long while. Maybe thirty years." The only remnant of the once-bustling ice cream parlor was its yellowed menu still taped to the front window.

"It's sad to see places like this close."

"I agree. Pop's was a family owned store. The last of the siblings passed away over a year ago, and their kids couldn't manage it. Americus has done a lot with revitalization since the nineties, but they still have a ways to go in keeping these storefronts occupied, especially with sweet shops. Those seem to be among the first to go when the economy tanks."

"Aren't there plans for a revitalization of downtown Montezuma?"

He led them across the street and back under the green and white awnings toward his car. "Montezuma's downtown died a watery death in the flood of '94 and never recovered. But we're working on restoring it—have been for a number of years. A big Atlanta land developer has met with the town council, and they've worked on a proposal to unveil soon. Andrew Jennings is the guy's name. You know him?"

She shook her head. "Atlanta's pretty big."

They exchanged a look and laughed. "As you're learning your way around small towns, guess I need some reminding about big ones."

Ashley stopped a few more times to look in the windows of thriving businesses that were closed on Sundays. "I hope stores like these will come to Montezuma."

"Me too." Then maybe he'd follow that old high school dream and move on as most of his buddies had done. A few came back, like him. More left and started over in someplace big.

As much as he loved his hometown, he missed the faster-paced life of Atlanta. Late nights talking with fellow counseling students, dreaming big dreams in a place where the streets didn't roll up at six in the evening. It wasn't too far away if he and Ashley continued dating. But he couldn't go back until things were settled in Montezuma and the revitalization well underway.

That should happen soon.

CHAPTER FIVE

He pulled the book of matches from his pocket and searched the grove of trees for any signs of life. No one could see him. They wouldn't ever know he was here.

They didn't care anyway.

A flick of the first match lit the night with beauty. When he had matches or a lighter, power flowed through him. He could do anything.

Except make his family care. They seldom spoke. His parents were too busy. His father? It didn't matter.

He ripped out another match and struck it. The orange flame flickered in the darkness.

Too many responsibilities. He was practically running their business now. But they treated him like a child.

Not that anyone else would see it. To all their neighbors and business partners, they looked like every other happy, busy family. Pretending.

Faking happy. He agreed to do whatever was asked of him. They had no idea who he really was.

That would work in his favor. He'd show them. One day he'd make them proud. One day soon.

✍

A good night's sleep did wonders. Ashley stood in front of her foggy bathroom mirror, sifting through a messy drawer of hair stuff. She still dreaded going back to Bradley's farmhouse today and talking with him and his mother. Poking her nose into others' business was a natural part of her job, but she hated butting into the lives of grieving families, remembering well the folks who "helped" after her brother died. Their questions hurt. She hoped to avoid doing the same today.

She'd get answers, but show compassion as Patrick had with her. Time with him and some laughter had chased away enough of the shadows to see Monday in a more hopeful light.

She combed through her hair one more time and fixed it up in a tight black bun. Hopefully, her hairdo and simple denim skirt and white sweater would be respectful to the Mennonite people she'd see today. Leaving off all her jewelry, she checked the finished look in the bedroom mirror.

Plain.

But plain was good. Today, anyway.

A now cold piece of toast called to her from the countertop where she'd left it. It'd have to do for breakfast today. Maybe she'd stop at Yoder's for lunch before catching a nap.

First things first, she had to settle the questions about Bradley Yoder. Then she'd paint. It was the only thing that corralled her mind and kept her from doing what she'd done the first few years after Eric's death. Scouring her file of newspaper clippings and copies of police reports hadn't accomplished what detectives ten years ago failed to do—mete out justice for her brother.

Swiping away the memories along with the crumbs, she scoured the counter and tossed the sponge in the sink. After plopping her empty plate in the dishwasher, she was ready to go. And the day all planned, no less. Margo would laugh. Mom would be thrilled. But days never went as scheduled. She'd learned that lesson as a rookie long ago.

Not that twenty-eight was all grown up and mature. She'd met artists in their seventies who'd never completely grown up. That wasn't her plan.

The drive to Will Miller Road took about twenty-five minutes. But downtown Montezuma struck her today with the same sadness she'd experienced in Americus yesterday evening. The dingy windows and dilapidated storefronts left to drug dealers and troubled teens screamed for attention.

Maybe she should attend the city council meeting tomorrow. It'd help her learn the ropes of this small town better than gossip from Emma.

She pulled into the Yoder's unpaved driveway, pebbles pinging against her Silverado. Just like last time, Anna Yoder stood on the large white porch. This time, the petite woman wore a plain purple dress, dark coat, and her white prayer covering.

The smell of cow patties and cut grass assaulted Ashley's nose as she climbed out of her truck. How did they stand this every day?

"Good morning, Miss Walters." Anna Yoder's pleasant greeting didn't hide the fear in her hazel eyes. She tucked a strand of light brown and white hair into her covering and waited.

"Good morning." Ashley climbed the front porch steps and held out her hand. "Thank you for talking with me today." Mrs. Yoder shook hands gently and then pointed Ashley into the living room without comment.

Warmth enveloped her.

"May I take your coat?" Mrs. Yoder held out her hand.

Ashley surrendered her old blue pea coat and surveyed the first Mennonite home she'd ever been invited into. The wood floors and immaculate front room reminded her of the Travelers Rest Bed and Breakfast. Only here the decorations were handmade quilts and needle-work or embroidery with Bible verses. If church greeted her with this kind of peace and simplicity, Ashley might go back. Someday.

She sat on a wood-framed sofa with soft blue cushions and waited for Mrs. Yoder to hang up the coat and sit before asking any questions.

Anna remained standing, the muscles of her forearms showing as she clasped her hands together in front of her. "Would you like some tea or a doughnut?"

"No, thank you. I just ate breakfast." Ashley hoped her growling stomach wouldn't betray her today. Maybe she should have one of those doughnuts. They were supposed to be the best around.

Anna sat in a rocking chair next to the sofa. "Bradley and my nephew from Indiana will be here soon. They are working in the barns today."

Ashley half expected Mrs. Yoder's bishop to join them, but that concern was probably exaggerated from police station scuttlebutt.

Anna spoke first. "We know Bradley ran away from Shipshewana, Indiana, out of anger at being sent away. He has not always had an easy time with our decisions."

Nothing like a wide open door. "Has he been in much trouble?"

"None of our other children displayed such a strong temper as Bradley." Anna met Ashley's gaze and held it. "But we understood it was difficult for him to be left as a three-year-old in a world far different from his own."

This much she'd gathered from asking Emma a few questions. "Has Bradley spoken to you about his biological mother?"

Anna broke eye contact and sighed. "Yes. On occasion. More since Peter's health grew worse." Her voice wavered. "And now the questions are continuous. Thankfully, there is much work to be done here."

"He's working at Harvey's grocery store too."

A quick nod and a softer voice. "He will work morning to afternoon, between milkings. His chores come first. Then he will spend many hours serving at the store for his misdeeds."

Already Ashley respected Anna Yoder. And uncharacteristically, trusted her. "Do you know where the bruises on Bradley's arms and face came from?"

Anna rose from her chair and forced a smile. "I will get some water for us, yes?"

"Thank you."

A male voice filled the farmhouse. Anna returned first, a tray of water glasses and doughnuts in hand. Then a tall, handsome man entered, holding a black hat. He nodded to Ashley without making further eye contact.

She stood and held out her hand to this blond, blue-eyed stranger. "I'm Officer Ashley Walters."

Something in his eyes changed, hardened. "I am Jonathan Yoder." He took her hand fast in his strong, callused one and released it faster. The contact bothered him as much as it zinged her.

In the last ten years, there'd been little attraction to any man. And now, in the span of a few days, she'd met two who caused her to stand straight and think hard lest she babble the wrong thing.

They all took their seats as uncomfortable silence reigned, broken only by the back door crashing open and thundering footsteps echoing through the kitchen.

Bradley entered, hands, face, and new coat dirty with mud. He wore no hat. Guess hats were just for the adults. Though still dirty, his face had a healthy glow, and his eyes brightened as he focused on her. The bruises were already less noticeable.

"Bradley, please wash first."

"Yes, Mamm." He nodded at the older woman and flashed a timid smile Ashley's way before leaving to obey his mother.

When he returned, energy vibrated around him. Not only did his countenance show a huge improvement since Saturday, there was much less hurt in his eyes, less fear.

Bradley brushed brown bangs from his eyes and took a doughnut before sitting down on the sofa beside her. "Thank you for helping me on Saturday." He held the doughnut near his black trousers. "I apologize for the trouble I caused you. Please forgive me."

"You've done nothing that requires forgiveness from me, Bradley."

Neither Anna nor Jonathan agreed, as evidenced in their furrowed brows and tight lips.

"Yes, ma'am, I have."

When in Rome, do as the Romans do. "Then I forgive you." The words passed through her lips with an ease she'd never experienced before. Just being in the presence of this Mennonite family was changing something inside her.

"Mamm said you asked about the bruises. I'm sorry I didn't explain Saturday night when you asked." He ate half the doughnut in one bite and swallowed before continuing.

Jonathan cleared his throat and Bradley nodded. He acted like a father to Bradley, even though the tall and muscular man had to be closer to Bradley's age than hers.

"I was in Columbus getting off the Greyhound bus when some men, maybe older teenagers, I am not sure, asked for a few dollars. I was going to give them some, but they pushed me behind the bus station and took it all. They were very rough, and one of the men was meaner than the others. He gave me those bruises."

"I'm so sorry that happened to you, Bradley. I'm also confused. How did you get from Shipshewana, Indiana, to Columbus, Georgia, alone?"

He hung his head lower. A few deep swallows came before Bradley laid down the rest of his doughnut and popped every one of his knuckles—smallest to largest.

Only one other person she knew had that weird backwards habit. Her brother. At dinner every night, Eric would pop his knuckles pinky to pointer finger as fast as he could before Mom fussed at him to stop. Then he'd pop one more. Ashley shoved away the memories and ignored the burning ache in her chest.

"Bradley?"

Very quietly, his words spilled out. "I took money from Cousin Jonathan. A boy from town, who visited my cousin's carpentry store often, helped me hide and then get the tickets and sneak away."

Jonathan's deep voice surprised Ashley. "Bradley will be working this summer with me to repay this behavior."

"In Indiana?"

"We will see."

She refocused on the boy beside her. "Bradley, did you run away because you found out about your father's death?"

The boy clenched his teeth. Silence stretched.

"I didn't find out for sure until I came home." He inhaled and exhaled twice. "He was getting worse. I had heard that much. I don't want to talk about this anymore."

More than the outside air chilled the Yoder's living room, and Ashley understood her time here had come to an end.

Bradley stood and swallowed hard, his face clearing of emotion. "May I walk you out, Officer Walters?"

"We must return to work, Bradley. It is not time for lunch yet." Jonathan stood only when Ashley did. "Your Mamm can see her to her car."

His young face crumpled into heavy, resigned sadness.

Eric had made a face like that every time Dad had promised to come home from work early then never showed. Her brother would fist away the tears when Ashley asked him what was wrong.

It always broke her heart.

Bradley's identical sorrow had the same effect.

She couldn't find her voice to intervene and ask if Bradley could walk her to her truck. If that simple courtesy could restore his smile, she wanted that more than anything right now.

Bradley picked up the tray of uneaten doughnuts and carried it to the kitchen, his shoulders slumped, his eyes not making contact with anyone in the room.

Anna stood motionless, her head bowed as if in prayer.

Ashley zeroed in on Jonathan. "I'd appreciate it if he could walk me to my car. It might help him."

"He will be fine."

"Do you have children?"

Surprise lit his deep blue eyes. "No, I do not. But why should that matter to you, Miss Walters?"

"I taught the youth in my church when I was in college. I learned that a little compassion goes a long way."

"You are instructing me on how to help my nephew?"

She stepped closer, having to look up to hold his intense gaze. "I'm trying to help Bradley."

"Why? You have the answers you came for, and you will not see him again."

"He reminds me of my brother. I want to be sure he's okay. Getting mugged at a bus station is no easy thing to recover from, even for an adult."

Jonathan's eyes softened and focused over her shoulder. "I will go speak with him." He turned and disappeared into another room.

Anna leaned down to pick up the unused glasses of water. "Good-bye, Miss Walters. Bradley will be back in a moment." She left the room the same direction Jonathan had.

The boy returned, his brown eyes brighter. "Mamm said I could walk you out." He glanced toward the back of the house. "She and

Cousin Jonathan don't want me to find my birth mother. But Mamm said I could ask for your help."

"I wish I could help you, Bradley, but I'm not sure what I can do."

"I have her name, and she was in trouble with the law before she left."

"Criminal records are for law enforcement only. You could try some Internet searching. That might turn up something."

He stared at the floorboard a long minute before responding. "Thank you anyway, Miss Walters. I understand." With that, he left the room and was out the back door in a flash.

She could have slapped her forehead. Of course he didn't have access to a computer. She should have done more. Maybe she still could.

Anna entered the room and stood at the front door, her pinched expression not masking her heartache. This woman had recently lost her husband. Now her son wanted to find his birth mother but didn't want to talk about his father's death.

No one else wants me.

Bradley's words at Harvey's grocery store flashed through Ashley's memory. There was more happening beneath the surface of this family than the trouble her family had endured. They were so alike in many ways. But she could do nothing to help any of them.

"Thank you for talking with me, Mrs. Yoder." Ashley walked onto the neatly swept porch, the pristine rocking chairs all in a row.

"May God direct your steps, Miss Walters."

Ashley walked out to her truck, not looking behind but feeling Anna monitor her every step.

Bradley's crestfallen eyes hounded her. No matter how fast she drove away, she couldn't outrun the boy's sadness. Or his resemblance to Eric.

∾

Jonathan followed the police officer's departure, holding the unfinished block of pine that would soon become a child's toy. He should not have engaged in conversation with her. It did not help him ignore her beauty.

Mary had never frustrated him as Miss Walters did. His wife was quiet and sensible, not given to emotional outbursts. He still could not believe she had tried to intimidate him by stepping too close and then lecturing him. No woman had ever done that.

Ashley Walters was as different from the women in his community as wood was from water. So much so, it did not hurt to think about her. She was protective and concerned for Bradley, something he had not witnessed from a non-Mennonite.

This should not matter to him. He could not allow his mind to focus on Miss Walters.

The sound of her truck died away, and he forced himself to return to the barn.

Rubbing his thumb along the smooth, pale wood in his hand, he saw the simple toy that would bring delight to some child. These were the most requested by tourists, but the hardest to create. Each toy stirred the memory of his son or daughter, the other children he and Mary had longed for but would now never have. Instead of allowing sadness to swallow him, his deep loss only drove him to work harder to serve those who came into his small carpentry shop.

He made the first deep cuts with his whittling knife and became so engrossed in the work that a pile of thin white curls appeared before he took a moment to rest his hand. Bradley stood in the barn doorway.

"You want to learn?"

Bradley shook his head. "I have no skill for this work. But I like to watch you."

This pleased Jonathan. His brother, Mark, would talk and talk while they worked side by side, both carving wood into furniture, toys, and custom items as their father had done long ago with simple tools and strong hands. But Bradley spoke little. He did not need to. His eyes told more stories than words ever could.

Jonathan continued carving and ignored the cold until the graceful head and tail of a mother duck appeared. Sanding would come later, as would the second piece of the toy, the three small ducklings.

Maybe he and Bradley would continue what they had started in Shipshewana, a friendship based on God's love and mutual respect. Respect he did not deserve for how he had treated Bradley.

"I am sorry for not telling you about your father, Bradley. I did not understand how it would affect you to not know what was happening with your parents."

Bradley nodded. "You explained. I forgave you."

Still, the guilt tightened Jonathan's muscles into knots. This was not a new experience, not since Mary's death. His bishop warned him not to allow these negative emotions a foothold. He needed to speak with God again about this. He longed to be free, even if he deserved this punishment.

"I want to find my mother."

"Yes, I have heard you speak of this many times. It is not wise. Your Mamm has explained. You must trust your elders, Bradley. They want what is best for you."

"Maybe..." He turned away, but not before Jonathan heard the quiet words voiced for no one to hear. "They don't really want me though." The boy walked quickly away and headed for the warm house.

Jonathan carved. He would find Bradley soon and they would complete the necessary work before dinner.

Anna's fears about Bradley's heart and concerns about Peter's dairy farm spread into Jonathan's bones. Anna would have to sell the farm soon if other men in the community could not continue to help as they had done for months now. Even with many hands giving extra time and sweat, the farm would still be sold if Bradley continued to ignore his growing responsibilities.

Responsibilities very great for one so young and unwilling, so full of hurt he would not express. But the boy must learn, as all of their people did, to work hard and serve his family and community well, as unto the Lord.

Jonathan drew near the house and stopped outside Anna's open bedroom window as a strange clattering caught his attention. Anna would not be using her computer when the noon meal needed to be prepared.

It was not Anna on the computer, but Bradley, something frowned upon in all Mennonite homes. Children should never be unsupervised with such a thing that could draw their young minds into dangerous places.

Jonathan walked into the house and headed straight for Anna's bedroom. "Bradley, what are you doing?"

The boy jumped out of the chair and began to search the ground for something. "I…I lost a book Mamm asked me to read from today. I was looking for it."

"You were looking for this book on the computer?"

Bradley stared at the floor. "I'll finish at Mr. Harvey's store after next week. Then I can help you with your woodcarving orders to pay you back for what I've taken from you."

Yes, this was what he and Anna had discussed. Everyone hoped this would strengthen the boy's mind and hands for the hard work ahead.

But for the first time, Jonathan was unsure this was enough. If lying had taken hold of the boy as stealing had, more trouble than ever would darken their future.

∞

The hands of the paint-pallet clock on the studio wall pointed to midnight. Ashley needed sleep and a long, hot shower. Desperately. But she couldn't tear herself away from the easel. The pastoral scene evoked such peace from deep within her that she continued to stare, surprised it had come so quickly from the strokes of her brush.

The blues and greens were the same ones she'd admired for weeks as she drove through the area. But the tall Mennonite man with blond hair and calm conviction still shocked her. He'd appeared on the canvas almost of his own will, and there he stood in black pants and dark coat, facing away from her.

Joy and sadness swirled like autumn leaves in her heart.

She turned to the other easel and ran her hands over a rough sketch of another scene. This one changed the heavy feelings to softer ones. Patrick, a dab of chocolate on his mouth, smiled as the elegant lights of Windsor Hotel shone above him. This was only a first impression of their date. But it would become a fascinating Impressionist painting with dabs of color joining with light to dance across the canvas.

The deep ache of the past began to yield, like the frozen fields of winter giving in to spring's thaw. That realization both thrilled and terrified her.

CHAPTER SIX

Ashley gawked at the crush of people overflowing the council chambers for Montezuma's city council meeting on the second Tuesday of January. She'd hoped to blend in and investigate both the revitalization situation and various bigwigs without anyone doing the same to her. She'd been scrutinized quite enough.

Farmers in their overalls and hunting coats, businesspeople in suits, and a number of the Mennonites in their plain dress all clustered in their own little groups. Almost every one of them waved or nodded as she passed them.

Blending in unnoticed. Right.

Up on the dais sat Mayor Johnson, whom Ashley had met briefly. Janet Hardy, the downtown development manager, and a few other council members took their seats as well.

Thankfully, they were too busy to acknowledge her and cause the rest of the folks seated at the front of the room to turn and greet her. Maybe the novelty of her singleness and big city past would wear off soon.

In minutes, the people behind the dark-wood barrier assembled in their seats and Mayor Johnson called the meeting to order promptly at 5:30 p.m. The white-haired man's voice boomed in deep, rich tones. "We have with us today some of our Mennonite neighbors. I'd like to ask Bishop Overholt if he would deliver the invocation."

She craned her neck to get a good look at the man most of the town assumed was head of the Mennonite community. In her subtle questioning of Patrick and fellow police officers, she'd learned there were three separate Mennonite churches. All had bishops, and none of them ruled with an iron scepter. Instead, they led the people much as caring pastors led churches of other denominations.

A stocky middle-aged man with dark brown hair and beard stood and walked through the barrier gate to the podium. Black hat in hand, he prayed without the need for a microphone. "Dear God, we ask that Your mercy and wisdom be poured out today. Guide our words and our actions to bring honor to Your holy name. Amen." He returned to his seat while the packed room sat in silence.

Mayor Johnson spoke into his microphone. "The only item on our agenda tonight is a proposal from Andrew Jennings of the Jennings Company, an Atlanta-based community development and master planning company. Mr. Jennings has been hard at work with our chairman of the planning and zoning commission, Thomas Hendricks." He motioned for the two men to take the podium. "Welcome, Mr. Jennings."

A well-dressed, athletic man with salt and pepper hair strode to the podium with an ocean full of confidence coming off him in waves. Mr. Hendricks quickly filed forward in Jennings's wake.

"Thank you, Mayor Johnson. And a special thanks to the good people of Montezuma for allowing me to work within your community to develop the best revitalization plan possible for this great city."

A smattering of applause received a stern look from the mayor and died away fast.

"What I'd like to present to the town council is a highly researched and detailed plan that includes two million dollars of privately donated funds to build and restore a variety of businesses that will bring tourists and locals alike flocking to downtown Montezuma."

More applause, louder this time. The mayor held up his hands for quiet and the people obliged, a little slower to comply.

Ashley stifled a chuckle. Crowd control wasn't the mayor's strong suit.

Jennings pointed to his unveiled sketches and to scale mock-ups, becoming more animated, like one of those old-time preachers driving home a fiery point. Except there were no comb-overs flapping out of place. Only polished perfection in a pinstriped business suit.

"Taking into account Montezuma's proud heritage and the surrounding historical treasures in Andersonville, Pasaquan, and the neighboring Mennonite community, as well as the overflowing resources of nearby Georgia Southwestern State University, our revitalization plan provides for entertainment with a quaint but elegant restaurant, an old-time ice cream shop, an antique store, small boutiques, and two museums: a veteran's museum that would house rotating exhibits and direct visitors to Andersonville, and a Mennonite museum to honor the traditions, crafts, and farming of this revered community. There would also be an art gallery to house local artists' wares and provide community classes taught by GSW students for very reasonable rates."

The crowd erupted, Ashley included, and Mayor Johnson waited until the applause died down to speak. "As you can see, Mr. Jennings, we have many residents who clearly love their hometown and are excited about the prospect of new jobs and the return of our once-thriving downtown."

An art studio, right here? Maybe she could try something new and offer free classes to middle school students, a very at-risk demographic.

"At this time, the council and Mr. Jennings are prepared to hear any questions and concerns from our citizens." Mayor Johnson flashed his politician's smile as he searched the faces in the crowd.

An elderly woman stood slowly and faced the men at the podium. "I have jus' one question. An' it's important." Her voice belied her petite form. "My question is about our houses. Are you gonna take our land for new roads and businesses and pay us pennies in return?"

A murmuring rose from the crowd around her, many directing their concern toward Mr. Jennings. The man exchanged a glance with his wife and son seated on the first row. The younger Jennings turned to survey the crowd. Confident like his dad, sharp brown eyes alive with energy, and far more tanned than anyone else in the room. Probably a recent college grad still using Dad's money for tropical vacations or tanning beds.

The mayor shook his head. "No, there are no plans for rezoning residential areas or building new roadways. Our infrastructure will stay much the same, with only a slightly expanded downtown area built up and improved."

Satisfied, the woman slowly took her seat.

After some quiet talking amongst themselves, one of the Mennonite men stood with Bishop Overholt. "We would like more information on the proposed Mennonite museum. Will you be purchasing our crafts and food to sell?"

"Absolutely." Jennings stood off to the side but spoke loud enough to be heard without the microphone. "We want this revitalization project to benefit all the members of this community."

Ashley glanced across the room toward another group of Mennonites and found Jonathan and Bradley sitting with Anna Yoder. Jonathan met her gaze and nodded.

She smiled in response, but he broke eye contact fast.

"But we also wonder if you will seek to employ members of our community to speak about our heritage and—"

"Again, Bishop," Jennings rocked forward a little and spoke up so all could hear. "This project will financially benefit all members of the Montezuma community."

"And will we be able to share our faith and speak to visitors about Jesus Christ?"

For the first time, Jennings fidgeted. So did the mayor. A little tie adjusting, some shuffling of notes. Interesting.

Jennings spoke first. "This two million dollar grant is from a private donor whose express wishes include no religious proselytizing within the confines of this project."

Ashley's hackles rose. How could they dismiss a valid question from these gentle people who did so much to help this community? What possible harm did their donor fear would come from the Mennonites sharing their faith?

She stood. "Have you considered modeling the Mennonite

museum here on Menno-Hof in Shipshewana, Indiana? It's an Amish and Mennonite museum that serves as a highlight for tourists and an opportunity for their culture and their faith to be shared in a non-threatening way."

Jonathan stared. As did most of the other Mennonites and towns-folk in the meeting.

Yes, she'd done some online research about the Mennonite culture. Why did that shock everyone into silence?

Jennings returned to the podium. "We value your input and will look into your suggestion. Thank you." He turned his attention to the bishop. "Any more questions, sir?"

The bishop and the other bearded Mennonite man nodded to the council. "Thank you for answering our questions." They returned to their seats and engaged in a quiet conversation with the Mennonite men around them. Their faces revealed no anger or worry. Only peace.

A few more citizens asked questions about job projections and timelines, but Ashley couldn't keep herself from watching the Mennonites.

Mayor Johnson reclaimed the microphone. "If there are no further comments or concerns, we'd like to adjourn this public meeting so the city council can proceed with business."

Bishop Overholt stood alone and addressed the council, not Mr. Jennings. "We as a community desire to see Montezuma thrive and jobs return so the townspeople can provide for their families. This is a good thing. But we have much concern over this Mennonite museum. Our faith is an irremovable part of our life and heritage."

Murmurs of agreement whisked through the crowd.

"As things have been presented here, we cannot in good conscience support the museum portion of this proposal. We will, however, continue to pray for this city and its people as we have always done. Thank you." He returned to his seat with the room in complete silence.

Good for him.

The mayor and other council members' reactions spanned the gamut. Some were stony. Others wide-eyed. Tension zipped around the room from one granite face on the dais to a small group of businessmen.

The meeting was dismissed, but most of the people lingered. Ashley stayed and listened to the conversations floating around her.

One angry voice cut through it all. "This is unbelievable." An older teen crossed his muscled arms and jutted his goateed chin toward the Mennonites. "Those people could ruin all the hard work you and the rest of the council have done."

Janet Hardy shushed him. "This could be a very small setback, maybe just a minor delay. You worry about graduating from college. I'll handle the real world battles for now."

The young man flipped his bangs out of his eyes and skulked away. Mrs. Hardy turned to fellow council members and rejoined their discussion.

A gentle hand at Ashley's elbow turned her around. "Fancy meeting you here."

"Patrick." She smiled. "I was looking for you earlier and tried to save a seat, but this isn't high school and seat saving is strictly prohibited."

"Some of our older citizens like to make sure things proceed by the book. Thanks for trying. Good suggestion about the museum too." Then he focused on something over her shoulder. "Hey, would you mind waiting for me a minute? I need to talk with a few people before I leave. But I'd love to take you out for coffee if you can spare a few minutes."

"There's a Starbucks close by?"

"City girl." He shook his head, eyes twinkling. "Nope, no overpriced coffee here. But I have someplace even better."

"We'll see if your coffee place measures up."

He winked and hightailed it over to the growing group of pressed-pants gentlemen. Rather than butt in there, she wandered over to a group of Mennonites.

A number of non-Mennonites stood with them, all speaking at once. Strains of "We support your stand" and similar sentiments floated over to her.

"Hello, Miss Walters. How are you this fine day?" Ashley recognized the spry, white-haired and bonneted woman from Yoder's restaurant but had never been introduced.

"Great, thanks. How are you? I mean with this meeting. I'm sorry things became so tense."

"We will continue to pray and trust the Lord."

"Oh. Yes. Right."

The blue-dressed woman smiled all the way to her eyes. "Thank you for your concern for us. We appreciate that."

"I wish I could do more." Ashley scanned the room for Patrick but couldn't find him.

"Join us at our sewing circle next Tuesday?" The older woman's kind eyes drew Ashley in. "We could talk more and answer any questions you might have about our faith."

The offer took her completely by surprise. "I can't sew a lick. I'd probably cause more trouble if I tried."

The woman patted her hand and grinned. "We'll just have to see about that, yes? Come to the fellowship hall of the Montezuma Mennonite Church. I'll be looking for you." She turned away, then came back. "I'm Vera, by the way. Just ask for me if you don't see me when you come on Tuesday."

Too stunned to object, Ashley nodded and watched as the sweet woman melted into the crowd.

∽

Jonathan followed Miss Walters's movements, surprised to see her talking with Vera Yoder, a distant relative of his uncle, Peter. Maybe the inquisitive police officer would find the answers she sought through talking with one of the older Mennonite women. That would be best.

He would rather not be on the receiving end of her questions again. That did not help his focus on Bradley. Even if this police officer wanted to help, her ways would conflict with the ways of his people.

That was only one reason he should keep his mind from the vibrant, confident woman who seemed to care about his people.

After Miss Walters finished her conversation with Mrs. Yoder, she joined a man who placed an arm around her and said something that made her laugh.

This was none of his business. He turned away. But when he tried to find Bradley, the boy had disappeared.

Jonathan started toward Miss Walters to ask if she had seen the boy. Bradley had spoken of her often today. But he did not have to ask. Bradley stood at her side talking to Miss Walters's friend. The boy smiled like he had not in many months. A tight pinch in Jonathan's chest made it hard to breathe.

"Cousin Jonathan!" Bradley called over all the other voices in the room. "Come meet my new friend." The boy pointed to the man with his arm around Miss Walters.

Something about Bradley's words and tone of voice struck Jonathan as odd. He hoped Bradley was not developing a case of hero worship, especially for a man who would show his private affections in public.

"Hello." He met Miss Walters's green eyes.

A slight blush colored her face. Did that have something to do with him?

She rubbed her arms as if she were cold. "Jonathan, this is Patrick James. Patrick, this is Jonathan Yoder. He's helping Bradley on his mother's dairy farm."

"I am a carpenter. My shop is in Indiana."

"Mr. James is a family counselor." Bradley's eyes remained focused on Mr. James. "He's helped some of the people who work at the Deitsch Haus restaurant, and he said—"

Jonathan leaned close to Bradley's ear. "Bradley, the personal business of others is not for our casual conversation."

The light in Bradley's eyes dimmed. "I guess we need to go."

"Yes." Jonathan nodded to the two adults. "It was nice to meet you, Mr. James. Good-bye, Miss Walters." With that, he followed Bradley from the suffocating room to the cold outdoors.

Here he could breathe better with fewer confusing thoughts to clutter his mind and no Ashley Walters to distract him from helping Bradley and Anna. The sooner they were doing well, the sooner Jonathan could return home where he belonged.

CHAPTER SEVEN

Ashley adjusted her duty belt and surveyed the small, Pine Village apartment. Not the greatest of neighborhoods. She hurried up the rusted stairs to apartment 301, Officer Elizabeth Rey fast on her heels.

The early morning darkness and apartment's paltry heating unit did nothing to abate the frigid January air.

"I done told you, officer." The young, white guy huffed and postured like a gangsta rapper, his eyes never quite meeting hers. "I got no idea who took my flat panel TV. All I know is, I want it and my theater system back, like today."

Sure. She'd just wave her magic wand and make it all appear. First she'd wave that magic wand and get the truth here, the whole truth.

Elizabeth, the only other female officer on the night shift, stifled a laugh, but her blue eyes couldn't hold the humor in. She brushed short, red bangs off her forehead and refocused. "Sir, if you could write down the serial numbers of every item stolen while we finish up here, it would be helpful."

He tilted his head to the side and squinted his dark, almost black eyes into slits. "Uh, yeah. I'll go work on that."

A little girl, about five or so with a bird's nest of blond hair, stumbled out of the back bedroom in a faded, blue-flowered bathing suit. She had to be freezing. "Daddy, I'm hungry. We gots any Pop-Tarts left?"

"Still night. You gotta go back to sleep." He hefted her into his scrawny, tattooed arms and disappeared into the back room.

Elizabeth pointed her camera and took a few more close-ups of the nice oak entertainment center. "I've taken all the overall shots and some of the entryway."

Ashley nodded. "Except for some scratches on the doorknob, I don't see any signs of forced entry."

"That's the only way in. No one could climb up to the third floor from the outside without being noticed."

"Maybe they had a key." Ashley studied each piece of worn furniture, each dirty plate on the scratched up, plastic-looking coffee table. Except for a leather recliner and the electronics, the place was a dump.

And the kind of place their resident burglar frequented. They had to catch the guy or gang responsible before stealing became the least of his offenses.

"Let's be extra, extra thorough here. Our burglar had to leave a clue, and one clue could break this costly string of thefts." Ashley surveyed the surroundings one more time, excited about the chance to make a difference she hadn't had on the Atlanta force. There the detectives would have taken over as soon as she'd interviewed the renter.

"Sounds like a plan." Smiling, Elizabeth snapped on some gloves and went to work dusting for prints at the entryway.

Ashley did the same in the living room, dipping her brush into the powder and starting into the familiar twirling application. She'd gotten out of practice on the Gwinnett County force, but here, they got to do more than write tickets and take people to jail. She liked it.

"Nothing at all on the door frame." Elizabeth pushed her silver-framed glasses up with the back of her wrist and spoke in a quiet whisper. "I find that a tad odd, don't you?"

"I doubted this was a smash and grab or some teen prank like our renter postulated." Ashley sat back on her feet, knees touching the worn brown carpet. "It isn't exactly like the others in our burglary spree either. My best guess is we're dealing with a different person, or a rotating group of people."

"Brilliant deduction, Watson."

"Sherlock, remember?" They smiled and went back to work.

The least enjoyable part of the job was taking sets of elimination prints of the family. Two sleep-deprived, whiney kids and two adults with secrets in their eyes made things worse.

"So, we all done here?" The man wiped his inked fingers with a paper towel.

"Yes, sir." Ashley held up a scribbled description of the missing items, including a note about a little daisy sticker his daughter had attached to the TV base. "Thank you for this. We'll get back to you as soon as we know anything."

He opened the front door wide. "And bring my stuff back, right?"

Elizabeth nodded. "We'll do all we can, sir."

They returned to Ashley's car and got in quickly. No need to be sitting ducks in the still dark morning.

"I'm surprised he coughed up this much information. No serial numbers though. Think it'll help us find his electronics?" Elizabeth squirted hand sanitizer from the bottle she'd thrown in Ashley's car earlier. "Want some?"

"No. Thanks." Ashley preferred washing up back at the station to sticky hands and the nasty smell of antiseptic. "Hopefully, we'll catch a break." She shook her head. "I just wish guys like that spent more money on food and clothes for their kids than electronics. That ticks me off."

"At least the guy isn't a deadbeat dad."

Yeah. There was that. Still. There was more to this story too. Maybe one of the prints would come back in a few months and point them right to their burglar. And maybe Mr. Gangsta Rapper would finally tell the truth. All of it.

The taste of lies and dusting powder mixed in her mouth and hung there, bitter and unshakable. She hated being lied to more than anything else.

Well…almost anything else.

They drove through downtown, slow and quiet, but nothing stirred tonight. Thursday had been uncharacteristically calm. Maybe the drug dealers were gearing up for a busy weekend.

Back at the station, Ashley tackled reports and catalogued evidence, stretching and yawning the whole time. Morning watch and trying to live like a normal person on her days off left her groggy. What she wouldn't give for day shift again.

"Got a minute, Ashley?" Lieutenant Shafer rubbed a hand over his dark features. He was getting close to retirement, but stayed on top of his game by working hours no one else wanted.

"Sure, sir."

He rolled a chair over to her desk in the squad room. "You know Officer Destiny Edwards, right?"

Ashley nodded. They'd spoken a few times during shift changes.

"She's having a hard time finding a babysitter to watch her kids in the evenings, now that Reggie is traveling again. Her neighbor can watch the kids overnight, but not during the day."

Destiny hadn't mentioned anything the few times they'd talked. But that was par for the course. Ashley was still the newbie with something to prove.

"You wouldn't mind switching from morning to evening watch, would you?"

She sat up straighter. "No, sir. Especially if it will help Destiny. I'm glad to do it."

He stood and let out a long breath. "Good. You're off this weekend, so we'll start the new schedule Monday."

"Great. Thanks, sir."

As soon as the clock ticked a suitable time, she'd call Margo and get her down here for a visit to celebrate. Ashley finished the report in front of her with new energy.

Within minutes of the lieutenant's departure, Elizabeth perched on the edge of Ashley's steel gray desk. "That happy face because of Patrick James?"

Ashley just shrugged, not ready to dish about her personal life. Then again, Elizabeth had been the first person at work to welcome Ashley and make her feel like she belonged. So maybe she should return the friendship with more than shoptalk.

Ashley pushed back from her desk and exaggerated the shrug, adding a grin. "Could be."

Elizabeth laughed. "Good for you. Too many wagging tongues think Patrick should be all married with kids. Maybe they'll hush up now that he's dating you."

"We're not, you know, dating really." Ashley squirmed in her desk chair. In high school one date meant serious, and she'd been quick to tell everyone about Harrison, her brother's best friend. But this wasn't high school. So why did it feel that way?

Elizabeth nodded. "Um-hum. That's not how it looks."

How could Elizabeth be so sure of that? She hadn't seen the two very different paintings at opposite ends of Ashley's studio. She'd finished both, but had decidedly mixed feelings, different emotions stirred by each of them.

"Patrick's a catch. Don't go on saying one thing with your mouth and another with the rest of you." Elizabeth's kind eyes softened the advice as she combed through her red bob with short, manicured nails. "You got a date this weekend?"

"Yes. He's grilling out with his brother-in-law and sister Saturday. His mom is supposed to be there too. I'm meeting the whole family at once."

Standing, Elizabeth smiled wider. "Have a good time. Just don't walk into any of Chip's jokes. Bless his heart, he's a character. We went to school together, back in the day." With a wave, she disappeared into her cubicle.

Like that advice would help the muscles tightening in Ashley's neck. Meeting Patrick's family was one thing. The whole town knowing about it and blowing things out of proportion was a whole other thing. But what could she do about it?

Control over her life was slipping through her fingers once again.

∽

Patrick punched in the numbers for Ashley's home phone. They'd talked a few times this week, mostly on his way home from working late. This Friday drive home would be more of the same, only earlier.

All day, he'd looked forward to sharing corny jokes just to hear her laugh.

Now he'd get to see her too.

Checking the rearview mirror, he could still see Jonathan Yoder's old white truck behind him. The day grew more interesting by the minute.

Ashley picked up on the first ring. "Hey, Patrick. On the way home already?"

He imagined her long black hair and striking green eyes. How quickly they'd fallen into a comfortable rhythm. "Yes, but I have something I need to talk over with you before you go into work tonight."

"Oh. What?"

Turning right onto Highway 26, he switched the phone to his left ear. "Would you mind if I brought a new friend with me to get your advice on a family matter?"

"You're the counselor. I'm not sure I have much to offer there."

"Ah, but you can help because it involves an expert opinion. One I know you're qualified to give."

"Okay...when?"

"We'll be there in about twenty minutes. Will that work?"

"I guess. See you then."

She hung up quick. Probably needed to go clean up the living room before they arrived. How Ashley lived with that kind of disorder baffled him. Kath was like that. He'd survived.

Jonathan's truck left the two-lane road at Yoder's Gift Shop. They hadn't talked about stopping.

Patrick's cell buzzed. "Is everything okay?"

"Yes." Jonathan spoke clear and clipped, as he had the entire time he and Bradley had been in Patrick's office. The other Mennonites he'd met at Yoder's or counseled hadn't been nearly as hard to get talking. "We will only be a moment. You can go on and we will meet you at Miss Walters's house in a short while."

"Do you know how to get there?"

"Yes." Jonathan disconnected the call.

Patrick continued to Ashley's house. Jonathan couldn't be described as hostile. None of the Mennonite men he'd met fit that bill. But he wasn't friendly either. Very closed. Patrick guessed the younger man was lonely, especially since he acted like a parent to Bradley without even being married.

He pulled in right at the twenty-minute mark like he'd planned and parked his Mustang behind the house. Up the wraparound porch steps to the side door. He knocked and waited.

Ashley got there quickly, but more out of breath than if she'd just run from her studio. "Hey, come on in." She held the door open, tucking a strand of damp hair behind her ear. "I was just cleaning up a little."

He grinned, and she returned the welcome. Her blue sweat shorts and paint-dappled GCPD T-shirt worked for him, but for Jonathan's and Bradley's sakes he should suggest a change of clothes.

"So who's the mystery friend?" She poked her head outside and looked around before closing the door behind him. "Or was this just a ploy to see me today?"

"Tempting, but no ploy. Jonathan and Bradley Yoder followed me over from my office in Perry. They should be here soon."

Looking down at her short shorts, she grimaced. "I'd best go change." She started down the hall toward the staircase.

"Mind if I browse the studio?"

Wide eyes and then a neutral face piqued his interest.

"No, go ahead. I'll be back in a minute."

The smell of oils and the tang of turpentine hit Patrick full force as he entered the bright, sunlit room. He could see why Ashley chose this one for painting.

The array of canvases surprised him. Some looked more modern in style and others definitely Impressionistic. The largest one, a pastoral scene, reminded him of Montezuma. Maybe the city girl had finally fallen for the unpaved country after all.

Another painting caught his eye. Amelia's restaurant in vivid detail. The subjects, especially him with chocolate on his face, made him laugh. As he recalled, it was Ashley with the chocolate grin at their first meeting.

"So you've found my diary." She leaned against the doorway,

stunning in a simple denim skirt and green sweater, her eyes studying his face.

He held out a hand and she came to him. Had they been dating longer, he'd have kissed her right then and there. He ran his thumb over the top of her hand and focused on another painting, an abstract in vibrant reds and purples.

"Anger or passion in this one?" Okay, maybe not the smartest question.

"Not anger." She didn't meet his eyes. Double-edged electricity swirled between them.

He released her hand with a slight squeeze and walked to the door. "Mind if I get some water?"

"Sure. Glasses are..." She paused and chewed the inside of her cheek. "Maybe in the cabinet to the right of the sink?"

A chuckle escaped. "Would you like a glass?"

"Yes."

He found the glasses right where Ashley said they'd be and filled up two very nice Waterford crystal ones. No regular Cracker Barrel ones. Around here, even the most uppity folks had a few glass mugs from the country store.

On his way back to the studio, a knock at the door stopped him. "Want me to get that?" he called down the hallway, setting the glasses on a simple cherry wood end table.

"Is it Jonathan and Bradley?"

He checked through the lace-curtained front windows. "Yes."

"I'll be right there."

Why the nervous catch in her voice? He shrugged it away as Ashley hurried to the front door, smoothing her skirt and flipping back her hair as she walked.

Jonathan and Bradley nodded and entered, Bradley glancing around with awe on his face. Jonathan studied the floor, not meeting anyone's eyes.

"Welcome, please come on into the living room." She led them into the sparsely decorated front room. There were no boxes this time, just white furniture and blue throw pillows.

Bradley sat on the loveseat, Ashley on the couch. As soon as she did, Patrick took the seat next to Ashley. Jonathan slipped in beside Bradley and dusted off his immaculate blue pants.

"So." She smiled at Bradley and locked eyes with Jonathan for a few seconds. "To what do I owe this nice surprise?"

"Mamm and Cousin Jonathan agreed to allow me to talk with Mr. James and find my birth mother." Bradley thrummed with the energy of a locomotive at full speed. "But Mr. James suggested we talk to you before making plans."

Patrick wished Bradley's politeness and barely contained energy were heart-deep. Unfortunately, they only masked a pervasive sadness the boy struggled to verbalize about his father's death and his pattern of destructive behavior.

Ashley blinked a few times but said nothing.

"And I wanted to thank you for your help and concern for my family, for allowing me to explain my actions to my mother and cousin." He stood quickly. "I…well, I brought something to say thank you."

Jonathan handed him truck keys and the boy bolted for the door.

"Y'all didn't need to bring anything. Really." Ashley's eyes still asked questions no one was answering. "But it is kinda nice to be thanked every once in a while."

"You do not have to keep this gift." Jonathan met Ashley's eyes and avoided Patrick's. "I suggested he not do this, but we have not seen Bradley so excited about anything in many months."

Before Patrick could comment, Bradley jumped through the door and into the living room, holding a chestnut boxer puppy.

Patrick stared. A dog?

"Do you like him, Miss Walters?" Bradley held the puppy out to her, and she snuggled it close. The dog yipped and then licked her. "One of my cousins works at the gift shop and said the puppy was lonely after his sister was sold. They wanted me to take him, and I thought of you. He's about four months old."

Jonathan cleared his throat. "If you do not like the dog, I will be happy to take him home with me to Indiana. He has had most of his shots and has been bathed."

Ashley laughed as the puppy licked her face. "No, I'll keep him. I've wanted a dog for so long but never got around to finding one."

Ashley and Bradley played with the puppy, and Jonathan stood transfixed, a rare smile on his face.

Bradley rubbed the dog's belly. "My cousin said two little girls named him Chester. Is that okay with you?"

"He looks like a Chester, don't you think, Patrick?" She held the puppy out to him, and the dog licked his hand.

"Sounds like a great name." The puppy's friendliness reminded him of Abe, his favorite dog growing up. Abe had licked everything too and followed close on Patrick's heels after his father died.

Chester settled onto Ashley's lap as they all returned to their seats.

"Thank you, Bradley…and Jonathan for this gift." She rubbed the dog's brownish red back. "I can't thank you enough for Chester."

If Patrick had any clue that Ashley wanted a dog this much, he'd have gotten one for her first. Too bad he didn't know. Too late now.

"We also have a few things for the dog in my truck. A bed and some food." Jonathan flicked his eyes to the wooden mantel clock, and his seriousness returned. "We must go soon. But first, the business we came to discuss."

"You want my opinion on meeting Bradley's birth mother?" Ashley met his gaze with an unsettled face. "I'm not sure I can be of much help with that."

Bradley jumped in. "Mr. James and I agree this is a good idea. But Cousin Jonathan and Mamm don't like it."

Ashley and Jonathan locked gazes for a long minute. Then she turned to Patrick. "Can we talk in the kitchen?" She handed the puppy to Bradley. "Would you mind taking him outside? He needs to get used to the backyard." She ruffled the boy's hair before he took off and stood staring after him.

Patrick nudged her. "You okay?"

"Yeah." She shook her head, eyes unfocused and sad. "Bradley reminds me of my brother. A lot."

The heaviness of those words struck him. "You sure you're okay?"

She darted out of the room.

Patrick followed her into the kitchen. "Ashley, if we need to talk about things with Bradley later, we can. I'd rather talk about your brother if you need to."

"No. I'm good." She filled a glass with water and gulped it down. "I want to help Bradley if I can."

He cataloged her response and checked his concern.

"So what did you want to tell me?" Her green eyes cleared and she slipped into a business posture.

"You asked me to come in here. I'm not sure why since Bradley's outside." He leaned back against the kitchen counter.

"Oh. Right." She narrowed her eyes. "What I have to say is for you only. I don't think Jonathan would understand."

That pleased him more than it should have. "Okay, shoot."

"From the few things Bradley's said to me, his mother could well be a convicted felon, if she's even still alive."

"She is. Bradley found her. She lives in Americus."

"She dumped him on someone's doorstep and disappeared." Ashley worked her jaw. "My experience with people like that hasn't been positive."

"I agree with you. At the same time, Bradley has fixated on this woman and is ignoring his work and refusing to face the pain of his father's death. He's closed off to everything but meeting his biological mother."

Ashley softened. "I'd forgotten about his dad's death. Bradley must be hurting a lot to not show any emotion about it."

"Exactly. And there's a chance that meeting this woman will give him closure and maybe even help him see how much he's wanted and needed with his adoptive family."

She exhaled long and slow. "I still don't like it."

"She has no parental rights to contest."

Ashley paused in the kitchen doorway. "I'll go along with this only if you let me be there too. I want to make sure Brad is okay."

"Done." She'd used a nickname for the boy, a sure sign of her investment in his life. Had she even realized that?

He placed a hand on her back as they returned to the living room, and she relaxed into his touch.

Bradley had returned and was on the floor with Chester, wrestling with the puppy. Jonathan stood until Ashley took a seat.

She spoke first. "I'm not convinced meeting with Bradley's biological mother is the best idea."

"I agree." Jonathan's gaze settled on Bradley.

"But if, as Patrick believes, this will help Bradley with some closure and enable him to refocus back home, it might be worth trying."

Bradley and Ashley exchanged smiles.

Jonathan did not. "We will continue to pray." He motioned to Bradley. "We should go. I will bring Bradley back to your office on Monday, Mr. James. Perhaps after more prayer we can make final plans."

Ashley moved to the door. "Thank you for bringing Bradley and…" She bent down to pick up Chester. "And my wonderful gift. I love him."

Jonathan only nodded and walked to his truck.

Bradley rubbed Chester's ears. "Thank you, Miss Walters…Mr. James."

Patrick and Ashley stood on the porch until Jonathan unloaded the food and dog bed and drove away. Chester whined and wriggled.

"I hate to ask this, but…can you take us to a pet store? I don't know where any are and I need to get Chester a crate and some toys to get him settled in before I go to work tonight." She let the puppy down to sniff around the front porch.

"Sure. There's a pet store in Americus. We should be able to drive there and back well before you need to get ready for work."

"Thank you." She grabbed her purse and snuggled Chester close.

It wasn't the Friday night he'd planned, but he could adjust. He was getting to spend extra time with Ashley. For today, that was enough.

CHAPTER EIGHT

Ashley shot straight up in bed and fumbled for a light.

What was that awful howling?

Chester.

She dashed down the stairs, following the sound, and found her puppy sitting by the back door, quivering. His mournful eyes pricked at her heart.

Somebody had trained this little guy well. She patted his head and fumbled with the lock. "Here you go. Good boy, Chester. Good boy for waiting on me." She grabbed a coat off the kitchen chair and slipped it on.

The second she opened the door, he flew down the steps and to the back fence. She flipped on a way-too-bright porch light and groaned at the dark night. Nothing like a crash course on doggy care.

Her parents would just about die. That shouldn't have made her smile, but it did. She'd always wanted a dog, and they'd always been adamantly opposed. Now they had no say.

Chester trotted back and sat by her feet.

Breathing in the frigid night air, she sighed. "Thank you, God."

Chester tilted his head and yipped. She picked him up. "Yeah, that startled me too, a prayer slipping out like that. It's been too long."

Maybe Chester wasn't just a thank you gift from Bradley. Maybe all the prayers Margo prayed, and probably Patrick and Jonathan too, combined and bypassed the walls she'd formed between her and God.

Maybe.

She flipped off the light and stared at the stars. They were so much brighter here than in Atlanta.

The snap of a twig close by snagged her attention. Surveying the entire yard, she couldn't make out anything in the darkness. But her hair stood on end. Was someone hidden out there, watching? After years on the force, she'd come to trust the instinct that told her to get Chester in the house and grab her gun before she checked things out.

Sprinting upstairs to her duty weapon, she left Chester in the bedroom and rushed back into the dark. If someone was playing Peeping Tom outside, she'd hand deliver him to the officers on duty.

Quieting her breathing, she inched along the house, her eyes adjusting to the darkness. She hugged the fence and scanned the perimeter of her large, forested backyard. Step-by-step, she covered every millimeter.

A rustling sound closer to the house turned her around with her weapon trained at head height.

Chester howled inside.

But no one was there.

She retraced her steps toward the fence gate and found it unlocked. She hadn't left it that way, had she? Not possible.

Rather than rush out of her yard like she wanted to, she stayed in control and slipped through the gate and studied the street both ways.

Nothing.

Either someone was hiding in one of a hundred places, waiting to ambush her, or she'd gotten spooked by the wind and wild animals.

Given the new house and all the animals roaming everywhere, it was possible, however unlikely.

She slipped back into her yard, locked the gate and back door, and picked up the phone. To do what? Call her friends to investigate an invisible troublemaker? She didn't need that ribbing from the other officers. Besides, she'd done all they could do short of canvass the neighborhood for a suspicious person on foot.

No, she'd let it go this time and double-check her gates every night from now on.

She tossed the phone on the table and dumped her old coat on the floor, too tired to hang it up. Stumbling up the stairs, she made it to her messy bed and flopped into the blue and white comforter.

The next sounds she heard were birdsongs outside her window and Chester panting.

His warm, wet tongue raked across her cheek, and she flinched. It'd be a while before the happy puppy greeting would cancel out the yuck factor.

"Yes, master. I'm awake." She wasn't ready for kids if one little dog could turn her world sideways in twenty-four hours.

Together, they made their way downstairs, and she started a pot of coffee. "Too bad your Mennonite keepers didn't train you to fix coffee too."

Chester yipped and wagged his whole backside.

What a cutie.

The phone's shrill ring echoed in the huge house. Chester barked, then followed her on a hunt for the cordless.

Looking all through the kitchen, she found only the base.

Nothing in the living room.

She jogged down the hall and found Chester standing over a wet phone in the studio. Either the little mischief maker had been playing with it or he was a good hunting dog. Regardless, she needed to purchase some baby gates to slim down his roaming area. She wiped the phone on her pj's before answering it.

"Hello?"

"Exercising already?"

Patrick. She smiled. "Not exactly, just trying to find the phone. But after running to the studio, I could count that as exercise."

"You could. But it might be more fun for you and Chester if you explore the neighborhood too." Patrick sounded wide awake and thrilled about it. Ashley wouldn't get to that point until around ten o'clock tonight.

"We'll put that on today's to-do list before the cookout tonight."

Phone tucked between her ear and shoulder, she made her way back to the kitchen and washed her hands before plopping two frozen waffles in the toaster.

Chester yipped. She scooped some dog food into his new stainless-steel antiskid bowls, the ones that even matched the shiny silver appliances in the kitchen. Mother would be so proud.

"About tonight. Kath is glad to have Chester join us."

"Oh, good. I need to pick up some flowers or something for your sister. She's been so understanding and gracious about rescheduling the cookout for today. Yesterday was just too crazy with the vet visit, errands, and other dog-related projects. I had to fix the fence and all sorts of other home improvements to protect Chester." Still, she'd forgotten the gates and failed to put Chester in his crate. His plaintive cry broke her resolve when she'd tried to leave him in there last night.

"You could have called. I would've come over to help."

"You had work to do."

"I was supposed to go hunting, but a patient called. I still could have helped with something."

"There are some things I need to do for myself." Let him psychoanalyze that one later. "Back to your sister. Would she like flowers?"

"She'll love the flowers. And she's very glad to know that Chester got dipped and sprayed and shot and all that good stuff."

Poor Chester. Yesterday's errands hadn't been fun for anybody, but she'd been relieved to learn the dog had been well cared for and was healthy. Now he was super groomed and living in a relatively safe environment. And despite the late night bathroom trips, he was an incredibly well-behaved dog.

Jonathan was the most likely dog caretaker. That made her even more thankful for her new pet.

"...and so if you'd like to join us, we'd love to have you."

Ashley figured out too late that Patrick had been talking for a while. Oops. "I didn't catch all of that. Sorry. Could you push replay?"

"I was just asking if you'd like to join me at church today, and then we can pick up Chester before we go over to Kath's house."

Church. Today. She ran a hand through her mass of tangles and shook her head. No way could she make it from pj's to church in any semblance of soon. Not a chance.

"I'd like to, but I really don't think I can today." Funny, she meant it too. "Maybe next week?" If she didn't talk herself out of it like she had every other time she'd almost gone the past few years.

"Okay. I'll try and remember to ask you about it on Saturday."

"Sounds good. Thanks for understanding." Even though there was no way he could really understand all her reasons for saying no. If they kept going out and meeting family, she'd have to tell Patrick something, sometime soon.

But not yet.

Chester yipped and tugged at her socked feet. "Sorry, Patrick, but I'm being summoned by his highness." She bent down and picked him up. He nuzzled her hand. "I'd better let you get to church too. See you tonight."

"I'll pick you up at five."

Ashley placed the phone on its base and let Chester outside for a minute. Watching him jump around and play tugged at her heart. If only Eric were here to see it.

And as they had for ten years, the memories flooded back, unwelcome ones this time.

Before the move to Montezuma, she'd often stepped into the past by opening her high school yearbook or one of the silly scrapbooks she'd done of her and Harrison. Eric's pictures dominated many of the pages. Her brother had inserted himself naturally into most of her time with Harrison. They'd been inseparable, the three of them. From the first night Harrison picked her up for his and Eric's junior prom and her brother decided to make it a double date, to the last time she'd seen Eric alive.

She blinked away the tears pooling in her eyes. She would not go back into that dark time. She couldn't. It'd destroy all of her that was left.

She opened the door, and Chester bounded her way and hopped into her arms. She snuggled with him a while and then slipped back inside, setting him down on a special Chester towel just for keeping his paws wiped off and her house clean.

"Now it's my turn to get clean." Chester cocked his head like he was trying to understand her words. "I need a shower, pup. You coming?"

Once upstairs, Chester flopped down on his doggie bed and snoozed. She hurried in and out of the shower reciting ten-codes and analyzing burglary reports just to keep her mind busy. Same for getting dressed.

Then in the foggy mirror she saw it. The one memory that shredded her heart: Eric's crime scene photos. She'd only viewed the crime scene photos once. Without the photos, there were days she could review her files and shut out the emotion, pretend it was someone besides her big brother.

But Eric was why she'd gone to the police academy. Why she trained hard and took pride in putting violent criminals behind bars.

To do all she could to stop muggers and rapists and murderers, so no one else had to go through the searing pain of still breathing after a loved one was ripped away.

To pay Eric back for all the times he'd protected her.

"If you'd been there, you would have died too." Margo's tear-stained whispers reached through the past and jerked Ashley into the present.

So why was she still alive and her big brother wasn't? He was the good one, the one everybody depended on. Why couldn't Eric have lived?

Answers to impossible questions never came. How could they?

She slipped into the studio and lost herself in the only place where past and present joined and turned into something beautiful.

∽

Jonathan settled into the barn closest to the house and busied himself with another small block of pine and his whittling knife, this time for the pure pleasure of working with his hands like his Savior had done.

The afternoon was silent, except for the peaceful scrape of knife against wood. Anna and Bradley would return soon from visiting friends, a family activity Jonathan had enjoyed in his younger days.

Many, many days and years ago.

A car's powerful engine rumbled over the loose gravel of Anna's driveway. It grew louder and stopped abruptly. Not a lost person seeking a place to turn around.

He walked to the house, up the back porch, and inside before the first knock on the door arrived.

On the way to the front door, he passed a family photo hanging crookedly on the living room wall: Anna, Peter, and Bradley when he was about seven years old. Jonathan adjusted it and prayed for his aunt's family and for God's mysterious work to be accomplished here.

Another knock sounded. He hurried to open the front door.

Two people stood in the late afternoon sun, a dark-suited man of maybe fifty years and a younger, shorter woman, also in a suit. Both wearing what he guessed were very expensive leather coats. Odd dress even for Montezuma people on a Sunday evening.

"May I help you?" Jonathan stood in the doorway.

The woman spoke first. "Is Mrs. Yoder here?"

"No. She will return shortly, though. Is there anything I can help you with?"

The man stepped forward, a smile tugging his lips upward. "You must be Peter and Anna's oldest boy." He offered his hand for a shake. "You're a ways older than my son, but just as able to hold down the fort, I see."

"Fort?"

"Just a turn of phrase, my boy. So, maybe you can help us. Can we come in and talk a spell?"

"Could you tell me your names, please?"

The woman cleared her throat. "I'm Janet Hardy and this is Andrew Jennings."

He stepped out on the porch and closed the door behind him. "I am not Anna's son but her nephew, Jonathan Yoder. And this is not my house in which to invite guests." He motioned to the row of three rocking chairs. "Please, sit. I know it is cold, but we can speak out here, yes?"

The woman's made-up face turned red for a moment before she sat in a rocking chair on the other side of Mr. Jennings.

Mr. Jennings rocked a moment and stared into the front yard. "Well, seeing as you're acting as man of the house here, I'd like to ask you a few questions, if I might. Your aunt is having a tough go of making this dairy farm work, is she not? Her two daughters and both sons have moved away, and her adopted son is much younger than you. I'd imagine that makes running a hundred or so acres of dairy farm difficult work."

"Anna is managing the farm well."

The woman stared at him like those people he had encountered at the gas station in Atlanta. He did not wish to repeat such an unpleasant event.

"So this farm is making a profit and your aunt is able to save up for the future?" The man rocked slowly and stared out into the deepening blue sky.

"These are not questions I can answer for you, sir."

"Can't or won't?" The woman muttered under her breath.

The older man rocked as if he had heard nothing at all. "So are you planning to stay long, here in Montezuma?"

"I am not sure how long I will stay here."

"Well, son." The man stood with the woman close beside him. "Please let your aunt know we stopped by. One of my investors is interested in making her a very generous offer for her land."

"For her land?" Jonathan rose, too, and stared at the visitors. "I do not believe Anna is interested in selling." She might have to sell to other Mennonite farmers, but his aunt had not mentioned offering her farm to anyone else.

"Local grapevine's buzzing about how Mrs. Yoder's farm would make an incredible location for the Mennonite museum and maybe a store or two we're planning for the revitalization. It's close to downtown, yet surrounded by enough countryside to make it feel miles away. And our offer would make sure your aunt is well taken care of for a very, very long time."

"I will pass this information along to Anna."

"Here's my card." Mr. Jennings extended a white business card with the Jennings Company logo and a list of phone numbers and computer addresses on it. "Please have her call me, so we can meet and discuss business."

"I will speak with her when she arrives home."

The visitors left faster than they had arrived. Jonathan remained on the porch, watching sunlight poke out from behind the clouds. Sell the farm to non-Mennonites? It had been in the Yoder family since the first Mennonites arrived in this area over fifty years ago.

Jonathan bowed his head to pray and seek the Lord for wisdom.

Soon, his aunt's blue minivan pulled into the driveway and parked. Bradley was out the door and into the house with no greeting.

Anna plodded across the lawn and up the porch steps.

"Are you not feeling well?" Jonathan offered his arm for her to lean on and led her into the warm living room.

"I am fine. Sad, though." She sat in her rocking chair and folded her hands. "Please go speak with Bradley. Maybe you will help me understand this headstrong boy."

He left the living room and walked down the hall to Bradley's room. His first knock went unanswered, so he knocked louder a second time. "Bradley? I wish to speak with you."

The door eased open, and Bradley left it that way and returned to his bed.

"There was a problem tonight?"

Bradley nodded. "Mamm is mad at me. But it wasn't my fault."

This sounded much like the chatter of boys young and old who came into Jonathan's carpentry shop and roughhoused too much, causing injury to themselves or one of the items for sale. Bradley should know better than this. Peter and Anna had raised him to use self-control and treat others with respect.

"This thing that was not your fault..." Jonathan stood just inside the door. "Would you explain it to me?"

"One of the boys teased me about getting in trouble in Indiana and here and how hard I have to work now. He said all this in front of Amanda and Ruth." Bradley blushed and turned to the window. "I asked him to stop, but he didn't."

"And so you did what, Bradley?"

"An older boy, Paul, said they should tie me to a chair so I wouldn't run off again. The girls laughed."

Jonathan waited, sad for his young cousin. Sadder still for what the boy's temper was doing inside his soul and the minds of all who saw this event tonight.

"So I hit him." The boy's voice was almost a whisper. "He will not bother me like that again."

"But this will wound your soul until you take it to the Lord. Forgiveness is His way, Bradley. Forgiveness will free you." Jonathan turned to walk out of Bradley's room. "The Lord understands your feelings. Speak with Him about this."

Jonathan stood outside the boy's room and prayed for words of comfort for Anna and healing for Bradley. Peter's death, all the strange business in town, and now Bradley's angry behavior would not make the farm run well or the community remain strong in the Lord.

They would need to talk with the bishop tomorrow about Bradley and other matters concerning Anna's farm.

He checked in on Anna and left her to her quiet prayers in the living room.

Returning to the barn, he picked up his wood and knife and tried to make sense of everything. Even if he had no idea what to do or how to help, Jonathan knew the one who did. And it was at God's feet Jonathan would lay the ache in his heart for both Bradley and Anna's future.

CHAPTER NINE

Patrick set Kathleen's large oak dinner table while his mother filled tall glasses with ice and sweet tea. Outside, Ashley held Chester up to a tired and bundled up Susie-Q resting in Kath's arms. His three-month-old niece just stared.

Mom joined him at the window. "She's a lovely girl, Paddy."

"Yes, she is."

"Inside too?"

He turned to face his mother, startled once again by her graying hair and extra weight. "What did your endocrinologist say about the new pills?"

She rolled her eyes. "I'm the doctor, son, and you need not worry about me."

"The canines and felines in your care are happy you're a vet. But I'm worried about your diabetes and how you're managing. Talk to me."

"Always the responsible one." She placed a cold hand on his cheek. "I've depended on you too much since your father died."

The weight of those words rooted him in Montezuma.

"But you now have other people to watch over." Mom peered outside. "Be happy and stop worrying about me."

Kath, with Susie limp in her arms, strolled toward the house. Ashley and Chester played their way closer to the house too.

"This conversation isn't over, Mom. And don't make too much of things with Ashley. We're taking it slow."

"That's not what you want."

How could she still read his mind? As a kid, he'd believed in her superhuman abilities, thinking she was the only mom in the world who could see inside heads. He'd learned better. Most moms had that infuriating ability. Too bad he couldn't bottle that and sell it at work. He'd make a fortune ten times over.

Kath entered first and unwrapped a sleeping Susie. "I'm going to put our princess to bed." She held Susie out to Mom for a goodnight kiss. "Want to send her off to dreamland, Paddy?"

He kissed her soft wisp of red hair and whispered, "Sweet dreams, little one. God holds you in the palm of His hand."

Kath winked. "Go be host with Chip. He needs you."

Patrick looked up. Ashley stood in the kitchen, coat off and eyes fixed on their little family ritual. The longing in her gaze tightened around his rib cage. He couldn't stop being a big brother to Kath. There had to be some way to help Ashley though.

Rather than attempt a conversation that deep in front of an audience, he motioned her over. With a smile that didn't quite reach her pretty green eyes, she and Chester crossed the kitchen to his side.

Chip entered last, his Atlanta Braves hat riding high on his head and a monstrous pile of burgers in one hand. He strutted to the dining room table and placed the meat in the center of all the other dinner fixings. "I'm gonna wash up, and as soon as Kath returns we'll dig in."

Mom added a huge bowl of her famous homemade mashed potatoes and a heaped up bowl of sweet potato casserole to the table and sat down. "Ashley, dear, why don't you come sit by me?"

"I'd love to, Mrs. James."

"Please, call me Helen."

"I'd love to join you, Helen." She tugged Patrick's hand and together they walked to the dining room table, Chester on their heels.

Patrick caught Chip's smirk and ignored him. No one in his family missed Ashley's hand in his, and that didn't bother him one bit.

Ashley sat down and Chester collapsed next to her. "Guess he's worn out but good today."

Mom nodded. "He's a fine puppy. I'd be honored if you'd bring him to my clinic."

"Absolutely."

Mom lasered him across the table. He should have directed Ashley to Mom's clinic in the first place. He shrugged. How was he supposed to know Ashley would take Chester to Americus for a checkup yesterday? He was at work then.

Chip's smirk deepened. What Patrick wouldn't give for access to Chip's brain right now. His brother-in-law had promised to be on his best behavior, no jokes. But that was like asking a hound dog not to hunt.

Mom waved Kath over as soon as she entered the kitchen. "Come on, honey. Food's getting cold."

"Ah, but I'm not rushing through sweet baby cuddles. They're only little a short while." Kath grinned at Mom. "A wise woman once taught me that."

After everyone was seated, Chip slapped his hat on his leg and grabbed Kath's hand. "Let's pray. Lord, we thank You for this day and for this food. Keep us honest, wise, and remind Patrick what Saturdays are supposed to be for."

Everyone echoed Chip's amen and started passing food. He wasn't impressed. He wasn't a workaholic either.

As usual around this table, conversation didn't start until most folks had caused a few forkfuls of food to disappear.

Mom spoke first. "Patrick, Chester reminds me so much of Abe. Don't you think so?" She turned her focus to Ashley. "Abe was his Labrador."

"Abe was a great dog, but I don't see the resemblance with Chester."

Mom wiped the corners of her mouth. "They're both honest looking and playful. I love that in a dog. Reminds me of Misty too. Good dogs those two were. And I understand both Abe and Chester were gifts."

Abe was Dad's last gift to them, and Patrick's dog had stuck by his side until he'd left for college and old age had claimed Abe.

Maybe he should adopt another rescue dog and make more good

memories. Maybe when things settled down and there was time to give a dog the care he deserved.

"Yes, Chester was a gift from a Mennonite friend."

Kath caught his eye and lifted one brow, but he didn't need the mother hen concern.

He glimpsed Ashley's way, but she bent down to pat Chester. Rather than have her equate his dad's gift to Jonathan's, it was time for a change. "So, did y'all hear about the special zoning committee meeting Monday?"

Chip gulped down half his tea. "I'd rather talk about huntin'."

"I'll go next time, okay? Back down, bulldog."

"I'm more of a Georgia Tech guy, myself."

Even Ashley laughed at the dig on rival mascots of Georgia sports fanatics.

Kath harrumphed. "I think it's fishy, that meeting. Why are you going, Patrick?"

"I'm on the committee. Besides, you know what this revitalization project means to this town…and to me." To his dad. Too many good memories that shouldn't die with the Montezuma downtown.

"It's still weird. Keep things honest, Paddy." She picked at her burger and wouldn't meet his eyes.

What did his little sister know that he didn't? Probably not much in terms of the revitalization project, but she made up for what facts she lacked with uncanny intuition. He'd have to talk to her later about her concerns. And the heaviness they laid on his back.

∞

Ashley was full and happy. She hadn't eaten good Southern cooking in a long while. Her parents preferred fresh lobster and pressed linens.

Not Ashley.

The dinner company couldn't have been beat either. Good thing she and Patrick weren't alone this evening, or the intimate glances they'd exchanged could get her into trouble.

Over chocolate pie, his attention had even chased away the pain that pricked every time Patrick and Kathleen exchanged a knowing look. So like her and Eric during family dinners. Their parents had never figured out the silly signals the two of them used to talk without words.

Eric would have liked Patrick.

Chester roused himself from too much human food and a nice nap, stretching long and yawning wide. Then her little ball of reddish brown fur followed her to the kitchen counter. She placed her plate in Patrick's outstretched hand. "That was amazing pie, Kathleen."

Kathleen grinned her thanks and returned to clearing the table with her mother, the two of them engrossed in conversation. Ashley couldn't remember ever cleaning up after a meal with her parents like that.

Patrick touched her chin and she jumped.

"Just checking." He studied her mouth a minute too long and leaned close. "No chocolate to be seen."

Words escaped her.

Thankfully, Patrick returned to manning the dishwasher with Chip and putting leftovers in the fridge like a well-executed sports play. She could totally get used to this.

Kathleen grinned and locked arms with her. "You have to train them well right off the bat."

Chip snapped a dish towel at his wife. Chester yipped. "Trained? I don't think so. I'm just a great guy, that's all. Right, Paddy?"

Patrick raised his hands. "I'm not touching that one with a ten foot pole."

Chip laughed. "Besides, it's the rewards later that keep me cleaning with a smile on my face."

Kath groaned. "Show some manners."

"Manners? You've got your work cut out for you, Kath." Patrick shook his head and attempted a serious face. "I don't think Chip can even define the word."

Everyone laughed.

Ashley followed Kathleen and Mrs. James into the living room,

Chester again attached to her heels. Aside from a playpen and scattered baby toys, Kathleen's décor resembled Ashley's. Lived in.

Ashley scanned the green and tan furniture and accents. Kathleen had far more pictures of family displayed than Ashley even owned. One of Patrick as a young teen caught her eye. Wow, was he handsome, even when most boys that age were gangly and awkward.

Patrick's warm hand on her back startled her. "Glad you like the picture."

Busted.

Chip plopped down on the tan sectional and drew Kathleen close. "So, Patrick, any truth to the rumors about the new Mennonite museum and stores?"

Patrick stiffened. "What rumors?" He led Ashley to the love seat and sat next to her without touching. Chester plopped right on her lap.

Mrs. James shook her head. "It's probably nothing, honey. But some of the store owners were hoping to get lots of authentic Mennonite gift items and food to sell when their stores reopen. Seems they're not able to find any sellers."

Patrick shrugged. "Don't know one way or the other. I haven't heard."

"But if it's true," Chip leaned forward, "that means the Mennonites here are keeping others from selling to us." He sighed loud and long. "It won't make things easy for us, you know? We need those stores and the jobs and revenue the revitalization is supposed to bring."

Ashley jumped in. "But the Mennonites aren't standing in anyone's way. They just don't want their way of life distorted by half-truths in that Mennonite museum the Atlanta big shot is touting. I think he's the one in the wrong."

Everyone stared. Not the impression she'd hoped to leave with these folks.

Patrick broke the awkward silence. "But I see Chip's point. If the rumors are true, it's not going to help anyone."

Why couldn't she just let this go? Brad's and Jonathan's faces came to mind. They didn't deserve the slur on their character. "The Mennonites don't need this revitalization. Jonathan's and Anna's businesses will be fine without it. Seems to me the town council is trying to capitalize on the Mennonites' way of life without offering them a little respect in terms of their faith. In my book, that's wrong."

"Jonathan doesn't live here."

"But how would you feel if people tried to exploit your way of life and wanted the most popular parts of your culture but none of your God?"

Patrick shrugged. "No one's trying to exploit the Mennonite way of life."

"The revitalization project wants the museum for the visitors the Mennonites would bring without giving anything back. These kind, gentle people shouldn't need anyone's permission to share their faith." Ashley's skin burned but she wouldn't back down from what reeked of injustice.

Chip sat forward. "How long have you lived here, Ashley?"

She sat forward, matching his posture. Chester hopped down to the floor and flopped into another nap. "A little over a month."

"And how many Mennonites do you know well?" Chip adjusted his Braves cap. "I've lived here all my life and don't know many of them by name. What I do know is they aren't very much part of our community. We need their help now so our town won't blow away like tumbleweed. That's all we're asking for, really."

Ashley sat straight up. "Then stand up for their right to share their faith. That would go a long way." She leaned back. "Besides, I've heard that the Mennonites are the first to help anyone in Montezuma even if they don't attend many community events. That says a lot about their character."

Kathleen stepped in. "You're right. The Mennonites have rebuilt many of the farmhouses and barns, and even homes in town when they've burned or were damaged. If allowing them to share their faith is the only thing standing in the way, we should be able to work that out, right Paddy?"

Beside her, Patrick raised and lowered his shoulders but stayed a few inches away. That short distance echoed like a chasm. "Hopefully. But it's private money." His eyes flicked Ashley's way. "I'll see what I can do."

She reached for his hand. "Thank you."

Conversation turned to Braves baseball and SEC football, especially the Georgia Bulldogs. Not the same topics as her artsy family, but a similar tactic after a tense exchange. Maybe things weren't so different in big cities and small towns.

Chester hopped up and yipped at the back door. "I guess duty, or as I refer to him, my master, calls." Everyone chuckled.

She joined her puppy outside and closed the back door behind her. The fresh, cold night air shivered through her, giving her jumbled mind time to unfurl.

The whole conversation about Montezuma and the revitalization crackled with unspoken words. Why?

Voices streamed out from the open kitchen window.

"You'd better step it up, Patrick, or..." Kathleen's tired sigh cut off the rest of her words.

"Or what?" Patrick. Tense.

Ashley's neck hairs stood on end.

"Or those rumors might just be true and she'll be wooed into the Mennonite world. She's spent an awful lot of time on the Yoders' farm lately."

What? Why were her off time activities the subject of small-town gossip? She was there to spend time with Bradley. Nothing else.

But Kathleen, like Patrick, sensed behind and under mere words.

Kathleen's tight voice broke the night's calm. "I don't want you hurt again, Paddy."

Again?

Ashley would have to get to the bottom of the siblings' conversation. But that might mean trading pieces of their pasts better left alone.

She shivered again, but not from the cold. Maybe that discussion would happen. But not yet. She wasn't ready.

CHAPTER TEN

M onday morning dawned with its usual dullness. The short and sweet good-bye from Patrick last night didn't help matters.

Ashley rolled over and replumped her large body pillow. Chester snoozed on, nails clicking on the hardwood floor as he chased something in dreamland.

Today gave her no reason to hop out of bed. Brad and Jonathan would once again arrive at her home with Patrick watching every move, analyzing if Kathleen's words were true.

She flipped over and stared at the ceiling. Truth be told, the aha moment had hit her like a lightning bolt in her predawn sleepiness. Patrick had picked up on the currents that passed between her and Jonathan, and it didn't matter that she had no intention of exploring them.

Jonathan wasn't even interested anyway.

Patrick was. And, like everyone else in this small town, Patrick had made the two of them a couple. And Ashley hadn't said no. In fact, she'd clearly said yes with their daily phone calls and weekend dates.

So like it or not, she was half of a couple again. And there were responsibilities to live up to. She slipped out of her pretty blue and white bedroom and into the shower without disturbing Chester.

At exactly nine o'clock, a knock on the front door echoed through the house. Patrick. It had to be him.

She wrapped a thin purple hair tie around her ponytail and checked the antique mirror one last time. The white and purple slip dress fit well and modestly. Still, her shoulders were small boulders sitting atop her arms.

The knock echoed again and Chester barked, waiting for her to join him in running to the door.

"Coming!" She descended the stairs calmly, belying the jitterbug dancing up and down her spine. Undaunted, Chester attacked the front door with barks and happy greetings.

She opened the door wide and stepped outside, ready to greet Patrick with a hello kiss.

Jonathan stepped back. "Miss Walters?"

Ashley tried to quell the fire in her cheeks while she glanced everywhere but Jonathan's face, hoping her stupid move had gone unnoticed.

When she dared a look at him, he averted his eyes and stared at her left shoulder.

Chester danced around them.

"Sorry about that…I…I thought you were Patrick."

Jonathan nodded, a shadow passing over his face then nothing but his unreadable stare. "I told Mr. James we would meet him here." He peered over his shoulder toward his white truck. "Bradley and I brought some dog bones and a wooden bin to store his food."

"Thank you. But you didn't have to do that."

Without comment, he turned and strode to his truck to retrieve the items. Chester romped right alongside Jonathan's confident gait.

A quiet Bradley crossed the front yard, holding a bag of dog treats and a Ziploc with some meaty bones away from Chester's curious yips. Jonathan followed, strong arms easily carrying a beautiful wooden bin with Chester's name on the hinged door.

The two men stood on her front porch waiting for her to invite them in.

"Oh. Sorry." She opened the door and stepped back for them to enter. "Thank you both for the food and this wonderful bin. Did you make it, Jonathan?"

"Yes."

Chester led the way to the kitchen. As she started to close the door, Patrick's black Mustang purred into the driveway. She stepped onto the porch and waited, reclaiming the courage to do what she'd originally planned. He needed to know she saw them as a couple now too.

As soon as he exited his car, his blue eyes locked onto hers. They didn't twinkle. And when he stepped onto the porch, he stopped a few inches away.

She closed the distance, tilting her head up, and touched her lips to his.

Patrick's arms encircled her and drew her closer. Then he pulled away but stayed close enough to lean his forehead to hers.

She sighed, her skin tingling. Patrick could kiss.

"That was a nice greeting." Now his thoughtful blue eyes sparked.

Much better.

Before they could continue their conversation, Jonathan stepped onto the porch and closed her front door with more force than required.

Patrick didn't release her.

Ashley glanced between the two men and stepped just outside of Patrick's embrace. Close enough to be with him, but not so close it was uncomfortable with Jonathan right there.

Brad joined them on the porch.

"Mind if I drive?" Patrick addressed all of them, but directed the question to her.

Jonathan answered. "We are fine with that."

The three males silently turned and headed toward the car. Well... this was certainly shaping up to be an interesting day.

She monitored the three men in the car out of the corner of her eye, Patrick humming as he drove, Jonathan focusing out the window, and Brad drumming his hands on his dark pants legs.

She should say some words of encouragement to Brad. No matter how this day went, it wouldn't be easy.

Brad broke the quietness first, leaning forward. "I read something this morning."

"Tell me about it." She relaxed a fraction.

"I read in my Bible this morning, something Jesus said, 'I have told you these things, so that in me you may have peace. In this world you will have trouble. But take heart! I have overcome the world.'"

The words poked at the raw places inside. Jesus hadn't overcome the evil that had taken her brother's life. He hadn't prevented Brad from being dumped on a stranger's doorstep by a woman who didn't care enough to raise him. God wouldn't protect Brad from the truth of who his birth mother was either. If she was anything like Ashley suspected, today would hurt Brad more than he could handle. So she'd protect him. Better to take care of what you can on your own and make sure it's done right.

Jonathan's deep baritone filled the car. "This should comfort you, Bradley. God is with us, and He will give us peace no matter what happens today."

She wouldn't be the one to poke holes in Jonathan's faith or Bradley's. Hers had enough holes for all of them.

The rest of the ride droned on in silence until they pulled into a driveway in a decent Americus neighborhood.

She turned around in the front seat to wait for Brad's first move. He sat still and stared at the box-like yellowish house that matched the address the boy had given Patrick earlier.

"Ready?" She sounded like a kindergarten teacher on steroids.

He took a deep breath and straightened his coat. "Yes, ma'am." He leaned toward Jonathan. "She agreed to meet with us, right?"

Tenderness filled Jonathan's blue eyes as he placed a strong hand on the boy's shoulder. "We are here for you, Bradley. Do you want Miss Walters and me to wait outside for you?"

"No." Brad looked from Jonathan to her. "I want both of you there."

Satisfied, they exited the car en masse and trouped to the front porch.

Brad hung back. "Miss Walters?" He stepped toward the Mustang. She joined him. "Please don't ask how I found my mother, okay?"

She waited in silence for him to explain, a technique that caused many a guilty person to squirm.

He kicked at the gravel driveway.

"Brad. Tell me."

"I...well, Mamm." He shoved his hands in his coat pockets. "I need to see her. And Mamm had information hidden under her bed—letters from my mom with numbers and such—and I used those and Mamm's computer and found her." His eyes pleaded.

"Jonathan and your mother don't know?"

"No. They wouldn't understand."

"They agreed to let you see Mr. James and come today. That's a pretty big indicator of their love and support." She nodded toward the peeling siding and scraggly weeds in the tiny front yard. "Your Mamm and Jonathan love you, Brad. Don't forget that."

"Okay."

She walked with him up to the front porch and stood beside him while he rang the doorbell. The tinny sound vibrated around them and hung in the air.

Patrick's protective hand rested at the small of her back.

Seconds slipped away.

"She agreed to this meeting at ten o'clock, right?" Ashley surveyed the cookie-cutter neighborhood.

"Yes." Patrick's jaw twitched. At least she wasn't the only one on edge.

Brad knocked on the mud-stained front door.

Soon they heard banging inside and a woman's muffled curse. Ashley cringed.

"Yeah, wait a minute, will ya?" Scraping and thumping noises grew louder and louder.

Sweat trickled down Ashley's back and caused her to shiver despite her down coat. She stepped closer to Brad and put a hand on his shoulder to mirror Jonathan's stance.

At least the boy was well protected outside. She hoped that would be enough.

Locks clicked and a short, well-dressed blonde flung the door open. "Okay, well, here I am." She studied Jonathan a few minutes too long and then slid her gaze to Brad. "You, Bradley?"

"Yes, ma'am."

Patrick stuck out his hand. "Patrick James. We spoke on the phone."

"Joyce Stone." She appraised Patrick in the same open manner as she had Jonathan.

Ashley wanted to wipe the suggestive smile off the woman's face. Then she checked herself and slipped into cop mode. Joyce Stone presented no competition. But the nicely dressed and flirtatious woman could do a number on Brad.

Ashley slid past Patrick and into Joyce's personal space, homing in on the woman's mousy brown eyes. "Officer Ashley Walters. It's nice to meet you."

Joyce backed up.

Ashley's warning charged the air. Mess with Brad, and Joyce Stone would have more trouble than she could even begin to handle.

∽

Jonathan almost smiled. Even if he did not understand a woman wearing a badge and a gun, he recognized the mother-like protectiveness Miss Walters communicated with her greeting.

And for that he was thankful.

Joyce Stone turned on her heel and marched into a clean but cluttered living room. Jonathan allowed Miss Walters, Bradley, and Mr. James to pass, and he shut the door behind them.

Everyone took seats around a nicely carved cherry wood table. He admired the handiwork, most likely carved from a single piece of wood. As he sat, he studied everyone in the room. All were stiff, including him. Mrs. Stone's two brown couches were clean but not at all comfortable. No one spoke.

Then Mrs. Stone's crossed leg began to bounce like a children's paddle ball toy. It would have been funny if not for the grave reason for their visit.

Mr. James cleared his throat. "Thank you for meeting with us today. Bradley has been looking forward to meeting you for some time now."

Mrs. Stone stopped bouncing. "You his shrink?"

Miss Walters stiffened next to Mr. James, neither of their expressions welcoming.

"I'm Bradley's counselor."

Jonathan did not like Mr. James or the cheapening of Miss Walters's honor with the public affection he allowed. But neither did Jonathan appreciate the undercurrent of tension and un-Christlike behavior Mrs. Stone expressed.

Bradley scooted to the edge of the couch, his face hopeful. "I've always wondered what you looked like and…" He stared at his black shoes and breathed in and out a few times.

Miss Walters placed a hand on the boy's back.

Mrs. Stone looked at Miss Walters, then at Jonathan. "You his adoptive parents?"

Miss Walters gasped and covered it with a few coughs.

"I am Bradley's cousin, Jonathan Yoder."

Bradley fidgeted. "See, I've gotten into some trouble with my family and community. I…I think because I'm different and because of that I've always wondered why you left. If…if there was something wrong with me."

Mrs. Stone just shrugged, not meeting Bradley's eyes.

Bradley straightened and tried again. "Do you have trouble reading?"

His biological mother swatted her hand at the air. "No. But your daddy did. Couldn't read a lick, really. It always bothered him."

Jonathan looked between Bradley and this woman, his mother. There was little resemblance. They shared the same brown eyes and probably the same color hair if Mrs. Stone had not tried to cover it with a yellowish dye.

"So I look like my father?"

The high pitched excitement in Bradley's voice drew Jonathan's attention.

"Yeah. You look exactly like him." She tossed her long hair over her shoulder. "But I wouldn't take that as a compliment."

Mr. James and Miss Walters tensed.

"So where is my father? Can I meet him too?"

Jonathan held his breath. Something deep in his soul shouted they should leave soon.

"Naw. He's dead."

Miss Walters tightened her hold on the young boy's hand.

Even Mr. James moved closer as if to protect him.

"You should have mentioned that in our earlier conversation, Mrs. Stone." Mr. James narrowed his eyes at Bradley's birth mother. "I would have suggested a better way and time to share that information."

Bradley once again stared at his black shoes.

Mrs. Joyce Stone did carry and bear Bradley, and they shared hair and eye color. That was where any similarity ended. She was empty inside.

Jonathan bowed his head and prayed for this boy he had grown to love and his biological mother. He also prayed this meeting would end soon.

In a much smaller voice, Bradley faltered. "So if…well, if my father is dead…" He swiped at his eyes. "Is that why you left me with the Yoders?"

"No. He, uh, didn't die till after we left you at that farm." Joyce Stone shrugged again and stiffened her shoulders. "You was too much trouble, always cryin' and always busy."

Jonathan shook his head. Bradley was a boy, true. But a child that was too active was one the entire community needed to help, not one to be abandoned by his parents.

Mrs. Stone kept talking faster and louder. "I jus' couldn't handle it. You hafta understand, I didn't have the money or the time to—"

Mr. James held up his hand. "That's enough. Remember? We discussed this on the phone."

Nodding, Mrs. Stone sank into herself. "I left you with a ma an' pa an' a good house. They gave you more than I could've."

Jonathan returned to prayer.

"I sent you letters, you know. And money. I did."

Crumpled into himself like a little boy, Bradley studied the coffee table. "I never saw any of those letters. Just the one where you told Mamm that you were never coming back."

Mrs. Stone ground her teeth like a cow. "Well, those people jus' wanted me to look bad. I sent letters. Them Mennonites probably just threw them away is all."

At this Bradley jumped up, face red. "Do not speak of my parents like that." His voice cracked. "They wouldn't...."

Miss Walters stood next to him. "We need to go. Thank you for your time, Mrs. Stone."

Jonathan stood with Mr. James.

Mrs. Stone jumped up from the couch, wagging her finger. "I did what was best. None of you have been in my shoes an' you got no idea how hard this kid was to raise to three years old. I did the best by him, leaving him with the Yoders. I did what was best."

Miss Walters placed her arm around Bradley's shoulder and nudged him to the door. The boy did not speak and neither did she.

Jonathan followed them outside and into the car, but Mr. James remained inside for a while. Hopefully, the man would make it clear to Mrs. Stone not to pursue any further contact with Bradley. The boy would not want that now anyway. Would he?

Soon Mr. James exited the house, started the car, and backed out of the driveway a little too fast. Jonathan could not blame him.

Bradley stared out the backseat window. Miss Walters sat next to him, holding his hand and giving him a tissue.

Mary would have done the same.

If only Mary were here, this day never would have happened.

"Did she do what was best?" Bradley's soft question, like a kitten's mew, filled the car.

Miss Walters licked her lips and tried to smile. "Her decision wasn't about you, Brad. It was about her. Regardless, you have a mother and cousin and many family members now who love you. That's what's most important."

True. Still, the question remained unanswered. Was it for Bradley's or Mrs. Stone's good that she left her son on the doorstep of a stranger? Jonathan did not know the woman. He did know Peter Yoder had loved his son well, and Anna would continue to love Bradley.

City buildings disappeared and green trees now blurred together as they sped toward Montezuma. The car remained silent.

He prayed Bradley would see this anew and let go of his interest in his biological mother. This was the good choice Bradley would make, and then they could all focus on helping Anna with the farm so that his aunt could keep her home.

This was best for everyone.

CHAPTER ELEVEN

Patrick sat yawning in the council chambers of City Hall on Tuesday, waiting for the early meeting to begin, praying for a way to remedy Bradley's pain-filled eyes from yesterday's family reunion. It shouldn't have gone the way it had. But maybe it was best that Bradley witnessed his birth mother's behavior. Maybe now the boy would have much-needed closure, and they could start dealing with Bradley's anger and grief more openly.

That hadn't happened yesterday. Bradley wanted no part in a discussion.

Patrick fiddled with his Georgia Tech tie and turned his attention to the conversations buzzing around him. Talk of cows and barns, budgets and bills reminded him of his own stack of paperwork waiting on his desk. And his full calendar. His first appointment at ten o'clock would not wait calm and quiet in his small waiting area.

This meeting needed to start and end soon.

Finally, Janet Hardy, back straight and made-up face smiling, and Andrew Jennings, expensive suit and confidence oozing, entered the mostly empty room.

"Good morning, everyone." Janet tugged her starched suit in place and silenced all conversations with her greeting. "Thank you for attending this early morning meeting. This is not an official committee meeting, but Mr. Jennings and I would like your help and input on a few new options that have come to light so we can present a cohesive and unified plan to the full zoning committee on the thirty-first."

The revitalization committee members present all nodded their approval. Small-town living thrived on new information to share.

Mark Bricker, the revitalization chairman, stood. "Shouldn't we wait for Thomas Hendricks and Mayor Johnson?"

"They both send their regrets." She nodded as Alex Jennings, a younger version of his father, entered the room. "The first order of business is a research update from Mr. Alex Jennings. Alex..." She gestured for him to take her place at the front of the room.

Alex smoothed his dark blue suit jacket and stood, a relaxed and open smile reaching his eyes. "Along with Mrs. Hardy, I'd like to thank you all for being here. I'll be brief and to the point, so we can get back to our regular schedules and another cup of coffee."

A smattering of chuckles filled the air.

Patrick glanced at his watch. He had to leave by nine at the latest.

"As I've served alongside people both in Montezuma and in the Mennonite community these past six months, I've met wonderful, hardworking people, all of which love their families and their hometown."

Men sat a little straighter and dipped their chins in approval.

Patrick leaned forward to listen, his sister's and Ashley's concerns buzzing in the back of his brain.

Alex stepped closer to the small group of committee members. "Recently, I've heard talk of a tragic situation that I believe we can remedy." Alex made eye contact with each member present. "Many of you know Anna Yoder and how her husband's recent death has brought grief and difficulties throughout their community. We're in discussions with Mrs. Yoder about selling her farm for a very sizeable compensation. This would give her the money she needs without the stress of a large business to run on her own. And it would give us one hundred acres, as well as a perfect position for the Mennonite museum, along with the possibility of using a section of their dairy farm for tourism."

In their many conversations about Bradley, Anna Yoder had given no indication that selling her farm was a possibility.

Patrick stood. "I hate to interrupt, but the Mennonite community was not in favor of this museum. I see no point in hashing out zoning proposals until that issue is settled. Have you gone back to your investors to discuss the possibility of the Mennonites sharing their faith?" He held up a hand to cut off Alex's friendly reclamation of the floor. "Many of us have discussed this and agree it's a vital element to a successful relationship with the Mennonite community and for building a genuine tourism interest."

"We're in discussions with the investors on this very issue. Right now, I'm hopeful they will come back with a positive answer very soon."

Patrick resumed his seat. He'd deliver that news on his way to work, and Ashley would be thrilled. That just might earn him another sweet kiss. He forced himself to refocus on Alex.

"As you all know, unoccupied land is scarce in Montezuma and the surrounding areas. The Yoders' land would solve a multitude of problems we've encountered. Now we just have to finalize the deal and present our combined ideas to the zoning committee."

The handful of business men and women in attendance all clapped. Patrick didn't agree with moving ahead until the issues were settled, but he was in the minority.

"What about a bookstore?" Mark made eye contact with people all around the room. "It could go right next to the art studio. Did y'all know our newest police officer is an artist? My wife says she's really good too. Maybe we can get her on board with teaching classes. That'd be a huge hometown draw for the ladies. My wife and her friends are dying to get to know Ashley better." He smiled. "I'm guessing a lot of the single men will sign up and pay a nice fee for classes too."

Patrick sat up straighter. "Hey now, Mark. Watch yourself."

"No offense, Patrick." He held up his hands. "But you know I'm right."

Ashley getting involved with their plans would provide a huge boon for their committee and the revitalization plans. Many of the ladies sitting on the fence about the revitalization would drag their entire families onto their side. Not to mention Ashley's art would gain some much deserved acclaim. He'd never picked up a sketchbook before, but he'd sign up for classes himself, if only to protect Ashley from all the fawning suitors.

The room exploded with one excited idea after another. He sat back, sifting through his motives and emotions. If the Yoders sold their land, which he still couldn't believe they'd do, this could be a win-win situation for everyone. The town, the Mennonite community, the Yoders, everyone would benefit.

So why the nagging in his gut? The Holy Spirit cluing him into something he was missing?

No clear answer materialized.

∞

Patrick pulled into his office parking lot early, startled to find Bradley waiting on the sidewalk.

"Mr. James?"

Patrick turned at the youthful voice. "Bradley? What are you doing here?" Neither Anna's nor Jonathan's vehicles were parked in the lot. "Are you okay?"

The boy kicked at the sidewalk and stuffed his hands in his pockets. "I need to talk to you."

Concern for Bradley overshadowed his already full calendar. "Come on in."

Jennifer swiveled in her receptionist's chair to face the front door as they entered. Her welcoming expression dipped when she saw Bradley. "Good morning, Patrick. Bradley. Sir, your ten o'clock should arrive in thirty minutes."

"Call and see if we can push appointments back a bit. Thanks."

"Yes, sir." She brushed gray bangs from her eyes and turned her attention to the phone.

Once in the office, Patrick headed to his easy chair, not his desk.

Bradley flopped onto the couch across from him. "I can't take this anymore. No one listens to me. They don't even want me around."

Patrick jotted a note on his yellow pad. "Why do you believe no one wants you around?"

"Mamm is too busy with office work, and Jonathan is always carving or telling me to do my chores. They just want me to work and be quiet when I come in for dinner."

"You used to talk to your dad when you came in from evening chores."

Bradley's eyes hardened and he shot up from the couch. "I don't want to talk about that."

They'd played this same game during their last session. Anna and Jonathan confirmed that Bradley never spoke of his father at home either.

"Want to talk about the meeting with your birth mother?"

"No." The boy flung his hands into his pockets and clenched his fist around something.

"What do you think about your mom selling the dairy farm?"

Surprise flicked in the boy's eyes. "She won't sell. The entire community is against it."

"Do you wish she would?"

Bradley shrugged. "I don't want to talk about that either."

"Okay. What do you want to discuss?"

"I hate it here. Nobody sees what I do. No one's proud of my taking on my father's work. I don't complain and I do my best. It doesn't matter."

"It matters to your mother. She sat on that couch and talked about what a big help you are to her. Remember?"

"So?" Bradley worked his jaw and turned away. Whatever he had in his pockets crackled as Bradley tightened his fist.

"What's in your pocket? A new baseball card?" Their shared love of baseball had gotten them off to a good start last week. The boy followed the Braves through the newspaper. No TV or radio in Mennonite homes, so they could only talk stats.

"No."

Patrick waited in the silence.

The boy spun around, crossing his arms in front of him. This was the most defensive posture he'd seen from Bradley. Maybe they were getting somewhere.

Still no one spoke. Patrick caught a glimpse of the matchbook in Bradley's hand. "Does your mother know you have matches?"

Bradley shoved the contraband into his pocket. "They belong to my friend who dropped me off here. I'll give them back when he picks me up."

"Those won't make a good security object."

Bradley relaxed his features. "I am sorry I picked them up. I have not had matches since the last fire I set before I went to stay with Cousin Jonathan."

He'd slipped back into his more formal speech and demeanor. They would get nowhere today in the short time they had left. But Patrick would break through Bradley's walls. The boy's future depended on it.

∞

The run-down buildings of downtown and the liquor store next to Highway 224 gave way to a more peaceful view outside Ashley's truck window. The drive into the Mennonite area never failed to calm her. Was it a city girl learning to appreciate the country, or something else?

A nudge in her heart shouted something else. Something deeper. The same something, or Someone she'd tried to ignore for so long now.

Then why had she agreed to show up at the Mennonite church for a sewing circle?

She actually hadn't. Vera had asked and then disappeared. Smart woman.

Turning left onto Whitehouse Road, her stomach tightened. What if they didn't like her? What if her tan skirt and blue sweater were too much or not enough?

Great. She'd turned left into the past and high school all over again.

Pecan orchards to her right and left, she soon spotted the simple country church and pulled into a gravel parking area filled with mini-vans. Sitting in her truck for a moment, she took deep breaths and listened to the CD Patrick had loaned her yesterday.

The mellow voices of Casting Crowns soothed her, just as Patrick had promised. One song stuck out and pricked at her conscience—"Somewhere in the Middle." It detailed her life, being stuck in the middle of yesterday and today, wanting what she could never have. God and control of her own life.

She turned her truck off, silencing the song she'd never listen to again. The minivans filling the parking area snagged her attention. She should be driving one of those.

If Eric had lived and Harrison had…she couldn't go down that path again. Harrison's pain-filled eyes mocked her. They would have been married by now, and she'd have her own minivan with 2.5 children.

A longing like nothing she'd ever experienced gripped her. For the first time, she listened to the longing instead of rejecting it. Was it for Harrison and a family?

No. Not now.

Sitting in a church parking lot, getting ready to face the most truthful and caring people she'd met, forced her to be honest.

She missed God.

"Okay, so I know You're listening." Not the most respectful prayer. "I'm still mad at You. I haven't been able to get justice for Eric, but You can. And You haven't."

Her lungs tightened and a shiver trailed up her spine. This part of talking to God she didn't miss. A long-forgotten Bible verse filled her mind. *Be alert and of sober mind. Your enemy the devil prowls around like a roaring lion looking for someone to devour.*

That was God's comforting answer to her prayer?

Lions she could handle. She faced them down every day. The unseen, however, she hated. The out of controlness of handing over her life to a God she couldn't see was too much. She'd handled the ugliness of the world on her own just fine.

Like she'd do today.

One slammed door and a few deep breaths later, she walked through the fellowship hall door. All chatter stopped.

No sign of Anna Yoder. But a dark haired woman stopped stacking blankets and met her eyes. "Hello. Can I help you?"

"Hi. I'm Ashley. Is Vera here?"

Vera Yoder stood in her blue dress a shade lighter than Ashley's bright sweater. "Welcome, Ashley. I am so glad you came."

One by one, the groups of quilting women returned to the work before them.

Welcome back to high school.

Vera led her to a table and pulled out a chair. "Here you go, have a seat."

"Thanks." Why had she agreed to this again? For answers she couldn't find anywhere else.

"Girls, this is Ashley Walters. Ashley, meet my nieces, Rebecca and Lisa, and their friends Prudence and Anna. These young ladies have quilted most of their lives."

And she'd spent zero days on this hobby. Maybe she could ask her questions about Bradley and scoot.

Vera handed her a needle and thread. "You can take over for me, right here." She pointed to a green section of the ring-patterned quilt. "This quilt is almost finished. We only need to stitch down the pattern."

Time after time, Ashley pricked her finger and slipped it into her mouth. So much for appearing casual.

The teens sewing beside her giggled. They missed nothing.

Prudence bit her lip and grinned. "My fingers bled often when I started too."

"I don't think quilting is my thing."

"You will improve with time." Vera finished another section of a blue ring. "These quilts will go to Christian Aid Ministries and then to wherever they are needed, as will the blankets and other handmade items."

"Ladies, we will break for lunch." The dark haired woman who'd first greeted her waited for silence. "Please gather around."

All the women, teens, and young children that were part of a home-based Mennonite day care gathered around the perimeter of the large room, holding hands.

The singing startled Ashley.

"God is great. God is good. And we thank Him for our food. By His hand we are led and He provides our daily bread."

It was beautiful.

"Come, join us in line, Ashley." Vera pointed the way.

Ashley nibbled at the soup and bread she'd chosen from among a huge spread of homemade dishes. "Thank you for inviting me today, Vera."

"You are always welcome."

It was now or never. "Do you know how Bradley Yoder is doing? He had a rough day yesterday and I haven't gotten ahold of Anna to check on him. I was hoping she'd be here today."

Most of the women focused on their plates of food. Vera tsked. "I am sure his family appreciates your concern and the help you have given Bradley. He is doing as well as can be expected."

One of the children piped up. "Except for the messed-up milk."

"That is enough, Jenny. We should pray, not gossip."

The child skipped away to help with cleanup.

"What's happened?" After yesterday's disaster, Ashley expected some acting out from Bradley, but not enough to destroy their livelihood.

"They are fine." Vera shook her head. "Accidents happen to everyone. And Anna's farm is old, but we will help her fix what has worn out."

"People in town say Anna is planning to sell her farm, but that can't be the best thing for Bradley right now."

A few of the ladies excused themselves from the table.

Vera stood. "I do not believe so. The land has been in her family for over fifty years."

A loud crash outside sent a few of the women hurrying out the door. Ashley followed.

"Where are the children?" Vera searched the area.

A cold wind swept over them and one of the older women shivered. "They are all inside. No one was left unattended out here."

Ashley studied a large tree shadowing the fellowship hall. "Looks like someone was in the tree and broke a few branches coming down."

"The children do not climb this tree. It is too large for their little hands."

An open window caught her eye. Then who was in the tree, listening in? And why?

∾

Tools in hand, he trudged to the outermost farm building. The old, wooden structure creaked in the wind.

He slipped inside, unnoticed as always.

Old tractors, rusted shovels, and rubber tubing greeted him. He kicked things out of his way as he crossed the dusty space.

The tractor hood screeched as he lifted it. They would use this soon to move hay bales.

He snipped two of the wires and tossed four bolts across the barn. They thumped and skidded across the dirt floor.

That should do it.

Next, he crept closer to the farmhouse. The smelly milking barn loomed large before him. If he could get in, he'd do more damage than the other day.

It hadn't been enough.

Today would push them over the edge.

Sooner or later, he'd find their breaking point.

CHAPTER TWELVE

Ashley drove behind the patrol car of the one cop who'd showed a genuine interest in friendship. Thankfully, Officer Elizabeth Rey had transferred from morning to evening watch with her—a kindness from the lieutenant. Or more likely gratitude for her making an early shift change easy. They'd all rotate shifts every three months now. She dreaded nights again, but at least she'd be in the rotation with Elizabeth.

They parked their cruisers a few houses down from the nice brick house they'd been tasked with visiting today. The late afternoon sun highlighted their path as they followed up on a Neighborhood Watch tip and a suspicious activity incident from the previous shift's briefing.

This could be a minor, boring blip on their day's report.

Or it could be a drug house.

Elizabeth approached the door first and knocked.

No one answered. Nothing moved inside or out. No nosey neighbors peeked out their windows either. Ashley surveyed everything at once, the hairs on her neck standing on end.

Elizabeth pounded again. "Police. Open up."

This time a stumbling, thumping noise filled the front hallway. Two deadbolts clicked, one after the other.

Elizabeth backed up a step. Ashley guarded the other side of the door.

A girl in her early twenties with serious bed head cracked the door open and glared. "Yeah, whaddaya want?"

"Are you the homeowner?" Elizabeth rested her hands on her gun belt and raised her eyebrows.

"Uh…nope. It's Kevin's house. I'll get him." In her sleep-deprived state, she flung the front door wide open as she headed toward the basement.

The house reeked of cat urine and ammonia.

Meth.

Elizabeth nodded toward a table in the dining room, the only piece of furniture on the main level. Decorating the beat-up brown table were two blenders, cold packs in various states of destruction, tubing, dark-colored cookware, and a couple banged-up chemistry sets.

"You did what?" A man's screeching voice split the silence.

The young woman's whimpering barely reached their ears. "I…I'm sorry. Please don't…"

The following silence screamed louder than the short exchange of words.

Her pulse rate hammering, Ashley unsnapped her holster with steady fingers.

Elizabeth did the same.

The young woman reappeared, an ugly red splotch covering her cheek.

Ashley itched to question her about the abuse, but they needed to see Kevin first. She'd come back to the wide-eyed and twitchy woman soon. No matter what she was strung out on, she didn't deserve a beating.

Heavy boots crashed against each stair. A gaunt man poked his tangled mass of brown hair through the open basement doorway and then reached his scrawny bare arms to the ceiling. Even from a hallway away, his open sores were visible.

Elizabeth squared off with him. "Are you Kevin?"

"Yeah. Why?"

"This your home?"

"Uh…yeah." He slipped his hands down. "There a problem?" His crooked teeth poked through his scowl. The meth head was waking up.

Elizabeth pointed her chin toward the dining room table. "Those your decorations?"

The young woman jumped in front of Kevin. "Those're mine. All mine."

Kevin pushed her forward. "Yeah. Take her." He stepped toward the basement.

Ashley zipped to his side and had him in handcuffs before he could blink.

Elizabeth danced the same dance with the young woman. Neither put up a fight, and both stayed silent the entire walk out the door, down the steps, and along the street toward the squad cars.

"See you in Oglethorp." Elizabeth sighed and tucked her weeping charge into the back cage.

Ashley placed the sullen Kevin into her backseat and shut the door. A lone onlooker caught her eye at the edge of a tan house two doors down. His defiant posture—arms crossed over a nice black jacket, chest puffed out, chin raised—dared her to notice him.

Was he part of the meth operation? Doubtful since he was hanging around watching them without the nervous energy of most druggies. She stepped closer, and the figure darted off.

His mannerisms registered in her memory.

Kevin slammed his shoulder into the back window, causing her cruiser to rock.

Great.

She'd return after her trip to the Macon County jail. Maybe then her black-jacketed friend would appear and answer some questions.

∽

Jonathan supervised Bradley's evening chores, waiting for the boy to explode any minute. Since the meeting with his biological mother two days ago, he had remained sullen and mute. That could not last long.

Bradley and two of the other young men from the community herded large black and white cows into the brick milking barn. The normal smell of the dairy increased with each cow that turned his way. In the almost two weeks he had stayed in Montezuma, the smell of manure had become more normal. He was still not comfortable standing this close to the huge cows.

It surprised him every time how the cows obeyed and took their places, filing into the building, up the ramps, and into their metal stalls.

Yesterday they had spent the entire morning and afternoon gathering parts to fix the damaged milking machine. Church members pitched in to pay for parts and offer for free what they could not purchase.

Some of the other dairy farmers joined his small effort to fix the machine. The day had been full of quiet camaraderie. This was what he missed most from his carpentry shop.

Bradley shoved at the back of one stubborn cow, and the big beast moved forward up the ramp to take the last stall. It was time for the first of many rounds of milking.

Jonathan wished to engage Bradley in any conversation requiring more than a yes or no answer. But Anna instructed him not to push Bradley to talk. He prayed her counsel was wise. Anna's bishop would come for dinner tonight, and Jonathan would speak with him in private concerning Bradley's meeting with his birth mother. There were details Anna need not hear.

He joined Bradley at the first milking machine and marveled at how well the boy had adjusted to leading the morning and evening chore. It was long and draining work, but he did it with little to no complaint.

The boys attached long black tubes with silver cups to each of the cows' teats. They had already flushed the lines and washed the cows' udders. Now they would collect the milk and send these cows on their way after another washing.

As the machines hummed and the cows stood still, Bradley checked each line. All of a sudden, tubes attached to two different cows spurted warm milk over the entire small barn, covering the men.

Bradley rushed to shut down the machines and inspect the damage.

"These lines have been cut through."

Jonathan leaned over Bradley to see what appeared to be very worn tubing lines in Bradley's hand.

"Who would do this?" Bradley threw the apparatus down.

One of the boys spoke up. "I have known lines to wear thin and separate from use. I will run home later and we can replace these lines after the milking is done."

"It will take hours longer without the use of these two stalls."

"Ja."

Bradley stiffened and set his focus on work, as did the other boys. Jonathan's heart ached. So much going wrong for one young man, and no father to share the burden. Rather than watch, he mimicked the boys' earlier actions and directed cows, washed udders, and attached teat cups. He longed for the more familiar work of his carpentry store.

Hours later the exhausted group parted ways. Bradley stormed ahead. Thankfully, the bishop had not yet arrived.

He touched Bradley's shoulder and the boy jerked away. "Bradley, we must talk."

The boy stood rigid on the back porch steps. "There's nothing to say. Except I hate the smell of manure and cows and boring work that takes all day. I hate this dairy farm. I wish Mamm would sell it!"

Before Jonathan could stop him, Bradley ran into the house and to his room, slamming the door behind him.

Jonathan cleaned up in the utility sink and removed his boots and outer coat, setting both in the neat places Peter had assigned them. He washed his hands one more time and entered the kitchen.

Anna stood, tears spilling over her eyes. "What has happened today?"

He hugged his beloved aunt and explained about the worn tubing as best he could.

The deep lines around her eyes and mouth deepened further. "I heard how much my son hates this life. Maybe selling this farm is for the best. I do not know anymore."

"We will speak with the bishop after dinner, and we will continue to pray." Loud crashes interrupted their quiet conversation. "I should check on the boy."

Anna nodded and returned to dinner preparations.

Before he could reach the door, the banging stopped. He knocked. "Bradley, I would like to come in."

No answer.

He knocked again and after another round of silence, he opened the door. The disaster that greeted him shocked him so he could not find his voice. A wooden chair lay splintered on the floor. The desk that had once been Peter's was battered, long angry scratches covering the entire surface.

"Bradley?" He called into the room, knowing already the boy was not there. The opened window showed how he had escaped.

He passed Anna in the kitchen without comment and tucked his arms into Peter's coat once more. Following the worn path into the nearby pecan orchard, he prayed. Soon scratching noises that did not come from an animal reached his ears.

Three rows of trees ahead of him, sparks of light burst into the night and dimmed as fast as they had appeared. What was Bradley doing?

As he stepped closer, he focused on the book of matches in Bradley's hand and grabbed it from him before the boy set the entire orchard on fire.

"Do you not know how fast and hot pecan trees burn? You could destroy your neighbor's farm in one minute of foolishness."

"I don't care." Bradley scooted around so only his hunched back showed.

"You do care, Bradley. These people are your brothers and sisters in Christ. They love you and you love them."

"No one here really loves me."

Jonathan crouched down closer to the boy. "They may not express their love as your father did. I am sorry for that. But they love you and want to help you. They want to understand you."

Bradley whirled around. "No! They just want me to stop causing trouble and be like them. I'm not. I'm not quiet. I'm a troublemaker like my mom said. And I'm not a dairy farmer, and I never want to be. I don't belong here."

Pulling the boy into his arms was awkward, but necessary. As if God had spoken direct instructions. "Your mother loves you, Bradley. More than you can imagine. So do I." The words spilled out in such a rush, he had no time to check them.

They were not enough to heal Bradley's hurts, but at least the boy leaned against him.

Much quieter now, Bradley sat up and wiped his eyes. "They don't understand. Neither do you."

"That is correct. There are some things no one wants to understand, like evil and using fire to handle anger. This is not good for you, Bradley. Evil is trying to control you, to use you to hurt this whole community. Do not allow it, Bradley. Please."

The battle warring for the boy's soul was an almost physical presence. Jonathan prayed. It was all he could do. God was the only one powerful enough to change the course of Bradley's life.

"Thank you, Cousin Jonathan. I will pray. May I stay here a few minutes?"

Jonathan placed the matches into his trouser pocket and nodded. "The bishop will be here soon for dinner. Please return in time to wash up and eat with us."

"Yes, sir."

Jonathan turned and retraced his steps to the house, still listening for any further trouble with Bradley.

Anna stepped out of the kitchen while he washed. "The bishop is unable to come tonight. There are services and he was asked to preach at the last minute."

Another wave of relief spread through him. At least they would not risk another confrontation with Bradley tonight. "Will he come tomorrow?"

"Yes. Dinner is ready. Will Bradley join us?"

Just then, the boy entered, hung up his coat, and tucked his boots into their place. Then without speaking, Bradley scrubbed his hands and arms.

Around the table, they held hands as Jonathan prayed. "Dear Lord, we ask Your blessings on this food and the hands that prepared it. Teach us to walk in Your ways. Amen."

He ate salad, homemade rolls, and spaghetti in silence. No one spoke. Hopefully, he could enjoy the pecan pie that had teased his nose all afternoon. This was Bishop Overholt's favorite meal. It was possible he would eat this same meal tomorrow, with much thanks.

A knock on the front door startled him. After leaving his empty plate beside the sink, he crossed the living room to answer it.

Surprised to see Miss Walters in her police uniform, he could think of nothing to say.

"I hope I'm not interrupting dinner." She half shrugged.

"No, we have just finished." He held on to the door with a firm hand. "Is there a problem?"

"Can I speak to you for a minute?" She peered over his shoulder toward the kitchen.

"Yes. Let me get my coat and I will join you on the front porch."

She turned to the swing.

When he sat next to her, she didn't move or speak.

"Is there something wrong?"

She tightened the hold she had on her knees. "I heard yesterday that there's been some trouble on Anna's farm. Do you think someone is behind it?"

Her carefully phrased question gave him pause. Would someone deliberately damage Anna's property? Would Bradley? He could not imagine the possibility. "I do not. The equipment is old and in need of repair."

"Are you sure?"

"Yes."

She sighed. "Good. I was afraid y'all were in danger."

He longed to speak with her about Bradley, but was unsure of his motives.

"Is Brad okay?" She stared at him with her concerned green eyes.

"He was playing with matches today and will not talk about the visit with his biological mother. I believe they are connected."

She stood in a rush that pushed the porch swing back. "What? Why didn't you call me?"

"We have taken care of the situation and will meet with Anna and Bradley's bishop tomorrow." This was not police business. He should not have said anything.

"Will that help?" She returned to the seat next to him, far too close for his comfort. He should move, but he did not. "Maybe he should come back to Patrick's."

He stiffened, disliking the reminder that she was involved with someone who held her in such little respect as to kiss her in public. "I will talk with Anna and her bishop and let Mr. James know what we decide."

"Please call me too. I want to help. I care for Brad a lot."

He nodded. "Why does this teenager mean so much to you?"

After a long, silent moment, she took a deep breath and exhaled. "I'd planned to have a son like Brad someday. He reminds me of Eric, and I just…"

"Who is Eric?"

"My brother. He was killed ten years ago when we were in college."

He caught his breath, and released it slowly. That explained the deep sadness in her eyes. "I am sorry. I know the pain of losing a loved one."

She turned toward him. "You do?"

"Yes. My wife died in childbirth two years ago." He could not believe he had shared his deepest pain with a stranger, a woman wearing a gun no less.

She touched his arm. "I'm so sorry. How…I know this is a personal question, but how do you handle the sadness?"

He stood, leaving the dangerous place beside a woman who could never be part of his life. "I work. I carve things Mary would have loved, and I pray."

"I paint."

"I have heard you speak of this. Do you paint only sadness?"

"No. I actually painted Anna's home and farm when we first met." Her face turned red in the porch light. "I paint other things too. People and abstract art, anything that comes to mind when I have time."

"I can make you some frames." Why had he spoken such rash and foolish words? Now he had made a promise that would require seeing her another time. Maybe he should send the frames by Mr. James. That would solve a number of problems.

She stood but kept her distance, as if his face had given away his inner struggle. "I would love the frames. Thank you." She glanced to her police car. "My dinner break is almost over and I need to call Patrick. Thanks for putting my mind at ease about Brad. Please let him know I came by and that he can call me anytime. And…well, thank you for understanding."

He nodded, not trusting his rebellious mouth to speak again.

As Ashley drove away, he stared into the night sky. "I must accept this singleness. My remaining single is from God. He has given me this gift. I will accept it without complaint."

His speech to himself did not work.

Prayer was the only thing that would win this spiritual fight for his and Bradley's life. He must pray until the focus of his life was only the Lord.

He returned to the house unsure of how to accomplish this thing that used to be as easy as breathing. How could he truly help anyone with the way his mind and mouth rebelled at the slightest temptation?

The silence after much prayer was his deserved consequence. Unlike Ashley, speaking with God was the only way he knew to fight the battles before him. So he would pray until God showed him what to do next, and accept the results without complaint.

He hoped he could be that obedient.

Chapter Thirteen

Patrick knocked on Ashley's front door with a bouquet of multicol-ored tulips in his other hand. Good thing he hadn't dated in years. It was expensive.

But Ashley was worth it.

She pulled open the door and invited him in, a wide smile on her face. This time he held out the bouquet of tulips, no shaking hands shoving it her way like their first date.

"Thank you. These are gorgeous." She shut the door behind him and glided to the kitchen, her navy skirt swishing around her knees.

"You're beautiful, you know."

She arranged the tulips in an expensive cut-glass vase. "I'm not sure I do, but you could tell me every once in a while, if you want."

"Gladly." He stepped close and placed a kiss on her cheek. "Ready for a real Middle Georgia dining experience?"

"Sure. After the week I've had, I'm ready for anything that doesn't result in a visit to jail."

He helped her into her black coat and held the door open. "I can guarantee a jail visit is not in our future."

Ashley settled into the Mustang's leather seat as if she belonged there. Maybe she did. She'd certainly settled into his heart faster than he'd expected.

"So how was work today? I missed our drive home phone call."

Music to his ears. Melanie had wanted nothing to do with his work, found it boring and depressing in fact.

"Work was that bad?"

She'd read his face like an expert detective, but it was too soon to dump all the mess with Melanie.

"Wow, you have chameleon facial features. You went from the worst day in the world scowl to contentment in less than sixty seconds." She huffed and nudged his arm. "I'm impressed, if not a little worried."

The words spoken in jest pierced his conscience. "I'll tell you whatever you want to know." He prayed she didn't take him up on his offer.

"Why did you get upset when I asked about work?"

The million dollar question. "It wasn't work. I was thrilled you wanted to hear about my day, but then I let a stray memory take over." He glanced sideways. "A girl I'd dated, almost married, hated my work and claimed it mattered more to me than she did."

"Were you a workaholic?"

"Yes." He'd spent years unpacking all the emotions and lies that he'd bought into during his relationship and messy breakup with Melanie. "That's changed though. My work is important, but it isn't my life."

"Good to hear." She touched his arm. "You're always asking me if I want to talk about sad things. Do you need to talk about this girl?"

"I'd rather talk about what I learned."

"Please."

"First off, my biggest mistake with Melanie was to stop listening to the Holy Spirit."

Ashley grimaced.

He needed to tread lightly. "Second was to let her actions lead to believing lies about myself."

She turned in her seat. "What does that mean? You've talked about lies before, but I figured it was just a counseling term."

Okay, God, You take over. "Lies are about more than counseling. They're what you believe about yourself that isn't true. Lies are the work of the enemy of our souls who uses painful circumstances to destroy us twice—once because of the pain and twice because of the false things we believe from them."

"Like what?"

"After Melanie left, I believed I was completely unlovable, worthless really."

Shaking her head, she focused on him with compassion-filled eyes. "It's hard to believe you thought that about yourself. You have lots of people who adore you."

"I didn't say lies make sense. But sense or not, they're pretty strong sometimes. That's why we fall prey to them. I spent a lot of time ignoring God after the mess with Melanie and let myself spiral downward. It was ugly."

"I get the ignoring God part. It's less painful that way."

"Not really. Then you have no one to go to who really understands. No one to help you see the truth so you can heal."

She squirmed in her seat and stared out the window. "I know I asked, but can we change the subject? I'm not up for this talk before dinner. Maybe later?"

He'd done what he'd hoped to do and it was a good start.

"Will you tell me about work?" She took his hand. The softness in her eyes touched him.

He relaxed into his leather seat. "Two clients graduated to call-if-you-need-me status, and I had a new couple's first appointment. All in all, a good day's work."

"No screaming fights and pillow throwing today?"

"Disappointed?"

"No. Glad people in your world are getting along better than in mine."

Should he ask? She'd already shut down a deeper conversation once. "Work?"

"Sort of."

"What happened to make your week so rough?"

"I talked with Jonathan about Brad Wednesday night."

A flash of jealousy zinged him. But he refused to allow the emotion to overtake his tongue. Ashley wasn't interested in Jonathan.

"He's playing with fire and won't talk about the meeting with his mother. I'm worried about him. Can you talk to him?"

"I met with him yesterday." He couldn't say much. "He speaks like a normal teen when we meet, but only when his mother or Jonathan aren't around. You've seen that, right? It's like he's two different people."

"He's just trying to figure out where he belongs. Like every other teen."

"Still."

"You don't believe he's behind the damage to the Yoder farm, do you?" Her green eyes blazed. "He wouldn't do that."

"He wants his mother to sell the farm."

"That doesn't mean he'd destroy equipment or endanger people. I can't believe you'd succumb to small-town gossip."

Should have kept his mouth shut. Yes, he had doubts and he hated that for Ashley's sake. For Bradley's. He cared about the boy. A boy who needed help.

"I'm sorry. I shouldn't have said anything."

"If you believe he's done something criminal, you have to report it to the police." Ice tinged her voice.

"There's nothing to report." Yet.

She slumped into the seat.

"I care about Bradley too."

"I know."

They cruised the last stretch of Highway 224 in silence. Despite the control he had over his tongue, he couldn't convince his emotions all was well.

At a stoplight, he turned to face Ashley. "Still mad at me?"

"I'm not mad."

"I'm trying to help Bradley, and he's in my prayers every day."

She released a long sigh. "I believe you. I just don't like what's happening and how people are whispering and pointing fingers at Brad when they don't even know him. Like news reporters deciding guilt or innocence long before a trial."

"Maybe you could remind them that the Mennonites believe the damages have been accidents."

"It would help if you believed that too."

He'd work on that.

They arrived at the Swanson House right ahead of the usual dinner rush. He'd eaten here almost every week since moving back to Montezuma. Nothing in Atlanta compared to this slice of culinary heaven.

Rose, the owner of the beautiful antebellum restaurant, greeted them at the front door and hung up their coats. "Well, hey there, Patrick. So nice to see you again. We've been missing your stories lately." She extended a hand to Ashley. "And now I see why you've been scarce."

Ashley shook hands and smiled. "Ashley Walters. It's nice to meet you."

Rose shooed off the hostess and led them to a secluded table at the inside corner of the wraparound porch. "Follow me for a little tour. We'll come back to your table right quick." She pointed out the roaring fireplace and the display dishes, explaining which part of this room and the next were original and which were added later.

"This here's the yellow room, my favorite." Rose stepped into the foyer. "We also have a party room dressed in green and a cozy one dressed in red, right over there."

Eyes twinkling with mischief, Ashley followed their host and drank in every word, as if she would capture it all in a painting later.

"Y'all are stepping into more than two hundred years of Georgia history, so be very careful or you'll stir up some bothersome ghosts." She giggled her grandmotherly giggle.

Rose's hospitality never grew old, so he listened as attentively as Ashley and held out a chair for her when they returned to their candlelit table.

"This beautiful antebellum home started off as a livery stable in the seventeen hundreds. But no worries, there are no horse traces to be found here. Just history waiting to be uncovered for new eyes to enjoy." Rose handed out menus and rattled off soup and quiche specials.

Ashley viewed the menu, then returned her focus to Rose.

"The food here is purely Southern, served family style. Try you some fried green tomatoes and bread puddin' for dessert. Take your time to enjoy."

Leaning close, Ashley scanned the room. "It really does feel like we've stepped back in time. I should have worn a hoopskirt with gloves."

"You look perfect just the way you are."

"Be careful. A girl could get used to such words."

That was his hope.

Their server, a young girl, stepped up to the table the minute Ashley laid down her menu. "Hi, I'm Becca." She focused on him, not Ashley. "What can I get for y'all tonight?"

Ashley pointed to her selections on the menu. "I'd like the chicken and dumplings with a house salad and sweet potato soufflé. Sweet tea as well."

"And for you, sir?"

"I'll have the fried chicken with fried green tomatoes and okra. And a sweet tea."

Becca took their menus. "Coming right up. I'll be back with your drinks in a minute."

Brows knit together, Ashley cocked her head. "Why did she expect you to order for me?"

"That doesn't happen in Atlanta?" He shrugged. "I've grown up with that. Maybe it's a Middle Georgia thing. Or it could be they're a stickler for antebellum customs here."

"I wish they wouldn't. It makes me feel like I'm two and can't order for myself."

He puzzled over that for a minute. "Why does it make you feel like a kid?"

Becca slid two huge glasses of tea onto their table and left without a word.

"My mother used to order for me. She mistook me for a bird. Dad on the other hand, ordered the most expensive steak on the menu, medium well." She lowered her voice to a whisper as if her parents were sitting at the next table. "I hate pink meat and bird food."

He ached for her and the picture she painted of her growing up years.

Before he could delve into this, Becca arrived and served their steaming meals. "Anything else I can get y'all? More sweet tea?" Without waiting for an answer she hurried off for refills of their still full tea glasses.

He reached for Ashley's hand, and they bowed their heads to pray. "Lord, thank You for this amazing meal and the privilege of sharing it with an amazing woman. Guard our conversation and let all we do be pleasing to You. Amen."

He dug into the fried chicken, every greasy bite of it.

A glance Ashley's way made him smile. She sat, eyes closed, savoring each spoonful. Wiping his hands and mouth, he watched for a moment. It was nice to see someone enjoy food so thoroughly.

She opened her eyes and fixed them on him. "This is amazing. Can we come back often?"

"Absolutely. So what's your favorite? The pecan and feta salad with the melt in your mouth biscuits or the sweet potato soufflé?"

"Both. And the chicken and dumplings. Honestly, I don't think I can pick a favorite. Of course, there's still dessert. That might win the award."

He loved her smile. The Swanson House had done its magic. "You said something about a friend of yours coming into town next weekend? Can I bring you both here one evening?"

"Margo might rebel at the calories, but I'll tempt her with bread pudding. That should take care of any grumbling." She savored another bite of the sweet potato soufflé. "She's been my best friend since grade school, and she shared her ice cream when mine melted too fast. We used to talk every day, but crazy schedules and my move down here have all but obliterated that."

"How long will she stay?"

"Just a few nights. Thursday through Saturday. She'll want to get home for church Sunday. Plus she needs to prepare for a big show she's doing next week. She's a first-class interior decorator for the well-heeled of West Paces Ferry."

"Sounds like a fun job." He'd worked with some from that neck of the woods when he was in Atlanta, earning his graduate degree in counseling.

"I'd hate it too, but Margo loves it. That's why we'll spend a day at Pasaquan and tour some of the antebellum homes around here."

He finished the last crumb of fried chicken and wiped off with his napkin. "No plans to tour Andersonville?"

"Margo would be traumatized. I was. It's hard to look at the living conditions faced by POWs from World War II."

Shocked she'd visited, he blinked a few times. "Did you go by yourself? I would have gone with you."

"By myself. It was only a quick trip and only because you spoke so highly of it. I'm glad I went, but I don't handle death all that well, so I doubt I'll go back."

"What about death scares you?"

Stiffening, she pushed the last traces of food around her plate. "It doesn't scare me. I just have to deal with trauma all day at work. I don't want to invite it into my entertainment, especially a date."

"You're angry."

She swallowed and unclenched the napkin she'd been holding. "I'm not."

"Did you know anger is a secondary emotion, usually guarding a lie?" He was taking his life into his hands, but whatever she wasn't saying hurt her badly.

"We closed this topic for tonight."

"Something is eating you alive."

She leaned forward. "I appreciate your concern, but I'm not at a counseling appointment. I don't want to be either."

He lowered his head and sighed. He'd done it again. To protect himself, he'd slipped into work mode, the one place where he succeeded. "I'm sorry, Ashley. I was wrong to push."

Her reaction amplified his deep concern. For her sake, he intended to return to this subject at a better time. Whether she welcomed it or not.

∽

Ashley relaxed into the Mustang's sparkling clean seats and closed her eyes. Dinner and dessert had filled her to overflowing. She would have preferred the conversations before and after dinner never happened, for Patrick's sake and hers, but for a short snatch of time in the middle she'd enjoyed easy banter, laughter, and out-of-this-world food.

The steady hum of Patrick's Mustang lulled her. She let go of plans for a Saturday filled with chores and freezer waffles and rested her head back on the seat.

"Hey, sleeping beauty, we're here." Patrick nudged her arm and turned off his car.

Jerking up from her seat, she groaned. "Please tell me I didn't snore or drool." She touched her mouth to be sure.

He laughed. "You sleep like a princess."

"Liar." Shaking herself awake, she surveyed her house. All the lights were on and Chester howled inside. "We didn't leave the lights on, did we?"

"No." He crossed the front yard ahead of her and peeked around the corner. "There's a Mercedes in the other driveway."

She groaned again. "Champagne color?"

"Yep."

"Great." Biting her tongue against the volcanic words that boiled inside, she forced a smile. "Won't you come in and meet my parents?"

Hands clenching and unclenching, she marched up the front steps. Her parents were back on the job of running her life. She'd had to move away or die inside. Now that choice was stripped from her.

Patrick stopped her before she could slam the door open and let loose. "Wow, slow down. I've never seen you so steamed. You gave them keys, right?"

"No."

"They didn't tell you they were coming?"

"Again, no." She inhaled in and out for counts of ten. The stupid trick didn't help a lick. "They're probably spying on us from the window, so we might as well go inside."

Chester's howling split the air. She rushed to her puppy's crate in the kitchen and released him as fast as her fingers could unlatch the lock. No sign of her intruder parents, so she let the brown fur ball attack her face with kisses. "Why are you in here, baby? Did those meanies lock you away?"

Her father cleared his throat behind her.

Busted like she was thirteen and sneaking in past curfew.

She wiped off her face with a moistened dish towel and let Chester out into the backyard. He was safer there. Ignoring Patrick's worried face beside her, she squared off with her father. "Care to explain why you are in my home without permission?"

Her father extended a hand in Patrick's direction. "Randall Walters, pleased to meet you."

"Patrick James." The men shook hands, both smiling and ignoring the massive pink elephant in the room.

In flowed her mother, expensive winter white suit showing off her tanned skin. "Hello, dear. I do wish you'd answer your phone every once in a while. It would have been nice to have some directions."

"How did you find it?" Try as she might to feign calm, her words snapped.

"Your lovely neighbor—Emma, I think she said—told us all about the house and said you'd be out on a date with a counselor." She extended her hand to Patrick. "I assume that would be you. Emma speaks highly of you."

"Thank you. I think the world of Emma."

Their tone and mannerisms were civil and polished, as always, but Ashley sensed her parent's displeasure. They'd loved Harrison and wished she'd married him.

"Why don't we go into the living room?" She led the way, slipping out of her coat and laying it and Patrick's on the couch. Then she sat on the far corner of the love seat. Patrick joined her and squeezed her hand. It helped. "So, Mom and Dad, what brings you here while I'm away for the evening?"

Her parents exchanged one of their knowing looks, and unease prickled through her.

"We just wanted to visit. We'll be staying in Emma's B&B, so we'll be no trouble to you."

Patrick took over the role of host. "Do you have plans to visit any tourist sights while you're in town? I'd be happy to show you around."

Oh, no he wouldn't. Not after ten minutes in their company. She should have moved to the other side of the country.

They chatted about possible plans, and she ignored them, scanning the room to see what was different. Something had changed. What was it?

Then it hit her. They'd placed little interior decorator touches here and there. A potted tree she should have noticed right away, and some elegant glass frames with fake families still under the glass.

Talk about symbolic.

"Sorry to interrupt your itinerary, but I'd like to know why you're in town and why you think it's okay to take over my home."

If Patrick wanted a serious relationship, he'd have to survive this initiation into the Walters family and all its dysfunctional glory.

Dad cleared his throat again, the pitch and duration indicating excitement about what he was going to say. She'd hate it. "We've pulled some very influential strings with the High Museum and plans are in the works for a fundraiser at the Brandon Young Gallery. You will be their featured artist."

He sat back and crossed his legs, self-importance and satisfaction radiating from him.

Patrick turned to her. "This is a huge honor."

She scowled, and he backed off immediately. No doubt the fire flashing from her eyes gave him a clue.

"No. I'm a police officer first, not a painter. I have no interest in doing a fundraising event, thank you anyway."

Mother flipped her hand. "It's an offer you can't refuse, a once in a lifetime career building event. The plans have already passed their board's approval."

"I said no. You should have asked me first before making plans." She stood and Patrick followed her lead. "I'm going to walk Patrick out. When I come back, if you'd like to talk about something besides art, I'd be delighted."

Back straight, she beelined it for the door and closed it in a rush behind them. "I'm so sorry. I didn't mean for tonight to become a meet-the-family fiasco."

"No apologies necessary." He shrugged into his coat. She had no need of one right this second. "I'm sorry for my comments about the show. I didn't mean to side with the enemy." He tucked a strand of hair behind her ear.

A deep sigh escaped her lips. "They aren't the enemy. But they are suffocating. I'm still sorry you had to see all that."

"Let me pray with you before I leave you in the lion's den." She nodded, and he drew her into his embrace. "Lord, we come to You, asking that You be Ashley's protector and comforter. Help her show Your love, no matter how challenging that can sometimes be. Thank You for a wonderful evening. May all we say and do glorify You. Amen."

Her anger melted in the intensity of Patrick's blue eyes. He pulled her closer and held her face in his warm hands. "You are amazing. Don't let anyone make you doubt that."

The kiss, gentle at first, deepened into a promise.

Losing herself in the moment, she wrapped her arms around his neck. For a second their kiss made her forget.

She regretted pulling back the second she did, but it was too weird knowing her parents were sitting a wall away.

He touched his forehead to hers. "I'll be praying. Hang in there. I'll be back in the morning."

"Thank you." With her eyes, she followed him to his car and down the street, wishing she could run away and spend the rest of her weekend safe with Patrick.

With an exaggerated sigh, she opened the front door and found her parents donning their coats and gloves. "What? You just got here, and now you're leaving?" She should be thankful.

"It's late." Her mother pecked her cheek and stepped onto the porch. "We'll see you tomorrow and talk about the exhibit when you've had some time to think clearly."

Dad pulled her into a side hug. "Love you. Goodnight."

And with a wave, they disappeared into the night.

After letting Chester in the back door, she surveyed the entire house, finding no boxes left to unpack. Red hot anger bubbled up again, and she tamped it back down by rearranging every room her mother had touched. Then she found an empty box on the back porch and filled it with her mother's fancy decorating pieces. Crystal frames, designer pillows, color coordinated antiqued vases and knickknacks. They belonged in Atlanta, not here.

That task complete, she plopped down on her bed. Chester hopped up to join her, lying quietly by her side. Woman's best friend, what a gift. She stroked his warm fur and let her breathing return to normal.

Grabbing her Bible, the one Eric had given her for high school graduation, she flipped it open to 1 Corinthians 14:33, "For God is not a God of disorder but of peace—as in all the congregations of the Lord's people."

One glance around her messy bedroom and she flipped to another, more comforting section. "It would be helpful to read something encouraging, comforting, or just nice. Surely You can do that, God."

Her Bible fell open to 1 Peter 5, and her eyes scanned the words until they lodged on verse 8. She read it aloud, "Be alert and of sober mind. Your enemy the devil prowls around like a roaring lion looking for someone to devour."

Twice this week God had shoved this verse at her. She didn't appreciate His answers to prayer thus far in their trial reacquaintance.

Reading the verse again, she shivered. Not comforting at all. What lion was God warning her against?

Falling into bed twenty minutes later, she tossed and turned, unsuccessfully pushing away the memories her little Bible study sparked.

She hadn't sensed God's closeness since she'd studied the Bible with Harrison years ago. And for the first time in a decade, God had to bring with Him a message that froze her blood.

Your enemy prowls around seeking to devour.

Try as she might, she couldn't shake the old prayer she used to recite over and over no matter how badly it scared her. "Now I lay me down to sleep. I pray the Lord my soul to keep. If I should die before I wake, I pray the Lord my soul to take."

Chapter Fourteen

Driving along Highway 224, Jonathan hummed a familiar hymn. His spirit lightened, despite the struggles with Bradley and the possibility Anna would sell her farm. The song rose up inside, and he needed to sing. "Praise God from whom all blessings flow…"

Tears filled his eyes. His voice caught and the song died away. He had missed singing. But it hurt. Hurt not to have Mary by his side, praising God together at home and during a service. Silence fit him better now.

He glanced in the passenger seat at the beautiful cherry wood out of which he had fashioned a frame. God's handiwork gleamed in the grain of the wood. The deep, rich color pointed to a God of beauty, something Ashley would understand.

Ashley's sad eyes came to mind. Three days ago, she sat beside him on Anna's front porch and spilled out her story about losing a brother she loved very much. He understood. And he wished yet again that she was part of his faith, part of his world. Then he could comfort her and together they could grow closer to God.

Then she would not be involved with Mr. James. She could be…

No. I will not continue this, Lord. Forgive me. My focus should ever be on You and the blessings You have brought to my life. Bradley and Anna need me. Strengthen my back and my hands to serve them and show them the love in my heart. Guide us in the decisions before us. We need You, Lord.

Jonathan pulled into Ashley's driveway and turned off his truck. Through her open studio windows the strains of instrumental music—jazz, if he remembered his customer's words correctly—filled his ears. She swayed to the music and painted with bold colors, her unhindered pleasure drawing him more powerfully than anything he had ever experienced. This was the way Ashley worshipped.

He sat still, captured.

If he were wise, he would leave the frame on the porch and run for his very life.

He was not yet that wise.

As he exited his truck, he turned away from the scene in Ashley's studio and retrieved the frame. Even without seeing her, he could sense her movements to the music and the way her hands created beauty with a paintbrush.

On her front porch, he stood, waiting to knock until his mind was in a better place. Prayer alone could accomplish this. *Lord, protect me. Protect Ashley. She is Yours. Bless her relationship with Mr. James. Make him honor and respect her as You would have a man treat a woman. Help me accept the singleness You have given me. I praise You, Lord. You are the giver of all good gifts.*

With a decisive knock, he straightened his back and waited.

She opened the door and her eyes went wide. "Jonathan. Come in." Stepping back, she looked down at her paint smeared gray sweats and police shirt and frowned. "Sorry. I wasn't expecting company. I have to get ready for work soon."

This was good. Jonathan nodded and held out the frame he had made for her, staying firmly on the porch. Being alone with a single woman inside her home would be a larger, more dangerous mistake than watching Ashley paint. He must avoid all appearance of evil. To do otherwise was not in keeping with the behavior of his people.

"Come on in. It's cold out there."

He moved forward but stopped himself just outside the threshold. "I should have called first. I apologize." He held out the frame again. "I only wanted to make sure this was the type of frame and the size you had mentioned."

With gentle hands, she accepted the frame and ran her thumb over the polished wood. "This is gorgeous. Thank you." Stepping outside, she focused on the frame but could not hide her shiver. He should go.

Before he could say good-bye, she spoke again. "I'll run in and get the painting I had in mind for this frame."

He stepped back to the porch railing and leaned against it.

A minute later she returned wearing a sweatshirt and holding one of her paintings and the frame. She fastened them together with skilled hands. The dark wood highlighted the painting of Anna's house as if they were meant for each other.

"It's perfect. Thank you, Jonathan." She held it out, her eyes so filled with joy he could not help but smile in return.

"I am pleased you like it." He studied the painting more closely. Was that him, black hat in hand, back turned, gazing into the sunset beyond his aunt's home? It was not Bradley.

Ashley cleared her throat and lowered the painting to rest on a wooden rocking chair. A slight red in her cheeks caused an uncomfortable response in his stomach. She was embarrassed because she had painted him. He should not be pleased about this.

He broke the strained silence. "Would you have the time to paint Anna's home again? I would like to purchase this for Anna's birthday. If she sells her farm, this would be a treasured reminder of God's faithfulness to her family over the years."

"I'd love to." She walked down the length of her front porch and peered into her studio window. "Yes. I have extra canvases and can do it this coming week." She returned to where he stood and tilted her head. "Will Friday be soon enough?"

"Yes. That is very good."

She toed the porch with her white socked feet. "I'm worried about Brad. I don't want to see him hurt or have him keep taking out his anger and pain in destructive ways."

Her words came in such a rush it took a minute for him to form a response. Mr. James had helped Bradley, no one could deny that. And the mention of his name was a good reminder that it was a sin for him to wish anything about Ashley. She belonged to another.

She turned away to study the painting again. "So how is Brad?"

Heaviness settled over him. "He is worse. Many in our community have changed their minds and believe Bradley is breaking the farming machines, out of neglect or malice, we do not know. A few believe he is setting fires again."

Spinning around to face him, tears sprang into her eyes and her fists clenched. "I didn't hear about any fires."

"They were small fires on a few of the outlying farms."

"He wouldn't do anything like that out of malice. He's not like that. There must be another explanation."

He shook his head. "Bradley was sent to live with me after being caught setting fire to two older barns. He is capable of this."

Head bowed as if to pray, Ashley grew silent. He hoped she was praying and finding some solace there.

A car turned into Ashley's driveway and parked. Two older adults exited the expensive looking car and stood staring at him. He should go.

"Ashley, dear." A tall woman, with dark hair the color of Ashley's, hurried up the front walk. Once on the porch, she turned to him and extended a hand. "Hello. Are we interrupting anything?" She shook hands with him and turned to Ashley. "I didn't know you allowed art clients to come to your house to purchase paintings."

A gentleman with dark brown hair, dressed in a very nice suit, joined them on the porch and wrapped his arm around the woman. No wonder Ashley welcomed such treatment from Mr. James. It seemed to be common among her acquaintances.

"Mother." The harsh tone of Ashley's voice surprised him. "This is my friend, Jonathan Yoder." She turned to him. "These are my parents, Randall and Jacquelyn Walters."

Jonathan nodded. "Pleased to meet you."

Mr. Walters smiled in a way much different than Ashley. "Nice to meet you too." He turned to the framed picture of Anna's farm. "You don't have time for boring pastoral scenes. You need to focus and create pieces worthy of the High Museum. You also need higher quality materials for framing."

Mr. Walters's words pricked like glass. How could Ashley's father not see God's beauty in the simple frame?

Ashley did not speak but worked her jaw back and forth. He should leave now. He did not belong.

She turned to him. "Thank you for the beautiful frame. I love it."

"You are welcome." He nodded again to her parents. "It was nice to meet you, but I must go." He met Ashley's sad green eyes. "I will speak with you next week."

With nothing left to say, he hurried down the porch stairs.

He could not help but hear Mrs. Walters's words as he walked to his truck. "What is this, young lady? You suddenly get serious about dating and you have two men fawning over you. That is not how you were raised. You should have listened to our advice."

"Jonathan is a friend. Nothing more."

"He couldn't take his eyes off of you. Surely you can see that."

Adjusting his black hat, he sped to his truck. He longed to return to the porch to protect Ashley from the meanness of her mother's words and her father's demands.

But she was not his to protect.

∾

Ashley braided her damp hair and fastened it into a tight bun, staring at the mirror in front of her with a clenched jaw and fire still blazing from her eyes. The nerve of her parents. Not only did they insult a friend to his face, they harped on his lifestyle and claimed he was in love with her. There was no way.

And no interest on her part. Not any longer. She'd chosen Patrick. Even so, her parents had no right to speak so rudely. She should call him and apologize. If she had time, she'd do that on her break tonight.

Satisfied, she strapped on her sidearm.

One last look in the mirror and she ran through her questions. Could she do it today? Could she stay safe and protect fellow officers and the public? Could she use her weapon if necessary?

Yes.

Arriving at the station minutes later, she joined Elizabeth and the other officers in the squad room. Lieutenant Shafer stood at the front of the room, shuffling his notes for the shift briefing.

"Ladies and gentlemen, we have much of the same to report this weekend. Burglaries are still happening and drug dealers are still out there trying to poison our young people. Tonight would be a good night to catch more than a few of them."

He handed out patrol assignments and dismissed the group by three fifteen. She appreciated his short and to the point manner. And that the briefings weren't filled with the homicides and gang activities of her GCPD days.

She waved to Elizabeth and headed to her section of Montezuma to patrol tonight. Unfortunately, it was on the other side of the railroad tracks from the Mennonite farms. The streets were quiet, not much traffic out. The proposed revitalization was so needed for this town. Places like the railway museum should have been filled on a beautiful Saturday afternoon like this one.

Static on the radio snagged her attention. A domestic. "10-4. Unit 157 responding. ETA two minutes. Request backup."

"On the way."

These calls were the worst. Husbands reeking of alcohol and testosterone claiming nothing happened while a shaking and bruised woman cowered and claimed she made a mistake. That she didn't want to file charges.

Ashley's hands gripped the steering wheel. Hard.

Not only did the pain and sorrow of such toxic relationships drain her, they set her on edge, watching every second for the violence to erupt with police as the target.

More cops lost their lives at routine traffic stops and on domestic calls.

She forced her emotions to the back burner and steadied her breathing as she pulled to a stop one house down from the address. Elizabeth's cruiser turned the corner and parked nearby.

Together they exited and walked up to the house, Elizabeth speaking first. "This could get ugly fast, Ash."

"I know."

Ashley knocked this time and stood to one side of the door, Elizabeth at an angle behind her.

No answer.

She knocked again. "Police. Open up." She listened for any trace of evidence that would force them through the door to rescue someone from another beating.

A petite young woman with a black eye opened the door. "Yes?" Her voice wavered.

"Did someone from this residence report a domestic disturbance?"

She shook her straight, bleached white hair. "No. No one." She moved to close the door, but a large hand reached above her head and pulled the door back.

"This another one of your boyfriends you're tryin' to hide?" He reared his tanned, muscular arm back.

Ashley moved forward. Elizabeth followed. "Step back, sir."

He froze, eyes darting everywhere at once. "Officers…uh…um. What brings you here?"

Right.

The young woman shifted away from her abuser and closed the front door. "I'm Mercy Givens. This is my husband, Ralph."

The names matched those from dispatch. "Did you call the police, Mrs. Givens?"

The girl was younger than Ashley, too young to spend forever with someone who used her as a punching bag. Unless the red welts on her arms were from some freak accident and the bruises on her feet were from falling up the stairs.

She'd heard it all and believed none of it. But unless Mercy pressed charges, they'd leave her home with no one under arrest. That didn't set right.

"I, well, I thought there was someone breakin' into our home, you know?" She moved down the front hall and stood by a closed door.

Elizabeth stayed glued to Mr. Givens.

Ashley followed Mrs. Givens. "The report didn't say robbery, ma'am. Want to explain?" She puzzled over the young woman's odd behavior. Was someone hiding behind the door Mercy guarded?

"I guess the lady on the phone heard Ralph yellin' at the guy in our backyard." She shrugged. "That's all I can figure, anyway." Her eyes searched her husband's cold blue ones. "I…I just need to get somethin' real quick." She threw open the door and stood back.

Ralph exploded, curses streaming, and lunged at Mercy. "You stupid—"

Before he could blink, Ashley slapped her handcuffs on his outstretched wrist and turned him around, wrenching his arm behind him and snapping the other bracelet in place.

Mercy shook. "Thank you." She repeated the whispered words over and over. Then she pointed past the door she'd opened, into a small bedroom stacked floor to ceiling with electronics. "He…he stole all… all of that."

Ralph bowed his back and growled, straining against the hold Ashley had on him.

She shoved him into the wall, face first. "Stay still."

While she babysat Ralph, Elizabeth stepped into the room. "What do you know? This here flat screen TV with a little daisy sticker on the base matches the description of the one missing from Pine Village apartments."

"Mr. Givens, let's go have a little chat down at the station." Ashley paraded him out his front door and into the back of her patrol car.

Elizabeth did the same, a lot more gently with Mrs. Givens. There was so much more to this story.

She'd have to wait till tomorrow to hear what the investigators pulled out of this pair. What she wouldn't give for Mercy to be completely innocent of the theft and a willing participant in building a case against her husband.

It'd be one story in a hundred where the abused threw off her victim role and lived to stand up to her abuser in a court of law. Ashley hoped that would happen in Mercy's case.

If not, they'd be back at the Givens house once again.

Only next time, Mercy might not be alive for them to rescue.

CHAPTER FIFTEEN

A nother day stretched before her and another round of battling drug dealers. Too bad every time they locked one up, another one crawled from under the rocks to take his place.

At least their recent string of burglaries had ceased with the arrest of Ralph Givens. She and Elizabeth had done well bringing that one in.

Ashley yawned at her desk. She'd slept in Sunday and spent the day alone with Chester, painting up a storm. Her parents had spent yesterday with Emma, so she really shouldn't be this tired.

Elizabeth scooted a chair close and nudged her arm. "Saw Patrick at the grocery yesterday. He congratulated me on a good night of work."

Ashley grinned. "Yeah, he said the same thing to me Saturday night when we talked." Warmth filled her at the reminder of Patrick's over-the-top compliments. She should enjoy them while they came.

"So he came over after your shift?" Her blue eyes widened.

"Nope. Just a phone call."

Elizabeth nodded. "Good for you, girl. Enjoy being single and keeping them waiting. Marriage is tough when you don't start it out right."

"We're nowhere close to thinking about marriage. But please don't spoil my *someday* fantasies." She didn't have many of them left, but she could do without having her few illusions shattered by her friend's opinion.

Her desk phone jangled. Saved by the ring. Waving at Elizabeth, she picked up the receiver. "Officer Ashley Walters. Can I help you?"

"It's good to hear your voice, Ash." Detective Rich Burke's smooth baritone jerked her to attention. "You're a hard one to get ahold of."

"Rich. It's not like I moved to Siberia." Of course she hadn't left her new cell number with any of her cop friends in Atlanta, least of all with the only guy she'd dated on the force. "So, how are you?"

"Good. You?"

"Really good. I love it here. Small town, less trauma." She fiddled with a pencil. The silence following her answer caused her skin to crawl. "You didn't call to see how small-town living was, did you?"

"No. Ash, I hate to do this while you're at work, but I might as well get it over with." He sighed. "I've left messages with your parents and asked them to have you call me at a time that's convenient, but they haven't returned my calls."

"They're here visiting. Did you call their cell phones?" Unease pitched a tent in her stomach.

"Yes. Didn't they tell you?"

Deep breath in. Deep breath out. "No. They haven't told me anything. What should they have shared?"

"GCPD followed up on a tip by an inmate regarding Eric's murder."

Blood drained from her head and dizziness took its place. Had God really answered her prayers?

"And?"

"The guy's in jail. He's doing a nickel for drug charges, about to be released. But his rap sheet and DNA say he's our guy."

"His DNA matched?" *Please, God…*

"Yes. We're filing charges and he'll be tried for Eric's murder. We're doing all we can to make sure he spends the rest of his life behind bars."

"Who's in charge of the case?"

"Detective Karen Everett. She's new and has no connections to anyone involved. She knows about you though and may have some questions soon. You up for it?"

For years, she'd strapped on a gun, ready to face down the evil man who'd beaten and murdered Eric in cold blood for the contents of his wallet. But now…could she do it?

"You okay? I wanted you to hear the news from a friend."

She opened her mouth to speak, but nothing came out. Nothing but tears. The end of her ten-year ordeal was on the cusp of justice and all she could do was cry.

She grabbed a tissue and wiped the evidence of weakness from her face. She'd finish this for Eric and walk into that courtroom with her head held high.

"Ash? I should have come down there to deliver the news. I'm sorry."

"No. No, it's okay. Thank you for telling me. Please let Karen know I'm available to talk anytime. Here's my cell." She rattled off the ten digits and wished she hadn't. She didn't want Rich using it. Or coming to town.

"When are you coming home? I'd love to cook you dinner again."

And here it was. "Montezuma is home now. And I'm dating someone, Rich. He's a great guy."

"It's serious?"

How to answer that one? Saying no meant Rich would continue to call. Saying yes meant admitting to something she wasn't ready to face. Especially now that Eric's case would fill her mind every spare second.

"Serious enough."

He chuckled. "Let him know there are cops in Atlanta ready to deal with him if he ever treats you wrong."

She had no doubt they would. In a heartbeat. "Thanks, Rich. I'll let him know." Another deep breath. "And thanks for calling about my brother's case. I appreciate it."

"Anything for you. Take care, Ashley."

Returning the phone to its base, she couldn't ignore her shaking hands. How could she go out on the road like this?

Like every other cop in the country did every day, no matter what. Personal lives jumped in the backseat when they were on duty.

Compartmentalization at its finest. She was a master at it.

∞

Hours of mind-numbing ticket writing later, Ashley pulled into her driveway for a quick dinner break. Chester greeted her with happy puppy yips and kisses.

She sank onto the floor and held him close, tears stinging her eyes. "It's been a tough day, buddy."

He wagged his entire body and licked her face.

"Let's get some dinner and talk about happy things, how 'bout?"

She spilled out the details of Rich's call and the shift she'd served while heating up a bowl of chicken soup and popping some pastries into the toaster.

Nothing like a meal of comfort foods.

She put her pastries and steaming soup on the table and scooped food into Chester's bowl. Then she bowed her head. "Lord, please let that man be convicted. Bring justice for Eric."

Justice had to happen this time.

In a few bites, her soup and pastries disappeared. She still had about thirty minutes left of her break. Picking up her home phone, she dialed Patrick's number.

It rang and rang.

She tried his cell phone and got the recorded message. Of all times for him to be unavailable.

A quick check of her watch and she decided to return to work early rather than sit alone and ponder the past.

Down Highway 26 all was still and quiet. Pulling this section to patrol tonight was a gift from God. Her night might pass without drug deals or robberies to bust. Then again, a trip to jail with an unruly passenger in the cage would keep her mind busy.

She turned left onto Whitehouse Road and drove on autopilot to the Mennonite church. Surprised to find the lights on in the fellowship hall, she parked and exited her car, slow and silent.

Was someone dumb enough to turn on lights during a burglary? She wouldn't put it past 'em. Circling around back, she surveyed the entire area.

A white pickup truck was the only thing out of place.

Maybe this wasn't a break-in. Could be the bishop or one of the men working late. Still, she needed to put eyes on the late-night worker to be sure.

She tried the back door and found it open. Slipping inside, she catalogued everything in the large room. The quilt supplies were stored away and a damaged wooden bookshelf dominated the center of the room. Chairs and tables had been pushed back from the work area.

"Hello? Is anyone here?"

The sound of a flushing toilet turned her attention to the left side of the large room. A Mennonite man stepped out of the restroom, shaking his hands.

He stopped short when their eyes met.

"Jonathan?" Her shoulders relaxed. "What are you doing here at ten o'clock at night?"

"Working." He pointed to the cabinet. "The bishop asked me to repair his favorite bookshelf as soon as I could. The only free time I had was now." He didn't meet her eyes.

Maybe he was too tired to be friendly.

"Sorry to bother you. I'll let you get back to work."

He tilted his head to the side. "Have you been crying?" Stepping closer, he placed himself between her and the door.

"It's nothing. I should get back to work."

"Is it your parents?" He winced. "It is none of my business. I apologize."

"No, but they're involved. I haven't even begun to deal with my anger at them." She grabbed a metal folding chair and sat down. This was still her dinner break, late as it was.

He sat down a few seats away. "You are often angry with them, yes?"

That observation hit too close to home. He didn't know her parents well enough to understand, though. "One of my friends in Atlanta called them trying to get ahold of me, and they didn't bother calling back or even mentioning it to me."

"This is the reason for your anger?"

Yes. No. She hated the question. "I'm angry because of their disrespect. They show up at my house unannounced, try to boss me around like I'm five, and then they don't even want to spend time with me when I'm off work." She ticked off the points on her fingers. This could take all night. "Plus, a police detective calls and they don't think it's important enough to let me know?"

"They have hurt you deeply."

Now that was an understatement.

"Have you spoken with them about these things?"

"No. Well, I tried. I've tried for years to show them I'm an adult, but they still barge in and take over. It's why I moved away. Guess I should have moved farther." Not only that, but they wouldn't ever talk about Eric's death. Or his life. He was killed and they acted like nothing ever happened.

Jonathan shifted in his seat and rolled his gray shirt sleeves down. "It seems your problems have moved with you. Have you spoken to God about this anger?"

She flicked her eyes heavenward. She should have tried Patrick again. He'd have listened and commiserated.

"Forgiveness is a gift from God that will free you. I do not wish to shove this idea at you, but this situation with your parents is hurting you. I would not be a friend if I did not try to help."

She wished his help was more helpful. "Thank you. You're right. I do need to talk this over with God and forgive my parents. I'll work on that."

"It will work on you if you do not."

If only forgiveness happened at the snap of her fingers. It's not like she hadn't tried to forgive them. Over and over and over again.

"If this situation with your parents is not what made you cry, what is?"

Snapshots of that day flew through her mind. She pushed them away. Talking about them wouldn't help. "A detective from Atlanta called me today to say they've found Eric's murderer. They're building a case against him." Heat engulfed her. "He's spent the last five years of his life in jail, fed and protected while my brother died and I've been alone for ten years."

Despite her best efforts, hot, angry tears spilled down her cheeks. She swiped them away. Eric deserved her tears. His killer did not.

Jonathan leaned forward. "I am so sorry, Ashley. I am sorry for your loss and all the sadness this news brings you."

"Thank you." She sniffed back any further tears and checked her watch. She should get back to work.

"I know you must go. Please hear me, though. I wish you to be free of this hatred and pain. It will destroy you."

She stood. "Forgiveness isn't that easy. The man that shot Eric at point-blank range deserves punishment." He deserved worse, but Jonathan wouldn't understand.

"Your hatred is only punishing you. Leave vengeance to the Lord. He will repay, and you can be free." His kind eyes pleaded with her.

"I'll try, okay." She walked away and stopped at the door. "Thank you for being a friend and listening. I'd appreciate your prayers."

"You will have them."

Good. Because she had nothing left to lift up to God right now. Not to the God who had allowed Eric to die.

Nothing at all.

Chapter Sixteen

Patrick thanked God for a desk job as he shoved the last cow into its stall for the Wednesday evening milking. The smelly beast bucked every step of the way. How Bradley at his age and size managed the grueling work every day was beyond him.

"I'm finished, Mr. James. Mamm said we could talk in the living room." He led the way back to the farmhouse.

Anna met them at the back door. "Thank you for coming here, Mr. James. I am unable to leave the farm most days, and Jonathan has been very busy with his carpentry work." She glanced at Bradley washing up in the mudroom utility sink. "It is good that you are here."

Patrick catalogued possible land mines in the conversation ahead.

Bradley wiped his hands and pointed into the dining room. "If you wouldn't mind waiting in the dining room, I need to change my clothes before we speak."

Their home was sparsely furnished but large. Enough for the big family Anna had raised under this roof. Excellent carpentry on all the homemade furniture thanks to more than one carpenter in Anna's family.

Few pictures decorated the walls, but the ones that hung there spoke of a loving family who'd enjoyed many good years together.

That was what Bradley needed to hang on to.

The boy entered, coat in hand. "I still have to finish repairing a tractor before dinner. Could we talk while I work?"

"Sure. Lead the way."

Once they were out of Anna's earshot, Bradley stopped. "I have to fix the tractor, but that's not why I asked to meet out here." He slipped into a wood-planked old barn full of farm equipment in various stages of repair. "Mamm doesn't need to hear our conversation."

"What's going on, Bradley?"

The boy grabbed a large wrench from a toolbox and stalked to the tractor. "A friend of mine came to the farm last night after dinner to warn me that his parents were going to the bishop to speak about discipline."

"Is this the friend supplying you with matches?"

"No." Bradley worked his jaw back and forth. "My friend said everyone believes I've damaged the farm equipment on purpose and started setting fires again. They'll make sure I'm sent somewhere awful or add more work and more supervision."

"Everyone?"

"Not Mamm. Or Jonathan."

"But everyone else in your community?"

"It doesn't matter. I can't handle this anymore. If they add more work, I'll…"

Patrick waited, the silence pressing into him.

"Bradley?"

The boy stilled the wrench in his hands. "I can't go through it again."

"Go through what?"

"All the discussion and waiting for their decision on my punishment. You and everyone else know I set fires before. On the farms of boys who have picked on me." Bradley tightened engine bolts and slammed the huge cover closed. "I haven't set fires again."

"You had matches, Bradley. I saw them and so did Jonathan."

"They belonged to a friend from town. I only used them the one time Jonathan saw me. It was stupid. But it felt powerful, you know."

"That's not real power."

"It's hard not to use matches. They used to calm me down."

"What about now?" Patrick studied the boy for signs of deception.

Bradley met his gaze. "I don't want that anymore. I didn't set those fires."

"I believe you." Wanting to believe wasn't enough and Patrick hated that. This time, a little checking had convinced him of the boy's innocence. Bradley was working with supervision when the recent fires had been set. The damage to the farm equipment was another story.

"Tell me about this friend with matches."

Bradley began working on another piece of equipment. "He's nobody."

"Did you know him before you moved to Indiana?"

"Yes. A family from our church used to babysit him and his two sisters."

Patrick moved to the other side of the tractor. "He's a lot older."

"A few years."

"Does he get in trouble a lot?"

Bradley nodded and continued working.

"What kind of trouble?"

"I don't know anymore. When he drove me to your office last week, he showed me this bag of white crystal stuff and asked if I wanted any."

"What did you do?"

Bradley rolled his eyes. "I said no. Then I called the police and gave them an anonymous tip. I saw that on a TV show at the bus station." He pointed his wrench toward the house. "No TV in there and I haven't been back on the computer either."

"Does your mom or Jonathan know about this?"

"The TV show?" Bradley shifted his attention from the tractor, his eyes wide. "No. Not about the TV or the phone call to the police. You aren't going to tell them are you?"

"You should tell your mom. You did the right thing. She'll see that."

Bradley shook his head. "Can we talk about something else now?"

"How about moving to Indiana?"

The boy worked his jaw back and forth. "I hated it. It was boring and crowded. I wanted to come home."

"Why?"

The boy kicked at the huge tractor wheels.

Then he punched and kicked. Small hands pounded against the towering tractor.

Minutes passed. Patrick prayed.

Bradley slumped to the dirt floor, sniffling. "I tried to get back in time." He swiped away tears. "But I wasn't here when my father died."

Patrick shifted closer. "I'm sorry, Bradley. Sorry for how awful it was to not say good-bye to your father. How awful the meeting with your biological mother was. I hate all this right along with you."

The boy shot forward and wrapped his arms around Patrick's waist. Patrick jumped at first contact, but pulled the boy tighter. "Lord, Bradley is hurting. Please be his comfort and peace. Let him know You love him and are here with him. We know You are a healing God. Please bring Your healing to Bradley. Amen."

They sat there, Bradley tucked into his arms, for a long time. Neither spoke.

Then Bradley scooted a short distance away. "No one here tells me I'm doing a good job. I just get blamed when something goes wrong. I miss my father. He told me when I did right and helped me when I did wrong. Mamm tries, but it's not the same."

No it wasn't. Patrick's mother had tried to fill the gap after his dad died. But nothing replaced a father's love and encouragement. Nothing except the heavenly Father's love. "My dad died when I was young."

Wide brown eyes answered him.

"Yeah. I know a little of what you're feeling. Maybe not the same, but I know what it's like to miss your dad."

"How old were you?"

"Nine. My dad was hunting with some of his buddies and fell from a deer stand. He broke his neck and died before they got him to the hospital."

Bradley nodded. "You didn't get to say good-bye either."

"No."

They sat for a time in silence, Patrick's mind whirling about next steps. The line between counseling and mentoring had blurred tonight. He could no longer charge this family and treat Bradley as a patient.

He'd explain things to Jonathan and see if he could get him on board with the plan forming in his head.

"You ready to head back? It's about supper time."

"No homework?" The boy had learned fast the way most counseling sessions ended. He started toward the house.

"Not today. Except, I'd ask one thing."

Bradley raised his eyebrows.

"Take the anger and sadness and talk to God about it. Come beat the tractor if you need to. It'll help."

"Thank you for understanding."

"You're welcome."

Jonathan met them at the back door. "Bradley, you're needed in the kitchen."

"Yes, sir." Bradley turned toward him. "Thank you, Mr. James. You've helped a lot." He ran inside.

Patrick locked eyes with Jonathan. "Can I speak with you a minute?" The wind whipped the hood on his down jacket.

"Yes."

Nothing like a good conversationalist. "I'm going to end my counseling with Bradley, but I'd like to continue spending time with him as a mentor. Would you support that?"

"You believe this is wise? The boy has many things still binding his soul."

"Bradley needs more adult attention, apart from work, to guide him through his grief."

"I will support this." Jonathan motioned to the wooden deck chairs. "Please, sit. There is something I wish to speak with you about also."

That didn't bode well. But he sat and waited for Jonathan to speak first.

"Ashley has spoken with you about the news from her friends in Atlanta?"

Patrick blinked. "Yes. She talked to you about it?" Had Ashley shared more with Jonathan than she had with him? Had she come to find Jonathan first? He hated the thoughts surging through him.

Visions of Melanie's many male friends flashed through his mind. Surely Ashley wouldn't follow the same pattern Melanie had.

"She did not seek me out. I was working at the church at ten o'clock Monday night, and she investigated the lights being on so late."

Patrick released the breath he'd been holding. Ashley had called him before that. He was just too busy with paperwork after his last two appointments had run over.

"She is hurting. I wanted to be sure she was talking to someone about it."

"I'll make sure she's okay." He sat back and crossed his left leg over his right. "Did you know her parents left without saying good-bye?"

"I do not know any of the details. I met her parents once and can understand why she would struggle in a relationship with them. I tried to talk to her about how forgiveness will free her from the weight she carries with her."

"It's not that easy. They should have been there for her and talked to her about Eric's murder investigation. She has a reason to be angry. And hurt." He worked his shoulders up and down to loosen them.

"I agree her parents should have been honest with her in many areas." Jonathan leaned forward. "Ashley needs your help to talk through her emotions. She does not need you to share in her anger. That will only make things worse."

Patrick bristled at being counseled by someone with an eighth grade education. His conscience pricked at him. How arrogant. He should be able to learn from anyone.

They stared at each other for a span of minutes.

Patrick broke eye contact first. No matter how much it galled him, Jonathan was right. But it was Patrick's place to help. Not Jonathan's.

"I'll take care of it. Thank you for sharing your concern." He stood.

Jonathan joined him. "Good. I will pray for both of you."

"Thank you. Please tell Anna and Bradley I said good-bye." With that, he turned and headed for his Mustang.

He appreciated Jonathan's prayers. At the same time, he wanted that to be the extent of Jonathan's help. Shaking his head, he slammed the Mustang door. He couldn't suffocate Ashley or play the jealous boyfriend.

He was better than that.

And Ashley needed him to be better than that. Now more than ever.

❧

Ashley ran down her porch steps and hugged Margo the second her best friend exited her cute little BMW coupe. She was supposed to have arrived hours ago.

"Well, there, Miss Ashley. I do declare that is the most excited greeting I've received in a long time. This evening air must be doing great things for you." She tucked her shoulder-length blonde hair behind her ear. "Or maybe it's that Patrick fellow. When do I get to meet him?"

"Later." She grabbed one of Margo's many suitcases. "Let's get you settled first and have some girl time. We'll have ice cream, maybe some dinner, and then we can talk till the wee hours of the morning."

Chester barked as Margo entered, but quickly made friends when Margo bent down to rub his ears. "He's a cutie. Not much of a watchdog though."

That could be a problem. One she'd deal with later.

Margo followed her up the stairs to the biggest of the spare bedrooms. The only furnished one. "Here my lady may rest her weary head after all the gabbing and ice cream we're about to eat."

"You will destroy my figure yet."

"I'll let you unpack, and I'll get the ice cream ready." Ashley closed the bedroom door behind her and stared down the hall. She hadn't logged many hours of sleep since her parents' visit.

Margo would be awhile, so she returned to her latest easel and picked up her paintbrush. If she could just finish the other three paintings her parents had requested, maybe they'd be satisfied.

With a whistle, Margo toured her studio. "You've been a busy girl. No wonder we haven't talked."

"The phone works both ways."

Margo tsked. "What are you working on here?"

"The fourth of six rush paintings. My parents want as many as I can deliver for a fundraiser show in May." She focused on the Impression-istic painting of Emma's childhood garden.

"I was under the impression you said no. At least, that's what your father said on the many voicemails he's left me, begging me to convince you to change your mind."

"Dad called you?"

"As always." Margo pulled a stool over. "Ash, you don't have to do this. It won't make your relationship with them better."

"It might."

Margo huffed. "In all the twenty-two years I've been your best friend, I've never, ever, seen your parents treat you like you deserve. You're not a robot, nor do you have to do everything they say."

"They're trying to help my art career."

"I thought you were a cop. A grown-up one at that."

She stuck out her tongue.

"Seriously, Ash. They've controlled your life far too long. And you've let them. You have to stop. Doing what they want will not make them love you."

"That's not why I'm doing this. I love painting." She held up her brush but couldn't figure out what color to use next.

"You love your parents, like every little girl. But they can't tell you you're good enough. Even if they could get outside themselves, their love won't make you see that you are enough in God's eyes."

She should have known Margo would go there. Most of the time Ashley loved her directness. This was not one of those times.

Margo plucked the paintbrush and palette from her hands. "You said something about ice cream. Let's go have some, shall we?"

Ashley allowed herself to be dragged to the kitchen and served a heaping bowl of cotton-candy ice cream. Margo even plopped a tiny bit of the pink goodness in Chester's bowl. That would keep him busy for a while.

"Tell me about the call from Rich."

She shoved a humongous bite of ice cream in her mouth and talked around it. "I thought we were done with the lectures."

"Don't talk with your mouth full. It's disgusting." Margo crinkled her nose. "And you're doing it on purpose. Just for that I'm not talking about anything fun until you tell me about the phone call."

"How exactly is this different than my parents' controlling behavior?"

Margo put down her spoon and reached across the table. "I'm sorry, honey. I just care about you. You're pushing too hard. Exactly like after Eric's death. I can't let you try to destroy yourself again."

"Rich said they know who killed Eric, Maggie." She forced the waver from her voice. "He's going to be released on parole soon."

Margo peered outside and shivered. "That gives me the creeps. Let's talk about you, not the case again. Okay?"

For all the good things her best friend was, a tough cop was not one of them. "My friend Jonathan says I should just forgive Leonard Simms. But it's not that easy. I've hated him for almost half my life."

She scooted the melting ice cream around in her dish. "Patrick's been so busy lately we haven't talked much. When he's off work, I'm on duty. Our schedules aren't meshing that great."

Margo jumped up from her seat. "You know what? I have a great idea." Chester yipped at her and waggled. "Why don't I take this big guy for a little walk and then whip up some dinner? I learned some fantastic recipes from my last client. You'll love it. And you can go take a hot shower and have a catnap. You'll need it if we're going to stay up late gabbing."

She had a point there. "You win. I'll see you in an hour."

Margo grinned her most troublesome grin before turning away to find Chester's leash. Nothing good came of that look. Ashley headed upstairs. Maggie had met no one in Montezuma, so the worst she could do was burn dinner and they had to order pizza.

Please, God? Please let that be the worst thing that happens this weekend.

If only prayer were a guarantee. She knew better.

⚬

Patrick clicked the TV on and muted the sound. Ashley's best friend should have arrived by now. He'd hoped Ashley would call to invite him over for dinner, but that hadn't happened.

The painting he'd ordered online for her had come today. He hoped it'd provided the encouragement Ashley needed, a reminder that God was in charge of the world, and she didn't have to be strong for everyone around her.

He'd tried to be there for her between his patients and her work hours, but there was never enough time for a deep conversation. She hadn't wanted to talk Tuesday or Wednesday when they'd met at her place for lunch, so he'd held her while she cried. Now Margo was here.

He settled into his comfortable tan sofa and stared straight ahead. He should have taken off work early and asked Ashley and Margo to dinner. Instead, he'd waited for a phone call. Dumb move.

His cell buzzed against his waist. She'd called. "Hey, Ashley. How are you? Did Margo get there safely?"

"I did arrive safely, thank you for asking." A silky, Southern drawl poured through his phone. "Sorry, I'm not Ashley."

Margo? "Is everything all right?"

"Yes and no. I know we've never met, but I could use a favor. It's for Ashley."

"Anything." He sat up straight and pulled on his tennis shoes.

"I prayed you'd be this great of a guy." She paused. "Ashley said you've been really busy lately and she hasn't gotten a chance to talk with you about Eric's case."

"She's right. I hate that, but it happens sometimes."

"Well, she needs you right now. She doesn't usually let on that she has any weaknesses, but she does. Not asking for help is her biggest flaw."

"She's been looking forward to your visit for a week." She'd probably hate him for barging in. Talking behind Ashley's back didn't set right either.

"Bring Hawaiian pizza and Cokes and be here in forty-five minutes. I'll take care of the rest." She hung up without waiting for an answer.

Atlanta folks and their manners. Maybe he didn't miss the big city all that much.

Despite his misgivings, he followed Margo's instructions and stood on Ashley's front porch, pizza in hand at the appointed time.

Ashley opened the door, shaking her head. "She sucked you in, didn't she?" Her eyes flicked from the pizza to his face. "Thank you for bringing dinner. I've missed you this week."

He set the pizza down on an end table and pulled her into his arms. Not caring where Margo was, he lowered his lips to Ashley's.

She pulled him closer and deepened the kiss.

The evening couldn't have gotten any better. He pulled back and held her at arm's length. "We'll get our schedules worked out better from now on, okay?"

She smiled. "I'd like that."

Margo strolled into the room. "Patrick James, I presume?" She held out her hand and he shook it. "Our dear Ashley already looks better, doesn't she?"

He grabbed the pizza box and headed to the kitchen. Growing up around his mom and sister had taught him when it was time for a wise exit.

They followed him into the kitchen. Chester barked from the back-yard and scratched against the door.

"He can stay outside until after we eat." Ashley shooed Chester away from the door. "So what did Maggie use to entice you over? Inflated stories about my grief?"

Margo huffed. "I told him the truth."

He handed them plates of pizza. "I'm happy to be here, but we don't have to talk about anything you don't want to, Ash."

"Thank you." She studied her pizza. "But there is something I need to talk to you about."

His focus jumped from Ashley to Margo. She shrugged.

Slipping into the chair next to Ashley, he took her hand. "Okay, shoot."

"I'm going to ask for a leave of absence from the chief so I can help out with my brother's case. I don't know if there's anything I can do, but I need to be there for my parents and to make sure everything is on track. At least for a little while."

Of all the things she could have said, this was one of the worst. It would destroy all the gains she'd made in leaving the past behind.

But what could he do, demand she stay here? He would never do that.

So if she insisted on moving back to Atlanta, even temporarily, then he'd take an extended vacation. Stay with a friend. No matter what, he'd be there for Ashley.

As long as she let him.

CHAPTER SEVENTEEN

Ashley's mind ping-ponged from one definite decision to another as she pushed food around on her plate Friday evening. Yoder's restaurant had the best country fried steak and mashed potatoes she'd ever eaten.

But tonight everything tasted like sand.

Margo gobbled up her food. "This is fantastic. I'm so glad you talked me into this."

Ashley shrugged. "We spent the day touring historic houses and talking interior design, I figured you should round out the day with a down-home dinner."

"Patrick's on his way?"

"He said to go ahead and eat, he'd be here before we finished."

Margo leaned forward. "You are going to tell him what we talked about today, right?"

Deep breath in. Deep breath out. Maybe. Margo had offered her a place to stay during the trial. But no helping with the case. Not that she could have in any official capacity. Of course, she'd called Detective Karen Everett while Margo was busy. When she didn't get in touch with Karen, she'd agreed to Margo's plans. Only because it made sense. For now.

"This is my training for developing a backbone?" Ashley hated the snippiness in her voice.

"This is you doing what's right." Margo wiped her mouth like a princess. "You saw Patrick's face. The man was crestfallen at your big talk of moving."

He'd hid it well, but the sadness in his eyes had ripped at her heart.

"He adores you, Ash. Give him a real chance. Grow some roots here. Live."

In walked Patrick, deep in conversation with Janet Hardy, her son, and the three members of the Jennings family. "Don't control this, Maggie. Let me choose how to live my life."

Margo teared up but nodded.

The Jennings and Hardys moved to a table in the back room of the restaurant, away from most of the crowd. She would have liked to hear their unguarded conversation before the big meeting on Monday. No one had the scoop on what would happen.

She hated going into a potentially volatile situation blind.

Patrick slipped in beside her, distracting her from everything else. "Hey there, beautiful." He kissed her cheek.

"Thanks for coming." She sat close, and Patrick slipped his arm behind her.

Electricity zinged between them. Maybe she should stay.

Disloyalty seared her conscience. Her brother deserved her best effort. He'd loved her, protected her, stood by her side. She couldn't just forget how he died. She had to be sure Leonard Simms paid.

Margo cleared her throat. "I need a trip to this restaurant's famous Mennonite bakery. I'll be back in a few minutes."

Patrick laughed. "You'll love it. Best doughnuts in the world."

Ashley met her friend's eyes. "Bring me back something good?"

"Of course." Margo winked and all was right between them again.

Patrick slipped his arm from her shoulders and took her hand, giving it a slight squeeze. "Have you guys had a good day?"

"Yes." She filled him in on their grand houses tour, and he listened as if her words were the only thing in the world.

With her hand tucked in Patrick's and his deep blue eyes focused on her, she made up her mind to stay in Montezuma.

Then again. Voices from the past crept in, whispering that she wasn't strong enough to handle a real relationship again. Not enough. Not after what happened with Harrison.

Her parents' stern faces cut into her wavering. They'd love it if she came home. They'd try to make her stay. To control her life again.

Not this time.

She stared at her plate. The best she could do was stop trying to figure it all out and assert some control over her life again. "I'm staying in Montezuma."

Patrick's eyes twinkled. "I'm glad. Really glad."

Two Mennonite young men walked through the front door, one with a black coat draped over his shoulders, bleeding through a bandage wrapped around his arm.

An older woman in a light purple dress and white head covering stepped out from behind the buffet counter. "Matt, what has happened?"

The young, bearded man nodded toward the side door. "Let us speak outside."

Patrick bristled beside her. "I recognize them. Those men have been working at Anna's farm."

Ashley stood and approached the small group of Mennonites, Patrick at her side. "Do you need a doctor? Or I can take you to the ER?"

Matt shook his head. "It will be fine. Just a cut from an accident. We have a doctor that will see me shortly. But thank you for your kind offer."

They walked outside, leaving Ashley standing there in awkward silence.

She turned to Patrick. "We need to figure out what's happening. Old equipment can't be behind all of these accidents."

He led her back to their table. "I spoke to Anna about the accidents again. She doesn't believe Bradley is behind them. Others disagree. More and more lately. But their community is helping replace the things that have broken and caused injury."

"Do you think Brad's behind them?"

"I don't know what's going on or who's behind the so-called accidents. But I don't see how they're accidents. Someone is causing them."

"Who?" She scanned the restaurant. No one was beyond suspicion.

"There are people in town very invested in this farm sale happening. People who might stoop to mischief to ensure a sale."

"Give me some names. I'll go talk to them."

"I know a few who *might*. But there are no facts, no case to investigate. The Yoders haven't called the police. They won't." He returned his eyes to her. "Maybe Anna selling her farm is for the best, before anyone gets badly hurt."

"Running away is never best."

∾

Standing on the front porch with her coat pulled tight around her, Ashley waved to Margo's retreating BMW coupe. Her best friend turned the corner and was gone.

And she was alone again.

She hated the silence after someone left. The emptiness. The absence of laughter.

It reminded her too much of the days after Eric's death. He'd taken the life and laughter in their home with him.

She closed the front door and wandered around the house, trying to find something to distract her. Too teary to paint, she finally decided to haul laundry to the washer. One piece at a time, she flung sheets and some clothes into the wash.

Chester poked his head into the laundry room and backed away from her sniffles and flying laundry.

She didn't blame him.

"God? I know You're listening. Margo wouldn't stop telling me how much You're listening." She folded a load of towels she'd left in the dryer from last week. "I'm sorry. I know I should have talked to You about

Rich's phone call and the decision to move home. The decision to stay. I just…I thought I could handle it. Like I did after Eric's death."

That hadn't turned out so well.

A loud thumping noise in the backyard shot her pulse into hyperdrive.

She'd locked the back gate, she was sure. Swallowing hard, she searched for a weapon. Her gun was upstairs.

Her eyes landed on a baseball bat.

Hands clenched around her Louisville Slugger, she poked her head out of the laundry room, but couldn't get a good look at the backyard.

Chester's doggie door flapped back and forth.

He'd gone out to investigate.

She gripped the bat tighter.

Then Chester's happy bark filled the air. Maybe the noise had been her puppy getting into trouble. Of course, Margo had said he wasn't much of a watch dog, so someone could be out there befriending her trusting puppy.

She stepped out from the laundry and pushed her dining room curtain aside.

There stood Patrick on her back porch, and Brad roughhousing with Chester.

She turned the locks and opened the door. "How'd y'all get in?"

Patrick tilted his head. "Through the open gate?" He searched her face. "Are you okay?"

No. She'd locked that door. Checked it just an hour ago when she'd gone out with Chester. Shivers raced down her spine. What was happening?

"Sorry. I'm fine. It's nothing." She focused on the unbroken gate lock. "I could have sworn I'd locked the gate."

"It's not like the past few days have been easy." Patrick's eyes assessed her.

"That's true." She'd gotten absentminded after Eric's death. Maybe Patrick was right. She stepped back into the house. "Why don't y'all come in? It's cold out here."

Chester zipped through the door before Patrick could take the first step. He raced to his water bowl like his tongue was on fire.

"Hello, Miss Walters." Brad slipped his plain black coat onto a chair.

"Hi, Brad. It's good to see you." Chester stood by her and yipped. "Why don't you take Chester into the living room? His toy box is in there."

"Yes, ma'am." He bent down to touch Chester, then disappeared into the living room, curious puppy on his heels.

Patrick pulled her close. "I figured today would be hard with Margo leaving, so we're here to take you on a picnic." He lowered his lips to hers and slipped his hands into her loose hair.

Her arms wrapped around his waist. Losing herself here was a good idea.

He pulled back. "Happy Saturday. We're here to fill your day with fun."

"I have to work at three."

"Then we'd better get going. We have a long way to go before we get to this perfect place Bradley and I found for lunch."

Her stomach growled. What a traitor.

"Guess you skipped breakfast?" He grabbed Brad's coat and tugged her into the living room. "Let's get you into a coat and out the door."

"We hope you like lunch." Brad led Chester out the door.

"She will." Patrick winked at her. "It includes chocolate."

He hustled her out the door. "You go on to the car. I need to check something."

"Check what?"

"Trust me, will you? And have a little patience. I just need to check on one thing and then I'll meet you at the car."

Patience was not her favorite virtue. But she went to the car anyway. And waited.

Patrick exited through the front door and sauntered down the driveway.

"Did you lock all the doors?" She surveyed her front door from Patrick's Mustang. "I should go check."

Patrick shook his head and pulled out of the driveway. "Already done. I locked the back gate too. You're safe and sound. So is your home."

She wished that were true.

Patrick drove down Highway 26 toward Bradley's house. "Are we taking Brad home?"

The boy turned from playing with Chester in the backseat. "We're taking the scenic route."

Patrick circled back into town. What was he up to? "Where exactly are you taking me?"

Patrick laughed. "To find chocolate and good company, maybe a little something more, right Bradley?"

The boy nodded but wouldn't meet her eyes.

When they pulled into Emma's bed and breakfast fifteen minutes later, she sighed. "This could have been a two minute walking trip."

"Where's the fun in that?" Patrick was out the door and to her side of the car before she could reach for the door handle.

Brad and Chester raced into the backyard.

"I'm not surprised Emma is in on this."

His eyes warmed. "Just remember, everything that happens here was my idea." He led her to the backyard gate. "Close your eyes, please."

She cringed but complied. No use in ruining their fun.

Patrick led her by the hand into the backyard and up the porch steps.

"Open them."

She blinked a few times and took it all in. Tulips decorated Emma's screened-in back porch in three different vases. Three times as many candles lit the overcast day and the spread of food covering the small table. A painting she'd never seen before was propped in a chair.

"Like it?"

She nodded.

Brad took her hand and led her to the candlelit table. "I'm glad you like it. Mr. James said it would cheer you up today."

Did Patrick know this was the kind of pampering Harrison had done anytime she'd had a terrible day? Margo would never have told him.

She hated thinking of Harrison at a time like this, a time when Patrick was trying so hard to make things better for her.

She met his hopeful gaze. Maybe he was another one of the good guys.

"I found this painting online a while back."

She brushed a finger across the simple wood frame. The sad woman front and center carried a globe on her back. Angels surrounded her, helping hold the world in place. Not much comfort. Ashley didn't want help carrying the weight of the world, she wanted God to fix things her way or let her make things right.

"Let's eat." Patrick held out her chair for her, and she moved the painting to a table behind them before she sat down. He held her hand as they prayed. "Lord, we thank You for this food and the beauty around us. Let all of this speak Your peace to Ashley. Comfort and encourage her and guide and strengthen Bradley. We love You, Lord. Amen."

Patrick's gift and prayer touched her deeply, but it was too much like Harrison. Rather than let on, she filled her plate and ate in silence. Bite by bite, she searched for differences. They were in Montezuma, in Emma's house. A place Harrison had never visited. There were homemade tea sandwiches and chocolate croissants. Harrison always purchased their picnic foods.

This was now with Patrick. She met his gaze and smiled. She should stay in the present and enjoy this moment, not letting the past ruin this day.

A chocolate croissant would help. The pastry still tasted like sunshine and dreams and held memories of her first meeting Patrick. Minus the embarrassing smudges.

Tuning into Brad and Patrick's conversation, she wiped her mouth to prevent any repeat of her smudge-faced performance.

"So your mom is signing the papers?" Patrick studied Brad.

The boy waited until he finished chewing to answer. "We can't replace all the damaged equipment. Neither can our community. If we sell, Mamm can retire and not have the stress of running a large farm."

Ashley sat still and silent. "What? When did Anna decide to sign the papers?"

"She spoke with the bishop and many in our community that did not agree with selling. The bishop also talked to the revitalization people about the museum, and they said we will be allowed to tell visitors about our faith."

"Really?" The food in her stomach churned. "Where will you live?"

Brad frowned. "We will live with one of my older sisters in Ohio until we can find a small house."

"Were the damages to the farm equipment caused by old age or someone tampering with them?"

Surprise flickered in the boy's eyes.

She reached for his arm. "I never believed you caused the accidents. But I want to know if you think someone is trying to force your mom to sell when she doesn't want to."

"I…I don't know."

It was too convenient for a string of accidents to run the Yoders off their farm. She'd poke around until she uncovered who was behind them. No matter who in the community it offended.

∾

An hour before her shift, Ashley stood at the Kauffmans' white farmhouse and knocked on the front door. She'd gotten the lowdown on the Kauffmans from Mr. Harvey at the grocery store yesterday evening. What a fount of information.

Just like Anna's home, there were white rockers in a neat row and a porch swept clean. How did they have the time to keep everything so tidy?

Beth Kauffman answered, her eyes wide. "Hello, Officer. Is there a problem?"

"No. I need to speak to Matt. Is your brother home?" She adjusted her duty belt.

"He is out back repairing one of our fences. I can call him." She pulled a small silver phone from her apron pocket. "Matt, there's a police officer here to talk to you."

Matt's voice carried over the wind. "Be right there."

Beth stepped back and opened the door. "Please, come in. My mother is upstairs with my little sister. Do you need to speak with her also?"

"No. Just Matt."

"Has he done something wrong?"

Interesting. Most of the Mennonite women she'd met spoke little. But maybe the sight of a police officer on her doorstep affected Beth like it did many others. Often criminals and citizens alike couldn't stop talking.

The Kauffman home resembled the Yoders' in simplicity and order. Cross-stitched Bible verses and a quilt were the only wall décor.

Matt tromped through the back door and into the living room, removing his coat. "Can I help you?"

Gauze bandages showed through his white work shirt. He remained standing.

So did she. "I have a few questions about your injury."

"It is taken care of. I did not report the accident to the police."

Beth's gaze bounced between them.

"That's why I'm here. Some folks in town believe the things happening at the Yoder farm aren't accidents. I'd like to make sure there's nothing criminal happening there."

Matt pointed to the couch. "Please, have a seat."

She settled into the couch next to Beth.

"I do not know what is happening at the Yoder farm." He rubbed his hands over his dark pants. "But the accidents are getting worse. More people could get injured."

"What do you think is causing the accidents?" She couldn't bring herself to say who.

"I do not know. There are sometimes pranks played, but we have not seen anyone around our farm or the Yoders'. We have watched."

"You think a kid from town could pull off these pranks?"

Matt shrugged. "I have no way to answer that. I have not seen anyone."

"What about Bradley Yoder?" Her mouth went dry.

Beth gasped. "Bradley does not like working on the farm, but he would never hurt his mother like that. He would not do anything to cause the type of injuries my brother received."

Matt studied the floor. "I must return to work." He turned and left the room.

Ashley headed to the door. "Thank you for your time."

Her little errand proved worse than the lack of answers.

CHAPTER EIGHTEEN

Patrick surveyed the anxious crowd filling the council chambers for the big zoning meeting.

Janet Hardy adjusted her microphone and called the meeting to order.

Someone caused the accidents on Anna's farm. Ashley was right. But he'd grown up with these people. No one here would risk injury to any of the Mennonites just to get their land and their cooperation for this revitalization.

A few would pull a prank to cause trouble for a business rival. One or two might send threatening letters. But not the destruction that had occurred on Anna's farm.

Janet finished her short speech and left the dais to sit by her son, jabbing him in the ribs to wake him. Derrick didn't flinch. He just sulked in his seat with his back to the crowd, earbuds poking out from his long brown hair. Patrick had watched the same display every Sunday at church. Some things never changed.

Andrew Jennings strode to the dais as calm and confident as the first time he addressed this assembly. The people in his company were the only outsiders involved. But they would only benefit from downtown development projects and gain nothing from a small Mennonite museum.

Except for the tourist draw.

He shook off the mind-darkening suspicions. It might suit Ashley to doubt everyone, but it wasn't his nature. He disliked viewing long-time friends as suspects.

Tuning back into the zoning committee meeting, Patrick focused on Thomas Hendricks. The white-haired, soft-spoken gentleman occupied a small section of the dais and gestured with his hands, pointing to maps and the computer-generated models of proposed businesses.

"As you can see, if we vote to rezone an A-1 agricultural section of town to a C-1 for general commercial development, we open up one hundred acres of land for tourism businesses that will enhance our city-funded downtown revitalization in addition to the private funds the Jennings Company has secured for this project."

As had happened with previous meetings, the crowd erupted with murmurs and raised hands.

Thomas pointed to Mr. Harvey, and the grocery store owner stood. The crowd quieted. "I'd like to know how many new competin' stores you folks plan on addin' in the name of tourism. If you allow more groceries or a supermarket, I doubt I'll be able to support my family for long. Same with our local restaurants and clothin' stores. How will we stay in business when people flock to these newcomers' stores?"

Patrick shared Mr. Harvey's concern. From the bits and pieces he'd garnered from various meetings, it sure sounded like the Jennings Company and the town council wanted to turn Montezuma into another Lancaster, Pennsylvania. Although that plan might bring financial gains for some, it would cost the town in every other area. He'd signed on to revitalize his hometown, not turn it into a tourist trap and lose what the citizens loved about their town.

Thomas motioned for Mr. Harvey to sit down and then addressed the entire assembly. "I know a lot of you have the same question, and it's a good one. Our committee and the revitalization committee, along with the city council, have reviewed the projected infrastructure changes and prospective benefits to our community. We feel the gains far outweigh the growing pains we'll experience in the process of change and improvement."

Around the room, voices increased in volume and blended with one another. Patrick settled deeper into his chair and sighed, catching only the highlights. Newer business owners agreed with the committee. Everyone gained in cities like Shipshewana, Indiana, where both the Mennonite communities and non-Mennonite businesses thrived due to tourism dollars.

Plus, the new Mennonite museum in Montezuma could now resemble Menno-Hof, like Ashley had suggested.

Others cited crime statistics, construction nightmares, and all manner of problems that could occur with the proposed expansion of revitalization plans.

All the back and forth caused his head to throb. He readjusted his position in the uncomfortable chair.

One of the older members of Montezuma stood. Mrs. Adams waited until the mumbling quieted. "I don't doubt your projection numbers and the financial benefits. However, I've lived through a time many of you have forgotten. Some of our Mennonite neighbors used to open their homes to curious tourists."

Patrick had never participated in those tours. But he remembered why they'd ended.

Mrs. Adams gripped the chair in front of her. "It was good for everyone's businesses."

The city council members nodded.

Mrs. Adams took a sip of water. "But it trampled on the Mennonite families' privacy. Rude people asked intrusive questions. Some people stole items from the homes. It became an embarrassing testimony to all the bad things we non-Mennonites can be known for. I do not want a repeat performance."

She stared down every committee member. "None of your projections and studies can produce a guarantee that our peaceful neighbors will be protected. You can't promise our crime rate won't increase. None of you can promise our small-town living and the reasons many of you moved here will be preserved. Money can't purchase happiness. Mark my words."

Rather than erupting in voices, the room remained silent.

The chamber doors opened and the entire place turned as one to view the late arrival.

Patrick started to see Ashley in her police uniform escorting the Yoder family into the room. She hadn't mentioned showing up for this meeting.

Ashley's green eyes flashed a triumphant glare that zeroed in on the committee members sitting motionless on the dais. "Ladies and gentleman, before you continue your discussion and voting, I believe you need to hear from Mrs. Anna Yoder."

She motioned for Anna to speak. The timid woman visibly shrank from the curious stares of the crowd. "I apologize for interrupting your meeting."

For the second time tonight, Patrick studied the crowd. No Mennonites had attended the zoning committee meeting. He should have paid attention to that fact.

Ashley stood guard over the Yoder family. The spark in her eyes and her determined protectiveness were beautiful. But why hadn't she told him she was coming? What was she up to?

"I had agreed to sell my farm and had planned to sign and mail the papers today." She turned as more from the Mennonite community joined her. "But I have changed my mind."

She paused to touch Brad's shoulder. "Selling our land is not best for my son. Our farm has been in our family for over fifty years. He will one day run this farm and continue the traditions of our people. This stability and hard work is good for him."

Ashley whispered something in Anna's ear.

Anna bowed her head. "My family and friends have prayed for God's direction. We feel at peace with the decision to not sell my farm. I am sorry for not listening to God closely enough to hear this wisdom before."

Patrick studied Ashley. Why hadn't she talked to him about this?

And why wasn't she looking at him? Had he known this was her plan, he would have stood with her, beside her.

Now she stood next to Jonathan.

Jonathan gave a silent nod to the stunned chamber, and then turned to help Anna leave. Ashley followed.

He had to talk to her before she went back to work.

Exiting his row, he rushed to follow her outside but was too late to catch up. She drove out of the parking lot following Jonathan's white truck. A maelstrom of emotions swirled around his brain.

How in the world was he going to fix all this?

CHAPTER NINETEEN

H is hand itched to use the matches in his pocket.
Darkness hid his entry into Ashley Walters's backyard. Could he do what he'd come to do?

Her involvement yesterday stood in the way of everything he had planned. She had to be stopped before she destroyed his last chance to make his parents proud.

The image of his father's kind eyes intruded. That had been so long ago. So very long ago.

One slow and steady step at a time, he inched closer to the porch.

Ignoring the risks, he stepped on silent feet up the stairs.

He'd danced along the edge of darkness these past weeks. How far would he go to make his plans succeed? Would he kill for it?

Thou shalt not kill. The ancient words wouldn't stop him.

They couldn't.

Neither could Ashley Walters. He'd do whatever it took to ensure his plans, his future. That was all that mattered now.

Chester's loud barking filled the night air.

His breath caught in his throat and his hands started to sweat.

He couldn't risk being caught now.

❧

A buzzing noise dragged Ashley out of a dream where she was trapped in a cave, searching for the way out but finding nothing. She fought the noise to stay and finish the dream, to find her way to safety.

The buzzing noise stopped. Then her bedside phone jangled.

She sat up in bed and stared out the curtains into the darkness. Who would be calling in the middle of the night?

Her digital clock read 6:30 in the morning. Where was Chester? He should have been barking at the phone to wake her up.

The annoying device continued to shrill. She picked it up, ready to give whoever was on the other line a piece of her mind for disturbing her sleep.

"Hello?" Her voice cracked.

"Ashley Walters?" An unfamiliar woman's voice filled the phone line. "Is this Officer Ashley Walters?"

"Yes. Who is this?"

"Detective Karen Everett. It sounds like I've gotten you out of bed too early. I'm sorry." The woman exhaled. "You know how police work is."

Nope. Not this kind of police work. That was for detectives. She worked her shift and came home and no one called her in the middle of her sleep.

"Well, I hope you're sitting down. I have some news for you."

Ashley was wide awake in an instant.

"I got your phone message saying you'd be available to help with any questions I might have on your brother's murder case. I had planned to call you later today to discuss the highlights."

Ashley stood and stretched, wishing the woman would get to the point. While she waited for her to finish her business speech, she slipped downstairs to find Chester. Had he gone into his crate to sleep?

No sign of him in the kitchen.

She scanned the backyard and couldn't find him.

Detective Everett ran down what Rich had already told her about the DNA and their case plans. Why had she been woken up for this?

Ashley opened the back door and covered the phone's mouthpiece to whistle. She flipped on the outside light too.

The backyard was the same. Gate locked. But no Chester.

Goosebumps raised on her arms.

"Ashley, did you hear me?" Karen's voice registered mild annoyance.

"Umm, hang on a second, okay?" She ran toward the trees. "Chester?" Where could he have gone?

"Ashley? Is there a problem? I can call you back at a better time."

"Chester?" Her voice broke on the question.

The frigid wind blew her hair into her face. She needed a coat. She needed to find Chester even more. He had to be frozen by now.

"Ashley?"

She placed the phone back to her ear. "Sorry. My puppy is missing. I need to—"

A little chestnut form hobbled out of the trees. "Chester. Thank God you're okay." She bent down to pick up her shivering little puppy, nuzzling him close.

"I found him. Sorry, Detective. I must sound crazy."

Karen chuckled. "I understand. We have three dogs, and if they went missing at night I'd send out a search party in this weather."

She wrapped Chester in his favorite towel and set him down by a heating vent. How could she have left him outside all night?

Why hadn't he come in through the doggie door?

"I missed a huge chunk of what you were saying when I couldn't find Chester. I apologize. Could you repeat it?"

Karen paused. "I was telling you how we were convinced Leonard Simms was guilty of your brother's homicide."

The casual, businesslike words sliced away the years with frigid precision. She could see her mom crumple into her dad's arms as they listened to the news of Eric's death. How he'd died before the ambulance ever arrived. How Eric had been robbed. Beaten. Shot multiple times.

A homicide statistic.

And now Leonard Simms would pay.

"So he's going to trial earlier than you'd figured?"

"No." Karen sighed. "Unfortunately, that's not going to happen."

"What?" She shot to her feet. "You can prove he killed my brother. What do you mean he's not going to trial?"

Chester whimpered next to her.

She lowered her voice. "I don't understand."

"He's dead, Ashley."

She stared straight ahead and saw nothing.

"Leonard Simms died in prison from a heart attack while playing basketball. I'm sorry it ended this way."

It couldn't end like this. Where was the justice?

"Eric's case file will be closed. I wanted you to hear it from us before anyone from the media could get to you for a comment."

Forcing words out of her mouth, Ashley thanked the detective and hung up the phone with a trembling hand.

Stars dimmed as the sky lightened outside.

The kitchen clock ticked off the minutes.

She wanted to cry. To feel something. But there was nothing left. One short phone call had stolen everything.

She stood, and Chester raised his head. "Stay here, buddy, and get some rest." Following the hallway to her studio, she groped along without turning on lights.

Until she sat down at her easel. She flipped on a lamp and picked up paints. Purples and reds and blacks sliced across her white canvas. With each brush stroke her insides began to thaw.

∽

Patrick parked his Mustang in Ashley's driveway and waited. She hadn't answered any of the times he'd called after the zoning meeting last night. Same thing this morning. So rather than let his emotions go in dangerous directions, he stopped by before work to clear the air.

The wind whipped across his face.

He stepped up to the front door and knocked.

No answer.

A light in the studio said she was up and working. He hated to disturb her, but they needed to discuss what had happened last night. Why she hadn't come to him and given him the chance to stand with her and the Yoders. He would have.

He knocked again and heard Chester bark.

Still no answer.

"Ashley, it's me, Patrick."

Locks clicked and the door handle turned.

Slow as molasses.

Maybe this wouldn't be as easy as he'd hoped.

Ashley opened the door and stood there, hair in tangles and her pajamas splotched with paint. Her eyes were rimmed in red.

"What's wrong, Ashley? What's happened?" He stepped inside and closed the door behind him. Ashley made no move toward or away from him.

"He's dead." Her voice scratched like sandpaper.

Taking her hand, he led her into the living room and sat down next to her. "Who's dead, Ash? Talk to me."

She rubbed her cheeks, smearing a paint spot in the process. "Leonard Simms. He died in prison. The man who shot Eric and left him to die on a cold concrete sidewalk passed away of natural causes. A heart attack." Red tinged her pale cheeks. "He died from a heart attack after playing basketball with his friends. He should have suffered. He should have been beaten and shot. He deserved to die in worse pain than my brother did."

Ashley crumpled into his shoulder and sobbed. He held her close and stroked her back, praying. Words were inadequate to soothe a fire that had burned inside her for over ten years.

She shuddered and backed away. "I'm sorry. I should have expected something like this."

He handed her the box of Kleenex on the coffee table and tilted his head until he could see her watery green eyes. "Let's ignore the shoulds for a while, okay?"

She nodded.

"Want to talk about it?"

"No." She exhaled a long breath. "Maybe. I don't know."

He tucked her into his arms, wishing he could do something, anything to protect her mind and heart from the pain.

"I don't know if I would have been satisfied to listen to a jury find

him guilty and sentence him to life in prison. I've prayed for that day."
She shivered. "But maybe I should have done more listening than
demanding God do things my way. At least the guy can't hurt anyone else."

"There's more to it."

"I don't want to analyze it." She turned to face him, just outside of
his arms. "But that's what I've been doing since the phone call. Painting what I didn't understand and seeing some truth in what appeared
on the canvas."

She motioned for him to follow her to the studio. Once he stepped
inside, he understood. There in front of him were three canvases, two
filled with fury, pain, memories.

The portrait of what he guessed to be Eric held his attention.

Ashley stroked the painting with a feather touch. "This is my good-
bye." Her eyes watered. "I was yelling at God and fuming about how
He'd messed this all up. How He should have never let Eric die."

He pointed to the swirls and slashes of red and purple paint drying
by the window. "That one?"

"Yes. Not a pretty prayer."

"They don't have to be."

"Somewhere in the midst of that painting, I realized I wanted this
trial and sentence to happen so that I could live in a time when Eric
was alive. It was my way of holding on. Of keeping Eric in between me
and God." She focused on him. "Of holding everyone at arm's length.
Including you."

"I understand."

"I haven't told you about Harrison. I need to." She collapsed onto
her stool. "Harrison was Eric's best friend. We were almost engaged.
When Eric died, I shut down and pushed Harrison out of my life. It
was too painful to be around him. I haven't dated anyone seriously
until you. And now I'm messing that up pretty badly."

His mind reeled with this new information. No wonder she was
reluctant to talk about her brother's death in detail. That experience
had colored everything in her life with pain. "Is that painting Eric or
Harrison?"

She turned to the portrait. "Eric. I said good-bye to Harrison a long time ago."

The last of the three paintings was another abstract in yellows and greens. He couldn't begin to guess the subject matter. "What's this one about?"

"Regret." She sighed. "I'm sorry, Patrick, for shutting you out yesterday. For not trusting you to stand with us last night. I should have talked to you before I showed up at City Hall."

She was an expert at changing the subject. With her emotions so raw, he wouldn't push. Instead, he stepped closer. "I would have stood up with you."

"I know. But I was afraid you'd try to talk me out of it. So I charged ahead, trying to control it all."

"I'm sorry I gave you the impression I would have tried to change your mind."

She turned back to the painting of a young Eric, eyes hopeful, jaw set to take on the world. How she captured all that with paint, he'd never understand. "I guess I traded justice for Eric for helping the Yoder family. Brad reminds me so much of Eric at that age."

"You care about Bradley apart from his resemblance to your brother." He took ahold of her hand, waiting for her to say more.

She stayed silent.

"You care for Bradley for who he is, and he knows that."

"Yes. But there's more to why I fought for Anna and Brad to stay in their home. I love the peace I feel every time I'm in the Mennonite community, the quiet strength of the people. Their simple way of life and unshakable faith. Their contentment. I don't want to see that destroyed."

"You're a protector, Ashley. I admire that about you."

That brought a tiny smile. "I guess Anna's turning down the offer on her farm puts an end to half of the revitalization plans."

"Yes."

"Are people angry about that?"

He squeezed her hand. "Some. But things should settle down soon, and we can focus on the original plans to help bring downtown Montezuma back to life."

"Will the city council still support the Mennonites and the museum?"

That was what he'd pushed for at the end of the zoning meeting. Not everyone was on board. "I'm doing all I can to make sure that happens. I want the revitalization to benefit everyone."

"I hope that's how it works out."

It wouldn't be easy. There were a lot of powerful people angry at the end of the meeting last night. But that wouldn't stop him. Some things in life were worth the cost to achieve them.

CHAPTER TWENTY

They had need of one quiet Saturday.

Jonathan longed for more peaceful days like this one. The morning milking was finished, and the three of them sat on the front porch playing Scrabble. The air had turned warmer for the beginning of February, so they would enjoy the outdoors.

Bradley was ahead. He placed the letter Z on a triple letter tile and connected it with an open O by adding one more O. "Thirty-two points. That's my best yet."

The boy's happiness warmed Jonathan more than the unseasonably heated temperatures. "Good. This is a wise use of your letters."

"I want to go to a zoo again. Daed took us once, remember? I was louder than everyone else."

Anna's sad eyes brightened. "Yes, I remember being very tired the whole next week."

Jonathan could imagine. The boy had never been quiet and still. Not even after long car trips to visit family.

"My birth mother wouldn't have enjoyed that trip, would she, Mamm?"

Anna's eyebrows rose. "I do not know, son. I have not met Mrs. Stone."

"I cannot imagine she would have." Jonathan watched Bradley. "Do you wish she had taken you to the zoo or other places?"

"No."

Anna let out a long breath, as if she had held it waiting for Bradley's answer.

"I am glad to hear that." Jonathan praised God. He had asked God to show Bradley the true love of his family and to help the boy let go of his fascination with his birth mother.

God had answered.

A white car he had seen in town raced past their farmhouse. He could not see the driver. It must be someone from Montezuma visiting a nearby farm.

He turned his attention back to the game.

Anna played a funny word. *Zee.* She showed him the entry in her big, red dictionary. He had believed her that it was a real word, but he was not familiar with it. Maybe he should remember it for the next game he played with his brother. Mark would not believe this was a word.

"I miss Daed." Bradley's soft words filled the air around them.

According to Mr. James, Bradley's conversation was healthy. For him to talk about his birth mother without anger and to talk about his Daed without heavy sorrow was good. It did not feel as good to see how the boy's words affected Anna.

Anna stood and moved to Bradley's chair, laying a hand on his shoulders. "I miss him too, son. Very much." She walked to the front door. "I will bring out some doughnuts for a snack. Would you two like some milk to go with them?"

"Yes, ma'am." Bradley turned away from his mother to study their Scrabble board.

Jonathan and Anna exchanged a sad smile. So much good to be thankful for even in the midst of much sadness.

Anna disappeared into the house.

"Has your time with Mr. James helped you to talk about your Daed?"

"Yes. Mr. James lost his father when he was younger than me. We've talked a lot about growing up without a parent."

Jonathan stared out into the pecan orchard across the road. His heart twisted inside his chest. He had wished to be a father figure for Bradley, to be the one imparting wisdom. Since he could not, he should be thankful Bradley had listened to Mr. James. It had helped more than anyone had expected.

Anna's loud scream pierced the silence.

Bradley stared into the house with wide eyes, unmoving.

Jonathan pulled Bradley along, and they ran through the living room and into the utility room, stopping at the mess of doughnuts and milk all over the floor. But Anna was not in sight.

A moan from beyond the back door drew him outside.

"Anna, what has happened?" She lay in a heap at the bottom of the back stairs, her foot caught in the middle of a broken wooden step. Bright red blood poured from her calf and ankle.

Bradley froze in the doorway.

Jonathan jumped off the opposite side of the steps from Anna and rushed to her side. "Bradley, please call Doctor Christopher. Tell him we are on our way." He studied his aunt's pale face. "Tell him Anna might have a broken leg."

Bradley stood, staring.

"Bradley, you must hurry. Go."

The boy rushed away.

"I heard a noise outside, Jonathan. It startled me. I did not want a stray dog frightening the cows like has happened before. So I..." She paused, her face drawn up in pain. He had seen suffering like this once before, when Mary was in labor.

"You do not need to explain. We must get you to the doctor."

There was no way to gently remove her from the step. Any movement would cause her more pain. Maybe he should ask Doctor Christopher to come to Anna's home.

Anna tried to push herself up on her hands, but she collapsed back down to the ground. "My arm. I think it is broken too."

Jonathan prayed, even as he tried to figure out what to do. Her left wrist and forearm were turning ugly colors.

Bradley burst through the back door. "Doctor Christopher is on his way. He said not to move her. Just make her comfortable."

Anna shivered.

"Please bring the folded blankets at the foot of my bed. And a pillow."

Nails lay on the ground next to the broken wood, as if someone had pried them loose. Jonathan picked up the aged but sturdy nails. Had the steps been weakened on purpose? Who would do such a thing?

Anna's wide eyes met his.

His heart beat so fast he could barely remain standing. It was no longer possible to believe old farm equipment was behind all of the injuries. These steps were sturdy. He had checked them himself on his first day here.

Jonathan would never understand evil that would wish this kind of suffering on a grieving widow. "Please God, comfort Anna and ease her pain." He held his aunt's right hand gently. "Please put an end to this destruction and bring the person who is behind it to true repentance. Change his heart, Lord. He needs You."

∽

Ashley stared at the beautiful Mennonite church and the ugly red words spray painted on the white siding. Her hands clenched and unclenched. She didn't trust herself to speak.

Patrick jumped in to help the other men washing, wiping, and applying paint remover, his jaw set and eyes flashing.

No one spoke. But none of the Mennonite men matched Patrick's anger. Or hers.

A warm hand touched her arm. She jumped and turned to find an older Mennonite woman staring at her with kind eyes. Vera Yoder's face held no animosity.

How did these people do that? How could they not be angry?

She studied her jeans. She should have worn a skirt. If she'd had more time to go from asleep to dressed after Patrick's phone call…

"Hello, Ashley. Thank you for coming to assist us in this cleanup."

"I'm not doing anything, but I want to help. What can I do?" She wanted to get to the bottom of what happened and how they could have no emotions about it all.

Vera pointed toward the fellowship hall. "You could help me in the kitchen. The men will be hungry after this work. It is a good thing God has given us a warm day in which to clean."

Ashley followed her inside the fellowship hall where children played quietly with attentive teens. The women bustled about setting tables and preparing food. Not one of them cried. None of their faces held a trace of anger.

"Here, Ashley. Would you pull apart this head of lettuce for sand-wiches?" Vera washed a bright green ball of lettuce and handed it over.

She set to work. "Everyone seems so calm."

Vera nodded and chopped vegetables. "Yes. We work together like this often."

"But someone vandalized your church." Ashley struggled to main-tain a normal voice. "Why aren't you angry at the person who did this?"

Vera added the last of her cucumber slices to a platter and wiped her hands. "In all my years, I have never seen anger make someone more like Christ. Instead, it rips a person's soul until there is nothing but bit-terness left."

Ashley stood motionless. Her own soul highlighted the truth in Vera's words.

"The person who wrote such things must be in great pain to strike out like this. He could love his town and family very much and not know where to place his anger. This might be the only way he knows."

Ashley couldn't argue with Vera's reasoning. Still, the ugly words against a beautiful church, against a peaceful people, set her teeth on edge. She'd moved down here to get away from the ugliness of life. It had followed her.

"This is my fault. I shouldn't have suggested Anna speak before the zoning committee. That stirred up a lot of anger." She faced Vera. "I'm so sorry."

Vera touched her shoulder with motherly affection. "No one makes another person do anything. We must each choose how we speak and act, and we must each give an account for our own actions. No one else's."

The words soothed the burning anger inside. It didn't get rid of it though. If she'd just stayed out of things, this might not have happened.

If only she'd nudged Anna to call Mr. Jennings, not barge into the meeting in front of the whole town.

She went back to peeling another head of lettuce.

"Ashley?" Vera pointed to her pocket. "I believe your phone is buzzing."

She fished her phone out of her jeans. "Hello?"

"Ashley, this is Jonathan."

"I figured you'd be here, helping clean up the mess."

"I have heard about the church building. I am saddened someone would do such a thing, but we have prayed for him and trust God will use even this for our good and His glory."

She couldn't grasp that ease of forgiveness. Where was the justice in simply letting people off the hook?

"I was calling to tell you Anna has been injured. She has a sprained ankle and a broken wrist. The doctor is with her now, setting the bones. This is why I was not at the church today."

"What happened? Was Brad hurt too?" Her pulse jumped a notch. "It wasn't a farming equipment injury, was it?"

"No."

"No, what? Do you know what happened? Is Brad okay?"

He sighed. "Bradley is fine. He is staying with his Mamm. I did not see anything about the accident. Anna slipped and fell from the back porch steps. The fall injured her wrist and ankle, but she will recover."

He was holding something back. She shivered in the warm kitchen. "Do you know what caused her fall?"

"Somehow the wooden steps had been loosened."

"I'm so sorry, Jonathan. I'll get to the bottom of who's behind this and make sure he's put in jail."

"I would ask you to pray, Ashley. This is not your fault."

"But it is. If I'd just listened to Anna, she wouldn't have gone in front of all those people and stirred up a hornet's nest. I'll make sure whoever's doing this is stopped."

She shouldn't promise something that out of her control. But if good intentions were pennies, she'd be rich.

Voices in the background drowned out Jonathan's reply. He spoke to someone else and then returned to the phone. "Anna and Bradley would like you and Patrick to join us at church tomorrow. She wants you to see that none of this is beyond God's grace."

Ashley's mouth moved but no words escaped. She'd turned down Patrick's invitations to church, but this was different. This was for Anna. For herself. The Mennonites lived forgiveness and prayer and peace like she'd never experienced.

She longed for that more than anything else.

Maybe she'd find it tomorrow in this very church.

Chapter Twenty-one

Ashley clutched two paintings in her hands. One wrapped in plain lavender paper, and the other unwrapped, ready to give Anna as a get-well gift. Green scenery blurred as Patrick sped toward Anna's farm. She studied his profile.

He'd worked all day yesterday in the warm temperatures and then agreed to come with her to church without any questions about why she hadn't joined him for a service at his church.

She had no idea how to explain if he asked. Maybe working beside the Mennonite men yesterday had stirred something in his soul too.

"Thank you for coming with me today."

"I'm glad you asked."

So much for engaging conversation to calm her nerves. She'd wanted to come to the Mennonite church since her first visit to the sewing circle. Now that she was on her way, her shoulders knotted and her stomach danced.

Patrick reached over to take her hand. "Anna's right, you know. Nothing that's happened could be your fault."

"I haven't done anything to fix the trouble either. I tried to talk to the Kauffmans again last night while I was on my break, but they haven't seen anything suspicious. And Jonathan refuses to report the incidents to the police, so our hands are tied yet again."

"They've forgiven the person behind the trouble."

"I wish forgiveness and peace were as easy as the Mennonites make it look." She turned to him. "You know that's why I'm going today. It's nothing against your church."

"So my church family doesn't make forgiveness look easy?" He didn't face her, but a hint of humor teased his lips.

"It's not that. I'm not even sure I understand really."

He turned his bright blue eyes to meet hers. "Maybe my church reminds you too much of going to church with Eric and Harrison."

Tears pricked at her eyes. Yes, that was it exactly. How could she not have figured that out?

"It's okay, you know. I'm not interested in taking over anyone's place in your heart or pushing you to move on." He shrugged. "Just talk to me, okay? Let me know what you're thinking, what you're feeling."

"Sort of a tall order. I haven't discussed my feelings much in the last ten years."

He squeezed her hand. "There's no time like the present." He parked in Anna's driveway. "I've been told I'm a pretty good listener."

She chuckled. "I can see that. I'll work on my conversation skills."

"I care about you a lot." His eyes finished what his mouth refused to say.

She had a hard time looking away. Thankfully, Patrick remembered where they were and kissed her hand before releasing her and jumping out of the car to open her door.

They walked up to the Yoders' front porch, each carrying a framed painting.

Jonathan opened the door as if he'd watched them since they'd pulled in. Good thing she hadn't kissed Patrick like she'd wanted to.

Ashley extended the wrapped painting. "I'm sorry I'm a week late on delivering this. I hope I haven't messed up Anna's birthday by leaving you without a gift."

"Her birthday is tomorrow. She will enjoy this. Thank you." He stepped out onto the porch and closed the front door. "I will go tuck this into my workshop so it is not found before tomorrow."

He strode around the house and was back quickly. "We were just finishing breakfast. Would you like a pastry? We have plenty."

Patrick stepped forward. "I'd love one. Thank you."

She fought a yawn as they followed Jonathan through the warm house to the kitchen.

Anna sat at a small table with her foot propped on a cushioned chair and her arm in a sling. "Good morning. Thank you both for coming with us today."

"Should you be up and moving so much? We can come back next Sunday if that would be better for you. I don't want to cause you more pain."

Anna shook her head. "I have taken my medicines and right now I am feeling fine. I wish to attend church. It is where my mind is comforted and my spirit strengthened."

Patrick nudged her arm and she jumped. "Oh. Sorry. I'm still waking up." She took the painting he extended and offered it to Anna. "This is for you. A get-better gift. It's your church and the people helping yesterday. I wanted to capture the beauty." She'd completed it in a flurry after work last night. She'd tried hard to capture their faces in a way that could only be described as peaceful.

Jonathan took the painting and held it close to Anna. Her eyes moistened. "Thank you, Ashley. This is beautiful. I will always remember this day as one where God created beauty out of sorrow."

Brad slipped into the room and picked up a plate of pastries. "Would you like one before we leave?"

Patrick collected two. "Thanks for sharing. I've wanted to try one of these for a long time. Guess today's the day."

The gooey frosting made her mouth water, but she restrained herself and ate the cherry scone slowly. Delicious.

Patrick picked up a napkin from the table and pointed to the corner of her mouth with an intimate grin.

Seemed she always had something on her face when eating a sweet. One reason she avoided the stuff most of the time. Or maybe it was just when Patrick was around. He distracted her from food.

Jonathan's movement snapped her out of the silent conversation with Patrick. Without a word, Jonathan turned away and disappeared down the long hall.

She stepped away from Patrick a little. She'd forgotten how uncomfortable couples had made her for a long time after Eric's death and the disaster with Harrison. And she'd just brought that pain back to Jonathan. Maybe she shouldn't have come.

Jonathan returned with his Bible in hand. "We should go." He motioned toward the front door.

"Can I ride with Mr. James and Miss Walters?"

"Yes, Bradley. Remember this is a church day." Anna accepted her crutch and allowed Jonathan to help her toward the door. Every slow step was etched with pain.

Ashley had to find some way to help. "I could get you a wheelchair and bring it over this afternoon."

Jonathan nodded. "That would be wonderful. Thank you." He opened the back door. "I will work on a ramp first thing tomorrow."

Brad joined them for the short ride to church. The boy was uncharacteristically quiet. Ashley turned to face him. "Are you okay?"

"I am just preparing for the service."

She raised her eyebrows at Patrick. What had they gotten themselves into?

❧

Patrick stepped into another world as he followed Jonathan to a seat on the right side of the small sanctuary. Ashley sat all the way across from him on the left side next to Anna. She was surrounded by bonneted women, heads bent in prayer.

Children remained in the pews in complete silence. No one ran around. No one spoke.

A spirit of peace hung in the air.

He'd never witnessed anything like it.

He caught the wide-eyed look Ashley flashed him and shrugged. At least this was nothing like the church she'd attended with Eric and Harrison, so hopefully she'd be spared painful memories for today.

Rather than gape at the people surrounding him, he used the silent time to pray for Ashley. For peace to replace the turmoil, for healing to lift the sadness lurking in her eyes. Then he prayed for Anna and Bradley and even Jonathan.

Jonathan wore pain like a heavy outer coat. Compassion for this man he'd once seen as a rival grew within him. If he had time with Jonathan after the service, he'd find out if there was any way he could help. If the younger man even wanted his help. He doubted it.

The service began with an older man calling out a page number. Everyone flipped to the correct place and sang.

Patrick was lost. He'd never heard this hymn, but it was beautiful. He simply listened.

Two more songs were called out by different men. Each time he listened. No sound came from the man at his right. Jonathan hadn't sung a note. Every other man sang out with deep, rich notes. Not Jonathan. Why?

He turned his attention to the front where one of the ministers gave the announcements. "Let us give thanks to God for a successful cleanup day here. Our members worked hard. We must now pray for the person behind the spray-painted words. This person is hurting and needs our forgiveness and prayer."

That wouldn't have happened in his church. Ashley was right. These people made forgiveness appear easy. Maybe for them it was. But not for the people he counseled. So many struggled to even acknowledge legitimate hurts.

Patrick leaned forward to listen.

"We would like to welcome two visitors with us today. Patrick James and Ashley Walters. Thank you for worshipping the Lord with us."

No one stood to shake hands or introduce themselves. So very different from any church he'd attended. It was nice to be welcomed though.

"Please open your Bibles to John sixteen." The bearded, plain-dressed man read the entire chapter.

The verses about the Spirit of truth coming to guide us into all the truth struck a chord. He'd prayed through these verses every day when he'd first started counseling. Young and naïve, he'd understood how much he needed the Holy Spirit to guide him into truth.

He should have never stopped praying those words.

"'I have told you these things, so that in me you may have peace. In this world you will have trouble. But take heart! I have overcome the world.'" The minister looked up from his Bible and surveyed the crowd. "We have experienced trouble. But we must remember Jesus has overcome the world."

Patrick lost track of time. With no up and down for singing, taking the offering, or visiting with those sitting around him, he struggled to stay awake.

Glancing across the aisle, he discovered Ashley taking notes about everything the minister said. Why had he worried about her relationship to God?

The first minister finished his sermon and sat down. Patrick perked up. Now maybe he'd get that chance to speak with Jonathan.

But no one moved. Not even the children.

Another man, slightly younger than the first, stood and opened his Bible. This bearded man read from Psalm 130. "'If you, Lord, kept a record of sins, Lord, who could stand? But with you there is forgiveness, so that we can, with reverence, serve you. I wait for the Lord, my whole being waits, and in his word I put my hope.'"

Conviction slammed into him. If the Lord kept a record of his sins, Patrick's would have filled up pages and pages. Probably even more than he could imagine. So why was it easier to remember the record of sins others had committed against him than to remember his own sins?

He reviewed the score sheets he'd filed away in his mind. The longest was Melanie's. Her list of transgressions had always seemed much longer than his.

But according to the Bible, the length of the list didn't matter. God didn't keep one. And neither could Patrick if he wanted to serve God like he had at the beginning of his counseling work.

Why had he not heard the prodding of God like this before today? He was at church almost every time the doors were opened, had been since he was a kid.

Maybe the quietness of the Mennonite service made it easier to hear.

All around him men stood, hymnals in hand. Patrick scrambled up and flipped through the pages, but couldn't remember the exact number.

Jonathan handed him a hymnal opened to the song being sung all around him.

He joined the chorus and belted it out, new tenderness to the words growing inside him. "Praise God from whom all blessings flow."

He had some work to do with God before this day was over.

✑

Jonathan shoved his hands in his pockets as the men around him welcomed Patrick and thanked him for joining their service today. They thanked him for helping with the cleanup yesterday too.

He wished he could have been in two places at the same time. But Anna had needed him, and he would not have left her alone in pain to wait for the doctor.

His eyes drifted to a group of women whispering together not far from him.

Ashley waved, her tan skirt and white shirt very different from the women surrounding her.

Patrick stepped closer. "What's her name?"

Jonathan faced Patrick. "Who?"

"The woman you were smiling at just then." Patrick acted as if they were close friends.

He had glanced at Ashley but had not smiled at her. He looked back to the group, and one woman blushed and turned away. "That is Beth Kauffman. Her youngest sister is one of Bradley's friends."

"She seems very nice."

"She is. But I do not know her well." Jonathan walked toward his car. "It is getting late. We should return to Anna's house for lunch. The ladies in Anna's church have filled her refrigerator with food."

Patrick stayed under the pine tree. "Can you invite Beth?"

Jonathan's face heated. "No. Is there a reason you are interested in speaking with her?"

"Ashley's mentioned how lonely you seem, and I saw it myself today. You don't sing, don't talk to many people. Is that by choice?"

How could he answer Patrick's question honestly without saying too much? He had made that mistake with Ashley. Their conversations had drawn her into his world and that was not a good thing. He did not want Patrick and Ashley together to surround him or pity him.

"My wife died two years ago. I have accepted God's choice of singleness for me. I will not lie and say it is easy."

Patrick stared. "I'm sorry. I can't imagine what that must feel like. The closest I got to marriage was the ceremony."

"What happened?"

The counselor scuffed his shoe against the gravel. "My fiancée decided she wanted to spend her time with other men. Even after I forgave her, she didn't stop. She didn't tell me she didn't want to get married either. I found out on what was supposed to be our wedding day."

"I am sorry." He studied the clouds that floated across the sky and prayed for Patrick. "I see again how right the minister's words are. In this world we will all have trouble."

"Yes. I learned a lot today. Thanks for inviting us to church. God was in this."

"It is good to hear." What Patrick had heard had softened his countenance. He even seemed to breathe easier. Jonathan hoped the Holy Spirit had comforted Ashley as well.

"I still have a long way to go though." Patrick studied him.

"As do I." His eyes found Beth Kauffman again. Maybe someday God would remove the gift of singleness. Until then, he should stay focused on today.

Each day had enough troubles of its own.

CHAPTER TWENTY-TWO

Patrick prayed the meeting at City Hall tonight would be calm and civilized. No one needed the tension and fireworks of the last few gatherings.

If they didn't keep their cool, he had a mouthful of truth to share—fiery preacher style.

There was too much at stake to stay silent.

With a final prayer, he locked his Mustang and hustled to the beautiful woman waiting for him by the flagpoles.

Time with Ashley these last few days had been quiet—less talk, more walks. He couldn't draw her out enough to gauge what was happening inside her though, and she hadn't shared much about her experience at the Mennonite church. They certainly hadn't ventured into the subject of lies again.

"Hey there, handsome." Ashley smiled, but the weariness of the past week still showed in her eyes.

He brushed his lips against hers and then leaned away to enjoy the view. "You're stunning." Taking her hand, he led them into council chambers. "Thanks for meeting me here. I know this isn't your favorite way to spend a night off."

"Not by a long shot. Maybe it'll be fast and we can grab some take-out to eat at my place."

He liked the sound of that. But when they entered the overfilled room, hopes for a quick retreat vanished. Every seat was occupied. Standing room only. No one smiled.

This would be a long night.

He sighed and found a piece of wall for the two of them to lean into.

Thomas Hendricks, the zoning committee chairman, spoke into the microphone, his white hair standing on end like Einstein's. "Ladies and gentlemen, this is going to be a short meeting tonight. We only have one item on the agenda, and it's to announce the outcome of the city council's vote." He paused to adjust his wrinkled tie.

Patrick relaxed a fraction. Until the silence stretched and Thomas continued adjusting his tie. Patrick caught the tension lines around his eyes.

Finally, Thomas cleared his throat. "We have met and discussed all the opinions you have shared with us in person and via email."

Patrick studied the crowd. Conspicuously absent were the Jennings and the Hardys. Even if the decisions weren't in their favor, it was poor sportsmanship to not show up for this meeting.

"We have voted to postpone any further meetings and votes regarding the revitalization plans."

People all around him burst into objections. Men and women who had been friends for decades yelled across the room, blaming each other for this setback.

A shrill whistle blared through the chambers, silencing everyone. Thomas set down the coaching whistle and stepped back up to the microphone. "We will conduct independent research into the Jennings Company projections and take a hard look at what went wrong with the revitalization planning. Until then, there will be no public meetings scheduled to discuss this topic. Thank you and goodnight."

"What about someone from town defacing the Mennonite church?" A gentleman across the room yelled. "They should be arrested. Spray painting awful words about the Mennonites killing our town. Is anyone looking into that?"

Others chimed in their opinions.

Many heads turned toward Ashley. She opened her mouth to speak, but Chief Fisher answered before she had a chance. "We're looking into what happened." His deep baritone silenced the ruckus. "The Montezuma police department protects all members of Montezuma. We will put a stop to whoever is causing problems in our community."

Chief Fisher stood guard at the door while people filed out of the room, many still grumbling. Some small groups continued their animated discussions. Most were quieter than they had been leaving previous meetings.

Patrick placed his hand on the small of Ashley's back and guided her through the large group of people stationed just inside the glass front doors.

"Patrick! Do you have a minute, dear?" Emma waved them over.

He leaned close and whispered into Ashley's ear. "If you're ready to go, I can cover for you and meet you at your house in a few minutes."

She shivered. "I'll stay."

They made their way to a small group of ladies Emma's age, among them Mrs. Adams, the loudest supporter of the Mennonite community's privacy.

Emma spoke first. "I'm so glad to see the two of you together. They make a lovely couple, don't you think, Leanne?"

Mrs. Adams grinned. "I have to agree." She turned serious and locked eyes with him. "Patrick, thank you for speaking wisdom to all the nonsense at the zoning committee meeting last week. It's become so uncivilized here lately."

"I'm happy to stand up and speak for both sides of this debate. I don't think it should be a debate anyway. We should be working together for what benefits everyone."

Emma nodded. "I agree and am glad to see Thomas Hendricks doing the right thing. It's wise to sort out fact from gossip and get to the bottom of what's happening to the Mennonites. If people are threatening them, it won't be long before they come after us."

Angry voices stilled their conversation. A red-faced Thomas

stormed out of the council chambers. "I told you, I am not answering any more questions. You've had your say, now leave me be."

A trio of young businessmen followed him, one of them pulling Thomas to a stop in front of Patrick's group.

Thomas jerked his arm away and turned to face Ashley and Mrs. Adams. "You two are to blame for this whole thing imploding. They should be badgering you."

The older man slammed out of the glass doors, leaving a wake of stunned townspeople in silence.

Patrick had never seen him so angry. He pulled Ashley close. "He's wrong, Ash."

"I know."

He turned back to the group of women. "I think it'd be best if I escorted y'all to your cars. If Thomas is this mad, it's likely there are others who might not have enough self-control to stay out of trouble. I'd hate for any of you to get hurt."

Mrs. Adams tugged on her designer purse straps. "Yes, you're probably right. I need to get home anyway. Supper to cook for Mr. Adams and all."

Patrick walked Emma and Mrs. Adams to their cars and waved as they pulled out of the parking lot.

"Want to come to my house for dinner? I have some steaks already thawed and seasoned." He opened Ashley's truck door.

"Sounds good. I'll meet you over there after I pick up Chester." She buckled her seat belt and backed out of her parking place.

Standing outside of the crowd, he studied the small clusters of people and their animated discussions. Mob mentality was nothing to dismiss. If someone was stirring these people up and pointing them toward vandalism, there was no telling where the trouble would lead.

❦

He loved the power coursing through him as he snuck up behind Leanne Adams's small house. The tiny home matched all the others on her street.

Darkness shielded him from curious eyes. Tonight he'd complete his task and nothing would stop him.

Mrs. Adams had turned too many people away from his plans.

She would pay.

He slipped through the back door of the house and fixed his eyes on Mrs. Adams's snoring, wheelchair-bound husband. The man had been asleep since earlier this afternoon.

Assured that he would sleep through any noise, he entered the dining room and continued to the kitchen, stopping at the stove.

First he turned on all the burners to the highest setting.

Their blue flames glowed against the darkness.

Beautiful.

With a gloved hand, he yanked a knife from the silverware drawer and used it carry a dishtowel to the gas flame. It caught fire instantly. Dropping the towel and knife on the white counter near the kitchen curtains, he retraced his steps and exited the house.

He smiled, waiting in the backyard until the curtains caught fire.

No one else would dare cross him now. Not after tonight's fiery news.

Chapter Twenty-three

Ashley struggled to keep her eyes open. Chester snoozed in the passenger's seat as she drove home from Patrick's house Wednesday night. How stupid she'd been to fear a relationship with Patrick. He listened tonight like he'd listened since their first meeting—encouraging, comforting, drawing her out, and inviting her into his heart. And his kisses...

Her face warmed at the memory. Good thing she'd said goodnight when she had.

At the stoplight near her house, she tapped her finger against the wheel, waiting at the intersection with no one coming in either direction.

Out of nowhere, a fire truck bore down on her, lights flashing and siren screaming.

Chester barked.

She pulled to the side of the road, allowing the red lights and siren to pass. Then she followed it, instincts pushing her to forget her bed and find out what was happening to the people she had sworn to protect.

Cops were never really off duty.

She followed the fire engine up North Dooly and right onto Minor Avenue.

This was her neighborhood.

Her heartbeat kicked into high gear.

As the engine took a left onto Engram, her mind flipped through addresses and names of the people she'd met who lived in this section of town. One name stood out as the engine in front of her slowed down.

Please, God, no.

She parked behind the fire engine, leaving Chester safe in her truck, and ran to the crowd of onlookers clad in pj's and robes.

Smoke billowed from the back corner of a small brick ranch.

Mrs. Adams's house.

A scan of the crowd didn't salve her racing mind. No sign of Mrs. Adams or her wheelchair-bound husband of forty years. No sign of the woman who had stood with her at the council meeting earlier tonight.

"What's going on?" She tugged the robe of a young woman with a toddler on her hip. "Are the Adamses out of the house?"

Wide eyes stared back at her. "I don't know."

Ashley's heartbeat thundered. What could she do now?

She shifted side to side, again searching the crowd for any sign of the elderly couple.

No one in a wheelchair anywhere.

Firefighters scrambled into the house, others tugged water hoses toward the backyard. Soon, sprays of water hissed from the hose connections, adding one more noise to the deafening idle of the fire trucks.

"Does anyone know if they were home? Maybe they went out to a late dinner?" She held on to a thin strand of hope.

Heat and smoke pushed the crowd back into the street. Powerful strobe lights blazed holes in the night sky surrounding the house.

She couldn't shake Mrs. Adams's parting words. *"I need to get home anyway. Supper to cook for Mr. Adams and all."*

An older woman in curlers shook her head, shouting over the cacophony of yelling firefighters and their equipment. "Doubt they were out. Leanne's always home with dinner on the table by six. They'd be in bed asleep right about now."

Ashley held her breath, straining for a glimpse of Mrs. Adams somewhere. Anywhere safe.

The crowd parted as two firemen rushed out of the house carrying the limp forms of Mr. and Mrs. Adams.

She nudged her way past the crowd to meet the men at the ambulance. "Will they be okay?"

Parker, one of the long-time firefighters, turned toward her. "Clear a path, officer, will you? We need to get them to the hospital."

Like lightning, she switched into cop mode, loud voice and all. "Listen up! Everyone onto the sidewalk across the street." She flapped her arms from the side to the front, directing the crowd like a squawking mother hen.

They obeyed.

The ambulance rushed past the silent cluster of people, lights and sirens breaking the eerie night into crazy flashes of red and white light.

Wood crashed and glass shattered as firefighters worked to extinguish the blaze. She stood riveted to one place, the crowd around her frozen together, unable to look away. All eyes glued to the heroes in turnout gear.

Minutes passed. No one talked. A few people drifted off to their homes.

Firefighters emerged from the smoke, wiping sweat-drenched faces with the backs of their hands. The fire chief turned to the crowd.

"Anyone see how this started? Mrs. Rose? Mr. Turner?" He locked eyes with each neighbor in turn.

A teenager shot through the crowd. "Maybe it was that Mennonite kid. He set fires all over the place a few months ago."

Mrs. Rose gasped. "Derrick, you hush up. You didn't see anything."

He jutted his chin forward and glared.

Derrick Hardy? Now she recognized him. Same black jacket and defiant stance she'd witnessed at the drug house where she and Elizabeth had arrested two meth heads.

"Why are you here, Derrick?" She nailed him with her eyes and he froze.

"Do you live here?"

The crowd parted between them.

"No."

She stepped closer to the young man. "Then why are you here?"

His dilated pupils bored into her. "I was driving back to school with some friends and saw the fire truck. Wanted to see what was up." He'd lost weight, but his bravado hadn't lessened. "Not a crime. Right, officer?"

Fire Chief Dotson broke in. "Why would you accuse the Mennonite boy?"

Ashley studied Derrick. A group of three boys around his age stepped to his sides.

The air crackled with tension.

"Do you have any proof about who started this fire? Or are you just here to cause trouble? I have work to do, young man."

Derrick shrugged. "I don't know who did if for sure, but that kid has started fires like this before."

"You have no proof. So you're just here to cause trouble." Ashley crossed her arms.

Derrick glared.

The fire chief turned back to the crowd. "Did anyone notice any unusual activity around the Adams's house? Someone who saw something? Anything?"

Neighbors shook their heads.

Derrick and his three friends skulked away. Like lions. She shivered, all nerve endings on alert. This time the prowling lions wouldn't win.

Every criminal left something behind.

∽

Ashley had to do something to tamp down the fire in her gut. Pacing the length of the squad room didn't help.

Elizabeth turned from her desk. "There's nothing you can do."

The truth of that clawed at her stomach. "There has to be something."

"You talked to Mrs. Adams last night. She told you what she told Sergeant Culp. She thinks she left the burners on after dinner."

Mrs. Adams had looked so frail in her hospital bed. So glad she and Dale were alive. Ashley hadn't had the strength to push her for more information.

"It was a cooking accident, according to Fire Chief Dotson's preliminary findings." Elizabeth turned back to her paperwork.

Ashley's gut told her it was more. Much more.

Lieutenant Shafer sped through Thursday's briefing and handed out road assignments as if last night had never happened. They'd best continue to investigate the fire even though Mrs. Adams had provided a plausible explanation.

She'd already been told twice to leave it to the sergeant in charge of the case.

Why hadn't she become a detective? She should have put in an application when she had the chance in Atlanta. Then she could poke her nose in anywhere she wanted and call it official business.

Elizabeth cleared her throat. "You're going to burn a hole in the wall with that look. Best use it out on the streets. We have dealers and thieves to stop tonight."

And arsonists. No telling who else.

Ashley patrolled the quiet side of town, making extra trips through the Mennonite areas. If anyone had believed Derrick Hardy's gossip about Brad, there could be retaliation today. Tomorrow. Someday soon.

Small-town folks took care of business their own way.

Senses on high alert, she turned the corner onto Will Miller Road and stopped.

Minivans crowded Anna's driveway. Small groups of Mennonite men and women dotted the front yard. No one laughed. They just stood, staring at the farmhouse.

Ashley parked and exited her cruiser, hushed voices silencing as she drew closer. One glance at Anna's front porch and she understood.

Tan drapes billowed and snagged on jagged glass. Shards of window and wood dotted the pristine porch.

She turned toward the group of teary-eyed women huddled around Anna in her wheelchair. "What happened?"

The women focused on the ground.

The small group of men who had gathered around Jonathan turned to stare.

"Where's Brad?" Tension snapped the air around her. She had to protect him like Eric had protected her.

Jonathan nodded to the house. "The young men are helping clean up the broken glass. Others have gone into town to purchase another window pane. We will install it when they return."

"What happened?"

Anna sniffled. "Rocks crashed through the windows."

Why hadn't they called her?

They were just going to fix it and move on?

Not this time. "Did you see anyone before or after the rocks were thrown?"

"Bradley said he saw a group of boys running away from our house." Anna studied her shaking hands.

Another car pulled up and parked in Anna's driveway. "It has happened at our home too." Beth Kauffman joined the group and spoke to Jonathan. "Will you come to help us after you are finished here?"

"Wait a minute." Ashley struggled to keep the bite from her words. "Someone threw rocks in your house too, and no one called the police?"

She locked eyes with each person who would meet her gaze. No one spoke.

Jonathan stepped toward her. "It was a child's prank. This has happened before."

"How do you know they were children? It could've been the people behind all the other accidents. They need to be questioned and arrested if they're behind this attack."

Beth shook her head. "No. They were boys from town. I recognized one of them."

Ashley turned to her. "Who?"

"I do not believe I should—"

"Tell me the boy's name and the police will handle this."

Beth straightened her back. "My father and one of our elders have gone to speak with his family. His father paid for our glass last time, and they will do the same this time I think. Then it will be over."

Not likely. "If it happened before, it'll happen again."

No one responded.

"Rocks in windows are not a child's prank. Someone could have been hurt." She focused on Anna. "Others have gotten seriously hurt. We need to stop the people behind this."

Jonathan stepped toward Beth. "Was anyone injured?"

She shook her head and blushed.

Ashley waited. She would not back down from this. "Even if no one was injured this time, Anna was hurt by someone's malicious actions. Farm equipment has been purposely damaged. None of these were accidents. And they won't stop unless you help us stop them. The next time, it could be worse than a broken wrist."

The women studied the ground again.

The men exchanged glances with each other.

Anna spoke up. "The broken window is different from the other things. This was done to get our attention, not to sneak around and hide their identities. These boys could be angry and retaliating against us and our neighbors because they think Bradley was behind the fire."

"Bradley had nothing to do with that fire. I want the name of the boys who were seen here today."

Jonathan adjusted his black hat. "This is not our way, Ashley. We will speak with those who were recognized here today, and we will pray with them and for them. We do not need the police to become involved."

"So you'll wait until tensions explode and someone gets killed?" People were murdered every day for less than what was at stake between these two communities.

The women gasped.

The men frowned.

Jonathan held firm. "God is our protector, Ashley. We will trust Him."

But they wouldn't trust her to do her job. "I'll make sure patrols are stepped up in this area tonight." And she'd return tomorrow. And the next day. And the next.

"Thank you." Jonathan stepped close to her side and lowered his voice. "Please pray, Ashley. Do not let your anger lead you into trouble."

At one time his calm conviction had attracted her. Now she wanted to scream.

"I intend to see justice done in this whether you like it or not."

His face softened. "I know you will. Please trust that we will handle things the way we believe is best, a way that will lead to peace."

All she could do was nod and leave the people to their strange way. As soon as she got in her squad car, she pulled out her cell phone and called Patrick. He'd understand.

"So what happened?" Patrick's shuffling paperwork grated her ear.

"Two houses had rocks thrown through the windows. They know who did it, but don't want the police involved. Makes no sense." She drove out of the Mennonite farm area and toward town.

"They've always been like that, Ash." He paused with no paperwork ruffling. "You have to admit, this time their way is keeping those boys out of juvie."

"But what if those boys are behind all the accidents?"

He sighed. "Ash, I'm only guessing about the boys' identities, but like Jonathan said, broken windows have happened before. If it's the same crowd, they're rash and headstrong, but not the type to destroy farm equipment or hurt one of the Mennonites."

"Those rocks could have injured Anna and Brad or someone else. This was not a harmless prank."

"It was stupid and dangerous, I agree. And I agree with Anna, it seems like retaliation against the Yoders for not selling their farm or for the accusation that Brad started the fire."

Her hand tightened around the phone. "But you don't agree with me that these attacks need to stop? That the police should be involved?"

"Ashley, you're not the bad guy here. You care about these people and they know that. Brad knows. But you can't control this. You said yourself that you traded finding justice for Eric for helping the Yoder family. Maybe this is an opportunity to learn from the Mennonites not to live in anger. To learn to trust God, not play God."

"You and Jonathan live in rose-colored worlds: his religious beliefs and your detached analyses. Neither of you are doing anything to stop the violence before someone gets killed."

Before someone else she loved was taken from her.

She pulled into Yoder's restaurant and parked, her hands shaking. Was there ever an end to the tentacles of grief?

"I'm sorry I upset you. I should have prayed, not lectured."

"You sound like Jonathan. Only he didn't throw Eric in my face."

Silence answered her.

Right now she didn't care. Fighting tears, she grabbed the picture of Eric she always carried with her. She desperately needed her big brother right now.

Patrick should have understood that, not trampled on what she'd shared with him.

He should have agreed with her and not used counselor-speak to calm her down. He wasn't supposed to bring up Eric, not as if her brother were an insignificant part of history.

"I am not Jonathan." His measured words sizzled through the phone. "And I did not throw Eric in your face."

"You shouldn't have brought him up." Anger stilled her shaking hands.

"Ashley, if we're going to be a couple, there shouldn't be off-limit topics." He paused. "I'm trying to help you see how anger is clouding your judgment. There is a better way."

"I'm not your patient." Helplessness from the last few days and snapshots of Anna's and Mrs. Adams's injuries stole her better sense. She couldn't go through what she'd experienced with Eric again. She wouldn't.

"I'm not treating you like a patient. I care about you and what you're doing to yourself."

"You and Jonathan both believe God is in control and will fix all this. But He doesn't. People die all the time. I can't stick my head in the sand and wait to see what happens next. I've seen too much evil to forgive like Jonathan and too much violence to believe like you do that prayer and forgiveness fix things."

She shoved her car into drive and pulled out onto Highway 26. "I need to get back to work."

"I'm sorry I hurt you. I didn't handle this conversation well. Can I stop by in the morning? I'll leave my counseling at work. Promise."

Deep breath in. And out. Blowing up at Patrick only proved his point. There had to be a better way.

She drove toward her house. "You can come by. I'll try to be in a better mood."

"Be who you are, Ash. I'll adjust."

Of course he would. Just like Jonathan. Always calm.

Anna's and Brad's scared faces replaced Jonathan's calm one. "Patrick? Would you go by the Yoder farm first tomorrow? Talk to them about going up to Indiana until things are safe here."

Then she could focus on one thing.

Justice.

CHAPTER TWENTY-FOUR

Patrick pulled into the Yoder driveway and shut off his Mustang. He double-checked his watch. They should be done with milking by now.

Jonathan opened the front door and waited. The man must have bionic hearing. Or maybe, like everyone in town, he was hyper vigilant, holding his breath and preparing for the next attack.

The man didn't appear any different. No fear or wariness in his eyes. "Good morning." Patrick extended a hand in greeting.

Jonathan shook it. "Come in."

They sat in the living room, the house silent around them. "Is Bradley here?"

"He is in the barn repairing some equipment."

Patrick's eyebrows rose. "More vandalism?"

"No. Normal repairs." Jonathan sat back into the tan couch. "Are you here to check in on us because Ashley is at work?"

"Ashley's still asleep." Or painting. Either way, she hadn't answered the phone earlier. Patrick sat forward. "But yesterday she asked me to stop by and talk to you. She's concerned about your safety."

"As I told Ashley, we are trusting God to protect us."

He nodded.

"She needs to remember God's ways are not our ways, but He can

215

be trusted." Jonathan studied his shoes. "Why did she send you instead of coming herself?"

"Ashley's still upset. She was there when Mrs. Adams almost died in the fire Wednesday night. And she believes there's a connection with that fire and the vandalism here."

"She is so angry she cannot speak?"

"She's got a temper." He preferred it not aimed at him. But they'd survived their first fight. Today's visit was part of patching things up. "And she's convinced you won't listen to her suggestion."

"So you have brought it?"

"I agree with Ashley's suggestion. As a friend and as a counselor, I agreed to come so you and I could talk this over without emotions getting charged."

"I am listening."

Like a rock. The man hadn't moved since they'd sat down. That kind of stillness took patience and practice. Maybe he should try it. "Ashley and I believe the violence will only continue escalating until the person behind it is caught."

"We will pray."

Patrick leaned in closer. "It looks like your family is the target. People's lives and livelihoods are at risk if the revitalization plans don't move forward."

"I am sorry to hear that. We only did what we believed God was leading us to do."

"I understand that. But some of the townsfolk are focusing all their anger and frustration on you. It's irrational. And dangerous. There are a large number of hunters in town with access to weapons. Whoever is behind these attacks on your family has already wounded a number of people. They could injure many more."

"Is this supposed to scare us into selling the farm?" Jonathan's jaw clenched. "How is this different from what the people in town are doing?"

So he could get angry. Patrick hadn't intended to rile him, but Jonathan's anger made him more human. "I don't think you should sell the farm. Not at all. I just want you to see this situation is serious. Ashley's afraid the person who started the fire at Mrs. Adams's house will attack you all and accomplish his aim the next time."

Jonathan relaxed. "She is afraid to lose someone else she cares about."

Patrick narrowed his eyes and studied the man in front of him. This guy was a natural counselor. He saw more than most. Patrick didn't like how much he knew about Ashley though. "Yes. She's afraid to lose Bradley. She feels guilty that Anna has been hurt too."

"She is not at fault."

Like he could convince her of that. "I know. I'll keep praying and talking to her. But I didn't come to talk about Ashley. I came to ask you to consider taking Anna and Bradley up to Indiana until this mess is over."

"They do not wish to leave."

"But you could convince them. They'd listen to you." Patrick was sure just about anyone would listen to Jonathan. His calm way proved persuasive.

Jonathan sighed and bowed his head.

In the silence, Patrick guessed the man had turned to prayer. Maybe God would do a far better job of convincing Jonathan than he was. He could only hope.

"I do not believe our leaving is the right course of action. It would give Anna and Bradley and their community a reason to think running and fear is acceptable. It could shake their faith in God's protection."

Patrick shook his head. "I believe this community is stronger than that. Their faith is solid."

"I spoke pridefully." Jonathan bowed his head again. "I apologize. My actions do not have that kind of influence."

"Your family will listen to you. Taking them to Indiana for a short time will keep them safe. Please tell me you'll at least talk to them about it."

"There are people here who would be hurt by our leaving. I wish to stay and continue praying with our people. This will be the best protection."

Patrick sat back. "Who would be hurt by your leaving? Beth?"

Jonathan took a deep breath. "No. I do not think my leaving would hurt Beth."

"Ashley?" Patrick paid close attention to every bit of Jonathan's body language. The man's shoulders turned in and his eyes focused on his hands.

"Do you have feelings for Ashley?" Patrick held his breath, waiting for an answer.

"Yes."

"For how long?"

"Since she came to speak with Bradley about the bruises he had gotten from running away."

So the jealousy he'd experienced was not his imagination. Ashley had been attracted to Jonathan. And vice versa. He'd played the fool yet again.

Jonathan stood. "She chose you. That was clear the morning we took Bradley to meet his birth mother."

Patrick struggled to remember that day. So much had happened since. Then it dawned on him. That was the day Jonathan had walked out of Ashley's house and saw the two of them kissing.

Jonathan stared out the front window. "Ashley and I have never spoken about my feelings and never will. I would ask you to not share this information with her."

Patrick stood and shoved his hands in his pockets. "Whether you decide to stay in Montezuma or take your family to Indiana, I'll be praying for you. I know what you shared was painful. I'll keep it to myself."

Jonathan didn't move or respond.

Patrick sighed. "I should go."

Neither of them spoke a word as Patrick followed Jonathan out the front door. What could he say? Don't be Ashley's friend because male *friends* are what stole Melanie from him? No. He wouldn't ask that. *Please, God, keep me from going back to that life, that behavior. Change me.*

A scream pierced the silence.

"Bradley!" Jonathan took off running.

Patrick followed.

They rounded the milking barn and Patrick smelled smoke. He rushed toward it.

Jonathan matched his pace. "The old equipment barn. It…is…all wood."

"Bradley?" Patrick yelled louder. "Bradley, talk to me!"

No answer.

The heat of the barn stopped them in their tracks. "Could Bradley be in there?" Patrick studied every inch of the barn. Only one wall was in flames. They could get in there before it collapsed.

"Yes. It is where I left him."

"I'll go get him. You call the fire department."

Jonathan pulled him to a stop. "We will both go. I know this barn. Many obstacles. Follow me."

He complied and plunged into the darkness. Smoke filled the large barn. He fell to the ground and tugged Jonathan's pant leg.

Jonathan dropped to his belly and crawled ahead.

They aimed for the middle of the building, the flames licking up toward the roof. This place could collapse any minute.

God, please help us find Bradley. Protect him.

Jonathan groaned in front of him and stopped.

He crawled level with the man and felt ahead. A body.

Bradley. Unconscious. Or dead?

Together they grabbed Bradley's legs to pull him out. A flaming beam crashed within inches of Bradley's head.

Heat seared Patrick's face and hands.

He crawled up the boy's back and snuffed out the fire attacking him.

Then with draining consciousness, he pulled Bradley to the barn door. But it wouldn't move. He kicked it and nothing changed. He couldn't get it open. He coughed and couldn't stop.

Where was Jonathan? He had no strength to go back and find him.

God, where are You?

Blackness was coming.

He pulled Bradley close, covering the boy's limp body with his own. Then the darkness won.

CHAPTER TWENTY-FIVE

Jonathan woke in a strange bed. He was moving through space. Fast. Loud noises. Where was he? What was happening?

His heartbeat raced.

His eyes and throat burned.

He could not get a deep breath.

Something blocked his nose and pinched him. He reached up to remove it but could not get his hand to his face. None of his muscles worked as he willed them.

"Good. You're awake." A male voice spoke from somewhere above him. He could not see. His eyes were too heavy to open.

"We found you outside a burning barn. You're lucky to be alive." The man poked and pushed on his arms and neck.

The pain told him every touch.

He wished it to stop.

It did not.

"Do you remember what happened?"

He searched his memory. An uncomfortable conversation with Patrick James. He had confessed his feelings for Ashley.

Shame burned through him, heating his already hot skin.

He and Patrick had run somewhere.

A barn. A burning barn. Bradley was inside. He opened his mouth to speak, but words did not come.

He tried to shake his head. It did not move properly.

Had they gotten Bradley out? Where was Patrick? He willed his body to move. Only pain answered him. Hot. So hot.

His mind latched onto the only thing he could call to mind. *The Spirit also helpeth our infirmities: for we know not what we should pray for as we ought: but the Spirit itself maketh intercession for us with groanings which cannot be uttered.*

He groaned with all his being that Bradley and Patrick had survived. *Please, God.*

∞

Ashley paced through her living room and studio. Where was Patrick?

She'd painted for the first half hour after Patrick should have arrived. Then she'd called his cell. No answer.

Same with his home phone.

Then she paced. Called Emma. The dear woman hadn't heard from Patrick in days.

She'd even called the Yoder house, and no one answered there either.

Twice she'd climbed into her car to go find Patrick. Each time she figured he was busy talking to Jonathan, maybe even the whole family. And after her outburst yesterday, it was too soon to show up there again.

Prayer was the only other option…if God even listened.

Patrick insisted He did.

So she closed her eyes. "Lord, this is crazy. I shouldn't race into panic. Patrick is probably fine. Just talking longer than usual." She was lying to herself. "Please protect him. Keep him safe. Show me what to do."

This was too much like the time she'd waited hours for news of her brother. The news that finally came had plunged her life into the darkest black she'd ever known.

She peered out the window. Still no Patrick.

It was past worrying time.

She picked up her home phone, Chester jumping at her hands. "No. Bad dog. My phone is not your toy."

Chester gave a humanlike whimper and huffed down by the door.

Punching in Helen James's number, she prayed her overactive instincts hadn't steered her wrong. If they had, she'd look stupid.

If they hadn't...

"Hello? Ashley, is that you?" Helen yelled through the phone.

"Yes. Helen, are you all right?" Her chest tightened.

"I'm rushing out of my office. The hospital called and Patrick has been rushed to the ER. Meet us there."

The phone went dead.

Patrick was in the ER.

Hands shaking, she slammed the phone into its base and grabbed her keys. Her tires squealed as she backed out of her driveway and raced down Engram.

Come on green lights.

She hit them all and screeched into a parking space on Sumter, then rushed through the hospital's front doors.

She followed the hall to the ER department. No one stopped her. She searched every face as she made her way to the small ER waiting room.

Several Mennonite women and Patrick's family bunched together. Some cried. Some prayed.

She beelined it for Helen. "What's happened?"

Helen hugged her. "Patrick was found outside a burning barn on the Yoder farm. None of them could talk. They'd passed out. That's all the paramedics would tell me."

"Who had passed out?" This couldn't be happening. Not Patrick. Not Brad. She couldn't lose them.

"Patrick. Jonathan and Bradley Yoder. They all had passed out from smoke inhalation, and two of them had burns." Helen teared up and blotted her nose with a Kleenex. "That's all I know. No doctors have come out to speak with us."

Ashley's mind numbed. What had happened? What did she need to do?

Helen shook her. "Ashley? You're pale. Come sit down."

Kathleen and Helen flanked her on either side and led her to a hard plastic chair.

She sat.

Anna in her wheelchair entered the ER, pushed by Vera Yoder.

Ashley ran to her and took her good hand, kneeling down beside the wheelchair. The older woman leaned into her and wept. "We must pray, Ashley. Pray for my son and nephew, for Patrick." She pulled Ashley tighter.

Ashley fought for composure. She had to be strong. For Anna. For Patrick's family. She slipped out of Anna's strong embrace and stood, wobbly.

Helen caught her arm and sniffed back tears. "Careful, Ashley. We don't need you passing out to join our guys back there." She extended a hand toward Anna. "I'm Helen James, Patrick's mom. I'm so sorry our sons had to endure what they did today."

Anna grasped her hand. "Thank you." She motioned to Vera to move to an empty corner of the room. "Will you pray with us?"

Helen nodded.

Kathleen nudged Ashley. "Are you coming? You look like you need it."

She did. But she had some business to take care of first. "I'll be right back. Y'all start praying and I'll join you in a minute."

"Where are you going?" Kathleen's eyes widened. "Are you going to make them let you back there? That would be so good. We need to know what's happening."

"No. I...I'll try that when I get back." She rushed out of the ER, down the hall, and out into the blinding sunshine.

Checking her watch, she crossed De Vaughn and headed straight for Chief Fisher's office. She had two hours until her shift. Surely he'd find a replacement for her tonight.

The chief's receptionist stood. "Ashley. I'm so sorry, honey."

"Thanks, Jessica. I need to see the chief. Is he in?" She didn't pause until she reached his doorway.

He motioned for her to sit and pointed to the phone at his ear.

She stood.

The receiver clicked and he focused his dark brown eyes on her. "I'm apprised of the situation. We have two of our best investigators on it and we've called in the state arson investigator. We're doing all we can."

That part was easy. "I need to switch shifts with someone tonight. We don't even know what happened yet."

Chief Fisher nodded his graying head. "I figured you'd ask, so I called in some favors."

"Thank you." She turned toward the door.

"But we're short staffed as it is. I've got two officers pulling doubles to cover those doing the investigating. I can't spare you tonight."

"But, sir…"

He stood. "I understand, and I'm sorry. You can work this beat and check in with the hospital staff between calls. It's the best I can do."

She deflated. "Yes, sir. Thank you."

She plodded back to the ER, legs and arms heavy. But she'd do what she had to do. That was what cops everywhere did.

Even when their spouse and kids were hospitalized.

Sometimes she hated this job.

∞

Patrick shook his head to stop the loud buzzing all around him.

Then searing pain in his hands and chest tore him from his groggy state. Everything burned. He wanted to scream but held it in.

Barely.

His eyes focused on the woman in a white coat standing by his bed. Why was he in a white bed with steel bars on the sides?

The ER?

Memory blindsided him. The barn on fire. Bradley with flames around him. Pulling the boy to the door. No exit.

"How…here?" His throat burned worse than his hands.

"I was hoping you could tell me." The blonde woman leaned down to look into his eyes. "I'm Dr. Sarah Owens. Do you feel up to a few questions?"

"What…happened?" Every word ached. He couldn't get a deep enough breath either.

"You were in a barn fire. You sustained second-degree burns on your hands and chest. But you escaped the worst of smoke inhalation damage."

He pointed to his throat, too sore to keep up his end of the conversation.

"You'll be sore and raspy for a while. Rest your voice. I'll let the arson folks talk to you for a few minutes, not long."

He mouthed his thanks and closed his eyes. Did Ashley know? Was she in the waiting room worried out of her head?

A familiar older, stocky man flipped back the curtains. The whirring noise grated against his ears. His brain hurt. Maybe questions weren't a good idea.

"Sorry to bother you, Patrick. Fire Chief Dotson. I just have a few questions. Won't take long."

He nodded. That only made the pressure in his head angry.

"Did you see anyone around the Yoder farm before the fire?"

No. He'd focused on Jonathan, and then all attention turned to saving Bradley. Had they gotten the boy out alive?

"Bradley. Okay?" He needed a pencil. Then he remembered his bandaged hands. That wouldn't happen for a while.

"Yes. Bradley and Jonathan Yoder are here in the ER. They survived. Bradley was burned on his shoulders and arms. Some on his head. Least amount of smoke inhalation of the three of you."

Thank God. He released the deepest breath he could manage.

"Did you see anything suspicious before the fire?" Fire Chief Dotson stood strong and unmovable. Too bad. He'd really rather use his burning eyes to see Ashley.

He shook his head side to side. Once. That was enough.

"No idea who could be behind this fire?"

One more head shake. He could do this. But only if the fire chief stopped all the infernal questions. He had no idea who would do something like this. Not to Bradley. Not to Jonathan. Not to him.

"Is it possible the boy could have started it, playing with matches or working on some of the farm equipment?"

Patrick wanted to shout that they had all almost died. That there was no way on earth Bradley would have done something so stupid.

Was there?

He searched his brain for facts. Smoke covered everything by the time they'd gotten to Bradley. He was lying in the middle of the barn, facedown on the ground.

If he'd started a fire and fallen trying to get out, he wouldn't have been facedown. Would he? Patrick had no idea. No energy to wrestle it out or explain either.

He shook his head side to side and closed his eyes.

"Thank you for your time, Patrick. If you remember anything, call me. I'll leave my card with Helen." With that, the burly man exited.

Patrick slumped into the hard mattress. Could Bradley have caused the fire?

His eyes wouldn't open. His mind wouldn't focus. He needed to ask for Ashley before he fell asleep again.

He needed her to be there when he woke up.

To tell him Bradley couldn't have started the fire that almost killed them.

∽

She hated not being at the hospital. Fire Chief Dotson had spoken to Patrick first. Then to Brad and Jonathan. But they'd been too exhausted by that to have any more visitors before she had to leave for her shift.

At least they were alive. Conscious. Out of the most dangerous woods. No carbon monoxide poisoning. No burned lungs. No reason to be life flighted to Perry or Atlanta.

Her eyes watered. Thank God she wouldn't lose them.

She pulled her cruiser into the ER lot and parked. The chief had said she could stop between calls, and she'd written enough tickets to earn a few minutes here. She hoped someone had good news for her when she walked in.

The crowd had thinned out. Emma had arrived with food for everyone.

Her stomach growled, but she ignored it. If she ate anything, it'd just come back up, and she didn't have time for that tonight.

Helen sat with Anna and the Mennonite ladies who'd remained. Everyone else must have gone home for dinner.

"Ashley. I'm glad you're back. Patrick asked for you." Helen smiled, but the effort died on her lips. This ordeal had already exhausted her.

"Is he awake now? Can I see him?"

Emma joined them and hugged her. "He's asleep. I asked a minute ago to see him. Sorry, dear, but Dr. Owens is guarding all three of them from many visitors. I babysat her, but she won't even allow me a peek."

Sergeant Culp and Lieutenant Shafer entered through the ER doors. They zeroed in on her and made their way over.

She stepped away from the families. "Do you have any news?"

Culp adjusted his duty belt. "You mean do we know who did it?" He shook his head. "Patrick and the Yoders didn't see anything. No one saw anything. Just like the fire at the Adamses'."

Lieutenant Shafer sighed. "We're doing all we can, Ashley. I'm sorry we don't have more. There's an arson team combing through everything. They'll let us know what they find as soon as possible."

The night of the Adams fire flashed back to her. Only two days ago. Felt like a month. How could she have forgotten to tell the lieutenant about her suspicions of Derrick Hardy? Easy. Elizabeth had talked her out of it. Said the boy was in school at Georgia Southwestern and was only in town Wednesday night for church. He could have skipped out on church and set the fire.

"Have you talked to Derrick Hardy?" She kept her voice low and even. "He was at the Adams fire, acting suspicious. He could have been involved with both fires. He has motive."

"What, his mama's job? The boy isn't that interested. Not enough to set fires." Culp shook his head. "I've known that kid since his mama was pregnant with him. He's not an arsonist."

Lieutenant Shafer bent toward her. "He was acting suspicious, how?"

At least he believed there was a possibility. She'd about had it with small-town, everybody-knew-everybody-and-no-one-could-do-anything-bad garbage.

"He watched everything with no emotion. Like it was a TV show. And he had no reason to be there." She clenched her hands. "And he tried to blame Brad for starting the fire. Turned folks' heads with his nonsense too."

Culp peered over his shoulder. "Some folks in the fire department think Bradley Yoder started the fire today. He's done it before. Burned two barns to the ground."

"He almost died today." Her eyes blazed and she fought for professional distance. It didn't happen. "No firebug would start a fire and get himself stuck in the middle of it." Culp was an idiot.

Shafer held up his hand. "Stop the gossip, Culp. No more until we have facts."

Culp shrugged and left her alone with the lieutenant. "Will you talk to Derrick? He was watching the arrest of two drug dealers about a month ago. It's more than coincidental that he's showing up at crime scenes."

"I'll talk to his parents. He should be home from school later and I can talk to all of them then. I'll let you know what I find out."

It would have to do for now. Her first priority was to see Patrick and make sure he, Brad, and Jonathan would be okay.

A close second was seeing Derrick Hardy questioned for his involvement in today's fire. She'd stop whatever prowling lions were behind the violence against the Mennonites and the people of Montezuma.

She'd stop them dead if she had to.

Before they got another chance to hurt someone she loved.

Chapter Twenty-six

Ashley drove past the charred brick of the Adamses' house. There was so much ugliness in the world, even in Montezuma.

She had to get through a disturbance call nearby and get back to the hospital. If she could talk to Brad and Patrick and Jonathan, she'd be okay.

Maybe.

Driving around the block, she surveyed the surroundings. Garbage cans stood sentry in a few driveways.

No one ran from house to house.

No dogs barked, alerting her to the presence of a hidden prowler.

She parked her cruiser in the driveway of Mrs. Abigail Todd, a long-time widow and close friend of Leanne Adams. Mrs. Todd stood at the front window, peeking through her heavy green drapes.

The bright lights in the front room illuminated Mrs. Todd and everything in view past the draperies. The expensive furniture and paintings acquired from a life of travel with her military husband were well known to everyone.

The woman made herself a target.

Ashley would talk to her again about keeping her valuables safe and not telling everyone how much they were worth. Not only that, Mrs.

Todd should keep the lights off in the front room if she wanted to spy on her neighborhood.

Exiting her cruiser, Ashley adjusted her duty belt and strode to the front door. To any observer, her movements were crisp and in control. Her uniform pressed and her shoes shined. Command presence.

Appearing in control could mean the difference between a criminal cowering or attacking. She prayed there were none watching now.

Because the outside was all an act.

Mrs. Todd threw open her front door. "Officer Walters, thank the stars you're finally here." The older woman glanced both ways and ushered her inside. "Hurry up, before anyone sees us." She slammed the door and leaned against it, out of breath.

Under different circumstances, Ashley would have chuckled. Mrs. Todd was known for two things: her expensive tastes and her conspiracy theories.

Tonight the whole thing irritated Ashley. Three people she cared about were lying in hospital beds, the extent of their injuries unknown to her, and she couldn't get in to see for herself whether they were going to be okay.

Deep breath in. Deep breath out. She focused on Mrs. Todd's large, pink curlers and modulated her voice. "Dispatch said you were disturbed by some loud crashing sounds in your backyard. Can you tell me what happened?"

In Atlanta, she'd have been hauling dealers or burglars to jail, maybe even some DUIs to boot. She'd take spooky sounds in the backyard any day. Then she could get back to the hospital.

"Well." Mrs. Todd put a wrinkled finger to her forehead. "I was sound asleep. Nothing good on TV, you know."

Ashley nodded to keep the woman talking.

"Then all the sudden it sounded like lightning struck my flower garden and rattled all my wind chimes at once." Mrs. Todd flattened her palm against her heart. "It was horrible."

Ashley glanced over the woman's shoulder through the diamond-shaped window on her door. The black sky held only glittering stars and an almost full moon. No clouds, no rain. No lightning.

"Mind if I go have a look outside?" Ashley stepped toward the back door.

Mrs. Todd followed, hand still pressed against her chest. "Shouldn't you call for backup first?"

"Did you see anyone outside? Or did anyone try to break into the house?" Those things might necessitate a call for another officer.

Mrs. Todd paused, lost in thought once again. "No. I don't believe I did, and I didn't hear any other noises. I was on the phone with the 9-1-1 operator, though. I could have missed something."

Ashley forced calmness into her voice. "I'll be fine, ma'am. I'll just do a walk-through to be sure you're safe."

Mrs. Todd pressed her other wrinkled hand to her chest. "You're a good person, you are. Thank you for helping an old woman tonight."

Once outside, the night wind pushed all around her. Wind chimes added a tinny, horror movie soundtrack to the backyard.

She shivered.

Mrs. Todd had gotten to her.

Shaking it off, her eyes adjusted to the darkness and scoured every inch of the large backyard. A few trees. No animals.

Neat flower beds offset by rocks.

No footprints in the Georgia red clay.

She moved to the far right corner of the yard toward a scattered mess of metal buckets and large plastic pails. This could have sounded like a clap of lightning when it collapsed.

The wooden shelves that once stood tall against the back fence drooped, old boards broken in the middle.

A piercing yowl behind her sent a wave of goose bumps up her spine.

A cat. The thing darted into the bushes and jumped up and over the wooden fence.

The adrenaline zipping through her system propelled her back into the house to explain what happened.

"Well, bless your heart, dear. I'm glad that thing didn't attack you. There are some mean cats in these parts, ones that'll tear anything they can to bits. Guess I'll have to keep an eye out and call those animal folks to come get him if we see him again."

She needed to get back to the hospital. A sense of unease stalked her. No telling what awaited her there.

∽

The police station hummed with activity uncommon for regular shift changes. Tonight was about as far from normal as Ashley could imagine.

Firefighters had battled the barn fire all evening.

Arson investigators occupied every available corner of the precinct.

Officers pulling double shifts crammed themselves into already overloaded desks.

And Ashley had to get in and out so she could finally lay eyes on Brad and Patrick, Jonathan too if they'd allow her.

"Ashley." Chief Fisher waved her into his office. "Can I have a minute?"

She forced one foot in front of the other, bone weary.

Stopping speeders and dealing with a feral cat hadn't drained her.

The unseen lions had. The ones God warned her about during her Bible reading. They weren't the criminals she'd expected. Those she understood. The unseen lions like fear and worry stalked and confused her. She had no way to battle them, no way to handcuff them and toss them in jail. Those were what the enemy used to drag her down.

It worked way too well.

Chief Fisher motioned for her to sit. This time she did.

"Lieutenant Shafer has Derrick Hardy in the interview room. I understand he's followed you around to crime scenes?"

The chief's light tone raked across her raw emotions. Did he think she had some creepy secret admirer in the college kid? If he was behind the fires and accidents, he was far more dangerous than a teenage creep.

"Only one, sir. A drug-house bust."

"You can observe from the media room. No contact or involvement during or after the interview, understand?"

"Yes, sir." She wasn't a rookie. Before she let loose something she'd regret in the morning, she exited his office and shot straight for the observation room.

Lieutenant Shafer sat across from the college kid slouching in his cold metal chair. "Tell me about your day on Wednesday."

Derrick shrugged. "I went to classes. Came home for church and dinner at my parents. Then I saw the fire trucks and followed them over."

"Were your friends…" Shafer flipped through the notes in front of him. "Were Shawn, Greg, and Jerry with you all evening?"

"No. I dropped them off at their houses before church. They don't go. I have to because of my mom. It stinks."

So the kid could have set the house fire. She leaned forward.

"About what time?"

"Dropped Jerry off last around five thirty. Then I went straight to church."

"Were you with the adults for service the whole time?"

Sweat beaded on the boy's clean-shaven face. His bloodshot eyes darted around the room. "Naw. It's boring. I was outside smoking."

"Until when?"

"Eight. Then I went straight home and ate dinner. Picked the guys up after that."

Lieutenant Shafer scribbled notes on his yellow notepad.

Ashley fidgeted with her keys. Derrick could alibi out for the entire evening. So why was he sweating?

"Did you talk to anyone at church about the Mennonites?"

Derrick shifted in his chair and scratched at his arm through his sweatshirt. "No. But everyone's talking about those fools and how they're keeping our town in the dark ages. How they're killing Montezuma."

Ashley wanted to jump through the glass and strangle the kid. He'd spray painted those exact words on the Mennonite church. He could be behind other things too.

Push him hard, Shafer.

"Did you know Andy Hendricks threw rocks into some of the Mennonite homes?"

A red face glared across the table at Shafer.

"How well do you know Andy?"

What? Why did Shafer care about a little middle-school kid? He couldn't have done any of the severe damage on Anna's farm.

"Some. So?" Derrick refused to meet Shafer's eyes. The kid's leg bounced up and down and his hands shook. "It's not my fault he threw rocks into those windows."

"Tell me about the meth you've been selling Andy."

Ashley's breath caught in her throat.

Derrick was a dealer? To middle schoolers?

Her phone buzzed against her belt clip.

"Ashley?" Helen's shaky voice filled the phone line and snapped Ashley's mind from one dark situation to another. "Can you come soon? There've been some complications."

"I'll be right there." She ignored the curious stares following her out the station's glass doors and rushed across the street.

Please, God, let them be okay. Please...

CHAPTER TWENTY-SEVEN

Ashley entered the ER area and scanned the faces for Helen. Still in uniform, she forced calmness into her spine and face and took deep breaths to calm the inside.

"Ashley. Over here." Helen slumped in a chair and tracked her progress across the now crowded room.

"Is Patrick alright? What complications were you calling about?" She slipped into the chair next to Helen and took her hand.

"Patrick is improving. Last time I went back, his doctor was talking about releasing him tonight. But they weren't sure, so I didn't call. I didn't want to get your hopes up too soon."

Okay. Patrick possibly going home tonight was good news. Her pulse rate dropped a few notches.

But Helen didn't meet her eyes. If it wasn't Patrick...

"What's wrong with Brad?"

Helen shook her head and sniffled.

"Is he...?" She couldn't form the words.

"No. He'll be okay. In time. It's just so sad." Her voice trailed off.

Ashley sat still, her insides a jumble. She left Helen in her chair, surrounded by coughing children and bleeding adults, one with a towel wrapped around his hand, blood oozing from the cloth.

Approaching the desk, she was glad for her uniform. The reception-ist straightened. "What can I do for you, officer?"

"I'd like to see Bradley Yoder." No explanation. No information to refuse. She studied the eyes of the young brunette blocking her from Brad.

"Are you family?"

Ashley shook her head. To her right, a wheelchair exited the doors leading to the ER rooms.

"Ashley?"

She turned to the sound of Anna Yoder's voice. The woman's pasty-white face and tear-streaked cheeks caught Ashley like a punch in the gut.

"Anna, what's happened with Brad?" She knelt next to woman.

"He has just now woken up for any length of time. And he can-not..." She pressed her face into the handkerchief in her hand.

Vera patted her friend's shoulder. "Ashley, he has a severe concus-sion. The doctor explained his memory could return any time, but he needs rest and medical treatment. They want to keep him overnight. There is talk of sending him to a larger hospital in Perry."

Concussions weren't usually a reason to send someone to a large city hospital. She sorted through Vera's comments. *Memory. Medical treatment. Complications.*

"He can't remember the fire?" That might be a blessing, allowing him time to heal before he had to face horrific memories.

Anna shook her head. "Please, go see him. Maybe he will talk to you."

The receptionist nodded and pointed through the ER doors. "Go ahead, officer. He's in the fourth bed on the left-hand side. Dr. Owens is probably in with him now."

Ashley stiffened her spine and walked down the middle of the room until she drew near the gray-curtained area containing Brad. She stopped to listen.

Her pulse thundered in her ears. What would she say? How should she act? Blood and IVs didn't bother her.

Unless they were connected to someone she loved.

A blonde woman in a white physician's coat parted the gray curtain and stepped out. "Can I help you, officer?"

"I'm here to see Bradley Yoder. His mother asked me to come back."

She pressed her lips together, compassion shining from her eyes. "Yes, she mentioned she wanted you to talk to Brad. Apparently you two are close?"

She'd never talked to Brad about how much he reminded her of her brother. But now it was more. Brad had always acted like he understood. Like her acting as a big sister was the most natural thing in the world.

"Yes. We're close."

The doctor slipped her hands into her coat pockets and fixed her eyes on something in Brad's room. "Five minutes. Don't expect a lot. He might fall asleep in the middle of talking. He's had a rough night."

Steeling herself against a frightening sight, Ashley slipped into Brad's room and closed the curtain.

The boy's brown hair fell onto his forehead and his eyes were closed. So peaceful. So young. So like Eric.

With a groan, he turned his head away from her, revealing a gauze bandage streaked with red. A section of tape on one of the ends slipped and the white bandage folded on top of itself. Underneath, red angry skin was split with a stitched together gash.

The bandage covered the entire back of his head.

She swallowed hard and clenched her teeth against the acid rising in her stomach.

Images of Eric at age ten flitted across her mind. Eric had fallen from his bike and banged his head on the edge of a low brick wall he'd tried to jump over. She'd witnessed the whole thing in slow motion. Then everything flashed forward. Eric's screams. The blood. She froze in place, unable to do anything. But when Eric called her name, she rushed forward and clasped his bloody hand in hers, cooing words of comfort. *"It'll be okay, Ricky. You flew like an eagle."*

Despite his pain, Ricky—the name only she could call him— laughed. *"Thanks, Lee Lee. It'll be okay. I'll be fine."*

Even injured, Eric always tried to make things better for her. Always. And now she had to make it better for Brad. She'd hold his hand

and tell him how brave he'd been. How thankful she was that he'd survived, and they were all praying for him.

Moving to the chair next to the bed, she lowered into it and waited for him to open his eyes.

Groggy brown eyes blinked open and fixed on her.

"Hey, Brad. I'll only stay a minute. I wanted to see that you're okay."

"I answered questions already." He drew in a labored breath and grimaced. "What do you need?"

The irritated tone of his voice took her aback. "I'm not here as a police officer." She shrugged down at her now rumpled uniform. "I'm here as a friend. Ashley, remember?"

He closed his eyes. "No. I do not have a friend by that name."

The beeping, scuffling, metallic noises of the ER faded into silence and pressed into her.

How could he not know her?

A tear slipped down her cheek. She was losing her brother all over again.

∞

Jonathan strained to hear the conversation between his cousin and Ashley. How could Bradley forget her? His mind ran in many different directions.

Ashley's soft crying stopped all thoughts but one.

"Ashley?" His hoarse whisper caused his throat to burn. "Ashley?"

She moved the curtains aside, then wiped at her eyes as she entered. "Jonathan?" She slipped into the room and came close. "I'm not supposed to be in here, I don't think, but I'm so glad to see you. How are you?"

He longed to share how terrified he had been that they would all die. That the blackness surrounding them in that barn was no match for the fear in his soul that he had been too late to help Bradley and Patrick.

"I am…better." His voice was little more than a harsh whisper. He attempted a smile, hoping she would continue the conversation.

She pulled a chair close to the bed and sat down.

His conscience prodded him. He should not keep her here. She should be with Patrick, not looking at him as if he mattered to her, as if there were more between them than could ever be.

She looked behind her. Maybe she listened for the nurses that walked up and down this hall often.

In truth, she wished to find Patrick. As she should have. Jonathan had only convinced himself of her interest. There was none, only friendship.

Closing his eyes, he focused on the burning pain in his lungs.

Soft words stirred him from the sleep he must have drifted into. Ashley was still there, and she was praying.

"Father God, Jonathan is my friend. He's taught me so much about Your forgiveness. If it wasn't for Jonathan and Brad, I wouldn't have listened to You again. I wouldn't have opened my heart to Patrick. I would still be so alone. Heal Jonathan, Lord. Heal his body and comfort him in his loneliness. Bring him peace."

For a minute he listened and rested in her presence, her care.

Then he remembered. They were only friends. She should go.

He touched her hand and she quieted. "I'm sorry. I didn't mean to wake you."

"Thank…you." He closed his eyes again to hold back the tears. "Need…sleep."

She stood. "I'll go. I'll be praying for you, Jonathan. And I'll stop by next week to see how you're doing, okay?"

He did not answer. He would never again have the chance to talk to her as they had in the past. He could never allow himself to listen to her pray for him again. It stirred feelings in him that hurt far worse than the injuries that put him in this hospital bed.

This would be the last time.

✑

Patrick longed to hold Ashley's hand, but the painful bandages prevented it. Instead, he tilted his head and captured her watery green eyes. "Ash…Bradley will remember. You'll see."

It still hurt to talk, but Ashley needed him.

"It's stupid, I know, to be in here crying when you're all alive." She scrubbed her hands against her pant legs. "I'm so thankful you're okay. You and Jonathan are going home tonight I hear."

He nodded, slowly. When Dr. Owens had given that news, his mom was overjoyed. He wasn't. He'd have to stay with his mother until he could manage simple tasks on his own. Right now, with his blistered hands throbbing, he couldn't imagine being able to open a jar of preserves or a box of cereal, let alone drive.

"Talk...to Jonathan?" The doctor wouldn't discuss anyone else's condition.

"Yes, but only for a few minutes to pray for him. He seemed so sad, so alone, and in a lot of pain. Anna's the one who told me what happened. She was there when Jonathan talked to the fire chief."

Patrick squirmed to a more upright position. Then he coughed and couldn't stop. The wheezy, rib-cracking noise drowned out everything else.

He fought for control. Fought to make his ribs expand and his breathing return to normal. The raw skin on his chest screamed.

Ashley held a straw to his lips, panic covering her face.

He drank. Small sip. Swallow. Burn. Wait. Again.

The coughing finally stopped, and he slumped into the bed. So much for being the brave hero of the night.

Earlier, he'd gotten Bradley out of the barn. Protected him. He couldn't remember how. The last thing he could recall was enfolding Bradley in his arms and covering the boy as best he could.

Ashley returned the plastic cup to the bedside stand and sat down. "Do you need to rest? I'll come see you tomorrow at your mom's if you need some sleep."

"No." He should have shaken his head and lain off his vocal cords. "Tell me what happened."

She leaned forward, her sigh shaky at best, her elbows on the knees of her police uniform. Strong outside, quivering inside. He wished he could draw her into his arms. Something. Anything to comfort her, to wipe away the shadows in her eyes.

"Jonathan and you rushed into the burning barn and found Brad in the blackness. You dragged him to the edge of the barn, right next to the door, and covered him with your body." She wiped her eyes. "That was brave, Patrick. I wish there were more people like you willing to protect kids like that."

Her words salved his aches and pains.

"Jonathan found you and dragged the two of you out the barn door. He saved both of your lives."

Wait. He'd missed the door? How could he have missed it? He'd kicked and kicked, but the wood wouldn't give way.

He'd missed the door. He'd been close, but not good enough. Jonathan was the real hero.

I'm as useless as ever.

Never quite good enough.

"Patrick?" Ashley scanned his face, her eyes wide with concern. "Your look could burn through steel." She gasped. "Sorry, I didn't mean that. I just…you seem really angry is all."

She raised an eyebrow and waited.

"Angry…I failed." There, he'd owned up to it, spoken the truth out loud.

Shaking her head, she relaxed back into the chair. "A wise man once told me that anger is a secondary emotion, usually guarding a lie."

Like a slap, her words jolted him. He'd fallen for the old lies, taken the bait, and was hanging on the pointed end of a fish hook. A few more minutes spent hanging there and he'd have convinced himself no one could ever love him. He'd traveled that road far too many times. Not this time.

Ashley had stepped in with a few simple words and exposed the lie. "You're the wise one."

She studied the floor.

It was time he did the same thing for her. It was too easy to get snared by a lie and simple to escape the downward spiral. With help. He prayed she was ready.

He'd deal with his own mess later, after the pain subsided and he'd gotten some sleep. Then he could fight off the enemy's lies much better.

Right now, Ashley needed him. He studied the beautiful woman in front of him.

"Tell me…about Eric?"

"You want to talk about this now?" She pointed to the curtains. "Here?"

He shrugged and then pointed to his forehead.

"Are you saying it'll take your mind off of everything else?"

He nodded once more and then rested his head from further movement. They probably had hours until the doctor would hand out paperwork and wheel him out to his mom's car.

"Okay." She gulped in air and let it out slowly. "You know Eric was mugged and shot. I sort of told you that Harrison and I were at a party that night. Eric was supposed to meet us there. He never showed."

In bits and pieces she'd shared this much with him. He could imagine her loss. The death of a family member left a hole inside that nothing filled. He was young when his dad died. Ashley had been in college. She'd grown up close to a brother who bordered on Superman.

And he'd been ripped from her.

Ashley rubbed her hands on her knees, as if she could erase the words or actions she was about to share. "Eric had stopped to pick up an engagement ring." She shuddered and paused.

He waited.

"My engagement ring. He'd picked it up for Harrison." Her eyes hardened and she struggled to keep her tears at bay. "I've spent the last ten years of my life wanting justice for Eric and at the same time, trying not to go back and relive that night."

"Don't have to…it's okay."

She was lost in a trance, her terrified eyes trained on the past. A past he no longer wanted to understand. Not if it hurt Ashley this much.

∞

Ashley paused to listen for any nurses, half hoping they'd come and keep her from telling Patrick everything.

Deep breath in, and out. "Harrison and I argued earlier that day because he had forgotten to pick up our gift to Eric. It was Eric's birthday. The party was supposed to be a surprise." Tears slipped down her cheeks, one after the other. She didn't bother to stop them.

"When Eric called later that night, I was angry. He was hours late and missing his birthday party to run an errand because Harrison couldn't get the present and the ring before we had to be there to set up for the party."

The past crept into the present and took over. "Eric finally called to ask us to come pick him up. His car wouldn't start. He'd waited for a tow, but they hadn't come. By then, he was in trouble, but he wouldn't tell me what was happening." She shuddered. All around her people laughed and danced. No one cared that Eric was missing his party. That he was stranded in downtown Atlanta. "I demanded an explanation, but all he'd say was that someone was following him and I needed to hurry. So I grabbed Harrison's keys and drove, angry at the world."

A nurse came in to check Patrick's vital signs. The young redhead paid no attention to the conversation she'd interrupted and did her job, checking the monitors attached to Patrick and slipping her hand around his wrist to check his pulse. "Everything looks good. The doctor should have your release forms here soon." With that, she left the room as quickly as she'd entered.

"Please. Go on." The compassion in Patrick's eyes cracked her resolve to hold it all in.

She closed her eyes and stepped back into a day she'd tried a thousand ways to forget. "I drove even though Harrison tried to take away the keys. I got to his car first. So then he tried to tell me Eric was fine and we'd see he was just playing a practical joke."

Her jaw ached from clenching. Still, the tears came.

"When we found him, he was trying to pull himself toward his car. There was blood everywhere. The red stain on his shirt spread so fast." She stared at her hands.

"Three gunshot wounds."

"I'm so sorry, Ash." Patrick's watery blue eyes stayed fixed on her.

"I tried to stop the flow of blood with my coat and pressure. But he just kept bleeding. I held him in my arms and tried to keep him awake, to keep him talking."

"What happened, Eric? Tell me. Stay with me."

"Love you, Ash." His eyes blinked shut.

"Stay with me, Ricky. Please."

She dropped her face into her hands and her whole body shook. "And then he stopped breathing."

The blood was everywhere, she could still see it. Feel it on her hands.

"Harrison and I…did CPR until the paramedics arrived. It…it didn't help. Eric still died. I couldn't save him. My brother died in my arms, and I didn't tell him I loved him or say happy birthday. I didn't even get to say good-bye."

CHAPTER TWENTY-EIGHT

He stood outside the Mennonite church with other townspeople there to offer their condolences and prayers. Some brought food for the Yoder family.

He was not there for that purpose.

Both Mennonite and non-Mennonite mingled together after a three hour prayer service Sunday morning. Kids played outside behind the church. Their laughter the only happy notes in an otherwise depressing day.

Anna Yoder was wheeled near him. He stepped in front of her wheelchair, causing the two old women to jump, and infused his voice with compassion. "I'm very sorry to hear what's happened, Mrs. Yoder. How is your son?"

"He will be fine. Thank you for your concern." The two women left in a hurry.

Too bad. He'd hoped to find out if the boy's memory was still missing. If not, he'd have to take more drastic measures. He'd seen too much two days ago. Good thing a shovel took care of a multitude of problems.

Three television vans rolled into the packed parking lot where people gathered. Reporters spilled from their doors and rushed to surround Anna Yoder.

The Mennonite men jumped to her rescue.

He slipped back out of camera range but close enough to hear.

"Mrs. Yoder, is it true your son is still in critical condition following a fire he set?" A blonde woman ignored the tears in the old woman's eyes and shoved a microphone in her face.

How had these people gotten the scoop? No doubt the novelty of Mennonites being the center of such juicy gossip drove them toward a story. Had hospital staff dished? Firefighters' families? Angry townspeople? No telling who talked.

The Mennonite men tucked Anna behind them. The women hurried toward the fellowship hall with Anna in their midst.

Reporters jostled for position. "Mrs. Yoder, have your people forgiven your son for the damage he caused?"

Another woman shoved to the front. "Mrs. Yoder, are you planning to sell your farm now that this tragedy has happened?"

Mennonite children stuck their heads out from behind the church, their eyes wide. The men held their positions, unmoving. No anger showed on their faces.

The handful of reporters not discouraged by the lack of answers pressed the men for a statement. "Please, can you let your neighbors know what's happening here? They're worried about their children too."

One of the older men spoke up. "The Yoder boy is not to blame for the fire. He is stable. At home. We are praying for whoever is responsible for the fire. That is all we have to say. Thank you."

The men turned as a group to leave.

"What about the farm? Surely they'll have to sell to pay medical bills?"

None of the men stopped to answer, and soon the churchyard cleared of reporters and concerned citizens. He left with the last bit of the crowd.

The irony. He'd remain to the bitter end and outlast them all. And they had no clue.

◌

Ashley sat in front of her easel Monday evening, staring into the depths of a blank canvas. She'd turned her insides out telling Patrick about Eric's death, details she wanted to forget.

Then she'd gotten all dressed up tonight for Valentine's Day. A day she'd now spend alone. Patrick had called to apologize for being too exhausted after doctor appointments to make it over for dinner. Not that he could drive yet anyway.

He'd said Friday night that talking would help, but he was wrong. It didn't help to let it out. Talking made it all too real.

She preferred bottling things up.

Her phone rang, and Chester barked. "Hush." She ruffled the fur on his head. "It's just the phone. And no, you cannot play with it."

Silly dog.

"Hello?" She adjusted the spaghetti straps of her red dress and shivered. She should have changed into sweats after Patrick's call.

"Ashley, I'm so glad I finally caught you. You're never at home." Her mother's voice filled the phone line. "We saw the awful news story about your town. You really should come home now, before you get hurt. Your father and I worry about you."

For the first time, it hit her that her parents must miss Eric too. They never talked about him, so for years she hated them for forgetting. Maybe distance had been good for all of them. She'd begun to view them as human. Hurting like she hurt.

"I'm sorry, Mom. I don't want you to worry about me."

Her mother's silence almost provoked a laugh.

"Well. Thank you. Still, we'd love for you to come home. Then your May art show would be so much easier. You could…"

Ashley tuned out the details of the May show. So much for her mother appearing human. She had a one-track mind set on controlling every aspect of Ashley's life. Maybe it was her way of showing love, but she'd never suffocate under that again.

"And has Harrison arrived? We asked him to make sure you were safe."

Her mind skidded to a halt. "Did you say Harrison? He's coming here?" *No, God. Not now. Please don't do this.*

Prowling lions were the least of her worries. Dealing with another painful part of her past face-to-face scared her more than any image she could conjure. A gang of thugs and her unarmed. A domestic call with a gun toting, abusive husband. A hurricane, tornado, and earthquake all rolled into one.

"When, Mother. When did he leave?" She flew through the house, picking up clothing and yesterday's dishes as she went. Chester sat, tail wagging, to watch the show.

"He should be there by now. You two have a good time and don't be rude like the last time you were together."

Which time was she referring to? The time when she handed Harrison a garbage bag full of their special things and said she never wanted to see him again? Or the last time she'd seen him? That night her parents had surprised her with a graduation party. One she'd asked them not to throw. The guest of honor that night wasn't her. It was Harrison. She'd told him to enjoy her parents' favor without her. She didn't want the crumbs.

She excused herself from the phone call and dumped an armful of clothing in the laundry room just as her doorbell rang. Her heart slammed against her rib cage. She swallowed once, twice, again to settle herself down.

Chester raced to the front door.

With slow, deliberate steps she closed the distance between present and past.

Opening the door, she inhaled a deep breath and stared at the dark-suited man in front of her.

Harrison's teen-idol good looks had morphed into a dashing, GQ-esque man. He still sported the dimpled smile she'd fallen in love with.

"Hello, Ashley. You look lovely."

But this time his black hair and inviting dark eyes didn't move her. Not one inch.

The only emotion that registered was shame. She should have been mature enough to part ways without the temper tantrums, and more than anything else, she should have grieved with him.

"Harrison." She stepped back ten years as she moved to allow him inside.

Chester quickly made a friend. What a traitor.

"Nice dog. How long have you had him?" Harrison scratched Chester's back, and the puppy caved and flipped over, wriggling in delight.

"About a month." Hard to believe it had been only a month since all Hades had broken loose in this sleepy little town.

Harrison straightened to his full six foot three height, towering over her. "How are you, Ashley? I've missed you."

She stepped away from him, her red dress rubbing against the leather couch. She really should have changed into sweats and a sweatshirt. "Why did my parents send you? And why are you still doing what they say? You never impressed me as a yes man."

He moved to the love seat. "Thank you. I'll take that as a compliment." His smile slipped a notch. "My parents and I stay involved with your mom and dad to try and draw them out of the past. I care about them, Ashley. You might not believe this, but Eric's death is on their minds every day."

After the phone conversation with her mom, she doubted that. Then again, they'd lost their Harvard All-American to follow in their footsteps. Eric was the poster child for perfect, firstborn A-listers. But he'd always made time for her, loved her in a way that she could see.

Harrison cocked his head and looked straight through her walls, lasering into her soul, like he always had. "They love you and were scared after that fire and all the news saying the two communities here are at war. They don't want to lose you too."

She sat on the edge of the sofa closest to the door. "The news reports are inflated. Things aren't anything like they're reporting."

"I'm glad to hear it." His dark eyes locked onto hers.

The silence stretched long and taut. She wouldn't give in and talk about the massive elephant in the room. It was still too raw inside. So was the shame of how she'd treated Harrison in the aftermath.

He flicked his arm up to check the time on his Rolex. "Can I take you out for dinner? I'd hate to leave you alone on Valentine's Day."

A Hallmark holiday, not a real one. She'd used that fact to bolster her aloneness and convince herself singleness was a good thing all these years.

It hadn't worked. "No. Thank you. I'm dating a wonderful man now. He's a counselor and a good friend."

"Is he coming over soon?" He stroked Chester's fur. The mutt was in seventh heaven.

"No. Patrick was injured in the fire." Her heart caught when she remembered Brad's tear-streaked face yesterday. The boy wanted to remember her and the rest of the people who begged to see him. But he couldn't recall anything.

Harrison stood. "I'm sorry to hear that." His shoulders slumped a tiny fraction, the only chink in his confident armor. "Did your parents tell you I'm a pediatrician now?"

"You always wanted to be an ER doc. The adrenaline rush and all. What happened?"

"Eric." Harrison's eyes fell to the floor. "I tried. I really did, but I couldn't handle it. With every gun trauma, I saw Eric's face. I fought to save him over and over again and failed. I couldn't live like that."

"I'm sorry."

He crossed the room and stood at her side before she could blink. She shook her head and pushed past him. She'd already gone through this with Patrick, and she wasn't strong enough to do it again.

Catching her arm, he turned her around to face him.

His shoes held her attention.

"Ashley, please hear me out." He nudged her chin up with his hand, his touch gentle. "I've talked to doctor after doctor about Eric's wounds. There was nothing we could have done. I just wish we could have talked about what happened. Grieved together."

Tears pricked at her eyes. She stepped away. "I think you'd better go."

He sighed and slipped his hands into his pockets. "I understand why you don't want to see me or talk about this. It hurts too much."

He had that right.

"I came because your parents asked me to check on you. More than that, to say I'm sorry, Ash. Sorry I wasn't there for you after Eric died."

The walls she'd protected herself with began to crumble around her feet. Harrison understood better than anyone else what she lost that day, and she'd gained strength from shutting him out of her life.

She'd used that power to trap them both in a lonely and bitter cage.

"I…" The emotions lodged in her throat made talking impossible. She fixed her eyes on the wall behind Harrison, and the painting hanging there caught her attention. Patrick had given her a picture of her life, a woman with a massive globe balanced on her shoulders.

Not speaking to Harrison was her way of managing the loss of her brother, controlling it, her way of numbing the pain. That was what weighed her down like the woman's globe in the picture.

She was so tired of carrying it.

Her eyes moved to the angels flanking the woman in the picture and she gasped. The angels weren't helping the woman hold up the world. They were holding it for her.

Harrison moved to the door. "I hope you'll stay safe, Ashley. I'll let your parents know you're doing well."

This time, she caught his arm. "I'm sorry."

His eyebrows lifted into his bangs.

"I was wrong to shove you away, to shut you out because I couldn't handle the memories. I'm sorry." She swallowed hard, her cheeks hot. "Will you forgive me?"

The weight of the world lessened a little.

"I already did." Harrison opened her front door and flashed a final smile. "Thanks for seeing me today. It was a gift." He stepped outside. "Patrick's a lucky guy. I hope he knows that."

She studied the picture again. Could she let go of the control and see herself the way Patrick and Harrison did? The way God did?

Maybe it was finally time.

⁓

Patrick shook his head at the overflowing basket in Emma's arms. "I can carry something, you know. My arms are fine." He slowed his pace to her walking speed as they left the bed and breakfast. Streetlamps lit their way in the evening darkness.

She tsked at him. "Dear boy, you are not keeping your end of the bargain. I said if you take care of yourself and if you go to all your doctor appointments, I'd help you pull off the best Valentine's Day Ashley has ever had."

"I went to all my appointments."

She marched down the sidewalk. "You drove over here yourself. Nearly gave your mother a heart attack."

He'd pulled off some stupid things in his life. Today's driving was one of the stupidest. He'd almost wrecked backing out of the driveway.

But he'd made it. He couldn't leave Ashley alone today.

He escorted Emma the rest of the way down the sidewalk to Ashley's house, not carrying one item. It about trashed his male pride.

The snail's pace Emma set for their little walk suited him today. Soon he'd work back up to his daily run. For now, he intended to use his recovery to spend as much time with Ashley and the Yoder family as they'd allow.

Bradley still didn't remember him, but the boy had spoken with him about the fire and the pain from his burns. Something they had in common.

They arrived at Ashley's home to find all the lights off, even in her studio. Surely she hadn't gone to bed at seven o'clock.

"If she's asleep, we'll wake her up." Self-confident Emma marched right up to the front door and knocked.

Chester barked and slid to the door, jumping up and down at the wood blocking his attack.

"Hang on. I'll be right there." Ashley's voice came from nearby. She unlocked the deadbolt and opened the door. "Emma. Patrick." She smiled. He'd done the right thing to surprise her.

Emma pecked Ashley's cheek as she passed and went right to work, setting up candles and decorations in the living room, shooing Chester from the preparations.

Ashley stared and fiddled with her hands, nervous energy coming off her in waves. "I thought you were home asleep." She kissed the side of his cheek. "I'm so glad you're not, as long as you're okay."

"I'm fine. Dear Mother Hen has forbid my lifting a finger." He held up the two big bandaged reasons he couldn't do more. They hurt much less today.

Emma busied herself with the red tablecloth and white dishes she'd insisted on packing with the food.

Ashley moved into the living room. "How can I help?"

Emma tsked at her too. "I need you two to sit down here and prepare for a lovely dinner. I'll be your waitress for tonight. You just relax and enjoy." She slipped a CD into the stereo and the room filled with soft violins.

Ashley raised her eyebrows high as they sat on her couch. "Was all of this your idea?"

He laughed. "Not the music. I would have packed my eighties' love song collection."

Shaking her head, she tried not to laugh. It didn't work.

The doorbell rang and Ashley stood to answer it.

Emma beat her there. "I said relax. I'll only be a minute." Two men from the bed and breakfast staff entered and hefted their coolers toward the kitchen. They left without a word a few minutes later.

Patrick leaned close enough to smell her rose-scented shampoo. "I had no idea Emma planned to go all out and commandeer your kitchen."

"I don't mind. It's sweet that she'd do this. That you'd go to these lengths to make this day special. Thank you." Her eyes danced in the candlelight.

"You're worth it, you know?" He held her gaze and prayed to keep himself from rushing their conversation. There was so much he wanted to say.

Ashley eyed the wrapped package at the center of her coffee table, its shiny red surface catching the candlelight. "I have something for you too. Do you want your gift now or later?"

"Do I need to open it?"

"Nope." She exited the living room, and Chester barked at her from the kitchen and scratched at his crate. Emma had caged the little ball of energy. Smart woman.

A minute later Ashley returned with a framed canvas in her hands, the back facing him.

He sat up straighter. "For me? I'm honored."

"You haven't seen it yet." She paused in front of him and studied the painting in her hands. "I hope you like it."

With a dramatic flourish, she turned the artwork to face him.

She'd finished the painting of their first date…with a few noticeable alterations. Amelia's restaurant vibrated with living energy. Ashley had captured the elegant atmosphere with picture-perfect lines.

His favorite part was Ashley wiping a drip of chocolate ice cream from his cheek. "That's not quite how I remember our first date. Wasn't it you with the chocolate on your cheek?"

"Maybe." She slid into place next to him, still holding the canvas. "I wanted you to know I'd be there when life gets messy."

A rush of emotion filled him. "No one has ever given me such a perfect gift. Thank you."

She laid the canvas on the couch and turned toward him. "You're worth it." Drawing close, she brushed her lips over his.

He moved his hands to her face, but she stopped him. "Do not hurt yourself tonight. Not even for a kiss."

A soft growl rumbled in his throat.

She laughed. "That doesn't scare me one bit."

"Glad to hear it."

Emma picked that moment to enter with their sizzling filet mignon and two steaming sweet potatoes. "There's butter and brown sugar on the sweet potatoes. You both deserve some extra sweetness tonight."

"Mmmm. This smells heavenly, Emma." Ashley situated the plates on the coffee table. "Thank you."

Emma winked. "Enjoy." Then she slipped back into the kitchen.

Patrick situated his arm around Ashley's shoulders, careful to keep his hands from landing on her. "Mind if I pray?"

"That'd be great."

"Father of love and life, our Great Physician, thank You for today. For health to enjoy time together. For protection. You've walked with us every step of our lives. Thank You for carrying us recently. Restore Bradley's memory. Continue bringing peace to our families. Heal Jonathan. Guide Ashley and speak peace to her heart as only You can. We praise You for the reason we celebrate today—Your unfailing, perfect love for us. Amen."

Emma's steaks fell apart at the touch of a fork. Bless her. He managed to gently use his left hand to lift the delicious food to his mouth.

Ashley ate slowly, matching him bite for bite.

"You doing okay? It's been a rough few days."

She turned to him. "I've thought over what you said about forgiveness and the hold anger has had on my life. Something happened today that showed me how right you've been."

"Really?"

"Harrison came over."

Patrick stopped mid-chew and gulped down the dry bite in his mouth. This was not the breakthrough news he'd hoped to hear. But to his surprise, he didn't tense with jealousy. He listened.

"He and my parents are close, and they were worried about me. He came to make sure I was okay." She paused and looked him straight in the eye. "He invited me to dinner, and I didn't jump at it or get angry. I didn't really feel anything but shame for how horribly I'd treated him. I know I should have apologized when he first told me why he came, but I was in shock."

"So what happened?"

Her eyes filled with tears. "I'm sorry. I should have waited until tomorrow to tell you about this."

"No, this is good. I can tell a lot has happened since we talked."

She huffed. "That's a nice way of saying it. More like the painting you gave me finally made sense. It's not the woman holding up the world and the angels helping, it's God holding it all together." She stared at the picture. "I was able to ask Harrison's forgiveness because I saw that I wasn't in control of the past and I didn't have to stay locked there."

She'd finally gotten it. His eyes moistened. God had spoken through the painting after all.

"Thank you for not giving up on me, for continuing to tell me the truth even when I wasn't listening."

"I'm here, Ash."

She touched his arm. "I thought about all you've said, and I prayed I'd start seeing myself the way God does. Forgiven."

With his wrist, he nudged her closer. She tucked herself into his side. "I'm proud of you."

"I have a long way to go."

"We all do, Ash."

They sat in the candlelit silence. A minute later, he couldn't wait any longer. "Aren't you even a little bit curious about your gift?"

"Maybe." But she reached for it and carefully loosened the wrapping.

"Oh." Covering her mouth with one hand, she held the framed photo in her other hand, her eyes never leaving it.

He searched her profile for any sign of displeasure. He'd spoken to Margo a number of times over the past week before he'd decided on this gift. Many, many prayers went into his selection as well.

Touching the engraved letters, she smiled even though tears slipped down her cheeks. "How did you...where did you get this photo of me and Eric?"

"From Margo. She said it had been your favorite. Apparently she rescued it from boxes of things you threw away."

Ashley nodded. "Love never fails." She turned to him. "Why did you have that verse inscribed on the frame?"

"Because not even death is strong enough to stop love. Your brother isn't gone forever, and I hoped this would be a good reminder of truth."

"It is." More tears slipped from her eyes. "Thank you."

She rested back into his arms. They stayed that way for a long time, Ashley's eyes still locked onto the picture of her and her brother when they were in high school.

He'd succeeded at his one hope for today—to make this the best Valentine's Day Ashley could have had. But even in the celebration, what was left unsaid still pulled at him.

Someone wanted the Yoders out of the way or dead.

CHAPTER TWENTY-NINE

He paced the small downtown park. All his hard work. For what? A kid with a concussion held his future in his hands.

And Bradley Yoder could remember any minute.

He had to finish it. Today.

Returning to his car, he drove down Highway 26. The dilapidated buildings gave way to green pastureland.

His shoulders tensed.

He hated this area of town. Few cars passed by as he drove.

Had things unfolded according to his plans, this area would have swarmed with tourists, and the Mennonites would have thanked them for being included in the economic upswing.

But they were satisfied. His face twisted into a tight sneer. How could they be so stupid?

Turning onto Will Miller Road, he slowed his car and passed the Yoder farm.

They'd pay.

Anna Yoder's deserted farm pleased him. Now he would simply drive around and search for the Yoder's white pickup truck or minivan. Where would they spend a Thursday afternoon?

He should remember this from all the time he'd spent causing trouble on this farm.

But he couldn't. He couldn't recall their schedule or the other small troubles he'd planned so long ago. Even his day-to-day responsibilities and where he had to be when slipped from his mind too often lately. His mental state concerned his family.

What they didn't know wouldn't hurt them.

But his one last plan would hurt the Yoders.

Patting the Colt 1911 in his waistband, he smiled.

Yes, today was the day to end it all.

⌒

Jonathan sat back into the soft couch. All around him, Beth's family sang. Anna, without her wheelchair for the first time, sat next to Bradley, a smile on her face.

Something else that was a first this long week.

His throat had also stopped burning with every word, and he could speak without coughing today. This was a much welcomed change.

But Bradley did not sing. The boy did not even remember the songs he had sung since he was a toddler.

A dull ache grew in his chest.

Ashley's beautiful face intruded into his mind and caused the ache to grow.

He shook his head. No, he would not allow his mind to travel this path any longer. He had given his mind and heart to a woman he should never have developed a friendship with in the first place.

But he had. For a time, the joy made him forget his loneliness. Then it blocked him from sensing the presence of God. That he could not permit again.

One last time, he recalled his final conversation with Ashley. At the hospital Friday night, she had sat by his bed and prayed. He woke to her tears and soft voice calling out to God on his behalf.

For a minute, he saw Mary. Her sweet, wise green eyes watching him, her soft voice speaking his name to the Lord.

Then Ashley met his gaze and the illusion vanished.

She was a police officer. A woman who carried a gun. A woman who spent her days angry at God for the loss of her brother. A woman who did not believe forgiveness could free her.

The words of her prayer replayed in his mind.

"Father God, Jonathan is my friend. He's taught me so much about Your forgiveness. If it wasn't for Jonathan and Brad, I wouldn't have listened to You again. I wouldn't have opened my heart to Patrick. I would still be so alone. Heal Jonathan, Lord. Heal his body and comfort him in his loneliness. Bring him peace."

She had learned from him. Maybe the Lord had used the foolish path Jonathan had walked for His good, to help Ashley.

Tenderness grew inside.

He had experienced the awakening of emotion and interest in a woman for the first time in a very long, lonely season. But she belonged with another, and he could be happy for her and Patrick.

He thanked God for this promise of spring in his soul, for allowing him time with Ashley and for her friendship.

And he could now let her go.

Instead of the sadness he expected, a peaceful freedom filled his heart. All around him a familiar hymn wrapped itself around his soul, and he began to sing, "Praise God from whom all blessings flow. Praise Him, all creatures here below. Praise Him above, ye heavenly host. Praise Father, Son, and Holy Ghost."

Not even his shaky voice could stop him from expressing the praise that welled up from deep inside.

Across the room, Anna gasped.

He smiled at the aunt whose quiet, loving ways most resembled his mother. Together they sang the words to another beloved hymn.

Joy like he had not experienced in years rose up inside of him. He would not let go of this closeness to his Savior for anything. Not ever again.

The song ended, and they sat in a quiet peace.

Beth glanced at him and moved her eyes away quickly.

The back door slammed shut, but no one walked into the room. The wind could not have opened a door, could it?

Beth's father crossed the room, his brow creased with concern.

Jonathan stood and stopped him with a lowered voice. "I will see about the cause of this noise." He made eye contact with Anna and then Mr. Kauffman. "My aunt was injured after searching out the reason for some loud noise in her backyard. Please let me go look around. I will avoid the steps and make sure there is nothing wrong. I do not want anyone else hurt."

Mr. Kauffman nodded and returned to his seat with the older men.

Jonathan inhaled a long breath and let it out before he left the front room. His hands did not obey his will to appear calm to everyone else.

They shook.

He doubted anyone took this noise outside lightly. Too many accidents had happened. Bradley had almost died. He could not allow anyone else to get injured.

He was the only single man without a family at the house.

So he grasped the cold metal door handle and twisted. The door creaked as he opened it wide.

Checking the first step for damages, he found none and proceeded to place both feet on the stair.

Then the next.

Finally, he stood on solid ground and took note of every car in the back parking area, the trees and fields surrounding the house.

No wind blew.

Nothing appeared out of place, as if someone had set a trap like they had done to Anna's steps.

He moved to the other side of the house and with slow, measured steps rounded the corner of the white farmhouse.

No one was there. Even so, a cold shiver made him gulp.

Evil was near.

He could sense the reality of a world he could not see all around him.

If evil was near, God's angels stayed even closer to his side as he rounded the front of the house and released a deep breath.

No one was here either.

Feeling very foolish for his wild imagination, he shook his head and moved to the Kauffman's back door.

"That's far enough." A growling voice forced his eyes to the other side of the yard. A man in blue jeans and a dark jacket stalked closer.

Every step the angry man took caused Jonathan's heart to pound faster and faster.

The man's black gun, pointed right at his chest, did not waver.

CHAPTER THIRTY

He couldn't believe how gullible and obedient these people were. The tall man stood ramrod still even though a gun was pointed right at his chest. He didn't shake. Didn't run. Didn't holler or call out to anyone.

That made his life easy.

"Turn and face the house." He gestured with his Colt.

The man he'd heard called Jonathan turned and stared at the clean white siding of another orderly and neat little farmhouse.

"Now you're going to do exactly as I say, understand?"

The man nodded.

This was too much fun. "In a minute, you're going to call out to your aunt and cousin and ask them to come help you with the injured animal you just found."

"There is no animal in this yard."

He shoved the man's shoulder. "Shut up! I'm in charge here." *What a fool.* "You're going to call them or I'll shoot you now and keep shooting until everyone in that house is dead. Got it?"

"Then what will happen?"

"Then you and your family are going to take a little ride to finish some important business you've forgotten at home."

The Mennonite man said nothing else.

Things were going even better than he'd planned. It was about time.

∾

Jonathan's mind raced. What could he do that would not put his people in danger?

If he followed this evil man's instructions, Anna and Bradley would be hurt, probably killed. If he did not, every single one of them would die this day. No one would move to apprehend the gun from this man and use it to stop him. This was not their way. They might run, but this man would kill many of them. He believed this man would shoot until all of them were dead.

He could not allow that to happen.

Dear God in heaven, hear my prayer. Protect us today, Father. Stop this man from his evil plan. Save Your people this day. Give me courage and strength to act. Use me today, Lord.

He slipped both hands into his pockets, hoping to retrieve his car keys and use them as a distraction.

How he had no idea yet.

His hand closed around his cell phone.

"Anna and Bradley Yoder are in there, right?" The man's last word wavered.

Jonathan wished he could lie and stop this man right now, but he could not. Instead, he focused on the phone and began to push the numbers for Ashley's cell phone.

He prayed she would answer.

"Answer me!" The man's arm connected with the back of Jonathan's neck and shoved him into the house.

His face crashed against the siding. For a minute, Jonathan saw pricks of light and nothing else. He had to stay awake.

Fighting down his panic, he pushed numbers he prayed were the ones that connected him to Ashley.

"I'm only going to ask one more time." The metal of the gun pushed against his back. "Is your aunt in there?"

"Yes."

"Good."

The soft sound of a phone ringing reached his ears. He prayed the man behind him did not hear it.

"Now be a good boy and call them out here."

Ashley's soft voice broke through the man's angry words. "Hello?"

"Do you understand me? Call them to come out here or I'll shoot you right now." The gun pressed into him harder. "Call!"

"I cannot." He prayed the man would not follow through on the threat to shoot. If he did, Jonathan prayed his family and the Kauffmans would not freeze in fear but run away as fast as they could. He prayed this man behind him could not shoot them.

Jonathan whispered another prayer for their safety. Was he willing to take this risk?

Ashley's voice broke through the tense silence. "Jonathan? What's happening? Is someone threatening you? Talk to me!"

A loud curse erupted from the gunman.

Sharp pain exploded inside him. His limbs went numb. Then everything stopped and darkness washed over him.

∽

Ashley gripped the phone in her hand and pulled her cruiser to the side of the road. "Jonathan? Are you there? Talk to me!"

A groan had reached her ears and then static.

"Jonathan?"

Silence.

Another phone call haunted her as she sped out of town.

"Hey, sis. Can you and Harrison come pick me up? My car won't start."

"What's going on, Ricky? You're late. You should have been here hours ago."

"It's nothing. Just some homeless guy is hanging around here and the tow truck's not coming for a while. It's creeping me out. Hurry, okay?"

She'd asked Eric where he was and told him she'd be right there, but she was too late to make a difference.

This time she'd stop the violence before it started.

Please, God. Please get me there before anyone gets hurt.

Brad's tear-streaked face came to mind. The brown-haired, brown-eyed boy who didn't even remember her.

Still, she'd be there for him. Protect him.

Tires screeching, she turned onto Will Miller Road and sped toward Anna's farmhouse. She stopped and parked in the driveway.

No cars out front.

No lights on in the house.

Heart slamming against her ribs, she took a deep breath and exhaled. Then another.

When her hands stopped shaking, she unlatched her duty weapon and slipped to the side of the house.

No one talked inside. No loud voices. No quiet movements either.

She followed the siding around to the back and surveyed every inch of the dairy farm.

Cows swished their tails in the air.

Barns stood empty.

One charred piece of land stood barren, no barn, no equipment in sight.

She shivered. Patrick, Brad, and Jonathan had almost lost their lives there days ago. Could she prevent that from happening today?

Rounding the house, she headed for the back door and latched onto the cold handle. It wouldn't turn.

Locked up tight.

Moving around to the front of the house, she listened for any noise, however slight, to tip her off to anything wrong.

Nothing moved.

She slipped up the steps and tried the front door handle. Locked.

Brad's scared face filled her mind.

They weren't here, but they were in trouble.

She had to find them before someone got hurt. Or killed.

If Derrick Hardy was the voice she'd heard over the phone line yelling at Jonathan, she'd see him behind bars before the afternoon turned to night.

Once again screeching her tires, she rushed from Anna's home and hurried down the deserted road, deeper into the Mennonite farmlands. She couldn't be late this time. Not again.

CHAPTER THIRTY-ONE

He dragged Jonathan to the side of the farmhouse and crouched beside him. They'd come to check on him soon.

What if someone else came? Was he ready to dispose of however many it took to finish this job?

Yes.

Clearing his throat, he deepened his voice and tried it out in a whisper. "Anna, could you come? Wounded animal. Do not want anyone to see the blood."

Would that work?

He picked up Jonathan's phone and searched the contacts for Anna Yoder's cell phone. Brilliant.

"Hello? Jonathan? Is there a problem?" She spoke in a hushed tone.

"Wounded animal. Please help me. But do not scare the others. It is very bloody."

Anna gasped. "I will come right now." She hung up the phone and footsteps sounded in the kitchen.

Thump. Thump. The crutches echoed on the kitchen floor.

Soon the door cracked. "Jonathan?"

He jerked Jonathan's body farther around the corner. She had to come outside all the way or else he'd never convince her to come close enough without the others' knowledge.

"Jonathan?"

She slid her injured foot across the grass and plodded toward him, one slow step at a time. His back pressed into the siding, he edged closer to Anna Yoder.

Her white head poked around the corner and she froze, her mouth opened wide. No sound escaped.

"Do not say a word, or I'll shoot your beloved nephew here, understand?"

She nodded and fixed her eyes on Jonathan's still form.

"What do you want?"

She didn't recognize him. Good. That would make today go smoother.

"Mamm?" A young boy's voice filled the backyard.

He pointed his gun at the woman's face and whispered. "Tell him to come here and help you."

She nodded again. "Bradley?"

He pulled the old woman to him and her crutches fell on the ground.

She gasped.

Smiling, he snaked one arm around her neck and the other hand clamped around the gun.

Bradley stepped past the house and right into the sights of his gun. The boy halted and raised his hands, widening both his eyes and mouth.

He motioned the brown-haired boy toward his car parked on the other side of a line of minivans. He dragged Jonathan and the crutches with him. No use causing alarm too soon.

The boy searched around him before opening the car door. Too bad he hadn't killed the kid the first time.

He would today.

Both Anna and Bradley obeyed and started to climb into the backseat.

"Oh, no. There's no way you're both sitting back there." He dropped Jonathan behind one of the minivans and motioned the boy into the front seat.

Once the door closed, he pulled a rope from the floorboards and wrapped it around Bradley's wrists.

Then he pulled it tight.

Bradley winced but didn't scream.

"Good boy. Way to keep your family alive."

He drove in silence through deserted streets. No one spoke.

Tears slipped past the boy's tightly clenched eyes. Too bad. At least he wasn't blubbering. That would have pushed him too far.

"Why are you doing this?" Anna's quiet voice ruptured the silence.

He smirked into the rearview mirror. "You'll see soon enough."

In minutes, he pulled his car into Anna's driveway. Nothing stirred. No cars. No nosey neighbors for miles. This he appreciated about the Mennonites.

He flipped open the console and slipped a pack of matches into his jeans.

Opening both doors on the passenger's side, he yanked the boy up by the rope first.

He cried out in pain.

"Shut it now, or this gets worse."

Anna hobbled out of the car. "Please, do not hurt my son. He has been through enough trauma this last week. We will do as you have asked."

He followed Anna up her front porch steps, one slow movement at a time.

As slow as she could go, Anna unlocked her front door. He almost pushed her forward but restrained himself.

The boy he shoved ahead of him.

Bradley sprawled on the floor, groaning.

Anna rushed to his side. "Please, stop." Her lips moved, but she spoke no other words out loud.

Maybe she prayed.

He laughed. It wouldn't help her one bit.

"There's one thing I need you to do for me, Anna Yoder." He pointed his gun to her tidy desk in the next room, clearly visible from where he stood.

"I have prayed for you."

He shook his head and sneered. No more playing nice. "Your prayers won't change what's going to happen." He glanced at the boy still stretched out on the floor. "It didn't help him last Friday."

Anna's eyes widened.

"Yes. That was me. If it hadn't been for that meddling counselor, everything would have ended there. You would have run away from this farm full of bad memories and sold it for pennies."

"You tried to kill my son? Why? What could make a man become so filled with evil that he would take another person's life? A child's life?" Tears spilled down her cheeks.

Bradley pushed himself to sitting. They boy's brown eyes fixed on him. Then recognition lit a fire inside the small teen.

"I remember you. You followed me from the milking barn to the old one." His voice rose with each word. "I saw your face. I recognized you from town."

"You forced me to do what I did."

"You picked up a shovel and hit me from behind. I heard the metal scrape the ground, but was not fast enough to stop you."

The return of the boy's memory only fortified his resolve to end this entire nightmare with one stroke of a match.

"Enough talk." He turned to Anna. "Go to your desk and sit down." He followed her there, stepping sideways to keep his eyes on both the old woman and the red-faced boy.

Out of the corner of his eye he saw movement.

He jerked sideways as the boy jumped in the air and tackled him.

He fell against a shelf and books rained down on his head. Pain seared his back.

His gun crashed against the floor.

He and the boy fell against the hardwood, arms tangled together, the boy shoving and trying to twist around to end up on top.

Over and over, he turned, until his back hit a wall and he regained the upper hand.

Before the boy could do anything else, he punched Bradley in the face. Blood poured from his nose.

Scrambling to his feet, he grabbed the boy now lying crumpled on the floor.

"You'll pay for that."

First, he picked the boy up and held him off the ground. Gym membership paid off big-time.

The boy struggled against his hold.

Like hoisting a weight bar, he bent his knees and pushed with everything in him, hurtling the boy through the air and into the wall.

He collapsed in a heap and didn't move.

Anna cried out and stood.

He retrieved his gun and pointed it at the boy's knee. "Don't do anything stupid."

She sank into the desk chair.

"I'll be leaving soon. After the fire is in charge." He slipped his hand into his jeans pocket to retrieve the matches. "Enjoy the show."

But he couldn't find the matches. They weren't in his pocket.

He checked the other pocket. "Say your good-byes, Mrs. Yoder. The end is at hand."

∾

Ashley sped toward the Kauffman residence, the Yoders' closest friends, praying faster than her mind could translate. Vans dotted the driveway and lined the sides of the road.

She pulled into the front yard and parked, running toward the sounds coming from the backyard.

Ten pairs of scared eyes turned her way as she rounded the house.

Jonathan, sitting on the ground with a bag of peas on the back of his neck, stopped her cold.

"What happened here?"

"Someone attacked me. Hit me with a gun, I believe." His eyes remained closed as he spoke. "I must have been out for some time."

Beth spoke up, her voice trembling. "We heard a car leaving a few minutes ago and thought the Yoders had all gone home because

Bradley was sick." She wiped tears from her eyes. "Bradley rushed outside, upset. We did not understand."

"There was nothing you could have done, Beth." Jonathan's voice was slow and quiet.

Ashley's pulse sped up, her senses on high alert.

Beth sniffled. "We tried to call Anna and Jonathan, and we searched the backyard but found no one."

Jonathan coughed. "They found me behind Anna's minivan. He must have dragged me over there at some point."

"Anna's crutches." Ashley pointed to the crutches lying beside one of the vans. "She wouldn't have left them. Where's Bradley?"

Jonathan met her eyes. "They are not here."

She ran to her squad car, fear snapping at her heels. Keying the radio, she steadied her voice. "Possible hostage situation. Requesting ambulance and backup." She rattled off the Kauffmans' house number and what information she'd gathered, keeping her eyes on the group of people now standing beside the house.

Jonathan leaned on another Mennonite man's arm. Together they hobbled toward her. "I believe they have gone back to Anna's farm. The man with the gun wanted me to call Anna. He seemed desperate to find her. He said there was unfinished business at Anna's home."

"But why would he take her to the farm?" She strained her mind to fit all the pieces together. "Stay here, Jonathan. An ambulance is on the way. I'll check the farm first."

All the accidents with the dairy farm. Anna's steps. The fire. She already believed whoever was behind the fire was after the farm all along.

She keyed her radio again and filled them in on her destination.

Please, God. Please let me get to them in time.

Chapter Thirty-two

Jonathan refused to stay and wait for an ambulance he did not need. He wished to avoid another visit to the hospital.

In the passenger seat of Mr. Kauffman's van, he prayed as they sped toward Anna's farm. Beth remained quiet in the backseat. Fear as he had never experienced caused his entire body to shake.

He would throw up any second.

"Jonathan, you do not look well. We should have waited for the ambulance." Beth's blue eyes watered.

"I will be okay." He prayed his words were true. He prayed harder for Bradley and Anna. Bradley was in more danger than he had been the day of the fire. So was every person Jonathan cared about.

God protect them.

Mr. Kauffman slowed down and parked behind a line of police cars.

Jonathan opened his van door and steadied himself. He would not throw up now or faint. He must pray. Anna, Bradley, and Ashley needed him.

He caught himself. No, they did not need him. They needed God.

Walking slowly toward Ashley and another police officer deep in discussion, Jonathan had no idea what he would do besides pray.

That was all he could do.

Ashley froze as their eyes met. "Jonathan, you shouldn't be here. Get back in that van and leave."

The hair on the back of his neck stood up and his spine snapped straight. "I will not. My family is in there."

He had never spoken with this force to anyone before.

Ashley's eyebrows shot up.

The police officer with her cleared his throat. "Well, now your first priority is to protect these guys and any other bystanders." He started to walk away.

Ashley clenched her teeth, anger coming from her in waves. "Chief, I know this house better than anyone on the force. Better than anyone you could call in."

"It's too dangerous. Right now, we wait." The police chief turned and walked away.

Jonathan's headache pounded. His heartbeat thundered. Surely Ashley would listen to the wisdom of her commanding officer and wait with them.

Then they could all pray.

"Stay here." Her voice snapped at him. "Pray, Jonathan, and stay behind Beth's van." Her words ended abruptly, and she turned on her heel.

A second later, she was running toward the side of Anna's farmhouse, crouching low and moving fast.

She headed straight into danger.

"Ashley—"

A strong hand pressed over his mouth and jerked him backward. His mind went blank and his whole body tensed. *Please, God...*

A voice hammered in his ear. "You'll get her killed!"

∽

Every muscle in Patrick's body tensed as he followed Ashley's race into danger.

His mind fumbled through a desperate prayer. No telling who Jonathan had alerted to Ashley's presence.

Jaw tight, Patrick whispered into the stiff man's ear. "Do not say another word, understand?"

Jonathan nodded.

The handful of Mennonites gathered around them waited, eyes wide and hands covering their mouths. Every one of them focused on him.

He stepped back, heart hammering and his conscience pricking. Stopping Jonathan didn't require the force he'd used. "I'm sorry. I didn't mean to hurt you."

Jonathan adjusted his shirt. "You did not."

"Who's inside?" Cop cars filled the area in front of Anna's farm, most of the men and women crouched behind their cruisers.

He motioned for the group around him to get back behind their vans.

"A gunman has Anna and Bradley inside. That is what the police were saying. I have not seen anything or anyone in the house since we arrived." Jonathan's face was white. He massaged the back of his neck and winced.

"Did I do that?"

Beth handed Jonathan a bag of frozen peas. "No. The man inside the farmhouse struck Jonathan."

Patrick's mind whirled. What in the world was going on? What could he do now?

"Why are you here?" Jonathan crouched and sat back on his heels, the peas pressed into his neck.

"I was on my way to meet Ashley for dinner, and all these cop cars rushed past me. I followed them here."

Jonathan bowed his head and silence descended on them.

Eerie silence. Patrick's shoulders knotted. "Gather round." A group of terrified Mennonites crept closer, hunching down on their hands and feet. "Pray. Please pray for Ashley's safety and for all three of them to come out of this unhurt. I'll be right back."

The man inside Anna's house had scared these peaceful people more than anything he'd ever seen. He shuddered. He had to find out what was going on, and the only people not in shock were the cops.

Sergeant Culp sat in his cruiser across the street. Patrick shot straight for him. "Sam, what kind of trouble did Ashley rush into? What's going on in there?"

Culp held up a finger and pointed to the cell phone plastered to his ear. His hands clicked over the keyboard mounted in his car. Then Culp snapped his phone shut. "Ashley went renegade and is inside that house with a gunman and two hostages. That's all I know."

"Anna and Bradley?"

Culp nodded.

Oh, God... Words wouldn't form to finish his prayer. "Let me talk to the gunman. I can be the hostage negotiator. Just let me talk to him."

"No can do. No one's answerin' any of the phones we've called."

Patrick paced the length of the cruiser. "There has to be something I can do, Sam. Give me a way to help."

Culp reopened his phone. "Go talk to the Mennonites. Jonathan Yoder was held at gunpoint and knocked out. Anna and Bradley were taken from some family get-together. They're all shaken up. Go be a counselor and make them leave with you." Culp turned his attention to his phone call.

Patrick flicked his gaze to the men and women hiding behind two older minivans. Culp was right. Those people needed a calm, confident counselor to convince them to move to safety.

He wasn't that man.

He wouldn't be until Ashley walked out of that house—unhurt— with Bradley and Anna.

Chapter Thirty-three

Ashley regretted her bravado the second she rounded the farm-house and came face-to-face with the business end of a gun.

The man's eyes widened a split second at her weapon aimed right at his head. "Drop your gun, cop lady." His voice caught. Bravery tended to slip when staring down the barrel of a gun.

Her eyes didn't waver from his. "Not until you drop yours." She didn't recognize the man in front of her. A scruffy beard covered his chin and a skullcap hid his hair.

The shaky gun and crazy eyes she knew all too well. She'd faced down her share of criminals caught in a desperate situation. A situation so volatile it could turn razor sharp any second.

His jeans were covered in blood.

"Where are Anna and Brad?"

He shrugged, his cold eyes cutting into her, his courage returning. "Are they still alive?"

"Maybe."

God, please let them still be alive.

"I need you to put the gun down, and we can walk away from this."

He laughed. "No one's walking away today, cop lady." He stepped back toward the small porch, his blazing eyes never leaving hers. "There's someone here you should see. You might remember him."

The gunman stepped onto the porch backward until his left hand touched the doorknob.

Her trigger finger itched. She'd trained every day at the academy for situations like this. Now that it was here, her vision tunneled. All she cared about this second was stopping this man.

But whose shot would land first?

That was what mattered.

The gunman jerked Brad's body from the house, keeping his gun aimed at her head. Blood covered Brad's face and shirt.

She gasped. Training scenarios and options disappeared.

The gunman smiled. "Say a quick good-bye."

Brad's head bobbed up and his eyes opened.

Her knees weakened. Forcing herself to ignore the pleading in Brad's brown eyes, she focused her gun on the man's forehead.

He sneered. "You shoot and he'll die."

She steadied her breathing. "You are not getting out of here alive."

"We'll see about that." He inched down the porch steps and backed against the house. "I'd say it's time you put down your gun and let me and the kid walk out of here."

"Release the boy and I'll be your shield."

The gunman glared. "Not happening." He pushed the gun into Bradley's neck. "Tell her how much you don't want to die, kid. Tell her your life is in her hands."

The words shot through her. Sweat trickled down her back.

She waited, every muscle tense, for the right moment.

Brad lifted his eyes to hers. "Ashley. Please do as he says."

She blinked. He'd remembered?

"Yeah. The kid knows everything. Too bad really."

Ice filled her veins.

Anna slipped into the back doorway, her hair and clothes disheveled, her eyes haunted.

One more dangerous unknown crashed into the situation.

Ashley steeled her eyes and locked them on the gunman's. Anna wouldn't attack him from behind. Even if she would, there was no way Ashley could communicate what to do in time.

"Pray, Ashley!" Anna screamed and collapsed to the ground.

The gunman turned his weapon on Anna.

She pulled the trigger.

CHAPTER THIRTY-FOUR

Ashley rushed forward, her gun still trained on the man's unmoving form. She kicked his gun far away and stood over him.

She'd killed a man.

A shudder ripped through her. This was not the way it should have happened.

Anna rushed toward her but stopped and fell on the ground next to Brad.

Cops poured into the backyard, guns locked in front of them.

Sergeant Culp stepped into her peripheral vision. "Lower your weapon, Ashley. It's over."

One of his meaty hands enclosed her gun. The other one pried her fingers from it.

She turned to face him. "He was going to shoot Anna. I had to." But the words died in the air. They understood.

Nothing changed the results.

Had she done the right thing? Was God the one guiding her actions? Or was she?

Brad's small hand slipped into hers. "Thank you, Ashley. You saved our lives."

All control crumbled at his words. Tears flowed. She pulled him into her arms. "You're okay. I thought I'd lost you."

Anna wrapped her arms around them.

Voices buzzed. People filled Anna's backyard, scurrying around. Activity everywhere.

She held Brad and Anna close.

Elizabeth, her friend and fellow cop, slipped a blanket around her shoulders and pulled her away from Brad. "Let the paramedics take care of them."

Ashley nodded, her arms and legs heavy as lead. She'd done the right thing. Hadn't she?

❧

Patrick paced in Anna's front yard. Police made a human barrier, keeping him from racing into the chaos behind the farmhouse.

No one would tell him what was happening. Who had been shot?

Two paramedics hauled a white stretcher toward the waiting ambulance. He rushed forward.

"Stay back!" Two cops ran alongside, blocking anyone from getting close.

Medics and cops clambered into the back and slammed the doors. Screaming sirens and lights split the surreal scene and disappeared down the road.

Jonathan stood next to him. "Who was that?"

Culp strode toward them. "The gunman." He squared off with Jonathan. "I heard you got knocked out by the guy. I need you to go with the next ambulance. I'll meet you at the hospital."

"I am not injured."

"I wasn't askin'." Culp raised his eyebrows, his bulk backing up the silent challenge.

"Yes, officer." Jonathan eyed the ground.

Patrick strained to see around Culp. "Where's Ashley? Is she hurt?"

Culp shook his head. "In shock. We'll let you see her in a minute."

"Bradley and Anna? Are they…?" He couldn't find his voice.

Jonathan stepped forward. "My family? Please tell us."

"They need to go to the hospital. They're pretty banged up."

"But alive?"

"Yep. They'll be out this way in a minute."

Two ambulances backed into the driveway, one veering into the front yard.

Four paramedics with stretchers disappeared around the house. One group returned with Anna on a stretcher and headed for the ambulance. They were gone before Patrick could ask a question.

A minute later, a white stretcher with Bradley's limp form strapped to it came into view. Blood covered his face and clothing. Tears streaked through the dirt and smears of red. "Bradley?"

He followed along with the paramedics, guys he'd gone to school with, and clamped his hand onto the cold metal rails. "He's going to be okay, isn't he?"

Jonathan stood guard on the other side of the stretcher.

"He's alive. Stable. Busted up pretty good."

Bradley blinked as they hefted his stretcher into the ambulance. Patrick climbed in beside him.

"You can't go with us, Patrick. You know that."

Jonathan climbed in next to him. "I am family, and Patrick is coming with us."

"Thank you."

Bradley turned his head toward them. "Mr. James, Ashley needs you. She is very upset."

"I'll go find her." He climbed over Jonathan and stepped down the first step. "And I'll come to the hospital as soon as I can. You'll talk to me when I get there?"

"We will talk like we used to." Bradley smiled.

"Yes. I'll see you soon." He jumped off the last silver step and moved out of the way.

The ambulance sped down the street. Two police cars followed, and minivans also tagged along behind.

He hightailed it to the small group of cops standing around, blocking him from Ashley. "If Ashley is okay, can I see her now?"

Culp shook his head. "We know you're anxious, Patrick. Hang tight. She'll be out front in a few minutes."

More waiting.

"Patrick." Elizabeth Rey's blue eyes warned him to tread lightly. She led a near catatonic Ashley toward him. "We still need to debrief at the station. You'll only have a few minutes."

He pulled Ashley into his arms. She was as cold as ice and unresponsive. He kissed her hair. "It's over, Ash."

"I killed someone."

"You did what you were trained to do. You saved innocent lives."

She pulled back and focused on her hands. "Culp told me his name was Alex. He was in his early twenties. A kid. And I ended his life."

Alex Jennings? "The one involved with the revitalization?"

Ashley swallowed and hung her head.

His mind spun. Why would he do such a thing? He studied Ashley's pale skin and empty eyes. "Ashley, look at me."

She did.

"I can't fathom what you're feeling, but this I know. You did the right thing. You're a hero."

She stepped back, eyes on the ground. "I don't feel like a hero."

"Did you just charge in there and start shooting?"

She jerked her chin up. "Of course not." Red crept into her cheeks.

"Did you unload your clip into him?"

Fire lit her eyes. "I shot only once. He was going to kill Anna. I had to stop him."

"That's right."

Elizabeth rejoined them. "Chief wants you to know the gunman survived. He's in surgery now and expected to recover."

Ashley stumbled back. He caught her and folded her into his arms, peace stealing every last word he could think to say.

She clung to him. "Thank You, God."

He couldn't agree more.

Chapter Thirty-five

Sunday afternoon, Ashley flicked the remote toward the TV at the end of a good sermon. Chester yawned and flopped onto her lap.

She burrowed into the couch, closer to Patrick's side.

His arm snaked around her. "Want to talk about the sermon or what happened on Thursday?"

"Tough choice."

"We don't have to talk about either one. I'm okay with the quiet."

Reaching for a glass of iced tea, she jostled Chester.

He yipped. "Hush up, silly. I'm not going anywhere."

Patrick reached around her to ruffle the dog's fur. "I get it, buddy. It's a guy thing."

She settled back into the couch, eyeing both of her staunchest protectors, one of whom wanted to talk so badly but had remained patient and present without a lot of talking in the last few days. "There's a song that keeps playing in my head. It sums up where I've been and where I am now. I'll play it for you."

With the push of a button, the room filled with a song she'd hated a month ago. The song that asked if she was "caught in the middle." Casting Crowns' mellow and haunting melody danced around them.

She could picture the place she'd lived in since Eric's death. Wanting God, but wanting control more. The promise of life and peace as real and vast as the ocean, but she chose the security of the excuses she'd lived behind.

When the song ended, she listened to the silence a minute. Facing Patrick again, she took a deep breath. "I've always wanted a God I could understand, a God who did things my way. But that's not who God is. Having a gun pointed at you clarifies things fast. It just took me a while to process what happened and what God was showing me in it."

Chester yawned again. Silly dog. He'd followed her around ever since she got home on Thursday night, knowing in his weird puppy way that she needed him.

"I can finally see God's hand in my past and present."

Patrick's blue eyes burned with concern.

"I could have handled the day Eric died differently. I could have trusted God. Then even if my brother still died, I wouldn't have pushed God away and turned my back on Him. I wouldn't have used bitterness to manage my emotions and control everyone around me."

"You're not alone in that, Ash. We all use something to protect ourselves."

Yes. She'd used control. Her parents used busyness and avoidance. Alex Jennings had used threats and manipulation. And a gun. None of it worked for long.

She shuddered. Things could have turned out so much differently Thursday. "It's God's mercy that Alex Jennings wasn't killed. If I'd had my way in that standoff, he would have died."

"No one would have blamed you. He tried to kill Anna and Bradley."

"Instead, he'll get justice. Maybe he'll turn his life around. I don't know. God used this to show me His ways are higher than mine... better."

Patrick grinned and leaned forward, cupping her face in his hands. The contact zinged through her.

"So you're not caught somewhere in the middle anymore?"

She shook her head.

"You're ready to move forward?"

Most definitely.

His lips brushed hers, and she caught her breath, lost for a minute in the intense tenderness. Moving closer, she deepened the kiss and slid her fingers through his hair.

Patrick broke the contact and pulled her into his chest. "How about a nice walk outside in the cold?"

"You're a wise man."

Chester raced to the kitchen and back, leash in his mouth.

The phone rang as she bent down to attach the now wet leash to Chester's collar. "The answering machine can get that."

Patrick retrieved their coats.

The machine beeped, and Brad's voice stilled her movements. Even Chester stood still to listen.

"Ashley? I…we are leaving tomorrow. Would you come today to say good-bye? Mamm is not up to going out again after church." Brad sniffled. "I would like to thank you."

She rushed to the phone. "Brad, wait." But no one was there, only a dial tone.

Hanging up the phone, she turned to Patrick. "They weren't leaving until next month."

"Let's go find out what's happening."

∽

Patrick pulled into the driveway next to a rental car with Atlanta tags and turned off the Mustang.

"Who is that?" Ashley's voice pinched.

"They're okay, Ash." Patrick circled around and helped her out of the car. "Let's not go storming in there, okay?"

She took a deep breath. "You're right. Just a little shell-shocked still."

He tucked her under his arm and directed her toward the porch. Slowly. She relaxed into him by the time they reached the front door.

Bradley flung open the door before Patrick could knock. "You came. Both of you. I'm so glad to see you." He launched himself into Ashley's arms.

Patrick tousled the boy's hair.

"I'll miss you both." His watery words were muffled by Ashley's coat.

Jonathan opened the door wider. "Please, come inside."

A suited man with salt and pepper hair stood and straightened his jacket as they entered. "I should be going." He turned toward the door.

Recognition lit the man's eyes. "Mr. James. I'm glad you're here. I've already talked to the Yoders and the town council."

Andrew Jennings lowered his eyes to the floor. "I can't begin to make up for the injuries my son caused, but I need to apologize. I'm deeply sorry for my son's actions and what he has done to both of you. Alex's attempt to fix the revitalization problems with violence was a delusional attempt to prove himself to me. He won't have the chance to hurt anyone else for a very long time. Maybe he'll change."

"You don't owe me an explanation, Mr. Jennings."

"It wasn't much of one, but it's all I have right now." Jennings raised his eyes and focused on Ashley. "Thank you for sparing my son's life. You were doing your job…" His words died away.

Ashley stepped forward. "I'm thankful he's alive, Mr. Jennings."

The older man turned back to the Yoders. "I've given Anna a check that will cover all their medical bills and pay for a new barn." He adjusted his coat. "I've taken care of your hospital bill too, Patrick. It's the least I could do."

"Thank you, sir. You didn't have to do that."

"Yes. I did." He slipped into his coat. "I've left a sizable check with the town council. It should cover hiring a new developer. I wish I could do more."

Tragedy had a funny way of sawing off rough edges. God had changed Mr. Jennings for the better. He hoped the same would happen with Alex.

"We will keep you and your son in our prayers." Anna extended a box of baked goods. "Please take these with you for Alex, and please tell him we have forgiven him."

Patrick would never understand that quickness of forgiveness, but it shone from Bradley's, Anna's, and Jonathan's eyes. They had learned something he only hoped to emulate someday.

Mr. Jennings cleared his throat and hurried to the door. "Thank you. I'm still so sorry. If you need anything, if the amount I left doesn't cover any of your expenses, don't hesitate to call." Then he slipped out the door.

His car engine roared to life, and he disappeared down the road before anyone spoke.

Jonathan was the first. "We will miss you."

Ashley hugged Bradley close. "Why are you leaving now? Can't you wait a little while? We just got Brad back." Her eyes moistened.

Patrick understood. He was barely keeping himself in check.

Bradley pulled him into a hug. "I wish you could come with us."

That did it. Tears pricked at his eyes. Bradley had wormed his way deep into Patrick's heart, and there was no pulling away now.

"Anna and Bradley will return, maybe this fall." Jonathan stood separate from them, but his eyes were moist too.

"That long?" Ashley wiped her eyes.

Patrick almost picked up the argument until he met Anna's sad eyes.

Her eyes watered, but her voice held strong. "We need time to rest and recover without the demands of the dairy. I have family who will look after it while we are gone." She focused on Ashley. "We thank God for bringing you into our lives." Her focus moved to include him. "For both of you. Ashley and Patrick, you have taught us about God's protective hand and how He uses people and ways we would never have imagined to show us His love. Thank you."

Ashley nodded and grabbed onto his hand.

"We will write and call while we are in Indiana. And before you know it, we will be home." Anna hobbled forward.

Ashley rushed to her. "I'll be counting down the days."

Despite the tears, a sense of peace washed over Patrick. This time away would be good for the Yoders. Bradley would return, and they'd go fishing as he'd promised.

He caught Jonathan's eye. "I hope you'll be back to visit too."

Surprise flicked in the man's eyes. "I will do my best, but my home is in Indiana." Jonathan spoke volumes with his calm expression and his extended hand.

Patrick clasped it and pulled the shocked man into his embrace. Ashley laughed and stood by his side.

They had all come so far. One more thing and it'd be perfect. That one thing had to wait. For a little while.

CHAPTER THIRTY-SIX

Ashley warmed her face in the August sunshine. Atlanta's smog and honking commuters dampened the moment. That was downtown.

Patrick squeezed her hand. "Enjoying the big city bustle?"

She shrugged. "I'm just glad to visit the High Museum without an art show tacked onto the trip. No smiling and schmoozing attempts to sell paintings for me."

"Are your parents still meeting us today?"

She searched the crowd waiting for entrance to the High. No Mom and Dad. "I hope so. They haven't been very talkative since I cancelled the May show and their attempt to reschedule for October."

"They'll get over it."

Patrick didn't know her parents like she did. "Your sister said to make sure you saw some big city traffic while we were in town." She eyed his reaction, measuring it carefully. "Kath seems to think you'd rather be here than in Montezuma."

Eyes bright and contemplative, Patrick studied her face. His thumb traced circles on the back of her hand.

She shivered like a schoolgirl.

"Seven months ago, I was ready to plow through revitalization plans and see Montezuma back on the map. Then I was going to pack up my bags and move to Buckhead. I missed the big city energy. The coffee shops that stay open all night. The theater and nice restaurants."

"So what changed?"

His thoughtful blue eyes sparked.

She could guess but wanted to hear it out loud. "You decided small-town living was too funny to leave behind? I can see that, especially Thursday nights at the bowling lane. World-class entertainment."

He laughed out loud and kissed her forehead. "Yep. My idea of a good time."

"I can't think of anything else funny enough to change your mind about big-city living." She batted her eyelashes like a goof.

His smile was reward enough. "You want to know what happened to change my mind?"

"That's why I asked."

"You." He pulled her to him and kissed her soundly. She'd have to remember he enjoyed being teased a great deal.

A woman cleared her throat nearby.

Ashley ignored her. Whoever it was could step around them.

"Really, Ashley. Your brother would have told you to set a better example."

Face hot, Ashley pulled away from Patrick and locked eyes with her mother. The hint of a grin on her mother's proper and dignified face short-circuited her brain a second.

"Did you just bring up Eric?" Maybe she hadn't heard right.

Mom flipped a hand in the air and turned on her cute flowered heels. Her matching sheath dress swished as she strutted toward the High entrance. "Your brother was a fount of interesting sayings. It's high time we put them back into practice."

Dad shook hands with Patrick and shrugged, an odd smile playing over his face too.

"What is up with you two?"

"We've missed you." Dad pulled her into a sideways hug. "And we were wrong to pretend Eric's death didn't affect us, to shut you out when you wouldn't play along." He pointed his chin toward Patrick. "You have a good man there, Ashley. Listen to him."

Dad hurried ahead, catching up to Mom and putting his arm around her. Then he kissed her cheek.

She vaguely remembered them acting like that when she and Eric were little. Eric had always pretended to gag and moan. In all honesty, the sight of her parents kissing made her feel safe. Eric would have loved to see their parents act like that again.

He still would have gagged though.

"Still with us, Ash?" Patrick took her hand and nudged them forward.

"Just thinking about when Eric and I were little."

"You're smiling."

"Yeah. I'll tell you the whole story later." Stopping, she pulled him close to her. "Tell me what you said to my parents and why you didn't tell me about your conversation with them. It must have been earth-shattering."

"Conversations. Plural."

Her mouth hung open.

Patrick tapped her chin with his finger. "My dad used to say you'd catch a lot of flies that way."

She snapped her mouth closed and stared at him a second. "You've had multiple conversations with *my parents* about me and about Eric's death, and they didn't hire a hit man to silence you?"

"They're not like that."

He must have forgotten the first time he'd met her parents.

"They were scared when they found out about the gunman and all we went through. Apparently, it rattled them enough to pay attention, and they were open to hearing what I had to say. They love you a lot, you know."

"I know." And she did. They came today just to spend time with her. A step in the right direction.

"Let's head inside. There's something I want to show you."

Patrick showing her something at the High? The place where she'd practically grown up? This she had to see.

∾

Patrick shifted his weight side to side as Ashley examined yet another Impressionistic painting. Granted, the colors were magnificent and the skill of the painters stellar.

"Don't you just love the scope of Monet's work?" She stepped back to view the painting from another angle.

Ashley's mom eyed him with amusement. "Yes. Very romantic. His water lilies are still my favorite." She pointed to a line sketch on the wall to their right. "We should have a look over here, don't you think? It's a comparison of a painting from one of the early masters next to an Impressionist's rendering of the same subject."

This was payback. Slow and steady torture delivered with Mrs. Walters's jocular smile.

"You'll get used to it." Mr. Walters patted his shoulder. "In time."

He checked his watch. "Hey, Ash?" He stepped close and whispered in her ear. "Want to see my favorite painting?"

She shivered.

This was more like it.

"Which one is your favorite?" She crossed her arms, cool and challenging. Her green eyes twinkled. "You haven't really paid attention to any of the paintings in this exhibit."

He leaned in again, close to her ear. "I'm a bit distracted by the beautiful painter."

"You said you had a favorite painting. Which one is it?"

Mr. and Mrs. Walters flanked their daughter. Mrs. Walters spoke. "Yes, Patrick. Do show us. We'd love to see it."

Three sets of green eyes twinkled back at him.

Torture. Pure and simple.

"Let's head to the permanent collection. I think it's in there." He took Ashley's hand and led her toward the elevator.

"I've seen the permanent collection a hundred times. They don't usually have new paintings over there."

He punched the down button. "You never know."

Narrowed eyes scanned his. "What aren't you telling me?" She searched her parents' faces too. "Are you three up to something? Something that ends up with me hoodwinked into a new art show or something?"

"Trust me." He reached for her hand.

She snatched it away. "The fact that you're saying that all smooth and steady scares me."

"Have I ever steered you wrong?"

The elevator opened and they stepped inside. He enjoyed a silent ride down. No funny looks, no excruciating ruse to detain him with one more painting to view.

Soon they were walking up the ramp to the second floor of the permanent collection. The white walls and floors blinded him, reflecting back the sunlit afternoon outside.

Who knew you could spend three hours standing in front of paintings and survive?

He didn't stop to ooh and aah over the marble statues. There was only one thing he wanted to see. More like one thing he couldn't wait for Ashley to see.

They paraded past treasures of Early American art and furniture, Ashley's hand firmly in his.

He turned left and right and left again to find the exact place. This section was virtually uninhabited. He glanced heavenward in thanks.

"Okay. Close your eyes." He pasted on his most serious face.

It didn't evoke the desired reaction.

"What? Why?"

"No questions. Play along."

She raised one eyebrow into a look that would curdle milk.

"Please?"

She turned to her parents. "Do you know what this is all about?"

Mrs. Walters's calm and innocent veneer was Oscar-worthy. "I believe you should put us all out of suspense and do as Patrick asks."

"Hear! Hear!"

Ashley turned back to him. "This better be good."

"I promise."

Snapping her eyes closed, she held out a hand.

He waved his in front of her.

"I can tell what you're doing even with my eyes closed. Stop flapping and take me to wherever your favorite picture is hanging."

He smiled at the security guard investigating their little game. The burly man only crossed his arms and kept his eyes fixed on them.

Patrick stopped and turned Ashley to face his favorite painting in the world.

Ashley's mom covered her mouth in a silent gasp.

"Okay, open your eyes, Ash." Patrick stood to the side, waiting.

Her eyes narrowed in a question. Then shot up into her hairline. "How in the world?" She turned to him. "How did my painting find its way into the High Museum of Art?"

Raising his hands, he held them out in a shrug.

She turned to her father. "Is this part of your string pulling? Dad, I asked you not to do that. Why didn't you listen?"

Mr. Walters held up his hands. "I had nothing to do with this, sweetheart. No string pulling at all. You asked me not to, and I haven't."

"Then how?" She turned awestruck eyes back to him.

He studied the painting of him at Amelia's restaurant, chocolate smudge dotting his chin. He loved that. He loved even more that Ashley's painting now hung for a short time in her favorite museum in the world. She'd hit the big time.

"The curator might have returned my call and might have been willing to look at some samples of your work."

"He came to Montezuma?"

"No. I came here with a few samples. He wanted to do a show, even before I told him your name, just like your parents said he would. He loved them, Ash, because you're an amazing artist."

Mouth open, she blinked at her painting and then turned back to him. No words escaped.

A tear slipped down her cheek.

He wiped it away. "Surprise."

Lifting up on tiptoes, she wrapped her arms around his neck and buried her face in his chest. He relished every second of it.

"I have one more surprise. If you're up for it."

She held on to him. "I don't know if I can handle another surprise."

"I'll wait."

Mr. and Mrs. Walters waved as they slipped into the next room. But not before he caught their misty eyes.

"We're alone." He whispered into her ear just because it made her quiver.

Turning in his arms to view the painting, she exhaled a long breath. "Happy?"

"Ecstatic. I can't believe you'd do something like that for me. It's the best gift I've ever received."

He rested his chin on the top of her head and enjoyed how perfectly she fit into his arms. "I might be able to top it."

"Not possible."

"Really?" He fished in his pocket for the small green box that held his future. "Ashley?"

Her eyes searched his.

He held up the box.

She gasped.

Bending down on one knee, he held her hand. "Ashley, I've prayed about this every day for the last month. I'm surer than I've ever been about anything in my life. I want to spend the rest of my life loving you. Will you do me the honor of becoming my wife?"

Tears welled in her eyes.

The question hung in the air, unanswered. Was she not ready for this yet?

"Yes, Patrick. Yes. I love you." She knelt down with him and kissed him till he couldn't think of one intelligent thing to say.

The security guard cleared his throat. "You folks need a picture taken?" The large man's face beamed. "Not too often we get to see a proposal here, especially not when one of the couple is a famous artist."

Ashley wiped her eyes. "I can't believe this is happening. You. My painting here. It's more than I could have dreamed."

They posed for a picture.

"Thank you." Patrick shook the guard's hand. "Thanks for helping me keep this place cleared out for a few minutes."

Mr. and Mrs. Walters returned, eyes bright with laughter and tears, and hugged Ashley.

"You deserve this happiness, honey. I'm so thrilled for you." Mrs. Walters brushed a hand down his arm. "Well done, Patrick. I'm proud of you."

Mr. Walters wrapped his arm around his wife's waist. "Let's leave these two alone, shall we?"

Patrick brushed a kiss across Ashley's cheek. Her eyes stayed fixed on the painting. "I had no idea when I sat down to paint this that anyone would ever see it."

"I know."

"God sure knows what He's doing." Her bittersweet tone gave him pause.

He gasped. "The great Ashley Walters is admitting that God knows better than she does? That He's in control? I think I might need to call the newspapers next."

She elbowed him. "Whatever."

"It's not like that's a small comment coming from you."

"No, it isn't. But it's the truth. A severe grace ripped my world out from under me and then handed it back better than I ever thought possible."

Taking her hand, he turned her to face him. "He's good like that, Ash."

"I know. He gave me you."

Patrick pulled her to him and held her close. It'd take a lifetime to thank God for all the joy he'd experienced today. He'd take a lifetime expressing that thanks too. One kiss, one painting, one day at a time.

God was in control, and He was good.

Of that, Patrick was certain.

Author's Note

Dear Reader,

Thank you for journeying with me to a favorite small town of mine and stepping into the lives of Patrick, Ashley, Jonathan, and Brad. One theme in this story was control. It wasn't until the end of the story that I realized each and every character wrestled with this issue, all in very different ways. They called the issue by different names: doubt, unforgiveness, guilt, fear, arson, worry, justice.

If you think about it, aren't they all about the same thing? Different shades and situations, but the same overarching question: Who is in control?

Honestly, there are days I believe the answer is me, at least that's how I act. I'm a type A, firstborn perfectionist who doesn't want to disappoint anyone or see how frail and fallible I really am. So God, in His infinite grace and mercy, gave me a body that's broken. A body that would force me to face my limitations daily and depend on someone far greater than I could ever be. For over twenty years I've lived with diabetes. My doctors told me I'd never have children, I'd lose my eyesight by the time I was forty, and complications were inevitable. Add to that, every day I live with the reality that one mess-up with insulin or food could result in an ER visit or worse.

You'd think I would have applied that type A behavior and become a model patient. I didn't. I fought. I ignored. And I lashed out at God. Then, ten years into this journey with diabetes, I found out I was pregnant. A doctor looked me in the eyes and said that if I didn't keep my sugars perfect, I'd kill my unborn child. I was terrified. I became that model patient, but nothing I did kept my sugars normal. They were scary high or terrifyingly low. I was sure I'd failed at the most important responsibility I'd ever been given.

Then I gave birth to a healthy baby girl. Her birth and life (she's a teenager now) have taught me that I wasn't in control one second of my life. Three additional pregnancies further emphasized my inability to control basic things like my own body and eternal things like life and death. We lost a baby during my third pregnancy. I wanted to grieve with hope, but it simply hurt for a very long time. With the love of my family and friends pointing me back to God when I forgot my way, I've learned that joys and sorrows are not in my hand to dole out as I wish. I'm not in control.

I'm forever grateful. It's a huge comfort to know there is a good God who is all-knowing, all-sufficient, all-powerful, and always present. This is who I want in control, not me with my limits and weaknesses. I'm convinced that the more we taste His goodness and believe He is for us, the less we will strive to do His work for Him. Instead, we can rest and allow Him to do His work in us and through us.

My prayer for you throughout the writing of this story was that you'd see God's hand in your lives and be drawn deeper into the reality that the weight of the world does not rest on your shoulders. It rests on His. The One who spoke the world into being stands beside you, His powerful and gentle hands outstretched, His eyes filled with love for you. Come home.

Because of His grace,
Amy

To learn more, please visit the Dark Chocolate Suspense website:
www.amywallace.com
Or email: amy@amywallace.com

I'd love to hear from you!

Discussion Questions

1. Ashley uses unforgiveness to control herself and others. Was it effective? Why or why not?

2. Patrick is afraid of relationships because of his past. How would you counsel the counselor to heal?

3. The antagonist is convinced he is in control of his future and must alter circumstances in increasingly dangerous ways to achieve his goals. Have you ever pushed ahead of God's guidance or lagged behind? What effect have your choices had on yourself and others?

4. Ashley's parents pretended their son's death didn't change their lives. Have you ever tried to do that with a significant or painful event? What helped you heal?

5. Eric's death defined Ashley's life. What good or bad events define you?

6. The city council planned an elaborate revitalization for the city of Montezuma. Is there an area of your life that needs revitalization? How would you begin the process?

7. How do Jonathan's and Patrick's views of forgiveness differ? Which viewpoint do you relate to more?

8. Bradley feels alienated because he's different from the people in his community. How can you use your differences to show the uniqueness of Christ?

9. The differences between the Montezuma and Mennonite communities tore them apart. How can you use the differences in your church and community to draw people together?

10. First Peter 5:8 says, "Be alert and of sober mind. Your enemy the devil prowls around like a roaring lion looking for someone to devour." Ashley faced many prowling lions: criminals, the enemy's attacks, lies she believed, and a struggle with control. What prowling lions stalk you? What Scripture verses can you hold on to and use to defeat them?

∽

Some of my favorite Scripture verses to defeat the enemy are found in Ephesians 6:

A final word: Be strong in the Lord and in his mighty power. Put on all of God's armor so that you will be able to stand firm against all strategies of the devil. For we are not fighting against flesh-and-blood enemies, but against evil rulers and authorities of the unseen world, against mighty powers in this dark world, and against evil spirits in the heavenly places.

Therefore, put on every piece of God's armor so you will be able to resist the enemy in the time of evil. Then after the battle you will still be standing firm. Stand your ground, putting on the belt of truth and the body armor of God's righteousness. For shoes, put on the peace that comes from the Good News so that you will be fully prepared. In addition to all of these, hold up the shield of faith to stop the fiery arrows of the devil. Put on salvation as your helmet, and take the sword of the Spirit, which is the word of God.

Pray in the Spirit at all times and on every occasion. Stay alert and be persistent in your prayers for all believers everywhere. (Ephesians 6:10-18 NLT)

It's my prayer that you fight the good fight, hold on to the truth, and walk in the healing God has for you. He loves you more than you can imagine. Take His hand and enjoy the ride.

MEET AMY WALLACE

Amy Wallace writes Dark Chocolate Suspense—high-action suspense that delves deep into heart issues. Amy is a wife, homeschool mom, author, speaker, coleader of a young writers' club, and avid chocoholic.

Her novels include the Defenders of Hope Series: *Ransomed Dreams, Healing Promises*, and *Enduring Justice*. Amy is also a contributing author of *A Novel Idea: Best Advice on Writing Inspirational Fiction, God Answers Moms' Prayers,* and *Chicken Soup for the Soul Healthy Living Series: Diabetes.*

Amy says: "Besides my husband and children knowing how deeply I love them, if I could be remembered for only one thing, it would be that I glorified God by enjoying Him to the fullest and that I showed by example what it means to dream big and live a life that touches hearts and leads people into a deep relationship with Christ."

I'd love to hear from you!
Please visit me at my website, Dark Chocolate Suspense:
www.amywallace.com

— OR —

Connect with me on Facebook:
www.facebook.com/amywallaceauthor

— OR —

Hang out with me at my Heart Chocolate blog:
http://peek-a-booicu.blogspot.com